MAGNUS

Barbarian Invasions
A Roman Empire military thriller
by Brent Reilly

**The spectacular 31-book historical fiction saga
by Brent Reilly**

Author has sold **500,000 thrillers**, including 400,000 on Amazon.
(see proof in About the Author).

Enjoy the **First Battle of Britain**! 4 legions vs 5 armies! **Real hero, true events**: In **367 AD**, a historical evil genius named Valentinus gets 5 armies to invade Brittania to drive out Rome, killing 100,000 Brits in what historians call the Great Conspiracy. Assassins murder its top 3 leaders. Troops on Hadrian's Wall let enemies through rather than stop them. Frank and Saxon warships destroy shipping and Gallic ports to keep the conspiracy a secret. Unpaid troops mutiny, garrisons desert, and invaders burn cities while robbing and raping. Legionaries, posted to protect them, instead take bribes to attack loyal leaders. A year without harvests leaves it starving. **All that really happened** so Valentinus could rule instead of Rome.

Meet the man sent to stop them. With just 4 legions, Magnus Maximus must beat Saxons, Picts, Attacotti, Hiberni, and Scotti, restore order, and rebuild a devastated country without help or bullion. Watch a larger-than-life killer hero with fatal flaws and lethal aim win an impossible war under extraordinary circumstances as Magnus leaps off the page and runs for his life. See Rome fall, enjoy the 4th century now, take a global tour of antiquity today, and meet the greatest Roman you've never heard of. Rome will soon lose Gaul, Britannia, Iberia, North Africa, and most of the Med. With the Dark Ages coming, **witness the twilight of the most powerful empire to rule the West** and the only one to encircle the Med. The bloodbath starts with the Battle of Britain.

This exhaustively researched savage saga has brutal battles in nearly ever chapter, but is also quite quotable: "**I feel like a whore selling virginity**", "If I'm going to Hell, I may as well enjoy the trip", "Grandpa was an abusive drunk, so dad abuses me sober", "Life is precious, but lives are cheap", "Ever since mama drank my poison, I've had a pebble in my boot", "**I want immortality, but not if it takes forever**", "Orphans are children who lost their parents; there should be an even sadder word for parents who've lost their kids", "I'm great at lying and I'm probably good at statistics", "I *speak* gibberish, but I can't read or write it", "Luca had great parents, but most babies fuck that up", "I may be crazy, but I don't *suffer* from insanity", "British food is inedible, but at least there's enough for everyone", "**Until I lost my virginity, I didn't know what I was getting into**", "I feel like a donkey owner who just kicked his own ass", "I'm often smart", "**Why do men shake with the hand they masturbate with?**", "101% of negative numbers never lie, but 11 out of 9 statistics might mislead", "Being ordinary doesn't make you normal", and "I always finish what I star…".

Magnus Maximus 1 hit #1 in Historical Thrillers, #1 in Military Thrillers, #1 in War Fiction, #1 in Military Science Fiction, #1 in Historical Fantasy, #1 in Technothrillers, #1 in Post-Apocalyptic Science Fiction, #1 in Dark Horror, #1 in Suspense, #1 in Time Travel Science Fiction, #1 in Saga Fiction, #1 in Science Fiction Adventure, #1 in Greco-Roman Fantasy, #1 in Teen & Young Adult Military Historical Fiction Ebooks, and #1 in Alternative History on Amazon.com.

PRAISE FROM AMAZON VERIFIED REVIEWS: "Best historical novel I've read." "4th century historical fiction at its finest." "You can feel the fire as the Roman Empire implodes." "Learn why Rome fell. Magnus puts it all in historical context. Great historical fiction." "Ambitious, outrageous, and audacious in scale, depth, and detail. Brilliantly told… I could feel the fire as Londinium burned. A remarkable read that kept me glued to my screen." "I couldn't stop reading. Magnus flew off the page… The giant blue Pict was sensational." "How military fiction should be written. It's fast, fun, and full of fighting." "Highly addictive. Magnus shines." "Magnus is dark, daring, and dangerous." "Shines a bright light on a dark time." "Exceptional military history…Great portrayal of historical characters." "Magnus stands up and stands out." "Magnus Maximus is Julius Caesar with a killer attitude."

Get screenplays for the first 6 seasons on Amazon!

NOTE: Germany didn't exist until Bismarck united it in 1871, so Germans (as we think of them today) didn't exist until almost the 20th century. Germanic-speakers identified by their tribe. Romans called them Germani and so shall I. By the 4th century, West Germani mounted slinger to kill them outside the range of other archers. Whirling pellets loudly break bones or twirl grown men like ungainly dancers. This demoralizes the Germani and elates the Iberians. It takes only a minute for the kid to wound them all and return at a gallop.

Serapio points at the rider, 100 paces away, clearly recognizing him, and yells an offer.

"Flavius, if you stop, we'll let your uncle live."

This visibly enrages the teenager. Rotating his upper body, he slings a ball of metal, which whistles as it flies at the horrified Alamanni commander, who dodges a little too late. The impact spins him like a clumsy drunk. Two of his men catch him as he falls, but blood splatters one, who angrily spits some out.

"That's for calling me Flavius!" Magnus bellows. "Uncle Theo, for the glory of Rome!"

The legate raises his sword in reply. The distant legion gleefully chants his name like a drug. Magnus gives ground to avoid a saturation volley, then laughs at these grown men. The slinger roars like a defiant lion, startling both sets of men, then laughs loudly like a lunatic. His primal scream comes from a deep hole that better boys would bury. The killer kid hugs his handsome horse.

"Caesar, let's show them what's what."

The athletic stallion neighs an eager reply. Warriors look at him like a rabid dog that needs a quick death. Down the road, several thousand men continue killing each other. Within the beleaguered legion, the Roman commander shouts, clearly concerned:

"Max, get help!"

Magnus laughs at that.

The Alamanni have had enough and rush the damn boy, who looks pleased instead of afraid. Magnus kicks his horse closer to avoid another saturation volley, then resumes slinging again. He's careful to time it for when the horse bumps him in the air; he must tense up his legs to stay seated while twirling a sling over his head. Every heartbeat, a whistle announces another lead pellet.

Flying over 100 miles per hour, his one-ounce round bullets have as much penetrating power as a .44 Magnum, later researchers will conclude. Holes in the ball have an aerophonic effect, not unlike angry wasps, as they fly fast at furious fighters. The balls buzz in the air, with the ugly thud of impacts as they penetrate flesh and mortify men. With similar range as Magnus, many bowmen stop to shoot the teen, but he's always moving and moving unpredictably. He only allows a few Alamanni to target him at a time to avoid their projectiles and often darts in to fling fast before racing away. It's impressive and hard to counter.

A pellet enters an Alamanni eye and exits an ear with a disgusting sound. Another hits a forehead and takes off the top of his cranium, covering his friends in filth. More lead crushes a knee and a sprinting soldier gets thrown on his back by a pellet to the face. A mighty warrior's shin shatters and his scream is breathtaking. Another Alamanni gets a hole in the head when he turns to yell for reinforcements. His eyes lose light and he falls on his face with a puff of dust rising in a donut shape. An ugly bastard gets hit in the back, trying to shoot Romans, and it looks like he's diving without outstretching his arms.

The Germani charge, but Magnus just rides away and turns often to exchange

7

projectiles. As Alamanni chase the teen up the road, the 3rd Century rushes out behind shields to grab a few dozen bows and arrows from dead and dying warriors. They back up carefully to hold a uniform shield wall and chuckle at the impotent impacts. Once back with the legion, the best archers notch up and shoot between wooden plank shields within an iron frame. Now the Iberians feel confident and aggressive even as their rescuer retreats.

The teen lures hostiles from the legion. The fastest enemies leave behind the least athletic, giving the rider more time to focus on fewer targets. Magnus laughs, clearly enjoying this, which enrages and outrages the fools on foot. Focusing intensely while always in motion, the slinger tracks arrows and changes direction to avoid them, but the slow pedestrians are less able to avoid his fast pellets. Every other whistle, a man goes down or bellows in pain. The teen chuckles courageously, contagiously, and contemptuously.

"I win again! Uncle Theo, this is the best game ever! Tag can't touch this."

Re-energized by the unexpected help, Roman soldiers cheer him on. Looking grim under his plumed helmet, Legate Theo redeploys his force to better counter the assault, his voice booming indistinctly over the battle. Romans are now throwing as many Germani hatchets as the Germani, who don't enjoy armor. Exasperated and bleeding badly, Serapio screams like a frustrated planner losing his mind. The tide has turned. The killer rider lures furious fighters from the legion by laughing at them. Suddenly facing no opposition, the northern wing of the Iberian legion moves to reinforce its center, where the fighting is fiercest. Magnus sees them leave with Uncle Theo and smiles.

In contrast with the grunting and groaning by the road, the teen's voice sounds angelic as he sings a catchy tune, Girls of Rome, while slinging his heart out. Magnus loves how they hate it. A dozen arrows and hatchets hang limply from his iron armor, but Magnus does not seem to feel them. His helmet already has dings and dents that make him dizzy, yet he seems more stimulated than ever. A few hundred warriors form a skirmish line against the prodigy to their north. They show their backs to the Roman legion, to their south, as if this kid is more dangerous. Dozens of bodies litter the ground, some louder than others.

Magnus laughs at them. "Losers, you swam the Rhine River and walked all day just to fail like your fathers. As my mirror often says, I'd hate to be you."

20 or so Alamanni clearly understand his Latin and charge without orders. The rest slowly follow, each with two quivers over their shoulders. Reseated, Magnus slings pellets at the fastest, even as he rides away. It looks like adults on foot playing Tag with a master horseman. Hundreds of arrows seek him out, forcing Magnus to retreat. He knocks some shafts aside, but more hang from his shiny chainmail. Time and again he must lunge to one side of his horse or another, speeding up or abruptly stopping. The enemy doesn't maintain their skirmish line; instead, some run ahead, their faces furious, while the slow fall behind. A pellet flies 100 paces to crater a Germani skull that spills cerebellum onto others; another shatters a kneecap, dropping that dude like a horse shitting; a third get lead in his belly, making him walk, bent over, as he climbs the slope to safety.

With every step, these warriors move farther from friends fighting for their lives. Magnus continues disabling a dozen men a minute, which drives survivors crazy: They're beating a legion, yet losing to a boy. An Alamanni turns and curses at how far they've

8

come because the Romans seem far away. His face contorts as he decides whether to chase the boy or go after the Romans. An overweight comrade slumbers by towards Magnus, apparently exhausted, his breathing loud and heavy. A slimmer warrior runs to the main battle, his face fearful and frantic.

On his horse, Magnus expertly avoids their arrows until they run out of ammo. Some jealously hoard their last hatchet until the teen gallops after them, only to swerve to avoid their latest load. He pounces on helpless pedestrians, striking down one after another without mercy or hesitation. The kid screams in joy as his score rises because that infuriates the enemy. Pellets burst into craniums and break bones; they penetrate backs and enter throats with ugly gurgling sounds. The whistling visibly bothers many men. The warriors have little cover, but some hide while others run. The young rider has speed to avoid the armed while going after those without arrows. The smartest have recovered enough shafts to pose a threat, but the boy laughs at them. Magnus is obviously enjoying himself because he excels at this game. He cripples the last of the mobile and literally leaves the injured in his dust.

Yelling happily at a gallop: "Best. Game. Ever!"

Down the road, a few fleeing Germani look over their shoulders in terror as the boy slings when in range. One after another, these Alamanni go down, cursing and crying. With a range warrior in their rear, the attackers can't focus on killing Romans. The ambushers clearly fear the mounted slinger more than a legion of trained professionals. Magnus scans the scene to see his score: a few hundred bodies, some limping angrily, littering the old Roman road and nearby fields. Survivors look dejected, defeated, and demoralized because they got beat by a boy.

Bandaging his chest wound, Serapio sees his nemesis coming and frantically pulls his friend's corpse over him for protection while screaming for help. A few dozen Germani archers leave the Romans to give him cover. They shoot at maximum range to keep the killer kid away.

Magnus yells from a safe distance without stopping his slinging or riding. "If you tell me how you know my birth name, I probably won't sling you again."

That seems a fair trade. Warriors try swarming the teen.

"You're the general's boy from the bloomery who bores easily and often. Your dad plans to invade Alamannia soon. You have a birthday coming up and your father dislikes you for many good reasons. I assume he doesn't beat you enough. Oh, he knows you take coins from his payroll chest to bribe the metalworkers into teaching you. You bullied your father's engineers to fix the iron smelter's bellows to pump in more hot air. After removing iron ingots from the furnace, you hammer off the slag because your father hates you hunting without him. He told your mother you were a wild beast that needs a cage. That man fears and envies you, perhaps because your left hand works as well as the right, for some reason. You're a huge prick, so I assume you have a tiny cock. I didn't know you hate your name, but I'd love to know why."

Magnus leans into a hurl to splatter someone sneaking up on him. "Flavius is too common a name for me, so I call myself Max. My family alone has a dozen men called Flavius. I want fame instead of glory, power, wealth, or women. Like Caesar, I seek a spectacular death that future poets and playwrights talk about. I know what I want in life and I'm dying to get it."

"Boy, you're as odd as everyone says. I look forward to giving you the

9

spectacular death you deserve. I am Serapio, son of King Mederic, who you just wounded. With my uncles, King Agenaric and King Chrodomarius, we beat General Barbatio near Strasbourg last month, only to lose to Caesar Julian outside Argentoratum. After we kill your father and his army, we'll destroy Caesar Julian when he marches his army from Reims."

Magnus keeps turning in the saddle to study those closing in on him without pausing his slinging. "King Chrodomarius died of illness or suicide in Rome before Emperor Constantius could publicly execute him in front of an eager audience. I'll catch you later, Prince Serapio."

The Alamanni leader bristles at the news of his beloved uncle, grief painfully etched on his handsome face.

The legion is strung out half-a-mile, but the Germani focus their fighters in the center to reach the ammo wagons. Packed tightly together, deadly men fight hand-to-hand, often throwing darts or javelins when they see an opening. Dozens have died on both sides and many more are wounded. Everyone looks desperate, as if the battle is in the balance.

Moving south, Magnus keeps a slow trot over flat grassland to fling faster at unprotected backs from close range. Several hundred Alamanni archers shoot with impunity at the legion, which pisses the boy off. Riding behind these bowmen, metal balls puncture animal hides to burrow painfully into backs. Warriors scream from the pain and turn to see who has killed them. Many Germani men moan while Iberians roar their hero's name.

"Max! Max! Max!"

Happy to help his countrymen, Magnus gasps in shock upon seeing his younger cousin on a wagon. 6-year-old Theo slings with pellets at angry Alamanni holding torches and jars of lamp oil. The enemy breached the shield wall and are fucking his friends rather roughly. Dozens of dead and dying dudes form a mortal berm in front of the ammo wagons.

Magnus talks to himself. "Cousin Theo! No! You won't share my glory, you spoiled brat! Today is mine!"

Horrified, Legate Theo looks frantic at his badass son, slinging pebbles from the top of an enclosed wagon alongside Roman legionaries. The boy seems more angry than afraid as he hurts strangers at close range. The brave boy knows what they want and puts himself in their way. Like Magnus, he flings hard at men just a few strides away, his pebbles knocking men out, tearing off flesh, and breaking bones. Germani with torches try to burn just the enclosed wagons instead of the open ones full of food or tents. Warriors behind them shoot arrows at close range, punching through breastplates to pierce flesh. The stakes are high because the attackers sense victory. Alamanni archers have higher priorities than a small child, but an impatient spearman takes a pebble in the eye, blinding him. He howls in pain and his companion looks furious.

"Brother!"

That guy throws his heavy spear into the 6-year-old, knocking him down without knocking him out.

"Theo!" his father screams fearfully when a German arrow punches his back and nearly knocks him off his high horse.

Riding offroad while hurling lead into backs gives Magnus a clear view. Seeing his uncle get hit, Magnus loses his grin and nearly his grip. Possibly out of his mind, he races into worried warriors, knocking over Germani in his way as he draws two short swords. Two rows of enemy archers are shooting Romans with impunity, spaced just far enough apart so the back row gets a clear shot through the front row. Roman archers are too busy hitting more immediate threats overwhelming the wagons. These Alamanni bowmen support a few hundred spearmen fighting the Romans hand-to-hand. It's a mess that brave men look terrified they'll lose. The scale can be tipped in either direction as both sides throw everything they have at the other. With greater firepower, Germani are winning.

Enter the Lion.

Magnus gallops up from behind, then slows to pivot between the two rows. The archers at his end seem surprised a rider is pushing his way in, but assume he's one of theirs. The boy chops into necks and shoulders as he adjusts his pace to not miss any. Each second, he slices into two more. Focused on shooting legionaries, the Alamanni shooters are slow to see the new threat cutting through their flank.

He's bled a few dozen before others turn to shoot him. One hatchet hits his chainmail and then another bounces off his breastplate, but neither sink into flesh. Completely committed, Magnus can't stop now. His body jerks from unseen impacts. No matter what he does or where he goes, they'll have a clean shot, so he kicks his stallion into a gallop, ducks behind his horse's head to minimize his threat profile, and extends both swords as if flying. These won't be killing blows, but it forces the enemy to dodge or dive.

A warrior to starboard tracks him, so Magnus pulls his ride right to throw off the archer's aim. He then plows into five men on his left before again chopping into necks from a position of height. An arrow hits the boy from behind, but at a shallow angle that bleeds him. He leans back to avoid another from the front, then manages to stab three more men before he runs out of targets. Distant Romans roar approval.

Turning around, Magnus charges those getting up. Since he no longer enjoys surprise, an atavistic noise erupts from his throat and attacks the enemy as if fury can fly. The teen doesn't even seem to know he's roaring like a deranged drunk challenging a tavern full of sober soldiers. He's in the Zone and it clearly consumes him. Nothing exists in his micro-world except those he must kill before he dies. He runs over one, slashes at another, lunges out of the way of an arrow, tramples a big, bearded bowman, and loses his grip on one sword that gets stuck in a stubborn skull. These are custom blades that he helped forge, so he's pissed and feeling crappy. With a mind of its own, his free hand throws knives at surprised men as he rides amuck, prioritizing those notching arrows. He vents loudly again, not knowing how crazy he sounds, looks, and feels. His sword changes hands as he reaches out to cut warriors to his left or right. Being ambidextrous, his other hand throws knives at targets farther away. A hard-thrown hatchet sticks to his breastplate, so he throws it back and breaks that man's heart. A few fighters run and one cries over a comrade. Caesar charges into another mob of bowmen so Magnus can cut them down. The huge horse stomps and snorts without slowing, trampling one archer after another. The boy on his back leans out to slice and slash. It's impressive, effective, and seemingly suicidal.

Strong hands roughly pull him off his young stallion, throw him to the ground, and punch his face really hard. The first fist bloodies itself on his noseguard and the warrior howls in pain. The boy barks a command and his stallion rears on his hind legs as if boxing the sky. The enemy's focus shifts enough for Magnus to drive a knife under his chin to taste his iron blade. He himself licks a bleeding lip and bitter disappointment as his head rings like a bell. Scared, he scrambles up and throws three knives into two men with arrows notched before remounting his killer horse. Someone unseen shoots him in the kidney and the blow lands like a sucker punch that leaves the boy breathless. Magnus must leave to survive, so he spurs his stallion forward into another monstrous man who goes down with a grunt and a growl. With a rebel yell, he's free! He looks liberated and nauseous.

Rotating his stallion, Magnus notices dozens of Alamanni running down at him from up the road, Serapio bellowing like a madman and limping like a cripple. They look desperate, tardy, and pathetic. As he has more immediate threats, Magnus scans for targets. The deadly teenager doesn't have good options. Turning his stallion, he sees not all the men he's stampeded are taking it lying down. Some are standing up with an ax to grind, so he rides back to fuck them up again. Given the distance, he slings them from a safe distance. A few dive or roll away, but archers need to stand on both feet and enjoy use of both arms to shoot. Many are bruised, bleeding, or have gone bonkers. Many men impotently curse or threaten Magnus. Two able-bodied Alamanni are running, but don't look like they plan to stop this side of the Rhine River. Seeing so many slain, dozens of Alamanni leave the legion to fuck him, once and for all. Screaming hysterically, the precocious prodigy flees while still calmly slinging. They come from all directions, running to cut off escape. That virgin is fucked as they gang up on the teen. Magnus runs out of time and space, so it feels like the world's gonna end. And soon.

Frantically, Magnus looks around as his enemies gather while never slowing his slinging. Enemies are so close that impact knocks them down or the lead makes their heads explode, splattering neighbors with blood. It looks like he's in a stampede, the way Caesar expertly maneuvers through runners or into them while Magnus ducks arrows and clings to the far side of his stallion to avoid hatchets. Many objects barely miss him or bounce off his chest plate. Others still hit him, but not in the limbs, where he's vulnerable. Then he sits his saddle, hugs Caesar with his knees and nails another with an awful noise.

It's not unlike Tag.

Men scream the names of lost brothers, neighbors, and friends as they collapse like rag dolls. Other wounded warriors bellow cries of pain and beg for help that can't come. A few hold up mangled arms or twitch on the ground like epileptics. Limpers hurry up the slope for the safety of the forest, agonized and horrified by their injuries. The whistling, whizzing, and whooping noises echo like curses because each ends with a scream. Every heartbeat, another Alamanni goes down, goes quiet, or goes insane from the pain. The savage kid is in his element, having fun, and doing what he does best. The Alamanni think he's retreating under pressure, when actually Magnus is luring warriors away from the legion. Again.

That killer kid is loving this. His grin extends to his eyes. His mind is moving as fast as his horse as he expertly directs Caesar, often using just his legs, to where he needs to go. His head lowers so his lion helmet knocks aside hatchets and he turns so arrows impotently bounce off his breastplate. When his pellets sink deep or carve a canyon through flesh, he laughs loudly, giddy as a kid on Christmas, which Christians started celebrating in 336 AD. As men get too near, he throws a knife or swings a sword, but few Germani get that lucky because he moves fast across flat grass with few trees. In the distance, Magnus hears horrified pedestrians scream himself hoarse, which makes the clever kid chuckle.

Few are shooting at Magnus because he's riding fast, unpredictably, and because so many emptied their quivers. They just need to close the noose. Some line up along the slope so he can't get out. Smiling cruelly and laughing gleefully, they tighten the circle, a hundred men eager for a piece of flesh from the terrible teen who hurt so many. It's all he can do to avoid flying projectiles. Poor Caesar takes hatchets meant for his horseman. Too many Germani run at him, so Magnus slashes with blades to avoid getting separated from his best friend. His face is frantic and full of fear when a gap opens and he suddenly changes temperature. His gloomy mood evaporates as he addresses them like fervent fans.

"You fools let your friends die! I lured you failures away!"

The boy waves at the legion, several hundred paces away, then bursts into a gallop while laughing to infuriate his foes. The angry Alamanni realize he's right and converge on him, but he escapes in their only gap – towards the road. A brave badass gets in his way, but Caesar avoids the spear for his rider to slash down and cut the Alamanni up. A hundred livid survivors realize they fucked up. Their frustrated shouts sound pathetic, even to them. They visibly wince when Magnus, riding to the road, laughs at them again.

The killer kid returns with a vengeance. His breathing is tame, but his expression is wild with tense, taunt facial muscles looking like they're taking a dump after days of constipation. His eyes are clear, focused, and blue while his head traverses left and right to scan the tactical environment. Grimacing at a gallop, he adjusts his position as if painfully constipated. Everything aches, but nothing like his thigh muscles from tensing for so long when he slings from an artificial position. He stretches and massages his muscles while wincing from the pain. His humorous bone feels funny and he notices two more arrows clinging to his chainmail. An eye twitches uncomfortably and his left arm doesn't feel right. He shakes it loose to get the feeling back and looks forward to the grim fate that awaits him. The ambushers have overwhelmed the Romans and are burning several enclosed wagons, taking heavy losses with a light heart. They smash clay pots with lamp oil and watch the flames flicker. The ambushers certainly feel like they are winning. Roman legionaries try cutting their way in, but are poorly positioned.

Standing on a wagon catching fire, Young Theo is standing up and stabbing down with a Germani spear using both hands and an angry attitude. The 6-year-old concentrates and curses, knowing he's failing. He clearly thinks he's gonna die, but is too stubborn to flee. Alamanni warriors, in pelts and furs, climb up to strike centurions, but barely bother the boy.

With arrows and hatchets clinging to his armor, Legate Theo charges his charger into a mass of men and uses a sword to cut those trying to take down his son. The shield in his left arm conks ambushers on the head; some seem stunned and one drops like a rock. Both Theos look determined to fight to the death, but Alamanni are spearing the legate while pulling him off his high horse. Surrounded by hostiles and neck-deep in danger, it looks like he'll die any moment. Father and son make eye contact and say

13

goodbye with super sad eyes. A big, bearded bully swats Young Theo down and takes his spear while Legate Theo fights several desperate hands pulling him from the saddle. They both expect the other to die and feel the doom down to their bones. Each is scared shitless, but as much for each other as for themselves. With nothing less to lose, Young Theo scrambles to his feet, jumps on the bully's back, and climbs up to stab him in the eye with a short blade while bellowing boldly.

It pains Young Theo to ask for his cousin's help. "Maaaaaaaaaax!"

Magnus whispers to himself at a gallop as he nears the road. "Uncle, I'll trade my life for yours." Patting his stallion. "Caesar, let's go out in style. I'll make it up to you in our next life. Sorry this one didn't work out."

Leaning forward like he's flying, Magnus doesn't realize he's growling as his stallion accelerates to maximum speed. Caesar likes to run and loves to run fast. Wind blows in the teen's face, causing a tear to drop, as they speed up. Something raw erupts from his soul that fouls the air with animalistic fury, bitter regrets, and a lifetime of sad sentiments. His unnatural howl is loud and near enough for attackers to turn. Their reaction alerts and alarms their comrades, so some startled strangers scramble out of the way. Two buff warriors jam spears into the ground to puncture the stallion like a boar, but Magnus throws knives into both, his upper body rotating for maximum power. That he can stay mounted while doing that at a gallop amazes witnesses. Without stirrups, it's easy to lose balance and slide off. His baby face is tight and tense as Magnus concentrates fully with a fierce scowl. Nothing else exists except this moment and this cubic meter of space as he trades longevity for acceleration on his champion warhorse. He has a short sword in one arm and a long knife in the other as he plunges into the backs of a dense group of enemies overwhelming his favorite uncle.

Dozens of horrified Alamanni throw themselves out of the way, which alone gives his doomed uncle a lifesaving respite. A big bastard has his arms around Uncle Theo's waist to either hug him hard or use his weight to pull the stubborn Iberian down. Hearing shrill warnings, that Alamanni turns his head and loses his shit. He lets go, but too late and Caesar swats him aside. The Alamanni screams a curse as a leg bone loudly breaks. The terrified legate makes eye contact with his unusual nephew as he gallops by and nods in relieved thanks, clearly never expecting him to survive. As he flies by at top speed, Magnus thrusts his sword into another man while roaring like a maniac. He returns his uncle's nod and yells goodbye as he sinks into a mass of armed men. He looks ahead, loving being the center of attention for the last time.

Still with a dagger in his bleeding eye, the burly bastard has both hands around Young Theo's throat. He holds the boy a foot above the burning wagon, but lets go when he turns to see a ton of horseflesh flying at him. The demon in the saddle winks at him with a smile and the bearded bully freezes, confused, as Caesar carves a canyon through ambushing Alamanni. He leaves behind a field littered with dead and dying bodies, hatchets, bows, and quivers scattered about. The rabble, rubble, and wreckage is impressive, unnatural, and disturbing. Dozens of Germani get up and curse the child. Farther from the road, a hundred foolish fighters run to the wagons, fearing they'll arrive late.

The Alamanni fighting their way into and onto the wagons are clearly winning over the bodies of brave Romans with superior arms and armor. But some turn and their screams make others pause right before a ton of horse crashes into dozens of dudes at 50

14

miles per hour. The surprise and confusion is total. Magnus has never ridden this fast before and it shocks him to fly off his mount into wary warriors on a burning wagon. Caesar smashes into so many bodies that he also goes down, tumbling like a giant snowball over several ugly enemies. The crunching of bones stands out amid the screams of agony. A ton of horseflesh squishes and squeezes a dozen Alamanni who never imagined an Iberian stallion crushing them into cripples.

Caesar scores.

The kid's flying body knocks four off a burning ammo wagon and nudges another into the largest fire. Iberian legionaries gleefully stomp and cut them. The Alamanni had ignited the edges, but needed another minute to burn the arrow shafts inside. The burly bully stops his flight with a thud and the constipated teen needs a moment to pull his shit together. Still with a blade in his face, this angry Alamanni is kicking Magnus when Young Theo stabs him in the back with enough force to push him off the wagon, onto other Germani. He falls like a tree and flattens four friends. Romans regroup to push them away from their caravan. The teen's unexpected flight pauses the assault, giving the Iberians time to exploit their momentary advantage.

A few dozen meters away, a familiar face catches his eye like a fishhook. "Cousin Franco! Tell Baby Frankito I'll miss his huggies."

A large centurion, Franco looks horrified. "Max, don't you dare die on me again, dammit! You promised Frankito to live forever!"

On a smoldering wagon, Magnus' eyes refocus and he ignores his aches and pains to stab a grasping arm, then tries getting unsteadily to his feet. Hungry hands grab a meaty leg, but his short sword slashes flesh until the enemy releases him. As his eyes finally focus, the precocious prodigy sees a mob of men yelling something. They crowd the ammo wagons, often standing on the bodies of Iberians who didn't get out of their way. With long hair and longer beards, the Germani seem unkept and uncontrolled. Most men would retreat against so many hoping to hurt him. Instead, Magnus looks half-asleep as he roars into grown-ass men holding torches to wood. Several superstitious strangers back up in fear, unsure what's screaming at them. Some chatter in gibberish, clearly cursing. Germani torching other ammo wagons pause to assess the situation. Bewildered and terrified, they fearfully stare at Magnus as if trying to figure out what he is. This little kid is ruining their big plans.

"A demon possesses the boy!" a warrior wails. "Or the boy possesses a demon!"

Hundreds of deathly afraid men on both sides look up at Magnus, then hear him roar like a mama bear at a cave entrance or possibly a deranged animal with anger issues. He's both smaller in person and larger than life as he runs out of time and breath.

While some Iberians dump dirt on the most threatening flames, others counter-attack. Led by Centurion Franco, they surge forward effectively and risk their lives to save their odd hero. Larger than even the Germani, Franco cuts a path through flesh and bone to save his conceited cousin. He knocks aside spears to thrust and slice, completely committed and possibly out of his damn mind. Other Iberians help and soon he's plowing through a field of Alamanni towards Magnus, sowing death in his furrows. It's impressive and visually spectacular. Desperate and careless of his own safety, this monster of a man clearly adores his clever cousin.

"I'm coming, Max. Fight, damn you to Hell! You have too many plans to take the easy way out! Don't let your damn dad beat you again."

15

The tough teen pauses his slicing and stabbing to make eye contact, then smiles sadly at Franco. But someone pulls him down and he's back in the fight, literally kicking and screaming.

Back in the saddle, Uncle Theo rides up and doesn't slow down. Coming across as crazy, he smashes into strangers, smacking some with his shield and stabbing others with his cavalry sword. He's focused, yet frantic because he might lose his life and, even worse, his son. With Magnus on a wagon, they're at eye level. The legate is 29 years old, handsome, athletic, and could pass for sane once he catches his breath and exhales his darkest fears. He watches his oddest nephew struggle to his feet with big eyes and great discomfort. Magnus is bloody and bruised, but smiling happily, for some reason. It's such an odd day.

"You crazy boy! Do you want to die?"

Magnus shakes himself awake and seems surprised at the fighting around him. "Oh, hey Uncle Theo. I want immortality, but not if it takes forever. Tell mama I love her to death." He turns to address the legion. "Attack! Kill them all! No mercy! Fuck them and the horse they didn't ride in on!"

That comes out as a rasp, but this legion is now pumped up and ready to rage. They were desperate before, but now channel their fears and fury at the archers who ambushed them. Sounding desperate, Franco yells indistinctly at Max while his legionaries roar collectively and fall forward as if obeying a suicidal boy is a good idea.

In contrast, having snatched defeat from the jaws of victory, the Alamanni seem demoralized and deflated. One turns and warns the rest that they lost the 100 archers pouring 800 arrows a minute into their enemies. The wagons they started burning have been extinguished and no one feels like torching them again. Having lost the reason for traveling hundreds of miles, they might as well leave while they can.

But the badass boy insists on the last word. Standing on the wagon and happily predicting his fate: "I die for the glory of Rome!"

How ironic that turns out. He says it with a huge smile and sounds delighted by the idea. He even perfected Crazy Eyes because honest men recoil from the criminally insane. Happy folks fear death, but this teen apparently seeks it out as a remedy for misery.

"Boy, you crazy!" an Alamanni says with a heavy accent.

Laughing like a lunatic as he pulls himself together one final time. "I might be crazy, but I don't *suffer* from insanity."

Magnus jumps off this wagon onto another and gets some speed before leaping onto the most resistant Alamanni. A thousand eyes track him and every single one thinks he's clearly crazy. Both sides move in on him. The Romans fight forward, animated, energetic, and dying to kill enemies. Knocked-down defenders get up with an ax to grind, thanking their armor and the strange beast passing for a suicidal boy. Horrified, Uncle Theo tearfully spurs his stallion forward to save his lifesaving nephew. Team Franco advances from the other direction, cutting through packed enemies who can't counter a force of nature.

Magnus is drowning in enemies and needs a lifeline. Landing on a mob of filthy Germani, he stabs and slices like a cornered beast, harming several. He kicks a butt and takes a punch as strong hands grab him. Magnus scrambles onto a giant with his back turned, which makes him twirl in fear. Spinning, that warrior throws him off and smacks

16

him down, but this distraction has given Romans an opening. The Iberian legion is eager to save him, so they surge forward, roaring his name. The Alamanni focus on Magnus instead of the armed men wearing full armor slicing their way near. These warriors hate no one as much as they hate this small boy and his big mouth. These Germani despise Magnus and can't wait to kill him.

Down on the ground, but not out of the fight, Magnus swings with his short sword and long knife to cut anything around him, but Germani boots still stomp and kick him. Big warriors wielding long swords lack the room to use them, which is why Romans invented short swords centuries ago. Screaming Alamanni limp, staring in shock at cuts in their lower legs as if those minor wounds are fatal. Several stumble away, cursing the kid who cut them. A few fall due to the severity of their injuries and then cry as if their lives are over. Some say goodbye in German to loved ones they'll never see again.

One beefy badass plants his weight on the kid's center-of-gravity, then jabs Magnus with his shitty knife, but it doesn't penetrate the boy's new kickass chainmail. Frustrated, the warrior tries thrusting the blade into an eye, but the boy turns his head, leaving a lifelong scar. The iron gets caught between his head and his lion helmet. Terrified of losing an eye, the prodigy rolls in one direction to put the warrior off balance, then turns in the opposite direction to knock him off. Blood flowing from the wound near his eye, the hero crawls on top of this enemy and puts a knife so far into the warrior's eye that he can't retrieve the blade. Frustrated, he adjusts his position, but still loudly struggles to pull it out. With enemies kicking and punching him, Magnus gives up his expensive knife to see who's hitting him.

The fight by the wagons looks like drunks dancing in a tavern. Magnus disappears from sight, making the Iberians frantic. They're screaming like lunatics while the Alamanni are fully afraid. Romans yell his name, furious to lose him. The Germani back up and back out, but several want to first stomp the life out of this bold brat. With a command and a curse, Uncle Theo rides up and knocks some down. His sword thrusts into one warrior and back-cuts another. Alamanni attack, but Theo uses his shield to block some blows, then kicks his charger into some enemies and ends up smashing into a dozen to clear the space around his naughty nephew. The pumped up legion fights in full rage mode, lost to battle lust. Some roar "Max" while other simply roar, but the rational Germani barbarians can't compete. Angry enemies shatter like clay pots and run for their lives. The Romans gleefully pursue, sensing victory. The battle is won, but not over.

Theo finds his childish nephew in a fetal position, an infantile attitude, and with a sophomoric sense of humor. Though audibly aching, he's bruised and bloody, but smiling like a drunk, for some reason. The uncle looks down on him literally and figuratively.

"Max, how bad are you hurt?"

He sounds in awful agony. "Everything hurts but my pride. Why couldn't they kill me? I can't do it myself because it feels like giving up. I despise quitters." Shaking something off, he struggles to make his limbs work. "I lost my mind, but it's probably around here somewhere."

From an ammo wagon, Cousin Theo watches them, looking bitter, envious, and upstaged. Bleeding, bruised, and despairing, he talks to himself: "Why won't he die? He's good at everything except suicide."

Uncle Theo pulls Magnus up and rides to the stallion as his nephew hugs him from behind like a tree. Magnus changes rides by leaping onto Caesar and they both hunt hostiles as ambushers scatter in retreat. The Germani leave behind most of their bowmen, dead, dying, or too wounded to flee. Their mission to steal or burn cedar arrow shafts has gone up in flame. They failed and that burns. And now they've lost Alamannia's best bowmen in the bargain. All because one boy learned to sling from the saddle. Magnus rides through warriors while slinging soft targets with hard pellets. Every time he strikes a skull, that man drops dead like someone snipped his puppet strings.

Smoke still rises from a few wagons and *medici*, wearing white uniforms, treat wounded Iberians. Legionaries pick up enemy bows to advance aggressively, shouting to pump each other up. Their horsemen are few, but go after the ammo-less, chopping them with swords in a one-sided massacre. The tide has turned and the Alamanni run to the Rhine. As they lose their ammo or their archers, these Germani become little more than slow targets. A horn blows twice as they run uphill with troops in pursuit. Roman horsemen catch up to slice them down.

Seeking Serapio, Magnus pauses to study the limpers. Some Alamanni have ridden away and he fears the handsome ambusher escaped. Other Roman riders shout thanks, pat his back, and thank Magnus as they butcher the bastards who came to kill them. The tables have been turned and the legionaries are loving it. Once he runs out of targets, the killer kid stops at the dense woods and starts singing again. The legion joins him in singing Girls of Rome as they massacre men. Legionaries gleefully stab strangers in furs and thrust swords into chests or throats. Magnus takes out his flute to play along. The Iberians smile up at him like he's a huge hero and he soaks up their adulation like a greedy sponge.

Magnus smiles, the happiest he's ever felt. "Best. Day. Ever."

Fort Briga in the Briey Basin of eastern Gaul

A stone castle on a hill dominates the terrain. A large river bends sharply, making it wider, slower, and shallower, and thus easier to cross. A dozen docks have vessels supplying the army. Vast forests cover both sides of the river, except where logging has pushed it back. Many supply wagons come and go on roads cut through the trees. Several field camps line the river. Half of a pontoon bridge extends to the middle of the current. Dark smoke rises from a nearby town that shares the main road and riverport. Thousands of horses graze. Troops hurry to complete tasks.

A trumpet blows and a dozen uniformed horsemen ride through an oak gate into the castle, looking grim. Some wear white bandages. In the distance, Legate Theo settles them in, barking indistinct commands for them to find doctors, medicine, and bunks. General Gerontius jogs over, his face fighting conflicting emotions. A very handsome 30-year-old, he moves like a champion athlete and instinctively scowls at his son. A natural rider, Magnus canters on Caesar to the command post alone, a big smile on his excited face and a bandage by his eye. A few bad bruises cover his good looks. Soldiers pause training to greet him cheerfully and he calls a few by name. Dressed in uniform as a general, Ger watches a trooper ask Magnus for a joke. Others hurry to hear it.

"I just had sex for three hours and, man, my hand hurts!"

That cracks them up. Their loud laughter carries and other men turn to smile at the popular boy. He laughs with them and playfully orders them back to work.

The general growls. "That bastard keeps stealing my best material."

A girl greets Magnus with a huge smile and a happy puppy. Dad hears him greet the dog with more energy than the cutie.

"Who's a good boy?" the boy says to excited barking. "Maximo is a good boy!" The puppy tries climbing the horse until the teen moves on.

Stern and annoyed while pressing his lips together, Ger studies his son with tight fists on his hips. Stiff and stressed, he doesn't call him over or shout a pleasant greeting. The teen rides up, but doesn't get down. Though sore and in pain, he seems thrilled and satisfied. While thousands of troops do their thing around the busy fort, father and son are basically alone in a wide courtyard.

"Dad, the Alamanni ambushed Uncle Theo, but I saved the legion by slinging from the saddle! I even hit King Mederic and his slippery son, Serapio. I finally had the first happy day of my life; thank God you weren't there to ruin it." They make eye contact as the teen taunts his father. "Oh, you should have been there to see me save your little brother from certain death. No, don't thank me; I wouldn't recognize gratitude. I almost died saving Theo, so you almost won twice. I pulled through just to spite you." Suddenly bitterly disappointed. "And Uncle Theo brought Cousin Theo, for some reason."

Dad struggles with self-restraint. "Max, stop making everything about you and tell me what happened."

"The Alamanni lost a few thousand of their best bowmen, so your army will have an easier time invading Alamanni at the next full moon. Because of me, you probably won't fail this time. I never imagined you ever succeeding as a general, but I look forward to sacking Frankfurt if your shit luck doesn't kill you first. Theo's Jovii Legion is just a day's march away to join your Victores Legion. Theo brought 80 supply wagons, a million cedar arrow shafts, and 300 catapults, from small handheld ones to the big *carroballista*. We'll have over 60 Onager torsional trebuchets to throw incendiaries at the enemy. The Alamanni literally won't know what hits them. Our 32,000 troops can finally invade Alamannia! If you don't fuck it all up, then we'll stop being dirt poor! Oh, I'd love to grow up without folks looking down on me. Dad, I'm sorry I called you a cheap motherfucker yesterday; you aren't cheap, just broke."

He sounds like they already won the war.

On foot, dad throws his hands in the air. "Max, where have you been? Your mother is worried sick and your little brother is almost concerned. Marc can play with Young Theo since you're always too busy."

Disappointed at his reaction. "You told me to find Uncle Theo. I did what you wanted, for once; there's no pleasing you, is there? But it was nice to get out of the hot foundry. My burns now have bruises."

Magnus looks at his underarm to check his latest burn. He presses it gently because it's still tender.

"Yesterday, boy! You left yesterday to look for Theo."

"A few thousand Alamanni blocked his path, so I hit them until Uncle Theo could drive them off. I saved a legion, so some centurions made me a grass crown like Dictator Sulla, 500 years ago. Caesar wanted to eat it until Uncle Honorius fed him a nosebag of oats. My new design makes the lead pellets whistle in flight. Being lighter makes them fly faster and therefore hit harder. Now I almost don't hate you making me a

19

filthy blacksmith apprentice. I had to hug Caesar with my legs, so my thighs are tensed up, like I took a spear up the ass." Pausing theatrically. "Again. No thanks to you, all those years training with the sling on horseback paid off. I have another idea for improving my custom saddle, but this one shouldn't take long or cost much."

"Max, you're only 10. Wait a while before getting yourself killed."

Sounding skeptical. "I don't feel 10. I'm probably twice my age. I'm as big as most 14-year-olds and I want to be the best at everything like you, but less angry and irritating."

His father looks like he's cycling through various answers before finding one that will provoke the boy. Sounding dead serious, Ger makes eye contact. "Son, you'll never be better than me at anything and you'll never be great. I don't care how hard you try."

Not surprised, the teen shifts position in the saddle and literally looks down on his dad.

"Ah, so you're having one of those days. Did mama catch you with another tramp?" He chuckles softly, then piles on. "Are you sure you want to drive me away? Then you'd be all alone with your manipulative lies, blind ambition, and grandiose schemes. One day I'll prove myself worthy of you and then maybe you won't stare at me with bitter disappointment."

"A daughter wouldn't talk back to me. Marc's a good son; I don't know what the hell happened to you."

Theo rides up and gives Gerontius a brotherly head-nod. "Gerontius, Max says you almost died in battle last month, but he saved you by slinging from the saddle. I can tell you're still hurt."

"Max helped and yes, it was close. I told him to stay with the baggage train, but he disobeyed me, like always. Did he tell you I saved him from three Alamanni kicking him to death?"

Magnus scoffs at that. "You saved Caesar; I was an afterthought. Tribune Pelagius saved me. You watched me duel the last bastard as if you bet money on him; I still smell his unnatural stench. I saw your disappointment when I beat a grown man in an honest fight by throwing a knife in his back."

"Watching? I was bleeding out and fumbling with my medical kit. I taught you that killer move, but you didn't do it right, despite all our practice sessions. Very few fighters are fully ambidextrous, so you and I can do things that most men can't. You won because I taught you well, yet you never thank me." Turning to Theo. "Brother, thank you for coming and welcome to Fort Briga. 400 years ago, Caesar Drusus built this cemented stone *castra*, so locals call it a castle." He points across the distant river. "From the Swiss Plateau to the sea, the 800-mile-long Rhine divides Roman Gaul from barbarian Germania and this bend in the river is the easiest place for horsemen to cross for hundreds of miles in either direction. The Alamanni used Fort Briga as their western capital for a century before Caesar Julian, newly appointed second-in-command of the Roman Empire, forced them east of the Rhine. Alamannia has Bavarians to their north, Burgundians to their northeast and, along the Danube going east, the Marcomanni, Gepids, Thurvingi, and finally Persian-speaking Sarmatians along the lower Danube and the Pontic Steppe. For centuries, the Marcomanni formed a confederation against Rome with the Quadi, Vandals, and Sarmatians, but their new queen, Fritigil, signed a peace treaty after we threatened her capital at Bergenland in Bohemia last month. She even agreed to become Christian. Without the Marcomanni, the rest prefer the Alamanni weakening us."

Still high off victory. "Dad, is Queen Fritigil as ugly as her name?"

"Yes. She has enough facial hair to shampoo her cheeks. Boy, I wouldn't fuck her with your tiny dick. We decimated the Marcomanni last month, so I don't expect them to survive as a distinct tribe. Theo, when Caesar Julian kicked out the Eastern Germani from Gaul, the Western Germani suddenly offered to take Alamanni land as buffer states. While our legions bunk here, the Franks, Saxons, Angles, Batavi, Frisi, and Jutes made their own field camps by the river. Our success last month convinced these Western Germani to weaken the Alamanni before they grow too powerful, while the opportunity to raid Alamannia thrilled their warriors. I hear the Alamanni already number a million, after assimilating the Buri. Their three brother-kings are the best leadership they've ever had. If we don't stop them here and now, they'll soon raid Italy again. In 259, the Alamanni threatened Rome. They fought us in pitched battles in 259, 268, 271, and 298. Roman Gaul can't be strong until we weaken them."

Theo grunts. "Ger, I brought all the ammo and *ballistae* that I could get, but the governor of Iberia will be furious if we're not compensated. The banker's check you sent didn't cover a quarter of it. The vipers at Triers refused to loan you my Iberian legion so, officially, I'm giving my troops an extensive training exercise that might involve crossing a river under fire. I'll need immediate payment for the 80 supply wagons. We're 1000 miles from our base in Valencia so, in your official correspondence, I'm not here and you only have 18,000 troops, plus whatever Max is."

Ger nods. "Julian's army already left Reims, but he moves like every centurion needs a cane. The Alamanni beat Julian like a helpless peasant outside Reims last year and he's still hurting. We plan to execute the classic pincer movement, *forceps*, but rumor is Emperor Constantius wants Julian to contain the Alamanni without succeeding too well. Too much success will make Julian shine brighter than his cousin, the emperor. Neither Julian nor I have received the promised food, ammo, and even boats for a pontoon bridge, so we're wasting time like there's no tomorrow." Pointing. "My tribune, Pelagius, is the best educated man I've ever met. Though born in Britannia, his grandfather struck it rich, so he grew up in Rome. Their family library is bigger than their wine cellar. Crazy, right? We met in Rome when I studied there for the summer. You two can talk about the great men of Rome all night. A young Batavi commander named Dutch brought 8000 Batavi allies from the Rhine delta, so we have 32,000 men. Uncle Honorius lent me his largest ship, an ocean-going trawler that I turned into an artillery platform. Payroll is in the vault, in case something happens to me. King Mallobaudes brought several thousand Franks and he helps keep other Germani in line. He's an impressive man who speaks Latin like a resident of Rome. If I read the future right, then next month we'll all be as rich as Crassus, as powerful as Caesar, and as drunk as Cato."

The teen sounds worried. "Dad, the Alamanni ambushers called me Flavius. Not even mama calls me Flavius. Why would they know my birth name?"

Dismissively waving that away. "Someone stole a box of documents. My camp has more spies than combat veterans."

"Dad, the Alamanni can still field 150,000 warriors; shouldn't we wait until we can catch them by surprise?"

21

Shaking his head no. "Julian made deals with their neighbors. The Saxons, Franks, and Burgundians can't wait for us to hurt their biggest rival for them. If we lose this year, someone else will shine brighter next year. It must be now and I must win or I'll never get another independent command. I don't want to go back to Britannia. Max, your mother's father is no longer chief, their victuals are plain, and the weather is gloomier than my childhood."

Magnus smiles at his uncle. "British food is inedible, but at least there's enough for everyone."

"Theo, how bad was their attack?"

The legate sits ramrod stiff in the saddle as if his spine doesn't bend. "Bad. My son and I almost died. I lost 88 legionaries and Little Theo earned his first combat wound, but it should have been much worse. Max showed up just in time to save us all. It was almost funny, watching grown Germani on foot chase an expert rider. Your crazy boy cracked open a few hundred heads and limbs. I'm honestly impressed. I had no idea a mounted slinger could deal so much death. Max seemed more suicidal than usual, so I hope you don't still beat him. Oh! The Alamanni tried burning just the wagons that carried the million cedar shafts and fletches for your new iron arrowheads. I assume you have a spy in your cot and still talk in your sleep unless Senator Savelli is betraying you."

The general groans. "Luca Savelli needs me to fund improvements to his mines, forges, and factories. His family has owned this river valley for centuries and has bred with enough Alamanni to start his own tribe, but he didn't get his land back until Caesar Julian pushed the Alamanni east of the Rhine. Luca has been suspiciously helpful since I began buying his over-priced, ultra-pure iron with Rome's money. Our 20-year contract induced him to upgrade his bloomery and purchase pumps to suck rainwater from his flooded mines. The new waterwheel, Archimedes Screw, and the triple-pulley system must have exhausted our initial payments. That clever bastard has more engineers than I do, and all of them have been improving capacity. I personally find the technical challenges fascinating while Max has become an expert at pestering all the engineers at the same time."

The big boy excitedly turns in the saddle to his uncle with manic face and tone. "Luca has the usual winches, vacuum pumps, and levers, but also bevel gears, worm gears, and offset gears, plus camshafts, CV joints, universal joints, crank drives, chain drives, belt drives, and something called rack and pinion. If you suddenly slip on something slippery, it's probably my blown mind. It's a tourist resort for technicians. Did you know high math can be useful? I didn't, either! I might retire here after I become rich, famous, and immortal. Uncle, Luca still wears a toga in public. No one in Rome wears togas anymore, yet he has a silk toga for every day of the month, all softer than a baby's butt, if you still caress those all night. He looks like a whale walking out of water. It's disturbing and hilarious."

The general suddenly grabs Caesar's reins and inspects a bloody cut on his huge head. "Max, I let you borrow Caesar and you almost got him killed? He's the best breeder our ranch has ever had. Do you know what this fucker is worth? If I had more time and less trouble, I'd beat you more."

The son puts on his innocent face while lying his ass off. "The enemy beat you to it. Dad, Caesar is the best warhorse they've ever seen, so the Germani wanted to take him, not kill him. But I'll probably survive my many cuts, bruises, and wounded pride.

22

Thanks for your concern. I almost lost an eye, a limb, and my life, but why should you care? You have a better, quieter son who doesn't talk back or run off. I thought I was gonna die, but I was wrong, for once. I'm not sure I can live with the disappointment."

"Max, I don't like the enemy knowing your name. Once the boats get here, I want you to take your mother and brother back home to Porto Gordo (Portugal)."

Theo agrees. "My son should also leave. Young Theo insisted on finally accompanying his father in the field. Little Gratian goes with General Valentinian and my son wants a military career. I had assumed a 6-year-old would be safe in Fort Briga, but he almost died down the road. I still can't get over it."

"Let's discuss things over dinner. It's been too long since we've talked. If Uncle Honorius, Cousin Honorius, and our brother Honorius were here, it'd be a family reunion." Eyeing his dangerous son. "Dad would come back from the dead for that."

Theo is suddenly unsettled. "Let that mean bastard rot in Hell for beating his boys. Brother, I'm eternally grateful for you shooting that drunk before he finished me off. I owe you."

Ger feels pessimistic. "Brother, if I don't make it, you can pay me back by taking care of my sons. If the campaign against the Alamanni goes well, you'll share my glory. If not, then I'm ordering you to blame me while distancing yourself. Our ranch needs cash money and political connections. If I fall or fail, then only you can pay off our debts to keep our ancestral estate in Iberia."

Theo sounds bitter. "Those bankers will take our land over my dead body."

Ger lights up. "Last month, General Barbatio greatly outnumbered the Alamanni, yet still lost, instead of waiting for us, as ordered. I think he wanted all the glory to replace Julian as Caesar, then become emperor after Constantius, who now wants to execute Barbatio, his bitch-wife Assyria, and cavalry commander Arbitio for their failure. In contrast, last year I helped Julian beat the Attuarian Franks at Augst and the Rhineland Franks on the Lower Rhine by Toxandria. After that, Julian gave me three cavalry squadrons to hunt down Laeti raiders who thought Barbatio's defeat meant everything was free for the taking.

"Outside Argentoratum, after the Alamanni drove off our light cavalry, a shield wall fixed their infantry's position. The Batavi and I saved the day with what felt like a suicidal charge that fucked their infantry in the ass. Oh, what a glorious moment! I personally killed at least a dozen and wounded many more, thanks to Max coming with a thousand arrows. Because of us, our thin shield wall held. Before their light horse could counter, Julian himself led our mobile reserves, saving my life and winning the battle. My head was so high in the clouds that I actually hugged Julian and thanked him for saving me. The least cynical thing I've ever done earned me command of an army of my own. If he becomes emperor, Julian privately promised to make me his Caesar. Like Constantius, Julian is also an orphan without sons and his wife Helena is only good for miscarriages. Theo, imagine your big brother as second-in-command of the Roman Empire! Caesar Gerontius Maximus! If I outlast him, I'd become Augustus Gerontius Maximus. Crazy, right?"

The men savor the tasty idea before the boy's brutal tone bursts their bubble.

"Dad, it'll never happen because you have shit for luck. But don't worry: I might support your forced retirement when I become emperor. Cousin Theo can be my Caesar as long as he never leaves my giant shadow."

23

Dad grabs a fistful of tunic and pulls his son off the stallion. Magnus smacks the ground like horseshit. Ger plants a big black boot on his chest as the dazed boy lays on his back in the dirt. Clearly, father and son have issues.

Ger is furious. "I had Caesar's luck until your birth. Everything sweet turned sour after that. I don't want to believe in reincarnation, but I've always felt like we've bumped heads in previous lives. With the support of your mother's clan, I could have ruled Londinium, but you pissed on the wrong Roman and got away with it by passing for a baby. I saw your eyes; you did it on purpose, then laughed in the governor's face." He exerts great effort to control his rage. "Son, I expect you to be the death of me."

Hating being pinned to the ground. "Not me, father. I need you to see me outshine you. The sunrise is always brighter than the sunset. I'm the dawn and you're the dusk. I'll always be remembered while you'll be forever forgotten."

Tearing up. "Son, I think you were my father, Eucherius. I killed him, so you've come back to kill me. Personas pass from body to body, but not memories, but I've seen him in you. I'm probably sorry I killed you, but you chose this body to punish me and I can't take it anymore."

That shocks the teen, who deflates. He digests the info, not loving it, and can't wait to shit it out.

"That'd explain why you hit me so often and why I love Uncle Theo so much. But your dad was an abusive arsehole who may have cost us our ancestral estate. Hell, I'd hurt him too. Ger, get my abacus to see if we can do the math. If my own son murdered me in my last life, that would explain why I'm needy in this one and why I want to fuck grandma. Just kidding. But I do hate her for remarrying. Dad, no wonder I keep calling you a son-of-a-bitch when you're out of hearing. The Apollo Oracle at Delphi says, Know thyself; it didn't say shit about knowing my grandpa. If I'm not me, then who am I? I always wanted to be someone else's son. Funny how that worked out." Something snaps and his expression changes. "Nah, I'm not buying it. Motherfucker, you're just blaming your dad for beating your son. Just man up, you weak coward, and admit you like hurting me for its own sake. I know how I am, so I don't even blame you. A big mouth like mine begs for a beating. Just own your faults like I pretend to own mine."

Dad grunts and shifts more weight onto his son, which fucking hurts. "My beautiful dad also liked to call me ugly names. Is this the best time to bring out the worst in me?"

Magnus studies Theo from the ground. "Uncle, you knew about this and never told me? That's it; you're grounded, young man, and no more honey cakes!"

Theo dismounts to roughly push his brother off. Magnus gets up and marches off, confused and conflicted. Ger watches troops get out of his way as if they know his bad moods.

Theo sounds so tired. "Brother, you should not have told him that, especially if it's true. Did you see his eyes change without blinking? That's the scariest thing I've seen today and I almost witnessed the annihilation of my beloved legion. Without them, I don't have a job, income, or even status. Commanding a legion is the only thing stopping those bankers from foreclosing on our estate. You remember when dad first taught us how to roar, Glorious Victory? Your son did that today when he tried getting himself killed. He threw his life away to save me. No 10-year-old could do what Max did. He was an avenging angel who hit hundreds of hostiles. When Max got up dazed, from being

24

thrown, I saw dad's eyes, clear as day. Ger, dad saved me. Sure, he became a horrible drunk, but he still loves us."

Ger shits over all that. "Dad loves you. I'm the one who shot him in the back and then laughed as he died. I never told you this, but he called me a bitter disappointment, a loser, and a failure because Emperor Constantius banned me when I fought for his brother during their civil war, over a decade ago. Uncle Honorius tricked dad into using the estate as collateral, but I had warned dad not to gamble with our home. Dad deserved to die for letting that ruthless pirate manipulate him."

Pissed and pensive. "Ger, I gave you permission, but you still murdered our father in cold blood when he was drunk and defenseless. Max may have dad's soul, but he isn't our father. Your anger and abuse push him to the edge. Back off and ease up before you idiots destroy our family again."

Ger looks at Theo with pleading eyes and a tormented soul, then nods in agreement.

Magnus follows his father like an assassin. The hot smelter melts them as they enter. Metalworkers endure steamy charcoal to melt iron ore as several males walk into this burning furnace. They hear hissing and men moaning, but back away from the intense heat. Ger points at the buff guy in charge, ordering others about.

"Theo, that's Joko, the senator's son. I thought I knew a lot about metalworking until I met him. I've learned more in the last month than the rest of my life combined. Max shadows him like a hunter. Joko makes the purest iron ever, so I re-forged my brass balls here. Oh, here comes Senator Luca. Hold on to your coin purse."

A pleasant, chubby man in his 50s, wearing a bright red toga, waddles over like a mayor seeking re-election. He waves them into his office to be heard over the clanging and sizzling of a foundry. Luca closes the door so they can hear, then leans forward as if selling them secrets. Luca's whole body smiles with insincerity.

"Legate Theodosius, I'm Senator Luca Savelli, also the mayor of Briga. In my restless youth, I once visited your home province of Galicia. The northwestern corner of Iberia is beautiful country and the greenest area of that dry peninsula. Welcome to Europe's most sophisticated iron smelter. My factories are also very advanced. If properly developed, Lorraine Province could become the world's largest iron producer. Sadly, most of it is minette or lignite, polluted by excessive phosphorus or sulfur from sedentary rock that makes it ill-suited to iron products with existing technology. Happily, my Briga mines produce ore with 60% iron. Purer iron leaves less slag, giving it more homogeneous content favorable for shaping and sharpening. Romans use coal, which weakens iron arms and armor with sulfur impurities, whereas I use charcoal to make iron stronger with carbon. My iron has twice the purity, making it twice as strong. As General Gerontius knows, my iron tips can penetrate iron armor that common arrows cannot. My swords can cut through helmets and even breastplates. Gerontius is so impressed by my weapons that he put a down payment towards a million arrowheads, 100,000 Plumbata darts, 10,000 Pilum throwing javelins, and 10,000 sets of chainmail tunics that protect the genitals, with another 10,000 chainmail vests sandwiched in boiled leather. I've doubled my workforce and have never felt more flattered. I might just get out of debt. All my life I've chased financial security; I'll be shocked and satisfied if I ever get it."

Magnus sounds super excited. "Uncle, Luca's chainmail saved our lives this morning. One set of chainmail wasn't enough, so I wore two, plus a chest plate and back plate. A few arrows from close range punctured both sets, but not deeply. My custom lion helmet kept my head from imploding from heavy blows. I even wore chainmail chaps to protect my legs. Theo, you're alive because I sent you several sets by ship, one for every cousin who loves me. I sent Franco the extra-large set, meant for daddy. My abacus says you owe me countless huggies."

Theo laughs and hugs the big boy. "Little Man, I owe you more than that. You threw your life away, saving my son."

"That was for you. Uncle, it kills me to see you sad. Even as a baby, Cousin Theo refused my hugs. I've always assumed I was your son and he was Ger's. The Goddess Fate is a divine bitch to switch my father at my birth."

Luca looks harshly at Magnus. "So you're the damn thief who stole those suits of armor. I should have guessed." He turns to close the sale. "Legate Theo, assess this Spatha cavalry sword. It's longer, yet still lighter than ordinary ones, while being stronger and sharper. For his size, Max prefers the short Gladius sword. Lighter blades swing faster, so superior iron means the better armed man wins, not the better fighter."

Theo picks up the kickass sword, does the routine swings, and then studies it up close. "It's lighter and sharper, but your iron is not steel. My Uncle Honorius sold Damascus steel swords for enough profit to buy his first cargo ship. If Shapur the Second of Persia didn't conquer Damascus, the Maximus family would be merchants instead of military men."

Sighing hard, Luca continues in a tired voice. "My father sent trade missions into Persia and learned the Wootz ingots that Damascus turns into swords actually come from Kerala, in southern India. Indians started making steel almost a thousand years ago and jealously guard their secrets for purifying iron. Persians pay enormous amounts for steel ingots because Europeans pay far more for finished products. Wootz swords have distinctive banding with mottling that looks like flowing water in beautiful patterns. They are sharper, less brittle, less likely to shatter, last longer, rust slower, and are lighter, which means they can be longer. They say Damascus Swords can cut a human hair floating across its edge. We've looked for thirty years for an expert to come here. I've lost two uncles, three cousins, and a lot of patience; my son Bobo still has not returned from Kerala." He loudly exhales something invaluable. "The technique for controlled thermal cycling after the initial forging remains a mystery in the West."

The hyper boy is more manic than usual. "Uncle, did you now pig iron is made from actual pigs. Luca, explain why your iron is superior."

"I know Bobo reached Kerala because he sent me a letter with what he learned. He says purifying iron requires higher sustained temperatures than Roman coal-fired furnaces are capable of, plus better fluxes to remove impurities. Bobo told me to use charcoal for greater tensile strength suitable for arms, armor, hammers, saws, axes, hooks, cranes, springs, support structures, and cantilever loading. Indians use a two-step process and something called a blast furnace, but I haven't duplicated their process or their result. I have quite the technical library that Max reads when he should be working. My granddaughter Sasa sneaks them to him and lies when I catch her. I beat her once, when she let Max copy Bobo's letter, but she continues to indulge the dangerous boy. It must be love because neither have hit puberty. I offered marriage, but the evil ingrate says he'll never marry. The young assume they know everything worth knowing until

26

losing their virginity proves they know nothing. Ger, your energetic son can't calm down now, but constant sex may cure his odd disposition. Give him a few years and girls will become his new obsession."

The big boy is contagiously pumped up. "Luca has lost writings by Archimedes, Ctesibius, and Hero of Alexandria. During Christ's ministry, Hero used steam to make balls spin in the air and lift massive blocks of stone. Uncle, did you know Archimedes calculated the volume of a pyramid seven centuries ago? I doubt anyone alive could do that today, even after inflation. After articulating the mathematical Principle of Proportionality and discovering how to calculate the volume of a circle, Archimedes used steam cannons against the Roman siege of Syracuse. He even designed a vacuum-toilet that literally sucked ass. How is this not required reading? Luca's library is a gold mine. I hired a math pedagogue to learn how to do the calculations. Joko is a genius who only looks like a bearded barbarian brute. I had no idea how much I didn't know until last month. Luca has a Jewish Persian who should start a technical school. The throwing knives I've forged here with pure iron are so much better than the ones I made in Porto Gordo. I didn't want to become an engineer until I looted Luca's library."

Ger looks tired and Theo alarmed.

Luca loudly exhales. "I'm an indulgent man inclined to education, but this monstrous child exhausts my patience. Every morning he interrogates my experts as they pretend to work. Max uses my equipment to do experiments and speaks of the elasticity of air as if serenading an engineer. He goes through lamp oil like Cato the Drunk went through wine. Max can quote Euclid and thinks pivoting my waterwheel more into the current will increase the spin rate by 22% - he says numbers never lie."

Exasperated, Magnus corrects the record. "I said 101% of negative numbers never lie, but 11 out of every 9 statistics might mislead. It's grammar that's mendacious. Never forget to remember that I'm great at lying and I'm probably good at statistics."

Luca ignores that. "Gerontius, I feared Max had ill intentions for Sasa because he plays the flute beautifully for her and sings her to sleep, but spies say she kisses him a hundred times for every platonic kiss that he returns. Convinced he's an angel, my indulgent wife makes him sweetmeats and honey cakes as if those are cheap and I'm never hungry. Max purchases goodwill by sketching us on expensive canvas and pays compliments as if expecting a receipt. Some portraits are quite good. He's better at drawing than painting and feels fueled by flattery. I have ten portraits, but my wife has thrice as many that she hangs on every wall. She spends money I don't have to buy sexy clothing she doesn't need because Max makes her immortal on canvas. He paints himself using our full-body mirror and has accumulated quite a collection. It's not natural for a boy to gaze at himself so much, so I assume he's secretly female. He'll need a dedicated ship to transport his self-portraits to wherever he stores his vanity for posterity." The senator glares at the teen. "Max is annoying, aggravating, and irritating."

The terrible teen defiantly puts his fists on his hips like his mother when she gives That Look. "And you're repetitive, redundant, and superfluous unless that goes without saying. Don't make me say that again!"

Theo picks up an arrowhead. "Senator, it's too small, narrow, and light. It takes weight to punch through fur coats and thick hides."

Magnus jumps up and down as if eager to confess to the perfect crime. Amused, Ger smiles proudly at his son's back. Magnus can't see the love on his father's face, but

27

Theo does. The badass brothers make comfortable eye contact as they share a moment. The general adores his firstborn, but his son has no idea.

"Go ahead, Max; show off."

The boy twirls to see if his father has gone plum crazy. His eyes squint as he looks up to scrutinize his demanding dad as if he doesn't recognize him.

"You're gonna let me be *me*?" He pauses dramatically, throwing his arms around while screaming loudly as if angry. "Is that even legal?"

Ger tries reason. "Boy, your tutors always said they've never seen a kid absorb technical information faster. You ignore theology, philosophy, and rhetoric, but you love making and fixing stuff. For years I hired experts to teach you whatever you wanted to know while learning what little I could. Roman engineering teams basically adopted you as a helpful parasite. You have a rare gift that I've nurtured like a child. How many times have you modified your saddle? How many knives have you forged for throw-ability? You've hurt yourself more in our blacksmith shop than I have in battlefields. It's time you started repaying that enormous investment. Uncle Theo hasn't seen you in a long year, so go on, show him what you've learned." Chuckling. "Man, sometimes I wish I drank beer. Luca's wife makes apple cider that's to die for; I'll hit her up for some at dinner."

Ger beams with pleasure as Magnus excitedly turns on Uncle Theo with a manic look so intense that the combat veteran steps back warily as if the boy has cooties.

"Little Man, lay off the sweet meats. No wonder you have too much energy to sleep."

His nephew laughs loudly like he just escaped death today. "Uncle, it takes speed, not weight. Doubling the speed produces 4x the kinetic impact. No, really; I probably even did the math. An arrow flying twice as fast is better than one weighing twice as much because it will penetrate 8x deeper. Flight is propulsion minus weight and friction, so lighter projectiles fly farther, faster, and strike harder. Dad tried pine, cedar, beach, ash, oak, birch, and poplar. Pine is popular because it's everywhere, but certain types of cedar are lighter, harder, and straighter. Oak is a classic hardwood, but weighs too much for shafts, so dad asked Admiral Honorius for the million cedar shafts from Lebanon that you brought. At 100 paces, Luca's arrowheads penetrate twice as much boiled leather. That's the difference between a kill and an angry Alamanni hurling a hatchet. I just got hit by a hundred hatchets and they hurt like hell."

Ger seems proud. "Theo, you won't believe the results even after you shoot the shafts. Luca's experts modified the arrowtip to minimize air resistance. The fletches must be uniform and the shaft completely straight, so Uncle Honorius uses a machine rather than accept human error. Most troops can't shoot for shit, but I've been hosting a weekly archery competition, not unlike a pissing contest, with local whores as the prize. I've hired several thousand of the best West Germani shooters and put them on salary. Each legionary fires 100 arrows a day, so Max shoots twice as many from each arm because he's audacious, ambitious, and ambidextrous. Your Jovii Legion only has a few hundred archers; if you had 6000, this morning's battle would not have been competitive. The reason Roman heavy infantry conquered kingdoms around the Med is because archery is hard to master. Heavy infantry would lose to an army of archers. Uncle Honorius formed a factory in Lebanon to turn a cedar forest into arrow shafts using a machine press that renders them perfectly straight. The enemy must have heard about it to risk so many lives to steal or burn them. If Serapio destroyed your legion and my shafts, I could not invade Alamanni as planned. Now we must attach the million iron arrowheads that I bought from Luca to the shafts and fletches that you brought to make sure we win this campaign and thus save our ancestral estate. I can't take any chances. I'm dying to finally succeed."

Theo shrugs. "It's your neck. Unlike you, I'm a lousy liar, so I can't cross the Rhine. Officially, I'm on vacation and no Roman vacations in Greater Germania. Still, I'm impressed. It seems you've thought of everything."

Ger doubts that. "Then why have my bad dreams gotten worse? I brought the wife and kids in case I don't make it. Before battle, Romans must make out a new Last Will. I still remember filling out my first Last Will. Brother, I'm leaving my third of our father's ranch to you. Uncle Honorius will take care of Marc; my wife can return to Britannia, but only you can control my firstborn."

That infuriates Magnus, who looks violent enough to murder his own father with killer irony. Luca leaves like a man in a hurry. The kid is explosive and venomous.

"You're giving me nothing but grief? For half my life, I've followed you from one fort, base, or field camp to another, eating shit for food, mucking your stable, and cleaning your boots. I've done everything you wanted except keep quiet."

Dad is equally angry. "You think I give you grief? You've always been disappointing, disrespectful, and disobedient. You criticize everything I do and how I do it, just like you did as my dad. Being brilliant doesn't give you the right to question your father. I was smarter than you, growing up, yet I hardly ever made my father feel like a worthless piece of shit when he was sober or armed." He flies off the cliff, his soul crying in pain. Addressing his son using his father's name. "Eucherius, I had to murder you to save our estate. Your brother Honorius got you to sign our home as security, though I warned you against that lying pirate. The bank doesn't want our ranch; Admiral Honorius wants it because your dad gave it all to you instead of sharing ownership. If we don't loot Alamannia, Uncle Honorius will take all we have and kick out mama for choosing you instead of the pirate when you three were teenagers. That bitter bastard doesn't forgive and doesn't forget. You signed away our home and now that scoundrel will own it all!"

About to explode. "I'm 10 and you're crazy! You're blaming me for what your dad did? Do you hear how insane that sounds? And yet folks wonder why I'm unusual. Children aren't responsible for their actions, yet everyone blames me anyways. Dad, you're a warehouse of normality housing a lot of crazy."

Still yelling from the clouds. "Boy, you didn't listen to me in that life and you don't listen to me now. Everything changes, yet nothing is different. We could have made a great team if you didn't fuck me over. I've never heard you speak to anyone like you address me. Even as a toddler, you'd hug your mother and stick out your tongue at me. I taught you trick-riding, how to make saddles, how to work iron, how to fight, how to read and write, but you've never thanked me for anything. I've devoted far more time to you than Marc, who actually hugs me. You don't deserve anything from me."

The boy shakes with raw emotion, like a volcano about to blow. "You're the meanest man I ever met! My first memory is running to your horse when you finally returned from a campaign, only for you to ride past me to fuck mama without even greeting me or glancing my way. It was like I didn't exist! You didn't say a word to me until you wanted something in the morning. Everything from you is a command, a question, or a complaint. You never take that tone with Marc. Never once have you asked how I'm doing or what I want. I once thought I could make you love me if I helped you enough. I warmed up your leftovers or chilled your water or scraped the crap off your boots after you walked all over me. But, no, you only valued my utility, so I worked hard to become useful. Even then, you complained I did a shit job mucking the stables." He looks down and inward, his voice softening. "Yet you never look at me like you look at Marc. You light up when your brothers visit. You somehow make mama stay in love with you, despite your frequent infidelity, so there must be something wrong with me. I tried to pinpoint it. I'd wonder all night, listing my many defects or grouping them in broad categories with many sub-brackets. But you're like a drunk who never drinks. Certain things matter to you, but I'm not one of them. Father, I killed a few hundred armed enemies this morning and wounded double that, which makes me a man in every way that matters, so be honest with me for once. Why don't you like me?"

Dad sighs in despair. "Because you remind me of me and I killed my father."

Not at all angry. "Grandpa was an abusive drunk, so you abuse me sober."

"That's not why I killed him and he only started drinking heavily when he lost the ranch. In a cash-poor enterprise, he used our estate as collateral to rebuild our home after lightning burned it down. But his brother, Admiral Honorius, talked him into it and probably started the inferno. So, after he beat me again when drunk, I killed him." Ger tears up because this is killing him. "Before he drank, Flavius Eucherius Maximus was a good man and a great dad. I named you after him, so every time I look at you, I see me murdering my own father, a man I loved and admired. But then I saw him in you; that's when we stopped calling you Flavius. We may lose our ancestral home because of Flavius Maximus. For what it's worth, I regret associating you with two terrible tragedies."

Magnus is going crazy, trying to reason this out. "If I was your dad and you murdered me, then you should apologize and treat me better. That's probably what most patricides do. If you start right now, I might award you a precious huggie."

Backing up and folding his arms. "I'm sorry, son, but I'll never apologize to you. You were a monster then and you're a monster now."

The boy stands there stunned, his eyes blinking uncontrollably until he snaps. Something replaces his fury, but it's hard to tell what.

"You confess to murdering me, when I was your father, yet call me a monster? I doubt even Euclid could circle that square." Ready to shatter like cheap ceramics. "Ger, I'm gonna move to Britannia and see if mama's family can tolerate my presence. Can I have one thing before I go?"

Dad smiles hopefully. "A hug?"

The boy is at his wit's end, super sad, and beyond impatience. "No. You've never understood me. I want Caesar because I've never seen you love anything like you love that fucking horse. I'd take Marc, but you'd miss him less. Since you'll die soon of failure, let's show Theo a training session. He mistakenly thinks all my bruises came from the battle. Come on, old man; let me show Theo my skills. He'll probably be impressed and appalled."

The training yard already has thousands of allies training with sword, spear, and bow. Many practice archery. As soon as they see father and son marching in, West Germani warriors excitedly tell others. Legionaries from the Victores legion hurry to see.

Each holding two wooden swords, Ger and Magnus are shirtless, muscled, and wear white bandages. That cutie, Sasa, and her happy puppy chase the boy and yell encouragement. Men run over with drinks and anticipation. Training pauses to see the spectacle. Thousands gather, whooping and cheering. It feels like a show rather than a lesson. Magnus jogs ahead, yelling names and making jokes. Achingly beautiful in simple clothes, mama holds her husband's hand, looking radiant, blond, and without a bra. Theo walks on Ger's other side, wary and worried. Behind them, 8-year-old Marc walks with Cousin Theo like good brothers instead of first cousins, both looking forward to the fight.

Young Theo smiles. "Oh, Marc, this will be great! Nearly dying will be worth seeing Max get what he deserves. He looks best when covered in welts. I even hug Uncle Ger when he out-does himself."

Marc's less sure. "Careful, cousin. Max trains every day with our best fighters and has a surprise for dad. If you didn't hate him so much, he'd hurt you less. You laughed in his face the last time Max asked for a hug." He glances at his horny mother. "Mama gets so excited by these training sessions that she doesn't wear underwear. I've learned to bring a medical kit because pain means little to either of these brutes. Dad says, ages ago, they were twins and have had a love-hate relationship ever since, which is a better explanation than anything I've dreamed up."

A Germani warrior cheers his hero. "Fuck'em up, Max! You almost got him last time. Oh, hey, General Gerontius. You gonna bloody him again? You left him limping last time, like normal fathers."

Dozens of armed men yell out the teen's name, clearly hoping he'll kick ass. His popularity surprises Theo.

"Ger, does everyone know his name?"

Sounding exhausted. "He's insatiable for attention, so he puts on trick-riding shows, sings, or plays his flute. He sounds like an angel, but behaves like the devil. Max makes money by drawing portraits. They chant his name like he's special. I'd rather bait a bear. I'm still recovering from last month's battle or I'd show them better tricks that dad taught me before he mortgaged the family fortune."

"The troops always liked Max. My Iberians think he's a hero."

Ger looks grim. "Every year he gets bigger, stronger, and faster because he's obsessed with becoming better than me in everything. His instincts are killer and his reflexes are crazy quick. Training with combat veterans sharpens his edge. He chops firewood or shoots hundreds of arrows most days to muscle his biceps. I needle him to sharpen his edge, but he's never appreciated me. I know he hates me for it, but I made a man out of a 10-year-old. If he survives childhood, Max could become another Julius Caesar. I'm very proud of a son that I despise. It's sad he can't talk to me without arguing. Must everything be a pissing contest? Our wooden training swords are heavy, giving me the advantage. I also have height and range, so he gets desperate and dangerous. Max hates losing. He stays up at night figuring out how to take me down. We're both ambidextrous, so... Max, the hell are those?"

Within a staked field, Magnus holds up his new wooden training swords over his brunette head and slowly rotates for his audience, screaming encouragement. His bright blue eyes reflect his devious smile and his face seems to glow. Oh, he's been looking forward to this fight.

31

"Dad, I soaked mine in tree resin, then varnished them so they don't break apart like my last ones. Yours are heavy oak, but I used cedar, for its light weight, because I need speed to counter your longer reach. Oh, God, I haven't felt this young since I lost my virginity!"

The crowd roars with laughter, which annoys Ger.

"Stop stealing my best lines, though you're welcome to the worst."

The teen gets serious. "Ger, disinheriting me means you no longer get to tell me what to do. Though I'm still sore, I need to repay you some bruises and I honestly hope it hurts. You ready, old man, to finally lose?"

In disbelief. "I'm among the best swordsmen in the empire, I saved our estate making money as a gladiator, and I'm twice your size with half your arrogance. I need to round off your sharp tongue and teach you some humility. You only see black and white in a world full of grey. Your cock isn't as big as you assume, so tuck it in and give our rivalry a rest. I'm tired of our pissing contests. Son, you actually think you'll win?"

The teen grins, circling Ger while swinging his wooden weapons. "I don't expect to be the last boy standing, but every bruise I give you is a glorious victory. I owe you at least a thousand. However, I'll thank you since we're attempting honesty. You always said you needed to toughen me to survive this cruel world and you were right. The Alamanni punched, kicked, and stomped me with gusto, but no harder than you. It pains me to thank you for your abuse, but you saved me today. I shrugged off their blows like an abused son and laughed at their hatchets, though I bled or bruised in a hundred places. I'm always in physical and psychic pain, so what's a little more? Though I've killed armed men before, it was usually in defense, from battlements or breastworks. Last month I slung hostiles while avoiding and evading attackers. This morning was up close and personal. I saw heads cave in and guts spill out. You said surviving your first battle was transformational. Well, now I know how you felt. The blood washed off my hands, but somehow stained my soul and crept into my conscience. Father, I'm not the little boy I was yesterday. You're a poor bastard who richly deserves a whooping; I may not give it to you today, but you'll get it someday."

Ger doesn't want to lose his son, but demands respect. "Max, you couldn't have asked for a better father."

Stunned exasperation as Magnus blows his top. "Are you delusional? I've asked God for a better father every night for years. It's unbelievable that God doesn't answer prayer. And I'm not shooting for the heavens. I just want a father who doesn't enjoy hurting me. Why do you think I spend more time with Uncle Theo when you're home? Dad, your heart might be in the right place, but your head is up your ass, which would explain your shitty breath."

Dad hefts the heavy training swords and considers his dangerous opponent. "Careful, son. Harsh words are like bloody arrows; you can only get them back from bleeding bodies. You're young and dumb enough to ruin our relationship, so I must get something off my chest."

A mocking tone. "A bra?" He smiles at the cheering crowd. "Again?"

The mob eats it up and echoes it back.

Offended. "Boy, I have a bone to pick with you."

His son chuckles. "Dad, that better be just an expression."

Giving up with a loud sigh. "Never mind. It's like reasoning with a rock. You sound dangerous, so I'll treat you as such. Always respect the threat. I've been having ugly dreams that suggest I won't be around much longer, so I better give you our last lesson today. Son, you always compare yourself to me, but you'll never be half the man that Theo is."

When Magnus drops his guard to gaze at his uncle, dad attacks. Both hold two training swords instead of one shield, so the boy barely blocks and dodges an intense series of blows that leaves him staggering around the grass. Every time dad knocks him down, Magnus gets up even angrier. The clash and clang is louder than the audience, screaming at the exquisite drama. Ger does not move like an old man, but like a 30-year-old champion athlete in his prime. That a mere teen can withstand the onslaught is impressive. Magnus accepts a body blow for the chance to smack dad's wounded chest. The general feels that and vents on the boy, turning aside his blades to whack the son on the helmet. Magnus lunges and lurches, but his father is equally adept and not built for mercy.

The brilliant sword fight awes Germani warriors and Roman legionaries alike. The audience watches, stunned, as the epic duel rages. Each fighter ducks, dodges, and dashes to avoid and inflict blows. The clash of arms echoes off the hills. Girls gasp and men moan as the brave boy escapes another attack from a superior foe. The sprint turns into a marathon as they swing their weapons increasingly wearily. Both are slow to block strikes, but neither has any inclination to end it. The open-faced helmets revealed their faces and they seem determined to win at all costs. The audience sees this and gets quiet as the duel bleeds on. Magnus takes his blows to the upper body while Ger gets hit in the legs a lot. Magnus manages a sucker punch to his recent wound that infuriates his father.

Worried, Theo yells out. "Ger, he plans to outlast you. Max has enough bottom-less energy to fill the sky. Finish him!"

Ger agrees. His hyper kid has limitless energy, so dad presses the attack, swinging and swiping both blunt swords with an intensity and insanity that Magnus finds increasingly unable to counter. Tired of backing up, Magnus takes some hits in order to hurt his father, only to get pummeled. A boot to the chest sends him soaring. The teen lands on his back in a daze.

Commanding loudly between huffing and puffing. "Say it! You must say the words, you stubborn ox."

When Magnus shakes off the shock so his eyes can focus, Uncle Theo has a muddy boot on his center of gravity, pinning him to the wet grass and a stiff arm keeping his brother at bay. He's furious.

"Enough! Stop fighting all the damn time. Sweet Jesus, give us peace or I'll leave with my legion." He looks down at Magnus as if preparing a loogie. "Little Man, say the damn words."

Ger still seems pumped up and ready to go, but his target can't get up. Theo had kicked away his training swords. Marc and Cousin Theo hold them like they won a bout. Obviously horny, Mama looks hungrily at her hunky husband rather than mourn for her beaten son. Rules apply to duels and this one won't end until the loser says the humiliating words.

In a heartbreaking tone. "I yield to the bigger boy."

Theo goes crazy. "I've never seen bigger fools. We could be one big happy family if you two reconciled. Little Man, take a bath. Ger, don't drink apple cider; enjoy a beer instead."

The audience breaks up and the family leaves without Magnus.

Ger hurts bad. "Theo, the bastard re-opened my chest wound on purpose. I'm either bleeding bad or I've peed myself again. How can I fuck my wife? When she gets flushed like that, she can go all night. She's dying to fuck me."

Reassuring. "We'll take care of you. Your firstborn didn't escape unscathed. After a year, I had hoped one of you had grown up. I don't believe in reincarnation, but you two act like you've hated each other for many lifetimes."

Magnus rides to the town market to buy a tunic, soap, and a towel, then heads upriver for privacy, away from thousands of armed men who may want to console or insult him. Riding his best friend, he looks sad and sullen. At the Rhine River and pretty paranoid, Magnus looks in all directions before he dismounts, disrobing carefully behind his stallion until nude. He groans at the aches and pains, then inspects his newest cuts and bruises while swearing softly. He tosses his sweaty clothes on Caesar. For a 10-year-old, Magnus is unnaturally lean, muscular, and athletic. He peeks out beyond Caesar to make sure no one is watching, sees nothing, but suspiciously senses something. He cocks his head to listen, then scans the threat board again. Something's wrong, so he waits, tense and wary.

"Caesar, someone's watching me. Please keep an eye out."

Shrugging, he grabs his soap and shivers into the cold water. Going deeper, he soaps his cuts and bruises, cursing when it visibly stings. He jumps, shocked, once he gets balls deep. Magnus dives in and lathers himself up. He starts humming Girls of Rome when Caesar unexpectantly whinnies. He twirls, furious at himself for turning his back on the shoreline.

Instead of armed men, a beautiful teenage girl walks to the water, not far away. She waves and smiles at him, puts her stuff down, then undresses to bathe while he watches. He tenses up and stresses out. This couldn't be more suspicious if she dressed in diamonds or farted flames. She's totally hot, so Magnus is frozen in fear. Not seeing anything else, Magnus squints at her like a snake and sees an odd anklet holding a blade. She drops expensive clothing and then enters the river, nearly nude and completely dishonest. Her tiny pink silk panties leave little to the imagination. Her big breasts defy gravity and scrutiny, but he's checking the woodline for threats because he's never known such terror. Magnus looks past her to focus on possible cover for ambushers. Nothing.

She ends up parallel to him, 10 paces away, hoping for a conversation. She cups her tits as if he didn't notice they're fucking fantastic. The eight beautiful rings on her fingers, each a different bright color, catch his eye like a fishhook. She must be Somebody to walk around wearing those so fearlessly. But Magnus is oblivious to all that. Instead of looking at her, the killer kid looks through her and beyond her, trying to figure her out. He's puzzled and scared, not horny or happy. Both are nude, but she's seductive and he's bewildered. Soaping himself quickly, Magnus can't help but scan the trees for hostiles instead of checking out the nearby nude. That offends and confuses her, but nothing compares to him leaving her in a hurry. Magnus has never felt more afraid and flees the water as if his life is in danger. He whistles and the hottie flashes him a sexy smile, only to see the darkly handsome hunk calling his fucking stallion. She says something that he doesn't seem to hear.

In his own world as he exits the Rhine, the teen shivers from absolute terror. The goosebumps on his arms are not from the cold, but he massages them anyways. Hurrying to his horse and indifferent to his nudity, he puts Caesar between him and the woods, then gets out his sling. Magnus scans the threat environment, wondering if he's about to die and eagerly looking forward to it. Seeing nothing unusual, the teen steps into a new loincloth to cover his genitals and then finally turns to study the naked threat.

Whispering under his breath. "Life shouldn't be this hard. Who's trying to kill me now?"

She's waist-deep to show her terrific tits, but he's in deep shit. She has makeup on and only the very rich can afford what she's about to ruin with river water. Holding up her pink panties and wearing nothing but a smile, she tries understanding how she fucked up. Staring at him in disappointment, her hot body glistens in the cold water, but she can't figure out what she did wrong. Unlike battling the Alamanni, Magnus is not just scared, but scared to death. It's obvious in his face and how his body tenses up as he dries off. He doesn't bother with his dirty Germani trousers or his oversized rough-spun shirt that's already falling apart. He slips on the plain linen tunic as if in a dream. After mounting, he reaches into his saddle packs, pissed he doesn't have his throwing knives or his swords. He looks all around him before concentrating on the improbable girl, suspiciously nude in the Rhine. The only threat he senses comes from her, so he kicks Caesar into the water to get closer. Magnus clearly plans kill her. She sees it, too, and backs up while hunkering down.

In a mocking tone. "Afraid of a girl?"

She's trying to taunt him, but his senses are on maximum. He rides into the river and her smile dies a painful death. Worried for her safety now, she wisely backs deeper into the river, ready to dive underwater.

He's cautious and afraid. "Socrates had a voice that sometimes told him to do or not do certain things. I have that. I once wanted to explore a cave, but a voice inside my head told me not to. I hate being told what I can't do, even from myself, so I went ahead anyways. I found myself looking at a growling mama bear so deep in the dark that I could only make out her bright eyes. I apologized and backed out. She graciously let me leave, rather than abandon her cubs, but I learned my lesson. When hunting, sometimes the voice says go left when I wanted to go right. My family moves a lot, which means new towns and unfamiliar roads. That voice has saved me many times. We would have been robbed by bandits, but I told my dad to wait, lying that I forgot something, until the thugs got bored and left the livery. In battle, it feels like I can sense half-a-heartbeat into the future because I'll move right before something comes at me. I've become very sensitive to that voice and it's now screaming at me to not let you live. It's never screamed before, so you must be very dangerous. I can't imagine why, but I've learned to respect the threat. For example, I think my dad would like to murder me again, so I must become better than him in everything. He must feel the same because he trains hard when he'd prefer to snuggle his horny wife. I was asking my future self – oh, I pretend-talk to an older version of me – about who sent you to kill me, but I don't sense anyone else here. Someone sent you, but you're alone. If you abandon your plan to hurt me, then I can let you live. You can start by throwing away the blade tied to your ankle."

She's pissed. "Boy, you are crazy. You'd kill an innocent girl?"

35

Deadly serious as he descends into deeper water. "You are not innocent. Snowmelt off the Swiss Plateau makes the Rhine River very cold, but you knew that going in. You threw off your clothes like a camp whore, yet you're too beautiful for that. Your silk clothing is expensive, but you dropped it in the mud as if someone else will wash it. You wear eight rings, all expensive. I've been here a month and I've never seen you, yet you're comfortable enough to go nude near 20,000 horny men. You spent more time in Rome than me to get that elite Latin accent. You strike me as very smart, so none of this happened by accident. You are nude in the Rhine because I had to bathe. Your only motive is to kill me. I need to know why. Lastly, you know I'm hostile. I can't leave until you give up, so either say who you work for or die."

Sighing in resignation. "You'll never catch me."

In stunned disbelief, he watches her swim underwater downriver, where the current carries her. The screaming in his head must be very loud because he starts slinging frantically, hoping for a lucky shot. If she swam across, he could have nailed her, but she takes the center of the current, which flows fastest, and continues swimming until she disappears around the Bend. Caesar is neck deep in cold water and wants to get out.

He whispers in terror. "That's the most dangerous person I've ever met. She planned to kill me in the river and I don't think she gave up. How will this day end?"

The family's home is humble. It's dark outside the windows, so they use a dozen candles, which create flickering shadows. Ger and his beautiful wife walk in the dining room, hand-in-hand, looking like they just enjoyed marathon sex. She's dressed in something tight and revealing, with cavernous cleavage and a spring in her step. He also dressed up to look great. She looks at Ger like he's a sex god and he smiles at her like she's the hottest thing this side of the sun. Theo recognizes that look and wishes his wife was here. The Maximus family gathers to eat around an oak table, two of the three boys loud and happy. Marc adores Cousin Theo. The kids and adults sit on opposite sides of the rectangular table. The legate looks puzzled as servants bring out plates of steaming food.

"We're not gonna lay on sofas like good Romans? Excellent. My back still hurts from the battle. I don't remember half the blows."

Magnus complains. "I'm so hungry. Mama, the food you left didn't taste right."

As he says that, he waves his left hand to the left, then his right hand to the right for emphasis, but mama ignores him, as usual.

By the dinner table, Marc turns on his cousin. "Theo, show me your scar again."

Cousin Theo lifts his tunic to show an ugly cut on his side and sounds serious for a 6-year-old. "Wish I had lead pellets. My pebbles hardly hurt them until they got really close."

Marc is impressed. "You kill any?"

"I doubt it, but I hit hundreds. Daddy told me to protect the ammo wagon, so I did. I take my duties seriously."

Magnus hates being left out. "I saw you, Theo. You were very brave. Even after getting speared, you kept fighting. You'll make a great legate."

Young Theo snaps back. "Max, since you're leaving with the stinking trawler, we don't need to be nice to each other. Next time we fight, we'll be the same size instead of you picking on someone four years younger."

36

Sounding defensive. "I was just trying to teach you, like I teach Marc."

Not buying it. "You never gave your brother a bloody nose. You've given me three, all after your dad beat you badly. I'm glad you're leaving and hope I never see you again. I'll be a better brother to Marc than you've ever been."

The adults don't seem to hear that and the teen feels alone in a crowd. Magnus studies the table as the men dig in. Dad wears trousers like a Germani and his beautiful wife gives him a hot plate before serving her sons. She kisses his forehead, clearly adoring Ger. The general flashes her a sexy smile that melts her heart.

In a sultry voice. "Girl, I never believed in love at first sight until I saw you. I love you forever. Thank you for being wonderful. Our anniversary is coming up. We should visit Rome again. I want to take you shopping. Poets say you can't buy happiness, but poets are poor, so the hell do they know?"

That turns mama's gears. Gushing with emotion. "Ger, I'm yours, only yours, and yours forever."

Seeing his father make his mother happy angers Magnus. He turns to his cousin like he sees him for the first time. Having lost his home, the orphan can't afford to burn bridges. It's almost possible to see his mental gears churning. Then a cantilever breaks, he blinks, and then he suddenly sees the world differently.

"Theo, you're right and I apologize. I took my anger out on you because you're cute and beloved. Even my mama prefers you to me. I'll leave you a thousand lead pellets because you're now a combat veteran. Uncle's ship can't leave until the battle is decided, one way or another. I could leave tomorrow if dad gets his ass handed to him again. That loser just can't catch a break."

Young Theo doesn't conceal his hatred. "When you leave, take your bitterness with you. It's hard to enjoy my mutton with that scowl on your face. All the pretty girls go crazy over you because they can't see the real you – all your ugliness is inside."

Unable to resist. "Cousin, if you don't clothe your naked anger, girls will go crazy over you, too. I feel like a prostitute who works hard for her money and a nympho who doesn't have time to fuck around. Did you know a woman can have an hour-long orgasm? I forgot her name, but that was one hell of an hour. Cicero said every minute, somewhere in the Roman Empire, a woman has an orgasm. We must find her and put her on stage."

Marc gets mad. "Stop stealing dad's jokes. If you're better than him, then come up with better material."

The hero recoils at the quip. As most enjoy dinner, the family talks to everyone but Magnus. Despite his glorious victory over the Alamanni, the lonely prodigy feels defeated and deflated. Picking his food, he slouches and sinks into his seat. He's gonna miss his family. He looks at them with longing, desperate to belong, but ignored by all. He whispers to himself when his dad makes everyone laugh.

"No one will even miss me."

Most start eating with their hands because sanitary table forks won't become common in Northern Europe for another 1300 years, though already popular in Constantinople. Dad wipes his greasy fingers on his trousers because napkins have not been invented. The agitated big boy takes the temperature of the room and finds himself out in the cold. He visibly adjusts his attitude and expectations as if trying to make the best of things.

37

Magnus sounds apologetic. "Uncle Theo, I'm sorry if I've troubled you. One day I hope to serve as your assistant."

"Little Man, you saved my life, you probably saved my son, and you definitely saved hundreds of my men, so you'll always have a place at my side. I thought you were a goner when your get-up-and-go just got up and went. Your big, dumb antics were nothing short of brilliant. Those Alamanni surprised the shit out of me. Literally. I almost died more times today than the rest of my life combined. Few Germani are good archers, but they brought a few thousand of their best. Killing their best shooters will save thousands of troops when we invade Alamannia. They swam a swift river on foot, probably at night, so they were determined to steal or burn a million cedar arrow shafts. I'm still curious how they knew I was bringing them. They didn't target the open-air supply wagons. Ger, how many people could have known the contents on those enclosed wagons?"

Ger curses. "Not many. I've been racking my brains trying to nail the traitor to a cross."

Dressed like she's selling expensive sex, Sasa comes in with two pitchers and Magnus seems surprised because the senator's very cute granddaughter has never served them before. But he's alone in his suspicions. Extra alert, he studies her.

Sounding sweet. "Sasa, you get me anything special before I leave?"

She's artificially cheerful. "Mama made you apple cider. I hope you like it." The brilliant boy gets an odd vib from her as she fills his cup. Her smile hides something malicious. "Would anyone else like some?"

She looks and sounds nervous. Magnus sits up almost quivering like an arrow, senses on all-alert. He stops eating and examines their food. Everyone but Ger holds up their cups. Sasa pours cider to mama, Marc, and Cousin Theo with one pitcher, but Magnus, Uncle Theo, and dad with the other. Something feels off and his danger bells ring. He's either constipated or scared shitless. Magnus studies her face, but she anxiously avoids eye contact. To serve Ger, she must go around him to serve from the same pitcher as Uncle Theo, when she could have easily poured from the other pitcher. Magnus visibly shivers as if a ghost entered his body. He doesn't know what to do, but knows he must do something. He looks like he's sitting on a snake. His eyes flicker fast as he dismisses options. His face is a cloud changing shape because he thinks that bitch from the river is about to poison them all. No one pays attention to him but, if they did, they'd worry. Cousin Theo is about to drink some, but Magnus roughly knocks the cup from his hand, then does the same to Marc while leaving his own cup untouched. His voice sounds unnaturally high and shrill, like he badly needs to pee.

"Sorry, cousin. Uncle Theo, you spilled on your tunic."

The legate was about to drink the cider, but pauses to look at his nice outfit. He doesn't see a spill, but Magnus makes eye contact with Sasa, who looks caught in the act. His face screams accusations and her eyes widen in fear. Sasa backs away as if pushed. Ger grabs his cup and Magnus watches him without saying anything, though he's practically shaking. The boy squints to see how much dad drinks and his father notices. They make eye contact. Magnus wears an expectant facial expression that Ger doesn't comprehend.

"To our health! *Salut!*"

After dad gulps some down, Magnus turns to see Sasa's face turn to terror.

38

Uncle Theo is about to imbibe, so Magnus rises to leap across the table to knock the cup from his uncle's grip with his cousin's delicious mutton. That shocks the room, ends all chatter, and messes up the mutton. Instead of being ignored, everyone looks at him, sprawled across the dining table like a roasted pig. They can't figure out his expression while Magnus can't kick his mind into gear. The leap leaves Magnus right in front of his father. The boy slowly pulls the lethal cup from his dad's shaky hand. Ger desperately tries understanding what's happening.

Magnus finally doesn't sound like a smart ass. "Dad, the cider's bad. Stick your finger in your throat to vomit it out. No one eat or drink anything. Push the plates and cups away. Marc, please get the *medicus* and then Tribune Pelagius."

The obedient boy runs out, his boots loudly stomping the wooden floor. Mama is young, blond, and gorgeous, but slow to appreciate the predicament. She looks very confused and sounds very scared.

Terrified at losing her husband. "Why do we need the army doctor?"

Ger instinctively reassures her. "I feel fine."

He didn't, though. Ger concentrates inward, his senses on fire. He touches his tummy and his face looks worried. Magnus hammers another nail in the coffin.

"Then why does Sasa look like she just murdered you? I want you servants to huddle in that corner. If you move, you die!"

The boy barks with authority and both peasants fearfully obey, though Sasa is slow. Theo the Elder turns in his seat, knows a guilty face when he sees one, then gets up and smacks the pitchers of cider from her hands. He roughly grabs Sasa by her long blond ponytail, drags her over, and pins her pretty head to the oak table. Her massive cleavage now looks awesome and out-of-place, like deceptive advertising.

Theo's furious. "Did you just try to kill me? The Alamanni had a hundred chances to murder me, so I thought today was my lucky day."

Her right cheek rests between two plates with food still steaming. Her face faces Magnus, still laying halfway on the tabletop. He props himself up on an elbow.

Magnus sounds sincerely troubled. "Why, Sasa? Dad was gonna make your family rich."

She's scared shitless and about to cry. "Cousin Serapio took the twins. They're just toddlers!"

Ger catches on and catches up. "Girl, you've been spying on me?"

"No, that's your quartermaster. Someone in power wants you to fail because he keeps getting orders that bypass the mail delivery system."

The teenager gets down and rounds the table with his father's poisoned cup. Theo pins her arms behind her back and then stands her up. Magnus looks lethal, holding a kitchen knife.

"Sasa, drink and your problems go away. Don't drink and your problems never end. Your whole family will suffer." She turns her head to avoid the goblet. "Sasa, you tried to poison me. If you don't drink, I'll gut you like a fish."

The girl shatters and cries like her life is over. Theo the Elder holds her up because she's lost all strength. Ger realizes the severity of the situation and stands up, not sure how to spend the rest of his life. He walks as if exercise helps and everyone turns to see how he's doing.

Sasa sounds like she has nothing to lose. "Max, it never crossed your mind to invite me to Britannia. Why?"

"Though I'm taller, you're a year older. I knew you hit puberty when you forced my finger between your legs, but I'm not there yet. I go to sleep thinking what I'd do in various tactical situations, how I could modify my saddle for a more stable shooting platform, or how I could sling with more power. But I don't dream of girls. Again, I'm 10."

Tears falling, the young hottie screams her heart out. "I loved you!"

The boy doesn't believe her. "Is that why you tried murdering me, my father, and my uncle? Drink down or I'll cut you up."

Mama's in the dark and needing a light. "I don't understand. Is Gerontius gonna die?"

Magnus shakes his head. "He didn't drink enough to die. He might get sick, though. However, Sasa is definitely gonna die."

In disbelief. "But I'm too pretty to die young! I'm still a fucking virgin!"

Magnus is not sympathetic. "Fucking virgins are the worst kind. Life is short, cruel, and unfair. We live in a world where good people suffer daily and bad people get away with murder." Pausing dramatically as if swearing on a Bible. "Since most folks die of violence, starvation, and disease, I swear by God to dedicate my life so everyone enjoys guaranteed food, shelter, and security."

As if the Universe hears, all candles flicker without a wayward wind. Everyone finds that suspiciously strange.

Theo shudders and shivers uncomfortably. "That hasn't happened since my dad died. Will this day never end?"

Resigned to her fate, the girl lets Magnus put the cup to her lips and drinks it all.

"What poison was in the cider?" Magnus asks.

She's beyond caring. "How would I know? An Alamanni cousin told me to put it in your cups or the twins would die."

That shocks the love of her life. "Was she a gorgeous girl with big boobs and small shame?"

Yelling defensively. "That whore isn't all that pretty!"

Shocked. "She told you to poison me? Not just the men?"

Finally enjoying herself, Sasa sports a wicked grin. "Serapio claims you're the most dangerous Roman here, including Ger and Julian. You attacked Alamannia's best archers, hurt several hundred, and yet somehow escaped unscathed. You saved the legion, ruined their mission, and killed their best bowmen. He said you must die."

Magnus doesn't know what to do with that. "I tried killing the only man who appreciates me? I need a dad; can I adopt a father? Is that a thing? Is Serapio a good hugger? That's Caesar's only flaw."

Ger groans, afraid. "Crap. I feel it now. Yeah, that bitch poisoned me. Whenever I'm about to succeed, something out of my control pulls it from my grasp. I assume I succeeded too much in my last life, so the Universe is balancing things out. The math pedagogue called it, reversion to the mean. Theo, I'm gonna lay down. See if the *medicus* can do anything when his fat ass gets here. I won't hold my breath, even if I could. Max, you saved Theo, but watched me drink poison, you lousy piece of shit."

"You assassinated your own father, but I didn't kill you, so you're a lousier piece of shit. I had no way of knowing the cider was poisoned until I saw Sasa's expression. Just admit I'm better than you and apologize for being such a terrible father."

Bent over, Ger tries throwing up, hacking with an awful sound, but only spittle and lost hope flies out of his mouth. Tribune Pelagius enters, astonished at what he sees. As a well-connected political appointee, he looks young, rich, beautiful, and brilliant. The killer boy walks over, powerful emotions washing over him.

"Pel, Serapio kidnapped Joko's twins to force Sasa to poison me, dad, and Uncle Theo, but only dad drank it."

Pelagius looks at his commander. Ger grimly nods his head, then tries vomiting again.

Magnus doesn't sound sorry. "Dad, you took my inheritance, so you're not a great piece of shit, either. We've had that land for almost centuries, when Paullus Maximus conquered Galicia in 13 BC. As your firstborn, I should get your share of the estate. You said I'd never be better than you at anything, yet I sensed danger while you did not. All your hard work, training, and preparation were for nothing. Just shit luck, as usual. You blew your big chance to make something of your little life, like in Londinium when you lost that large lot of land. Just vomit now and rest tomorrow. Maybe you'll appreciate me for the rest of your miserable life. You have plenty of failures to look forward to as I surpass you in everything."

Ger feels his life ebb. "Max, I always knew you'd be the death of me. That's why I beat you so often. I dream that we've been brothers, cousins, and friends before we turned on each other in life after life. I've seen me kill you and you kill me, millennia ago, though we started as identical twins. I still don't like the irony. You're a spiteful bastard, so in my next life, I'm gonna torment you like you tormented me. We'll see who gets the last laugh. Beware the punishment of a patient man." He turns to his brother. "Theo, please bury me in a pretty place with a view of the river. I don't want to spend eternity in a cemetery with strangers. I always wanted to be special, not ordinary. Dictator Sulla's gravestone reads, No Better Friend, No Worse Enemy. Make mine say, Killed By His Son's Treachery."

Theo's caught in the middle. "Ger, that's unfair. Max didn't kill you. He was the only one who spotted the treachery. I owe him my life again and I hate being in debt."

Spitting on the floor again. "Then he's your burden if I don't survive this."

Head in a corner, Ger tries vomiting a stomach. It sounds terrible. A candle flickers out, darkening the mood.

Mama is horrified. "Ger, you might die? But I can't live without you!"

Distraught, she collapses on the floor and sobs loudly. Without him, her life feels over. Grunting with stomach pain, Ger limps to his bedroom as if he needs to take a giant dump. Sasa also sinks to the floor and gasps like she can't breathe. She actually looks good, if she weren't dying.

Two oil lamps illuminate a large room with little furniture. Weak starlight comes through a window. The males wait with their backs to a wall, not able to believe what their eyes clearly tell them. Ger lays motionless on the cot, pondering his options and hating them all. Muttering to himself, he's angry, bitter, and beaten. The fat army doctor waddles in and examines him. He clearly doesn't know what to do and leaves to get something. Everyone looks at him scornfully. Ger's commanders come in and crowd the bedroom, looking stunned at their dying general, with his magnificent physique and

41

kickass outfit.

Ger becomes resigned to his unfair fate. "I'll die soon. I can really feel it now. No wonder I always hated Mondays. Pel, as the senior tribune, you command my army whether you want it or not. I think you're able, but don't know if you're ready. Dutch, serving with you and your Batavi heroes last month was an honor. I'm sorry I couldn't get you Frankfurt's loot or that strategic island. Cousin Franco, I was hoping to fight alongside fellow Iberians. Growing up, you were like a big brother. Give Baby Frankito a kiss for me. King Mallobaudes, you are the most impressive Frankish commander I've ever known. I bet your Salian Franks will become even more powerful than the Rhineland Franks. For what little it's worth, I told Julian you'd make a great governor of Gaul. These are my final wishes and last commands: execute the quartermaster for undermining our mission and question those close to him. Whoever has been sending him orders has been sabotaging us and needs to die; I suspect Emperor Constantius or his advisers, but just kill those ostensibly under my command. My brother brought supplies that I must pay for because Rome didn't send us what they promised. We didn't even have arrows and most of our swords are ancient. Pel, send someone to tell Caesar Julian what happened. I doubt he'll continue the pincer movement, so the Alamanni win this year."

Magnus feels bitter and helpless. "I'll destroy the Alamanni for this when I'm grown."

Laughing bitterly. "Boy, you destroy everything you touch, so hug them to death. If you talk enough, the Alamanni may kill themselves. Men, please give us the room so I can spend my remaining time on Earth with my loved ones. And maybe Max."

Resentful. "Dad, I underestimated you. You somehow managed to ruin the only good day of my life. It turns out you really are great at something besides losing, quitting, and failure."

But then the horrified senator bursts in, wearing a different great outfit, before the commanders leave. He must have diarrhea because it looks like he's losing his shit. Luca can't believe his lying eyes.

"Nooo. Nooooo! Nooooooo! What about the contract? I borrowed to buy what I needed to make your million arrowheads. Will Rome pay what it owes?"

"Senator, if I could predict the future, then your granddaughter wouldn't have poisoned me. I demand compensation for my life, so I ordered my troops to take all portable valuables from your properties. Dismantling Europe's best smelter may take a while. You've stockpiled a lot of iron ore and purified ingots, though I don't care for your fancy furniture. I'd take your integrity and decency if you had any."

His words shock the senator. Luca is desperate, stressed, and at his wits end. "After slaughtering my granddaughter, you're gonna take what's mine? Someone stole my grandsons! I've suffered enough! You'll punish me after I helped you? I had nothing to do with the cider. I need you alive to get paid for what I've produced. Without this contract, I can't repay what I borrowed. I'm finished if you do what you say. I've been good to you, so why ruin me?"

"Luca, other than your family murdering me, you've been a perfect host. I thought next month would be the greatest in my life, so I'm as bitter as that apple cider. However, I'm curious why you're so eager to invade the Alamanni homeland. You have scores to settle?"

42

Luca addresses the commanders. "I know where they hide their golden ore. Smelting is expensive, so they had me do it for a quarter of the final value until a few years ago. They must have stockpiled a mountain of gold by now unless they built themselves a smelter I don't know about."

The dying general chuckles weakly and his breathing sounds ragged. "You wanted us to invade so you could steal their gold? Pel, I'll let you and Theo decide whether to raid Alamannia, but I'd feel better if we paid what we owe. My father died in debt and I'd rather not echo him. The senator has been fair with us. Luca, our family has access to Europe's biggest mercury mine in Iberia. Theo can get you as much mercury as you want. Smelting gold and silver with toxic mercury requires special equipment and procedures, but costs far less than using heat. You can triple your operating margins, after the initial capital investment."

Hope breaches the despair infecting Luca's face. "The Alamanni have stolen from my family for centuries. They won't expect a raid after your death."

The officers light up at that. They look at each other eagerly to score big, then go home.

"Theo, I'm too sick to think clearly. Pel, you're the smartest man I've ever known, despite your religious convictions. What are your thoughts?"

Pel straightens up. "If you die, then most enemies will go hundreds of miles east to stop Julian, leaving fewer to face us. Sir, we should hurt those who orchestrated your murder while not going broke doing our duty. Plus, Caesar Julian expects us to do our part, with or without you. I'd rather not anger him."

Ger likes that. "You phrased that like you're running for office. In that case, I'm ordering my army to attack my murderers. I planned on taking Franco with me to sack Frankfurt with our best archers. To get the Alamanni to leave us, announce my death and that the army must wait for Rome to send a replacement general. Make it clear the invasion is canceled. That said, you should all ask the West Germani to stay, then invade as planned during the next full moon. By then, most armed enemies will be hundreds of miles away, harassing Julian. Your orders are the same: avoid pitched battles, retreat under effective fire, take their portable valuables, kidnap young women and small kids, and destroy everything else. This is a raid, not an invasion. I want you to return home rich, not dead. Commanders, the more men you have, the more loot you'll take. I suggest you send trusted recruiters to spread the word of plentiful plunder. Western Alamannia is a hot bitch with her legs wide open. Fuck her now and fuck her hard."

The commanders nod eagerly, but both Marc and Cousin Theo begin crying. Even Magnus can barely control his emotions.

Marc tears up. "Daddy, I don't want you to die. I love you and I'll miss you."

Now the general tears up because he'll miss his family and knows who to blame for his unexpected death.

"Marc, you've been a great son; I don't care what Max says. My Uncle Honorius thinks you'll make a great ship captain and an even better pirate. Maybe our new smelter in Porto Gordo can make an iron ship. Wouldn't that be something?"

Sympathy for Ger pisses off Magnus, who clenches his fists. "You're getting off easy! How are you so weak that one gulp of poison kills you? I want you to suffer, not die. You can't suffer if you die. The ancients say death is a sweet release; it's birth that's an agonizing bitch."

43

Theo seeks reconciliation. "Make peace while you can. Brother, whatever emotions you die with, you'll take with you. Heaven is where you have nothing to do and eternity to do it, whereas Earth makes Hell redundant. Be the bigger man and forgive the boy. His main flaw is he's just like you, only more so."

Neither say nothing, as if afraid to speak. They won't even make eye contact. The bedroom has as much anger as grief. Young Theo and Marc stand shoulder-to-shoulder, keeping a healthy distance from Magnus. Luca and the commanders flee the drama, with Pel rubbing his hands together like he's about to get golden.

Once the commanders leave, mama unsteadily stumbles in, holding Magnus' poisoned cup.

Sounding punch-drunk. "Ger, please make room for me. I can't live without you."

The males stare at her in astonishment. She drops the cup and it lands with a loud ding.

He's surprised and pleased by her devotion. "Girl, I'm dying to spend the rest of my life with you. I've always loved how much you love me. With Marc spending his life with our merchant fleet, I guess this is better than returning to your quarrelsome family in Colchester."

He exhausts himself, scooting over to make room in the narrow bed for his beautiful wife. They smile at each other as if still in love. His brother kneels to wrap them in a blanket, so it looks like Uncle Theo is praying. Never, in the history of the world, has a man seemed so sad. She cuddles the man that she can't live without, subdued and sleepy. Ger puts his arm around her, kisses her on the lips for the last time, then gestures for Marc to join them. The adorable 8-year-old climbs on the bed and hugs them both while sobbing quietly. That feels so good that Ger opens his arms for Young Theo to hug them. Theo the Elder joins the embrace and they weep together. The dying general kisses them all on the forehead, his approaching death finally kicking him in the mental testicles.

Magnus stares at them in stunned disbelief. Not even his family wants him.

Ger smiles at Young Theo. "Nephew, I wish you were my son instead of Max. After his lamp oil burns out, you'll go farther to become the great man he wishes he was. He may grow taller, but you have my permission to look down on him. Brother, you're a lucky dad to have both sons love you."

The unconditional love between those five makes them visibly glow. Their expressions look so tender as they whisper goodbye with soft smiles and sad eyes. Magnus' parents feel loved, but not by him. Compulsively clenching and unclenching his fists just a few strides away, the big boy can't comprehend his predicament. Magnus clearly isn't wanted at his parent's death. His wild eyes infect his face and bloat his body. He's tight enough to shatter and shakes enough for an epileptic. The boy looks about to break. A weak wick could ignite him like the driest tinder.

His voice sounds strange. "You all look happier without me. I wish I drank all the poison. I can't wait to die. I'm gonna kill every Alamanni to see if that makes me feel better. I might even take troops. Mama, you drank my poison? All of it? On purpose? You chose dad over Marc? Do we mean so little to you? Your out-of-control son needs a parent! I'm already an orphan before my mama and daddy die. Uncle Theo, will you reject me, too?"

44

Uneasy. "I'm too far in your debt, Little Man. Besides knocking poison from my lips, you saw the Alamanni pulling me off my charger and raced suicidally to rescue me. You probably saved my son by throwing yourself literally in the way. The mansion will belong to me and my brother Honorius, but I'll keep your room until we lose the estate."

Depressed. "You make me feel like a debt burden that you can't wait to pay off before I lose interest. If no one loves me, then why should I love anyone? I'll use people like people have always used me. That's only fair."

"Little Man, that won't make you happy."

Pacing the room impatiently to avoid erupting, the orphan loudly scoffs, eyebrows raised in disbelief. "Happiness? Oh, that ship has sailed, uncle. I can't be happy, but I might get some satisfaction before family turns on me again. If I'm going to Hell, I may as well enjoy the trip." He looks up and puts his hands together to pray. "Dear God, please save me from family; enemies I'll deal with myself."

Dad kisses his younger son again on the head. "Marc, we'll miss you. Mama and I love you so much. I couldn't have asked for a better son. I'm sorry we can't see you grow up. My Uncle Honorius chose you over Max because the sea is no place for an angry fool. Maybe you'll visit India and China like you've always dreamed. Rome sent an embassy that was received in China two centuries ago. A ship full of silk would set up the family for life. Max will never amount to anything, but you can save the family and our ancestral home. You can become the hero that your brother wishes he was."

Mama kisses Marc and whispers lovingly, face to face, both full of tears. Still sharing their big bed, Cousin Theo watches Magnus watch them with poisonous envy.

Magnus is going crazy. "You two are dying, so why do I feel like my life is already over? Mama, you gonna say goodbye to me?"

Suddenly furious. "Boy, I saw you watch your daddy drink that poison. You interrupted Theo without warning your father. He's never done anything to deserve what you did. Instead of taking your beatings like a man, you poisoned my happiness. Flavius, you are dead to me."

The irony strikes deep. The bad boy paces the room, crazed and crazy. He can't see past his sense of doom. It's all just too much.

"Stop calling me Flavius! Man, I need a better name. A great name. The greatest name ever. Caesar Maximus Optimus sounds uncommon. I hardly know anyone with that name. Or maybe Penis Maximus Erectus? That's a wonderful name for a big dick like me."

Dad can barely speak. "Max, I'll give you Caesar the Stallion if you let us die in peace. You don't have to leave; as my dying wish, just stop talking for once so I can die without hearing your annoying voice. I need calm silence to choose my next body once I leave this one."

That makes Magnus melancholy. His back hits the wall and he slumps to the floor as if someone cut his puppet strings. He has no energy left and looks half-dead.

"I was wrong for once; this is the worst day ever. Is it too late for a huggie? I promise to make it painless."

To everyone's shock, his brother turns on him, his face furious.

"No! Our parents' death is your fault. You chose not to save him. You'll always be my brother, but I'll never forgive you for taking mom and dad from me."

Horrified at losing his brother. "Marc, I'm very sorry. I didn't think he'd die.

45

Under all that muscle, I never saw how weak he was. By drinking my poison, mama fucked us both." Seeking punishment, he turns to Cousin Theo. "Hit me hard."

Cousin Theo doesn't hesitate. He flies off the bed to land towering over Magnus. Animated like he just got the best birthday present ever, the wiry 6-year-old rotates his torso to slap the shit out of his big bully. It pumps Young Theo up and puts a spring in his step. Despite bracing himself, Magnus bounces off the wall and topples uncontrollably to the floor, moaning like a kicked cat and crying from a killer day. It sounds incredibly painful and took whatever sanity he had left. Cheek on the wooden floor, his tortured expression cries for relief. His eyes see only the past. The bloody cuts and big bubbles from bruises stand out. Young Theo's lower legs tower over his prone body and pathetic posture. He's an empty vessel filling with misery, regret, and remorse. The light in his sky-blue eyes flickers and threatens to die out like a puff of smoke. Not even his parents look that dead. It's wicked crazy, strangely compelling, and would make a great movie poster. Ger roars hard with laughter at this unexpected gift, then mama, Marc, and Young Theo join in as if this is the funniest thing they've ever seen. The contrast between their hilarity and his misery cuts deep.

Magnus whispers to himself. "Worst. Day. Ever."

Knowing he's beaten, Magnus stays on the floor, sobbing quietly under all the loud laughter. Losing self-control, the dam bursts and dark emotions spill out to pollute the place. Tears flow, fueled by too many traumas. Spasms rack his body and torture his soul. After the glee of glorious victory over the Alamanni, the bad boy looks beaten on the inside as much as the outside.

Before sadness and sorrow swallow him in a coma-like sleep, Magnus hears his father's last whispered words, in a weak, croaking voice:

"Goodbye, brother. I'm off to the great (dramatic pause) Perhaps." His tone turns dark, deep, and vindictive with his last words. "Max, see you later, you great piece of shit."

On their backs, staring up at the heavens, the parents look great for corpses.

Cheek on the wooden floor, Magnus sees nothing, as if dead inside. With males crying pitifully in sorrow, his empty face, destroyed by cruel fate, twitches slightly.

CHAPTER 2

The hilltop castle and the field camps seem busier than ever. Men are moving with a purpose. Others swarm a large fishing trawler. The army has woken up in a fury. Even the West Germani look pissed, grim, and aggressive.

The aging, overweight senator struggles up the steep slope, slipping once and cursing twice, until he earns the summit. Out of breath, he needs a minute before moving on. A few dozen uniformed bowmen stand around, with Fort Briga behind and below them. With Commander Franco in charge, troops put a kettle over hot coals while others bring crushed rock from the smelter using wheelbarrows. Theo, his brother Honorius, Cousin Theo, Marc, and Magnus use picks to break up rock within a small crevasse on the side of the ridge. They balance themselves precariously because it's a lethal drop down the embankment. Blankets cover the corpses, but Luca looks at Ger and his wife anxiously.

"Quicklime? Theo, you know how to make cement?"

The males in the hole don't even pause their digging. Magnus is whacking it like there's gold underneath.

The orphan answers. "No, but he can quote Cicero all night. My favorite quip is, incest is a game the whole family can play. After Marc Anthony cut off his head and stuck a pin in his eloquent tongue, I wonder if Cicero still preferred defeat with Pompey over victory with Caesar."

Theo pauses his digging and points at a newcomer. "Senator Savelli, this handsome youth is my brother Honorius. I have an uncle and cousin with the same name. He arrived with my legion and serves as my quartermaster. He also works at our bank and helps manage our businesses, so you two have plenty to talk about. I'm sending him with some Batavi elites to Amsterdam to organize our plunder and re-supplies."

The grieving boy grunts unhappily as he hits the bedrock hard with a pick. "No damn Germani will ever dig up my mama. When she said I was dead to her, I gave her a piece of my mind that she didn't give back! Mortar isn't hard enough. It's why we're chipping and chiseling rock instead of burying my parents in loose earth. Luca, I had to take waste iron pellets, clinker, and some marine sand from your foundry. We borrowed your brooms to get enough rock dust. I never knew burying parents was so much work. I might just have to take a vacation in Frankfurt to get over my grief."

Uncle Honorius mops his sweat. "What's clinker?"

Magnus is the first to answer. "Overheating the ingredients of cement mix leaves hard clumps that often look like balls. Luca uses a heavy roller to pulverize clinker, adding this dry dust to crushed rock, gravel, marine sand, and water to make concrete."

"How is marine sand different from sand?" Uncle Honorius asked.

"Wind-blown sand, like in deserts, makes grains round. Cement mix better grabs sharp, angular sand found in rivers, lakes, and along coasts. Uncle, how could you not know this? I thought it was common knowledge. Though I've laid concrete, I've never mixed cement, so I hope I get it right. Hard slag will cover the coffin before we cement it shut. My parents will spend eternity laying almost upright, gazing down at the Rhine. Dad was always blind to his faults while mama pretended to be blind to his affairs, so I assume they want a view to die for. I sketched them this morning and will make copies

47

later. I've never seen dad look happier and finally gave him the hug he never deserved. Mama got an extra kiss on the forehead because I loved her so much, before that neglectful bitch disowned me. Luca, I wrote their biography on the back of one of your least useful religious scrolls. If an earthquake shakes them loose in a century or three, I want locals to know who they have disturbed so they can replant my parents in new bedrock."

Luca looks at Magnus in stunned disbelief. All stop digging except the orphan, sweating without his tunic. Topless, his bulging muscles look odd on such a young boy.

Luca speaks up. "Legate Theo, you can't bury your brother here. This is private property."

"Senator, you claim the entire Briey Basin, but you don't actually own it. Show me the deed. My brother was generous, successful, and well-liked. Many troops assume you had a part in his death. I'll hold them back if you grant me this tiny plot in perpetuity. I want it in writing by sunset if you want my help stealing gold from your Alamanni neighbors across the Rhine."

The orphan pauses his digging to wipe his brow, then gets out to gab. The other males then resume digging.

"Luca, today's your lucky day. I told our troops not to disassemble your foundry, forge, and factories because they'd rather kill my father's murderers than do hard work that requires hard thinking. You're welcome. Plus, they must attach a million killer arrowheads and four million fletches to a million cedar shafts. Even the West Germani want your arrows, but I'm monopolizing them for Frankfurt, along with our best archers. Not just from the Jovii and Victores legions, but from all the West Germani. Dad started weekly archery competitions, but then it grew into a giant dick measuring contest that I assume I won. I'm taking the best 7500 or so to sack the Alamanni capital, Frankfurt, while their warriors are far away battling Caesar Julian's army from Reims. I recruited volunteers by offering your chainmail armor sandwiched within two layers of boiled leather. That isn't as impenetrable as an iron plate, but it comes close and is easier to wear all day. A chainmail tunic over a chainmail vest can stop enemy arrows except at very close range – at least, with your superior iron. Etruscans had chainmail several centuries ago, but it took you to finally improve them. Luca, is your mine or smelter profitable?"

The senator laughs with enough bitterness to start a war.

"My grandfather made some money, but poured it back into infrastructure and improvements until he hit the water table. My father didn't bother, but I grew up obsessed with all that wealth just below my boots. I built the Archimedes Screw and the waterwheel in the river before the Senate sucked all life from me. Mining requires huge capital. The road to the mine alone cost a fortune. Cranes, hoists, pulley systems, pumps and pipes – the Senate would kick me out if they knew the depth of my debt. The poorer I feel, the richer I dress."

Magnus likes that. "How much to sell us 51% of everything you have in the Briey Basin? Not to me personally, but to Maximus Inc, our family's parent corporation."

Luca almost laughs, but sees the terrible teen is as serious as the mourning men. He rarely takes kids seriously, but Magnus is unique. "What do you offer? I need bullion, not trade."

"10,000 solidus gold coins. The pure ones that Constantine the Great minted 50 years ago, not the crap that Emperor Constantius is paying his troops, clerks, and contractors with. I want to monopolize your high-iron content ore. Maximus Inc will buy all of your relatively pure iron for 10% over cost, giving you a guaranteed buyer. Smelt as much as you can."

The senator swoons. "If I get better at pumping water from flooded mines, then I could smelt massive amounts of high-quality iron. What would you do with it all?"

"Arms, armor, farming implements, and ship hulls. My little brother wants our family to trade directly with India for silk, sugar, and spices. China has the world's best silk, porcelain, and something unknown in the West – called paper. That's obscenely profitable, but wooden hulls warp quickly or get eaten by bugs and worms. Tar, asphalt, and caulking only delay the inevitable. Expensive ships rarely last several years and often sink at sea with their precious cargo. Heat, humidity, and water shrink, shrivel, and stretch planks, which then leak, whereas iron hulls should last many decades if we figure out how to demagnetize them so they don't attract lightning. My great-uncle, Admiral Honorius, says he'll build his best oceangoing ship design in the Red Sea if we can provide him with iron hulls. Arabs have controlled trade with Asia for centuries and they make a killer living by monopolizing trade between East and West. Greeks and Romans have taken the trade winds off East Africa to India for a few centuries and a lucky captain can return with 100x his investment. Because sailing is so hazardous, traders either multiply their money or never return."

"Max, your family is broke. I'd accept, but you're offering me something you don't have."

"Joko said the Alamanni put their wealth in a tower vault in Frankfurt. He made the door and has the master key to the lock, but wants 10% of everything within. Dad's promise died with him, but that vault is still there. The price Joko pays to get his twins back is getting us in. I want your lawyers to write up a purchase agreement, conditional on us coming up with the money. 10,000 solidus or its equivalent. I don't expect to survive, but Uncle Honorius should be around. Agreed?"

The fat politico ponders his options, then shakes the boy's calloused hand. "Agreed. Since East Germani were forced east of the Rhine two years ago, they've given me very little golden or silver ore to smelt. I know they still mine because my family has bred with locals for centuries, but they use that gold to pay the Hanseatic League for deep-sea fish to feed them through the winter. You can't starve them without taking their biggest port, Frankfurt."

The legate climbs out of the grave to join the conversation. "I'm guessing you planned my brother's invasion along the best gold mines. I have his map; why do I need you?"

"They don't post signs or hand out maps; you need bilingual guides. The kidnapping of the twins has motivated my sons, nephews, and cousins to take teams to a series of sites. I reviewed them this morning and almost shat myself. Everyone knows the general died of poisoning. Julian's army crossed the Danube from Reims, so Alamanni non-fighters began hiding in the Black Forest, which has little food. They must harvest their small fields soon or starve this winter. Germani multiply faster than their food supply, which is why they must raid their neighbors. With Gerontius dead, warriors are already moving east to counter Julian. That leaves the mines, smelters, and warehouses unguarded. We could bankrupt Alamannia at little risk."

Theo points. "That explains your wagons. This is more than a simple raid. The more places we strike, the longer it takes and the more vulnerable we become. I can't afford to take time to steal ore that must be smelted."

"Theo, please; they took my twin grandsons to Frankfurt."

The orphan grunts angrily. He doesn't look or sound 10. "Luca, who's Serapio?"

The Roman cocks his head to think about it. "He's either my second cousin thrice removed or my third cousin twice removed. His mother was a Savelli who spent a few years in Greece, naming him after the Grecian-Egyptian god, Serapis. His father, Mederic, calls him Agenaric, after his beloved big brother. The uncle is called Agenaric the Elder and his nephew is just Agenaric."

Magnus grins mischievously. "Did she work at a temple in Corinth?"

"Not that I know of and careful who you call a whore. She said she studied philosophy in Athens. What do you know of Serapio?"

"That son-of-a-bitch speaks better Latin than me, though I studied a year in Rome to replace my Iberian accent. I wounded him with a shitty pellet. He says he's dying to kill me. Know where I can find him?"

"He lives in a tower in Frankfurt. My Alamanni family all speak excellent Latin and Serapio is the brightest. He studied three years in Rome's best schools and it cost me a fortune. When Alamanni controlled this basin, they squeezed my ventures like an orange."

"Sasa said Serapio sent a cousin to kidnap the twins to force her to poison me. Coincidentally, a beautiful blonde with big boobs bathed nude next to me in the Rhine. Who is she?"

Eyes getting big, Luca groans in despair. The brutal betrayal numbs him. "That's Serapio's firstborn. She must be the one who took the twins. Oh, Joko will be livid. Wait! Serapio did this to me? I sponsored that ingrate! His father and uncles became petty kings because my father educated and armed them with our iron. My food kept their clan alive during the last drought. A dozen of my bastard sons will demand revenge for Sasa and the twins. Oh, this will get ugly. My branch of the family depends economically on Joko, so they'll be out for blood. Who's in charge of Ger's army now?"

"Dad was the legate of the Victores legion, but now Senior Tribune Pelagius is in command. However, tribunes are political appointees from Rome, so I doubt our allies and vassals would follow an untested tribune into battle. Theo is a legate, but unknown and has never won a big battle."

Luca does the math. "Pel's father is also a senator. Our families intermarried twice over the centuries. Pel is smart and ambitious, though overly religious. I consider myself a Christian, but he's an ideologue. I find it odd that Christians believe they'll only live twice. Oh, but his Greek is flawless. Not even an accent. Pel must earn a name in the legions to leave as a Military Man and climb the political ladder to higher office. Elites in Rome obsess over status."

Magnus has nothing to lose. "If we're talking about executing my father's invasion, then I'm all in. While the tribune is technically in command, he's a battle virgin that centurions won't trust, so we need the Prefect, the senior centurion, the other centurions, and the lower tribunes. They'll require convincing. I've spent serious time with Pelagius, mostly pulling out my hair. If you need a theologian, he's your man, but the Romans in this army will want political cover to justify the evil shit they hope to perpetrate on our enemies. After subduing Franks and Saxons to pacify Gaul, Julian is very popular. The officer class won't do anything that displeases him. Our troops and allies need political cover beyond their dead general. Luca, you have six books on Euclid; can you square this circle?"

That angers Luca. "Why don't you talk like a 10-year-old? Were you born old? I'm in a desperate situation! I could lose everything. We must do something and we must do it now." They all stare at Luca until the obvious hits him like a right cross. Speaking softly. "Oh. You need someone with authority to blame in case things go to shit. Oh, my. So, I must go, too? My hand has palsy, so I'm not a fighter anymore."

The teen and the troops laugh at that. Magnus spells it out:

"Luca, I like to draw, but I can also paint, so imagine this: Alamanni cowards are so afraid of General Gerontius that they force a girl to poison him. Senator Savelli informs the deceased's brother, who marches here with his legion to get justice. They persuade our allies, vassals, and friends to punish the wicked men who murdered a hero using a woman's weapon. Let's invite everyone to the funeral, but I'll speak last. Uncle, please organize the expedition for the full moon, as dad planned, and dress dignified for your speech. You look good when not dressing badly. The time to hammer is when the metal is hot. If dad took his lethal luck with him, then we'll forge a fantastic future."

An eagle flies overhead and squawks a greeting. Ger's army packs the riverbank, pointing at where their brave leader will spend eternity. The powerful river flows behind them. Their killer mood is palpable. The large tomb of Gerontius Maximus towers over the Rhine where river traffic can see it. The army below, by the river, watches teams insert an open coffin into a crevasse overlooking them and listen to a priest sanctify the couple. They can see the general and his gorgeous wife, dead before their time. They're loud and angry. The white-haired senator gives a speech, then the general's brother, but they don't come alive until the orphan roars. The sun sets behind him, giving Magnus an angelic glow as he screams like a demon possessed. Between the ridge and the river, 50,000 angry armed men look up to Magnus literally and metaphorically.

His voice booms over the army below. "Senator Savelli and his sons have offered to lead our army into Alamannia because they knows the area intimately. He wants revenge for his gorgeous granddaughter, who loved me to death, and for his kidnapped grandsons. Serapio the Snake killed your general using poison because he knows he'd lose to real warriors. Tribune Pelagius is in charge, but he won't order us into enemy territory unless you agree, so let's decide right here, right now. By now, Caesar Julian is deep into eastern Alamannia and probably needs his second army for his pincer movement. He's one arm short of a hug. Since my dad's death, all the enemies facing us have gone east to fight Julian. We can either save Julian or let him die so Alamanni can soon rape your wives, mothers, and daughters again. We can either surprise Alamanni now or let them surprise us next year. We can let Julian's army loot Alamannia or we can take our share.

"After centuries of sacking, the wealth of Gaul now sits unprotected in Alamannia. We can let Julian sell a million Alamanni into slavery or we can take some of that sweet bullion. We can avenge our leader or we can tell the world that we'll do nothing when cowards poison our heroes. My Uncle Theo doesn't need all of you to

51

avenge his brother and take Alamanni gold; just the bold and the brave." The badass boy erupts vocally and it echoes over the river. The troops go crazy and roar back, pumped up and loud as hell. "Are there any heroes anymore? Have the giants who served Caesar perished from the Earth? I ask because I'm going into Alamannia, alone if necessary, and I'm gonna tear off Serapio's head, fuck his friends, take his wealth, and rescue Joko's twin toddlers.

"Which of you will be there with me when Caesar Julian rewards the men who defeated the enemy? Which of you will cut down the criminals who have plagued this land for centuries? If you're scared of warriors who got beat by a 10-year-old, then I don't want you. If you're too lazy to pillage these pillagers, then I don't need you. And if you won't avenge Gerontius Maximus, the hero of Argentoratum, then fuck you – you're not invited to this party.

"I need men who will cross that river wet and come back rich. Will you become the heroes that you always hoped you'd be? Because I'm not coming back until I've avenged my father, slaughtered my enemies, and haul my weight in loot. How much wealth do we expect to take? My Uncle Theo brought 80 wagons, my dad had 120, and Senator Savelli has another 300. That's right, brothers. We expect to load 500 wagons with loot, besides all that you can carry. We've added several thousand packhorses and most of you have sacks, bags, or backpacks. That's a lot of plunder! Your job is to impoverish the Alamanni while burning their crops, homes, and granaries. Your job is not to fight battles, but to remove everything worth taking, including their fuckable women and young kids to sell as slaves. I'm not asking you to die for Rome; I'm asking you to fund your retirement. Your family has suffered enough. You have been poor too long. Our enemies have gotten rich off your hard work. You can either grind it out every night like an ugly prostitute or take what you deserve if your balls are big enough. With their warriors in eastern Alamannia, now's the time to raid western Alamannia. So, as I bury my beautiful parents, I'm gonna ask one more time: are you heroes with me?"

The army roars loud enough to nearly drown Magnus out. With pent-up rage, he vents his fury in a primal roar and the armed men below eat it up. His father's army is now his.

Behind him, Magnus doesn't notice his uncles and Luca looking at him warily.

The invasion of Alamannia begins after dusk under a full moon. Ger's gunboats, each with a Scorpion catapult on the bow, beach themselves on the eastern bank of the Rhine. Hundreds of archers and shieldmen climb out to secure their beachhead as engineers extend the pontoon bridge so wagons can walk over water. By Briga's docks, Magnus watches the vanguard shoot shadows and advance into the scary woods across the river to take out sleeping sentries. He hears distant shouts, curses, and cries of pain. Leaders ignite two torches and wave them to signal success. The killer kid grunts approval.

Legate Theo, Tribune Pelagius, General Mallobaudes of the Salian Franks, and Commander Dutch of the Batavi each lead several thousand horsemen through the river in their units, careful not to get mixed up. Riders scramble up the gentle riverbank into enemy territory. No foes oppose them. Four rivers of riders take their place on the eastern bank. Magnus watches them disappear down trails through the massive Germani forest. 50,000 eager men will soon fuck Alamannia in an orgy of violence.

Satisfied, Magnus boards the artillery trawler just as it casts off. *Ballistae* are bolted to its deck. He waves at Uncle Honorius, a quiet banker looking uncomfortable on a freighter. Troops cover the weather deck and catapults line the rails. As the trawler enters the current, Magnus watches a dozen large troop transports, six small gunboats, and two horse transports try to keep up. The sad senator finds Magnus on the stern, gazing upriver at his father's army.

"Luca, I should be waving at my dad right now while mama weeps again. Every time he had to risk his life, she fell apart – it's why I learned to cook. Armies have invaded Alamannia, but never 50,000 desperate fighters seeking loot. Dad hoped to steal a million horses and cattle, but I doubt the forests of Germania offer that much pasture. I asked for all captured mules for our mines because horsemen value them less. Even the Saxons promised them to me when I demanded the general's share of the plunder. I'd be happy with a hundred, but I may leave Uncle Theo with thousands of valuable mules. Iberia's Almaden mercury mine is the world's largest, so last month dad asked them for a purchasing agent to buy our prisoners, mules, and even our excess cattle. They won't pay cash, but we'll get an enormous amount of mercury to smelt your precious metals. Luca, you've developed so much technology out of your own coin purse that you deserve wealth, peace, and security. Partnering with Maximus Inc will enrich you in ways you can't now imagine. I wish I were there to see it."

The senator sounds scared. "You're not afraid to die?"

He literally waves that away. "Life is scarier than death. Only the living suffer; ever catch a corpse complaining? My parents rejected me, so I'm rather ambivalent about my future. Dying is easy; living is hard."

"Max, why do those Iberian troops like you?"

"Most are from my home province of Galicia, in northwest Iberia. Like most Romans, I'm not from Italy. I train with them because I've followed my father in the field since I was 5 as his talkative pet slave."

"I know they know you because many call out your name, but I don't understand why they like you, usually excessively so. Do you get them raises or procure them women? It's strange to see grown men hug a perfidious boy."

The orphan turns sharply, offended, then shrugs it off. "I'll be mad if I learn what that word means. Until recently, everyone loved me except dad and Cousin Theo. I'm good at winning folks over. You saw me work our West Germani allies when they joined our expedition. Despite the language barrier, I made them laugh so hard they spilled their mead. They all know my name. I'm not usually angry, but mama drinking my poison put a pebble in my boot."

The trawler picks up speed as the current kicks in.

"Max, why attack now?"

"Dad told Julian he'd cross under a full moon to better coordinate their campaigns. They're more afraid of Julian, so dad always hoped to fuck them in the rear. Oh, and it's not a pincer movement; our armies never expect to meet. Dad wants to sack their settlements, kill their herds, and capture their families while looting as much as possible. Julian doesn't want a battle because the last few didn't accomplish much. Both sides lost many men, but we can't occupy a damn forest. Dad told Julian that winning battles won't win this war. We need fewer Alamanni, so that's how we should measure progress. We'll kill more enemies by burning their crops and slaughtering their herds than by battling armed men. Their warriors must decide to harvest a few weeks early or challenge us, but they can't do both. Their fighters are called up to defend their homeland, but are not compensated, so they risk losing everything. Dad floored me when revealing his Grand Plan; I'm still in awe. Imagine winning a war without fighting bloody battles."

Luca is skeptical. "This was never your father's plan."

"Starving them was always dad's brilliant plan. I was there when he proposed it to Julian. That beautiful man's eyes lit up. What dad told you was just bullshit to occupy the spies. Sacking Frankfurt just cemented the plan in concrete."

"Why Frankfurt?"

"At 50,000 people, including those riding out the winter, it's the largest city in Alamannia and their biggest industrial center. Most of their iron weapons are forged there. Happily for us, ships can reach it. Battles are won by warriors, but commerce and industry fund armies. Dad wanted to remove their metalworkers, businessmen, and professionals. Frankfurt sends ships beyond the Baltic to net fish off Scandia, in the North Sea, so we're gonna burn or bust their boats. Caesar Drusus started Frankfurt in the 1st century, but the Roman border retreated to the Rhine River in 260 when the Alamanni poured across. The Main River, the Rhine's longest tributary, goes through Bavaria, so we'll pass through a lot of hostile territory, but the opportunity to devastate the Main Valley is too good to pass up." He pauses theatrically. "Valleys are shaped like vaginas, but this one is hotter and wetter than most."

The cruel kid chuckles at his own joke.

Luca snorts in disgust. "Max, I know you spent the last five years with young, horny troops, but I wish you wouldn't talk dirty. Besides, they'll just rebuild Frankfurt after we leave."

"But we're not leaving. Caesar Drusus fortified Cathedral Hill, a river island and the oldest part of town. Its height dominates the city on both riverbanks and, most importantly, controls the crossing. Germani don't realize the Batavi see the Alamanni, Franks, Saxons, and Bavarians as competitors. Dutch has agreed to occupy Drusus Island as long as we supply his garrison. The Alamanni must recapture that hill because Frankfurt has good Roman roads to Mainz, Berlin, and other inland population centers. They can't let us stay, yet they can't force us out. Dutch will use Drusus Island to impoverish Alamannia. Mama's unexpected death has put me in a murderous mood. I expect to die fighting, so I need you to get my boys out with all that they can carry. Theo's brother Honorius will take care of you."

"You should have brought more men."

"I brought several thousand elite archers and didn't have transports for more. I'm doing what I can with what I have."

"I'm surprised Legate Theo loaned you his best bowmen. He may need them soon."

Magnus chuckles at that. "Rome didn't give Theo a legion. Julian let him raise a legion from Galicia so Julian could take Iberia's legion out of Iberia. Rome outfitted them originally, but the local government pays them – poorly. Instead of a militia, called upon only when threatened, Theo proposed a fast, professional mounted force to respond to danger anywhere in Iberia, stationed in Valencia, Iberia's busiest port because it faces the Med. The government agreed, but never came up with the money. Over three centuries, the Maximus family has bred with every Iberian clan that matters, so those boys protect their own homes and families, not invade Alamannia. That ambush shocked them because they did not expect to fight – escort prisoners to the slavers, sure, but no one was to die or kill. 80 or so died and a few hundred legionaries suffered crippling injuries; they all would have died without me, so the Jovii want payback.

"Many Iberians suspect my father lied to get them to come, but he's dead, so they now need to make the most of their situation. With the army's treasure chest empty, Pel can't even pay what dad promised. Theo wouldn't have brought his precious legion if dad counted on loot to pay their supplies and services. Emperor Constantius fucked his own army to make his own heir, Caesar Julian, look bad in case his latest wife gives him a son. That legion gives Theo high social status. He was a thin, bitter, miserable man until he got respect from Iberia's social elite. Frankfurt probably has more portable wealth than the rest of Alamannia combined, so enriching his legion will make Theo a pretty popular person. He won't have recruitment problems after this raid, unless too many die. Our family dominates northwest Iberia, so Alamanni plunder will fuel our local economy, enriching our port and province. That solidifies our clan's influence over the peninsula. You heard me right, Luca – we're taking all the huggies."

The senator is still skeptical. "But the other legions must scavenge. Theo assigned a century to each of my sons to empty ore, but moving heavy rock is a lot of work. Most Alamanni are dirt poor with nothing to steal."

"Theo's athletic peasants, the Victores Legion, and the West Germani must work for their treasure. Stolen horses are worth as much as slaves. Your guides will take them to towns while destroying everything within reach. I assume my uncle's richest raiders will share with the poorest, but I didn't ask because Theo's been in a foul mood after losing his beloved brother, his beautiful sister-in-law, almost losing his son, and expecting to lose his most annoying nephew.

"Dividing a force is a good way to lose badly, but our units will move fast and often. We'll destroy a large area quicker and capture thousands of young Alamanni to sell as slaves to mine toxic mercury in Iberia. Alamanni kidnap primarily to enslave, so this is just simple justice. Our West Germani allies do this for a living – plunder what they can and fight when they must. Romans have always tried defeating Germani in battle instead of destroying their livelihood. The enemy will wonder what we plan while we plan to leave with all that we can carry.

"Did you see the slavers salivating when the gunboats showed up? Oh, the auction will be epic. Every man who participates will share in the sale of those slaves and each will probably get a stolen horse. Dad commandeered two horse transports that Constantius wasn't using, but now they're mine. The Batavi promised to guard any stolen horses for me until I can send them to Porto Gordo. Dad doesn't trust Julian, so he rented an entire warehouse in Amsterdam that his brother Honorius will manage. Rome's share of the plunder will go towards paying you, Theo's supplies, and other campaign costs. After what Emperor Constantius did to us, Uncle Honorius will make sure no crumbs fall into royal hands. The Franks, Saxons, and Batavi will support us more if they profit off this campaign. Everyone wins except our enemies."

The senator is still confused. "So why are you here?"

"Great-Uncle Honorius wants to know what happens to his trawler. It leaks too much for ocean voyages, but it's big and high, so dad optimized it for artillery. Theo also wants to hear what happened and, if Dutch goes down, we need to tell Batavi leadership. Serapio murdered my dad and tried murdering me, so my hands twitch every time I imagine targeting him. I daydream of killing him all night long. I sleep so good that I can go years without waking. I always nurture obsessions, but I've never felt like this. I've always said I've never been a kid, but now I'm not kidding. Though she apparently didn't love me, Mama's death left me with rage, fury, and guilt. Is there a grist mill that can grind all that?"

Luca points. "We're leaving the Rhine to enter the Main River." He shudders as they lose sight of the Rhine. "Max, you're too young to be so angry."

Magnus spits angrily over the rail. The river water looks darker. "Julius Caesar commanded a cohort at 17 and saved them all at a siege, earning a decoration. I always wanted to be a young, decorated hero. I don't want to die a nobody and be forever forgotten. Fame is our only immortality. Luca, I'd rather live large than live long because this world is unnecessarily cruel, crappy, and capricious."

"Max, do not call me by my name. We are not social equals. My ancestors founded Rome a thousand years ago. You're an Iberian with a Briton accent that real Romans can barely understand. My family owns much of Italy while you're an odd orphan without ancestors."

The teenager laughs and leans back against the rail. "Oh, Luca. I'm a Fabian of the Fabia gens, one of Rome's Founding Families. I'm a direct descendant of Quintus Fabius Maximus, whose strategy of wearing down Hannibal saved Rome from destruction. Fabian Tactics is named after him. Consul five times like his grandfather, Fabius was dictator twice and named after an ancestor-hero of the savage Samnite Wars. My ancestor, Paullus Maximus, conquered Galicia and settled his sons there. My grandfather's grandfather, Marcus Pupienus Maximus, was briefly co-emperor in 238 when traitorous *praetorian* imperial guards killed both emperors as they set out to battle Goths and Persians. That's when my branch of the family left Rome permanently for our Iberian estates. I'm 5th-generation Iberian-born, yet still consider myself Roman. That's the power of Rome."

Shocked. "You are still not my equal."

"What does that matter? I won't see my 11th birthday. You only need to tolerate my presence a little longer, then you can kick my corpse. I'm sorry I had to take your darts, javelins, and chainmail, but I swear we'll pay for it all, if we can. Dad hated chainmail because it rarely stopped arrows, but now I know the purity of the iron matters. Roman senators usually sell overpriced crap to the military, so centurions distrust what the lowest bidder provides."

Luca sounds bitter. "The Senate refused to buy my chainmail because it costs twice as much as the crap they provide. I made enough for our field armies, but the cheap bastards said it was too expensive. Having half the impurities makes my chainmail twice as strong." He stares at their white-foam wake and speaks more truth than he knows. "Rome will fall if senators care more for their comforts than their cohorts."

The orphan fingers his chainmail, which fall below his knees. He jingles as he moves. "I customized my own chainmail vest and chainmail tunic, plus chainmail chaps for my legs. Imagine dancing with a dog on your shoulders. The breastplate pulled me forward until I added a backplate; wearing armor all day has turned my calves into cantalopes. If steel is just very purified iron, then steel chainmail must be incredible."

56

"Steel arms and armor would be both lighter and stronger. The blade's edge would be sharper, stay sharper, and last longer. A kitchen knife must be whetted often to cut meat, so I hope to live long enough to hold a steel sword."

"My brother wants to captain a ship to India. I'll ask him to steal their best steel experts. Luca, we'll get rich together if you stop treating me as your social inferior. My family has saved Rome before and will probably save Rome again. Pick your poison."

Luca feels old and exhausted. "Max, your company is harder to tolerate than my mother-in-law, but you seem serious, like your father. He was a man I could do business with and you're the only Roman who appreciates what my iron offers. That's how weird the world is. Max, I'll try to overlook your shameless sense of familiarity, your unearned arrogance, and the unspeakable things you say and hope you remember my social graces, goodness, and generosity. Your father also owes me a lot of money."

"The dead owe nothing to no one and orphans have no fathers. He disowned me before he died, left me nothing but contempt, and gave my inheritance to my uncle. Go after Theo; he only commands a legion and is a complete push-over."

Pulling back warily. "Your uncle is as stubborn and savage as the best of Caesar's spawn. I sense a cold ruthlessness and thoroughness in Theo that scares me more than your brilliant father. You must also know this because he's the only man you address with respect. Insults fly out of your flippant mouth like spittle, except with him. Theo gives you a look that makes you carefully rephrase what you initially wanted to say. I bet he's never hit you, yet he's the only man you have ever feared. The son is as fearsome as the father, so careful how you treat your cousin because he will become equally impressive. A 6-year-old defying Alamanni ambushers? Young Theo is made of strong stuff."

Magnus is pensive. "Dad was rarely home, so Uncle Theo is my real father. He's not the only father I've ever had, but he's the only father I've ever known. I'd kill or die for Theo. He never treated me like a child, which is why he calls me Little Man. He always insisted I was special." He pauses thoughtfully, studying the senator. "You've taken a different tone with me, so you must find me useful. Why do you need me?"

Luca laughs heartily, his belly jiggling under his bright white toga. "I'm deep in debt and doo doo. Bankers are snakes that slither upright. Bankers will loan as much as you want, as long as you can prove you don't need it. They'll smell my desperation and ignore my pleas. Ironically, I must count on you to regain solvency, which is maddening."

The teen invades his personal space. "Do you have a blast furnace?"

Smiling at the stars. "I have a design, but it requires a completely different smelting facility. I also need a higher-capacity stamp mill to crush ore prior to melting off the metal. I can make a bigger kiln easily enough, but I need volume to justify the investment. Max, you need what I offer and offer what I need, but you're a strange business partner. Rome no longer invests in its military. Since adding darts a century ago, they've done nothing innovative. Most legionaries are not Roman or even Italian, but Romanized Germani mercenaries who won't risk their lives without extra compensation. Natives of Italy avoid the army like the plague. General Valentinian cuts off thumbs to induce other Italians to do their duty, but who wants to risk their life far from home for 20 years in horrible conditions for free? Youth is our best thing and serving in the Roman Army is the worst way to waste it."

The orphan jumps up, bursting with emotion. Luca backs up warily.

"Dad started as a military engineer, but I must surpass him in every way. He was really smart, so I had to study harder. I surpassed him in higher math at 8 years old. It's strange to find someone with equal interests, but since I'll probably die tonight, let me toss you some advice. I told Joko, but he just grunted at me as if I'm aggravating.

"Now listen up, Luca. First, your shitty undershot waterwheel is too slow, small, and poorly placed. An iron frame would make them last longer. Installing them in the fastest current will cost more and interfere with navigation, but twice the spin rate gives you twice the power. You need to pump water to a high tower and then use gravity through pipes to turn a series of overshot waterwheels, which have a third higher efficiency. Owning a water tower is like storing energy because you control the flow of water that spins your waterwheels. Enough water towers effectively gives you unlimited power. Unlike rivers, which suffer from drought and floods, a water tower can send the ideal amount all day, every day. That makes all your machinery operate at peak efficiency. Gears that turn too slow are wasted while gears that turn too fast will burn up. A water tower could power waterwheels on your slope. I'd recommend two sets of ten, each getting progressive smaller.

"I spent a month studying Rome's mechanically driven Janiculum mills and they alone produce more flour than the rest of Italy. Anatolia's Hierapolis mill has been around for over a century, using a connecting rod, so I don't understand why every town doesn't have one. Crank-activated sawmills should be everywhere, plus similar ones that cut blocks of marble into floor tile. Stamp mills have been around for seven centuries, yet yours is the first I saw with cams and trip-hammers. Ore can't be smelted until ground up into tiny pieces, but almost everyone inexplicably does that by hand, like grinding grain with a pestle. And yet folks think I'm crazy for loudly advocating for automation and mechanization. Luca, hire the best experts because a poor design will cost you far more than their higher pay."

Luca looks at him like a dangerous snake. "Theo claims you're precocious, yet your father called you a monstrous beast. I didn't understand until now. You're fascinating and terrifying."

After they shake hands like good Romans, they watch the rest of their fleet follow them. Magnus waves pleasantly. A vulture flies over the ship and screeches angrily. From the foredeck, Magnus somehow hits it with a pellet and jumps for joy at his accuracy.

"Joko, you were right again: longer, more elastic leather gives me more power and accuracy. You're brilliant and, as a genius, I ought to know. I knew I liked you for more than your witty repartee. I'm gonna take a nap. Wake me just before we arrive." A sentry in the topmast yells something excitedly. "Oh, look, more hostile Bavarians. Let's take their ship. I always wanted to be a Roman pirate like Admiral Honorius instead of an Iberian orphan."

Joko grunts as if he wants to be left alone and the dying bird loudly hits the river. Magnus runs to the catapult operators, points, and watches gleefully as they track their prey. The Bavarian moves to avoid, but the trawler turns into them. Two Scorpions fire hooks and a winch pulls the enemy closer. Hundreds of archers line the trawler's rail to shoot unarmed fishermen. Magnus is the first to board by jumping to the smaller vessel. He rolls and comes up laughing like a kid before disappearing below. The suicidal teen soon returns with an angry old man that he stabs and throws overboard.

"They have fish and salt! Boys, we're not going hungry! This ship can probably hold 100 stinking prisoners. Can anyone of you sail? I can, but I'm busy and weighted down by guilt." They soon come across an even larger freighter at anchor. The grieving orphan leads a team that wakes up the crew and then yells to his trawler. "They belong to the Hanseatic League and have agreed to buy their lives by serving us for a month. The more shipping capacity we have, the faster we transport our plunder. I'm taking their captain and their flag. Who wants to sail to work?"

A strong wind moves the ship up the Main River. Magnus shares the Crow's Nest with a sentry. He's squinting his eyes and mumbling indistinctly to the sentry, who shrugs. Angered, Magnus carefully climbs to a rope and slides down to the deck. His hands burn, so he dunks them in a barrel of water. From there he marches forward to the bow. Joko is a big, bearded, barrel-chested bull of a man, but Magnus grabs him by the chainmail, puts a blade to his balls, and roughly pushes him against the rail. Beyond him, the ship heads to something massive upriver.

"Joko, the fuck is that? You mentioned a tall tower, but I saw something huge surrounded by a rock wall thrice my height. Tell me again where Alamanni elites have homes."

Struggling for self-restraint. "I said the three brothers pooled their resources to build a tall log tower. A stone wall encloses an entire neighborhood for security. They have their own docks and they fenced off great pasturage for their best horses." The big prick lets go, cocks his head at an odd angle, and looks through Luca without seeing anything. "Dad, Max says he sees words. I've never heard of such a thing."

"I also smell lies and hear flattery." He grunts angrily. "Joko, that's exactly what you told me, word for word. You fooled me with the truth; I'm impressed and distressed. I haven't felt this dumb since that tree ran into me. Joko, I should have asked you questions to plan better, like how many floors does it have?"

"Ten floors. A few thousand rich people live there, but hopefully their fighters have left or else we're in big trouble."

"Ten floors? That's important information you should have shared."

The big man stares him down. "Count your blessings if you can manage the math. I would have warned them you were coming if they didn't steal my twins. If Gerontius didn't die of poison, he would have died in Frankfurt. Either way, he was a dead man. Max, your father's death saved your life. He didn't, but his death did. I enjoy the irony."

Magnus' head spins. "Well, for Heaven's sake, don't tell him that; if souls are immortal, then I'd literally never hear the end of it. Dad had to die so I could live? Yeah, I can live with that." Sheathing his blade. "How do they farm so much? From the topmast, crops fill my visual horizon. Who do they sell it to?"

"The Hanseatic League, Baltic tribes, Scandians, Finns, and Ostrogoths, but not the Batavi, which is why Dutch wants to hurt them. The Batavi live in the Lowlands, so they must build expensive dykes and install waterwheels to pump out seawater to farm or ranch. The Alamanni conquered a quarter of Gaul for the soil. If you rescue my sons, I'll show you their secret. It's genius." He laughs for the first time. "Boy, you'll shit yourself."

"Stop laughing; you're scaring me." Magnus studies Joko suspiciously. "Honest men are hard to trust. I mastered rhetoric just to learn how to lie. Sorry, no, that's not true. I misspoke because the sun got in my eyes." He looks up, but it's still night. As they sail closer, they see a rectangular structure outlined against the full moon. Something bothers the boy. "Why would they build so high? That looks like a perfect square."

Joko pounces. "You say that after reading six geometry books? I can hear Euclid laughing at you. It's an exact cube, genius. Max, condescension is when someone talks down to you... Ah, forget it! I can't talk so slow!" He roughly pushes the boy out of his personal space. "I didn't design it, but I helped the Romans who did. Trees cover Germania, so height helps them see what's coming while giving them extra protection. All four entrances have iron doors in iron doorframes that I installed. Your father was not breaking into that without my master key. He would have died a loser-failure, just as you said. I liked Ger, but he wanted to kill my customers.

"All three brothers spent years in Rome so, like Romans, they equate size with power, unlike Greeks, who obsessed over beauty, yet failed to build a single arch. Not even a pointy Gothic arch. Everyone wealthy needs a home here, which has made the family the richest in all of Germania. They charge an arm and a leg for food, but even amputees pay it to sleep safely. But the real money is in the luxury stores on the ground floor. High-status ladies dress up to look down on others. Rich bitches enjoy one-upping their social circle to make rivals feel second-class. They have cotton, velvet, silk, satin, and something called sateen, whereas poor Germani wear rough-spun hemp, linen, jute, sisal, and maybe wool. A lady from Rome owns the jewelry store, but I know how to break her safe's padlock if you help me rescue my sons."

The orphan turns from the skyscraper to study the metalsmith. "You never offered me a key, so you knew this was suicide."

"Why would I help you kill my cousins? You wanted to die and I wanted to help you. Boy, I like you, but the prospect of seeing your death thrilled me like my first erection. Funny how that turned out. It galls me to rely on you to get my kids. They'll hail you as a hero instead of a suicidal murderer."

Glaring up at him. "Most men must lie to deceive me. You've taught me to distrust honest men, as if I'm not paranoid enough. I can't even fault you and that's what I excel at. Damn you for being perfect! Since I need a father and you openly dislike me, I'm tempted to adopt you." He returns his gaze to the log Cube. "How will we get in the tower?"

"With great difficulty. The Hanseatic League flag that you stole may buy us precious time. Instead of round wooden shields covered in leather, I made large iron shields. Not enough, but I didn't expect family to betray me."

Magnus whoops. "I hear you, brother. Dad thought me monstrous; I'm a virgin, despite Sasa's charms, but I'll show him a fucking monster. It's past midnight. No sentry has seen us, so all fighters must have left to challenge Julian. Maybe I won't die tonight after all. I'm not sure I can live with the disappointment. If a sentry wakes Frankfurt with a warning bell, we're doomed." He turns to the rocky island in the river. "Or if we fail to take Drusus Island."

A large quiet city sits on both sides of the Main River, one much older than the other. The big trawler leads several other vessels, all desperate to dock. Transport boats beach themselves on a hilly island with a castle on top. Batavi land to capture the citadel, shocked it has no sentries. The six gunboats land troops, then position their Scorpions to offer fire support. Foreign invaders scramble up to capture the castle before an alarm wakes residents to the danger. The stinking trawler sails upriver to the tall tower. Meanwhile, the largest freighter chooses the dock with the deepest water; the other ships hurry to moor. A gangway lowers and a few thousand troops flow off, all with backpacks and four quivers. Special teams target ships at anchor, overwhelming sleepy crews. Others quickly work their way through dockside facilities to assault the city. Two horse transports land more raiders. With remarkable efficiency, several thousand foreigners invade Frankfurt without anyone sounding an alarm.

The orphan studies the elite neighborhood. The foredeck is packed with people. "Frankfurt has no bridges? I guess that makes sense because the word, Frankfurt, means the ford of the Franks; it's best to build where it's easiest to cross the river. We'll take the newer, richer half of the city while the rest watches helplessly. I count twelve ships and countless boats worth stealing. I had no idea I'd become a killer pirate like my sneaky Great-Uncle Honorius. Grandpa's brother is the Med's craziest criminal, yet almost became a senator. My family's merchant fleet can't get enough ships because they rot so fast. Look at the size of that freighter! She's so beautiful I just hit fucking puberty. Dad once called me a fucking virgin, but I assume he was screwing with me. I see six freighters or cargo boats by the tall tower, plus two luxury passenger boats. I'll be rich if I don't die." Chuckling. "Luca, these illiterate barbarians live better than you. Stealing from others is not nice, but apparently pays well. Frankfurt is their Rome. The Alamanni don't guard their capital? They rely on a palisade to protect them? Why has no one sacked this city? Joko, why do you keep asking me rhetorical questions? No, don't answer; I don't want to know. Giving our men backpacks was genius and cheaper than paying them. We should make quiver baskets that hold more arrows. 30 each may not be enough. I bet a backpack quiver could carry 100 arrows, half my regrets, and most of my misery."

"Max, don't you ever shut up?" Joko asks.

"Not even when eating or sleeping. I'm oral in a world of anal, so I talk a lot of shit. I blame my existence on my fucking parents. Oh, and I babble when scared."

Uncomfortable and armed, Luca also seems scared while Joko is desperate to get his twins back. A lot of Iberians look equally anxious because that tower is massive. The ship seems slow, fighting the current with an unreliable breeze. They hear the Sack of Frankfurt starting downriver as troops move in for the kill.

Magnus squints. "The log Cube has a hoist on the roof to lift heavy cargo to any floor. Joko, why does it have a rope to the docks?"

"Residents use leather straps to fly down or to send cargo. It beats walking." He points. "They have underground tanks to store seafood surrounded by cold river water that often freezes at night so fish lasts longer. Frankfurt has a bulk-rate contract with the Hanseatic League for deep-sea fish – mostly herring and anchovies. Dangerous, but lucrative work. Most Alamanni spend their winters here because it has food, then leave every spring, deep in debt. The men must then fight for free to feed their families. The three brother-kings are quite clever to use food to unite all Alamanni. This neighborhood alone has ten granaries for old and fresh wheat, barley, oats, rye, and millet. Frankfurters eat wheat loaves, not that hard, dark bread made of course grains like millet. I can barely stomach that stuff, but northern Europe somehow lives off it during famines. Oh, Max:

famine isn't when there is no food; famine is when too many folks cannot afford food. Tired of gruel and barley porridge, northern Europeans take what they can get. Joko turns to the senator. "Dad, their factories and foundries are better than yours because I taught them how to improve on our designs. Both coal and iron ore are sourced locally; if they had more capital, they'd dominate European manufacturing. I can't wait to take their expensive machinery, equipment, and tools to repay them for their treachery."

That startles Magnus. "Germani aren't this smart. All Roman insults say so. Only Visigoths have a written language and that's really recent. Someone thought this through. If they stopped wearing animal skins, the Alamanni could pass for human." He turns on a Roman legionary, who backs up warily. "Tribune Piso, you're the Roman Army's best builder. Dad thought he needed you to fortify Frankfurt, but he didn't know the Alamanni built a log fort pretending to be an apartment insula. Please take a long look at that tall structure to determine how to defend it and how to burn it." He smiles up at the master builder. "Piso, for an engineer, you're well built. I once knew a constipated plumber; do you know any well-designed architects?"

"Make up your mind: do you want to defend or destroy it?" Piso asks.

"I want to lure all Alamanni fighters here so I don't have to chase them in a forever forest. Once I tire of killing them by hand, I'd like to burn them all inside so they feel comfortable in Hell. I brought fewer fighters, but superior ones, because we must look beatable if they just throw enough bodies at us. Your job is to keep my men alive until the enemy gives up or runs out. You don't need to die with me, but I wouldn't blame you for escaping this cruel world."

Piso tries making sense of the boy, then shrugs.

Luca is clearly terrified. "Max, combat doesn't unsettle you?"

"Why would it? I have nothing to lose but my worthless life. I have no future unless I steal enough to live on. Life is too brief to be poor – I think Jesus said that. I won't miss my mean daddy, but my neglectful mama left me like month-old fish. She broke my heart and shattered my mind. I'll always hate her for loving Ger more than me. She only had me to fix dad's location for a Sodomy Attack. You won't believe this, but I'm just a tool so mama could get what she wanted. I know I shouldn't blame her, but I do. She loved her man more than her firstborn. Guess that makes her a better wife than mother. But, man, I still want a refund. Luca, I can't commit suicide because that feels like quitting, so I need someone to do me a favor by killing me. Joko, sheathe that damn blade! Apart from suicide, I also need help with masturbation if anyone can spare a hand. I'm curious how many Alamanni we'll kill. There's nothing quite like taking all a man has and all he will ever have – that's real power. With my blurry vision, I don't see how sex can compare."

He turns on his teams as the trawler gets into position. "Helmsman, dock us between these two big freighters. Team Alpha, take the one on our left; Team Omega, seize the one on our right. If you don't burn the ships, I'll sell them to Uncle Honorius. Delta, we must storm the log Cube. Yeah, I'm also surprised to say that sentence. Again. Cousin Franco, your shieldmen ready? We need to get in before the city wakes up to its doom. At least, that's how I start my days."

Looking up, Joko loudly and pleasantly greets a resident.

Magnus shivers in dread. "I see an old woman looking down on us, but she doesn't seem to recognize our catapults. Scorpion operators, prepare to snipe archers on high balconies. I doubt we can reach the roof. I've never seen a taller edifice. Stealing the Hanseatic League flag may save some lives. Boys, let's walk off like sailors and hope our Germani coats disguise us. If you speak East German, talk loudly while bitching about your boss. Brag about your massive penis and complain about bathing every decade."

Before they tie mooring lines, the gangways lower and three teams jog out. Some yawn as if just woken up, but most sport a predatory look. Magnus practices insults in East German as if opening a new play.

The Lion has landed.

The old Alamanni woman finally screams in horror and the tower slowly comes alive. Tenants look out windows and stumble onto big balconies in their night clothes. Sleepy eyes try puzzling it out. Most look more confused than alarmed because the intruders wear fur coats over their uniforms.

Jokes glares at Magnus. "Serapio is mine. Max, his three sons are about your age. You can do what you want with them, but his vicious daughter is the one who stole my twins and forced Sasa to poison you. I've fed and housed her, so she needs to die hard. That bitch thinks she's the sexiest girl alive. We call her the Universal Target because everyone takes a shot at her."

The teen laughs. "Dad's jokes aren't the only ones I should steal. You can kill Serapio as long as I can kick his corpse. His neighborhood better be rich because I'm feeling poorly. Germani have raided Romans since Gaius Marius, 500 years ago; it feels good to balance things out. I'm glad they didn't wall off the riverport. Joko, can you run with those iron shields? I don't have all night and my impatience is killing me."

The fighters burst into a brisk jog through dockside warehouses while Luca, left behind, uncomfortably waddles all alone. Downriver, transports land the last of the troops. They walk to work, moving from shadow to shadow. A dog barks, then many others, but they sound like they're barking at each other. Harsh voices in East German tell them to shut up but, for some reason, they don't.

Several thousand raiders fan out, going through muddy roads to the best homes, but waiting for residents to sound the alarm. They ignore commercial buildings to prioritize people. Most structures look old and dilapidated with trash littering the streets. The Plan is to position everyone to maximize surprise and thus minimize casualties. Though it's very late, someone finally yells a warning that others respond to. Pairs of men kick in doors or shoot through glass-less windows. They rush in with swords and twine to kill or capture enemies. As the screaming gets louder, neighbors pour out into the dirt street, but few are armed because Frankfurt has never been attacked by sea. As always, the armed beat the surprised. The victors tie up the saleable outside, then move on to other homes. The dirt streets soon have thousands of bodies struggling to free themselves. Most scream in pain or yell for help. As the raiders advance, the size of the city thins them out. The first locals destined for the slave markets are driven at sword point to the harbor just as resistance picks up deeper in Frankfurt. Leaders hear the clash of metal and the thumping of arrows piercing flesh. Even the screams sound different.

Unlike Old Frankfurt, this new neighborhood has cobblestone streets with nice shops and eateries within the outer wall. Residents whitewashed these structures like the Batavi do in Amsterdam, so moonlight reflects off them, creating dancing shadows. The tower has glass windows, drapes instead of tapestries, and balconies starting on the 3rd floor. Many rooms light up, which means they have expensive oil lamps. Hearing fights in the city, many locals face the wrong direction and can't even see the armed trawler blending in with theirs. Dozens of archers crowd riverside balconies and take aim at those running up, but Joko says something that buys them a lifesaving minute.

Magnus rambles while jogging. "That looks like Caesar's insula, except several centuries newer and four stories taller. When I snuck into Caesar's old bedroom, the wall partially collapsed and I thought I'd die. The open center had piles of garbage and enough rats to feed Frankfurt. One day I want to burn it down and build something better."

"Max, you sure talk about yourself a lot," Franco points out.

"It's true. All 80 memoirs say so."

"You have a lot of plans for a boy seeking death."

The kid shrugs. "Death is my solution, not my problem."

Joko butts in. "Brothers Mederic, Agenaric, and Chrodomarius pooled their resources to construct something that Greater Germania has never seen. Flaunting wealth is a proven way to acquire power. Their father and uncles had been the most aggressive in expanding west of the Rhine, forcing my father and grandfather to mate with more Alamanni." He suddenly sounds sad. "I thought our branch of the family was off-limits, but Serapio always enjoyed breaking the rules. Alamanni arrogance grows with their military strength. We need to teach them a lesson and I need a famous Roman to blame."

Still jogging to keep up with grown men. "I'm famous and Roman? I thought I was infamous and Iberian. I hope my arrogance doesn't grow with my military might or my head will explode." Armed residents exit the ground floor entrance. "Oh, look, they've come to greet us. I didn't think we'd be outnumbered and my belt only holds twelve throwing knives. We need to get closer, so who should I challenge?"

Franco barks: "Max, put on your damn helmet."

"I need them to see my innocent baby face or else I've wasted a lot of time in the mirror. I've practiced ten smiles for distinct audiences. Julian responds most favorably to #3 and Sasa fell for #1. I'm gonna give the Alamanni my world-famous #6."

Joko points. "The big one with the bandage is Mederic. Don't let his white hair and ugly beard fool you. He's the best of this bunch."

Magnus agrees. "His longsword is almost as big as my cock, which also takes two hands to hold, or so Sasa said. After I kill him, I'm gonna run inside and force his friends to follow. My short swords will give me an advantage in a narrow corridor. Jog like you're going around the Cube, then give them a saturation volley."

The non-Iberians laugh at that while Magnus draws a knife with his left hand and a short sword with his right, which he holds out as if fencing. He waves it back and forth like an accusing index finger to focus their attention on it instead of the hidden knife by his side.

"Max, Theo told us not to let you die," Franco says.

"But he doesn't expect you to succeed. I saw it in his hard hazel eyes when we said our goodbyes. Even Cousin Theo almost seemed sad to never see me again. But I plan to confuse them by defying death by becoming immortal. The last thing I want to do in life is die in battle after saving humanity. Is that really too much to ask? Oh, they're about to shoot us; time to work." Waving his sword like a toy. "Mederic! Hi! Remember the boy who killed you? Is that your sword or are you just glad to meet me? Hey, he understands my Iberian Latin! Mederic, where's your fucking son? Serapio owes me a mama, but this time I want one who loves me for me, if that's not too much to ask."

64

The Alamanni archers on the balconies let the boy approach while keeping a wary eye on the Iberians jogging around the Cube. Joko holds back to see this unfold. Hundreds of women, kids, and elderly look out windows or balconies. Moonlight casts strange shadows and shade. Someone with massive lungs blows a conch seashell horn and residents go into a frenzy. The teen can't see them mobilizing, but fears it. The dangerous orphan yells up at three boys on a high balcony who look down at him with absolute hatred.

"Can Serapio's kids come out to play Catch The Sword? I'll win against all four if they have the balls to face a fun 10-year-old. And tell your bitch-sister I want to see her with her clothes on."

The two iron doors reveal a dark interior. The warriors look past their prime and ready to run.

Mederic yells in East German. "Joko, your boys are safe with their grandma. Serapio acted on my orders, so you can only take his life over my dead body."

Joko replies in East German. "Why aren't you fighting Julian?"

"The demon-boy killed my best bowmen and wounded me, so the other chiefs are jostling to replace me as king. Serapio says the general's boy is more dangerous than the general. I thought that stupid until this child brought a small army into my big city. I might remain king if I kill him. If you walk away, I'll return your twins once the Romans leave Alamannia."

Getting close, Magnus screams arrogantly. "Talk Latin, you barbarian brute! You killed my parents, so I demand an honor duel. They didn't love me, but I might miss my mama's mutton. Prepare to die, you stinking savage who speaks great Latin and lives better than any Roman."

"Boy, varnish that tongue. You're not big enough to kill me."

The orphan continues jogging while bowmen on balconies track the hundred or so Iberian bowmen running behind the building. They hear the sound of distant fighting raging across Frankfurt.

"That's not what 2200 corpses said on the road to Fort Briga. They said I was the deadliest boy in Alamannia. Defend yourself, old man, before you bore me to death."

A full moon gives them light. The warriors by the ground floor entrance seem tense, bunched up, and ready to retreat. They look more at the archers running around the corner than the loud teen attacking them alone. Then Team Franco pivots to sprint at them. The Alamanni defenders get ready to retreat inside, then lock their iron door. Magnus waves his short sword awkwardly, as if he's never touched one before. The easiest attack was obvious: the king raises his long heavy sword over his head with both hands to chop this intruder in two. Expecting this, the teen's left hand throws its knife into a leg as Mederic rests his weight on it. The plain blade sinks to the hilt and the look on his royal face is priceless. Horrified, the Alamanni king totters like a logged tree as the athletic teen speeds past him, drawing a short sword with his left hand while puncturing a royal chest with the right. The sword breaks his heart and the king falls to his knees as if eager to gag on cock.

Magnus yells while running. "Fire!"

Franco blows a trumpet for the ship's artillery while his shooters saturate the elite Alamanni. The trawler had positioned wagon-size catapults on the foredeck to supplement those already lining the bow. With the captain's command, they fire a volley

65

at enemy archers. Burning barrels land on balconies and cook Germani alive. Bolts puncture people while survivors hear laughter from the artillery trawler. A bunch of fighters fall, so other Alamanni try and fail to hit the ship, but don't have heavy weapon range. After losing another exchange, most angry Alamanni bowmen on the balconies escape the danger by darting inside to run to the roof.

Spotting arrows in the air, Magnus surprises the warriors ready to retreat behind their iron door. The kid dodges a sword and knocks aside a spear to chop a leg and slice into an arm before diving in a roll into the dark hallway entrance. Two big men charge him, but the club is too heavy and the spear too big for the small space. The boy nicks one and thrusts a blade into a boot, then ducks to chop open a leg so the body blocks the door from closing. Most warriors turn to attack him when a saturation volley from Team Franco strikes them down. Magnus laughs, surprised he made it, and takes off running into the skyscraper.

Magnus talks to himself. "Seeking death has made life tolerable. I hope mama misses me."

He sheaths his short swords while running down an unlit hallway to take out his sling and a handful of pellets. Hearing hundreds of feet, he hides in a shaded area near a large courtyard illuminated by a full moon. Behind him he hears the grunts of men in pain.

Magnus whispers at them unsympathetically. "I'm not just a boy! I'm an angry orphan with nothing to lose."

While the log tower is shaped in a perfect square, the open center is a perfect circle with a spiral-shaped ramp against the structure. It's plastered and painted to look nice. Like Caesar's insula, the structure surrounds an open atrium with a garden, playground, and open plaza.

In deep shadows, the boy whispers to himself. "Fucking Alamanni circled the square. I gotta tell Euclid."

He looks up to see the full moon beaming down at him and smiles until he sees expensive marble tile cover the courtyard. Snorting, he smells fresh bread and looks through a glass window into a big bakery. His grin turns into a groan as he scans the threat environment.

Whispering like a kid seeing a candy store. "Oh, man! They have their own bakery? I want my own bakery! Wow, they can afford marble tile. Just what kind of barbarians are these Alamanni? Damn these savages for stealing Roman culture!"

Like army ants, several hundred terrified folks move their valuables from the ground floor stores, up the ramp to the penthouse vault. Some have perfume or jewelry, but most carry clothes. Scared kids, women, and the elderly walk up the wide ramp with all they can take with them. To Magnus it looks like a river of people flowing up. Unarmed tenants wearing night clothes look down at him with alarm, shock, and disgust. None have bows because the bowmen went to the roof to battle the boat, but the courtyard has a few dozen men with clubs, swords, and spears. Through windows, many more men can be seen arming themselves. Instead of charging, some squint to identify Magnus in the poor lighting.

"Boy, who are you?" an armed man asked in East German.

Magnus sees a path to the ramp that leads to the upper floors, but a few fierce fighters stand in his way. A big badass approaches to challenge him. He hears a whooshing sound and stops. The first lead ball enters his left eye at a right angle and blows his mind along with his brain. The detritus sprays two warriors behind him, who wipe the crap from their eyes while cursing and crying. Magnus flings the next nearest threats and nails four more before they charge en masse. They're badly wounded while he's up to no good. The teen runs down the wide corridor, pausing to throw lead at a dozen hostile shadows. Backing up, he knocks them down, then finishes them off with his short swords. The last one begs for mercy.

"What mercy did you show my daddy? If I'm already going to spend eternity in Hell, then I should enjoy myself while I can. Whether I murder one man or a million, I can only burn for eternity. I think that's what Jesus said. I'll ask Pelagius if I survive this hell."

The teen cuts him open and watches his guts spill out as the victim screams in agony. He sees Franco coming in with Team Delta, then smiles as he finally puts on his lion helmet and jogs to the courtyard. Magnus hurls lead at everyone armed, but not at the army of human mules, moving valuables upstairs. Mad men attack him, holding up improvised shielding, but he retreats while smashing their shins, then ending their lives. One desperate group after another charges, but die as failures. Team Franco is shooting down everyone who gets back up. Impacts knock men down, twirl others around, and collapse them like killing is easy.

The kid laughs loudly. "Worst dancers ever."

Three men with swords and shields block the entrance to the smooth, wide ramp that circles the open interior. Fewer mules are moving valuables now. Team Franco fans out to shoot and dozens of residents rush to attack them. The teen exploits the distraction. Bursting from the shadows, Magnus throws a knife into the chest of the first man, kicks him hard into the next, then whacks the third. He feels smart until he notices the ambush: Folks pour out of ground floor shops, armed with anything. One lady wields a killer painting in a bronze frame that, apparently, she doesn't want. Maybe 100 quickly cover the white marble tile. Team Franco shoots arrows as fast as they can while retreating down four corridors. Seeing so many run at him, Magnus sprints up the smooth wooden ramp as residents come down from upper floors without range weapons. None look in their prime; these are older men, fat folks, big kids, and crippled veterans. Most hold household items like pots, pans, and kitchen knives, except some veterans with old swords. Many scream at him or hurl insults because his mere presence enrages and outrages them. They feel violated, like their raiders have violated a million innocents over the centuries. Karma's a patient bitch. Alamanni have him sandwiched, some running up at him while others charge down. With nowhere to go and no time, he's scared, alone, and out of options.

He sounds terrified. "Fuck me! I should have thought this through."

A laugh from three floors above makes him look up as he slings for his life. It's that hot bitch from the Rhine, flashing him her fantastic tits while blowing him a killer kiss.

"Flavius, I'm gonna cut off your tiny cock and shove it down your big mouth while you die."

"Again?" He laughs at her. "Last time, my son shot me in the back when I was drunk and unarmed." He studies her a moment to sink a zinger. "Like most crazy bitches, you were cute until you spoke."

67

Too many Germani attack, so he empties his knife belt at the biggest threats and defends himself with two swords. As they are poorly armed and untrained, the angry orphan ducks and dodges, dancing within them to cut as many as he can, even as he backtracks. With his blades a blur, he's cutting a hostile every heartbeat and even that's not enough to avoid their manipulative hands and stinky breath. They try tackling him, but he's too short and fast. One Alamanni flies over the railing and another falls after a hard push by a desperate teenager. His retreat leaves a trail of blood and bleeding bodies, whimpering for help or cursing his parents.

An angry Alamanni holds a bleeding belly a few meters away points at him. "You son-of-a-bitch!"

Blocking a blow while slicing a shoulder. "You know mama?"

A thrown hatchet strikes Magnus in the back and embeds itself in his chainmail. His back plate has more dents and scratches now. He looks down to see two more hatchets hanging from his front chainmail like limp dicks. The big boy throws them back at the easiest targets and laughs at their pain.

"This is a great way to die. I've finally lucked out."

He assumes this is it, as he recovers throwing knives, hatchets, and javelins. His face shows true fear – not of death, but dying forgotten. As one arm tires, he switches, flinging projectiles with equal strength at sprinting strangers within spitting distance. His lead breaks legs, but otherwise the bellies or chests of those holding weapons over their heads. He dodges strangers as they fly past, stunned and defeated. Their expressions show raw, visceral emotion as utter despair replaces grim determination. Some paw, pat, or whack him as their momentum carries them down-ramp, with Magnus getting out of their way without interrupting his slinging. Objects bounce off his helmet and ring his bell, but the teen shakes it off as if his life depends on it. Pots, pans, jars, and pots trip up his footing.

A man with an ax gets a pellet in the face and another with a mace twirls as lead punctures his right shoulder. With a moment to burn, Magnus swings the ax into one enemy and the mace into another's knee, before pushing her under the railing and off the ramp. The screaming gets louder, but Magnus is in his own world, in the Zone, focusing on the next second without worrying about the next minute. He hears Franco frantically call his name from the courtyard and knows his boys are engaging the ground floor hostiles. Too many bodies have piled on the ramp, slowing them down, so Magnus turns to fling at enemies climbing the ramp to fuck him from behind. Team Franco is vastly outnumbered, but better armed. An army of dying Alamanni have shafts sticking out. They look like stupid zombies as they either limp-charge bowmen in armor or desperately crawl away. Team Franco blocks the ramp entrance to fight shoulder-to-shoulder as hundreds charge like desperate maniacs. Frontline troops block blows with swords while the rest shoot Alamanni elites from point blank range. The red carnage bleeds into the boy's brain for future nightmares.

Magnus needs a moment to take his temperature. Looking around him, he sees dozens of bodies dying too slowly. Strangely, no one is attacking him. He seems confused until it dawns on him that he survived.

"I thought I was a goner." He holds out his hands and sees them steady. "Either I'm the best at winning or the worst at losing. Maybe my mean mirror will stop insulting me now."

With his rear secure, Magnus concentrates on those above him, but also notices something strange. While those willing to fight take whatever is at hand to block the ramp, the non-fighters on the upper nine floors hurry to move their valuables, just like those on the ground floor.

"There are more people moving wealth than defending it. Residents must have a plan in case of attack."

Alamanni flow into a penthouse room. Magnus sees paintings, busts, coin purses, stolen bullion bars, and sacks of jewelry. An elderly man grunts under the weight of his silverware, actually made of silver. Bejeweled weapons, goblets, and furniture flow up the ramp on human mules to an iron storeroom on the penthouse floor. Old ladies, shorn of jewelry, carry organizers made of exotic wood and often gilded with precious metals. All small kids flee up the ramp, most carrying their personal possessions. The riches astound and motivate Magnus.

With the teenage intruder striking a dozen targets a minute, the crowd backs up and yells for shields. This gives the boy a breather. He looks like he has a new lease on life as he calculates the rent in this place. He checks out the luxury penthouse apartment where tenants store their valuables and wonders how to reach it. It will be hard, but he has nothing else to live for. His chiseled face get a determined look as he slings with renewed vigor at anyone armed. As he eyes all that wealth, he starts chuckling like he has found the pot of gold at the end of the rainbow. His laughter pumps up the troops below, but pisses off his angry enemies. Walking through wounded enemies is dangerous. A wounded woman faking death grabs his leg and tries stabbing his calf, only for something to blunt the blade. Magnus hacks off her forearm and explains while she howls in pain.

"I wear chainmail chaps sandwiched between two layers of leather. Getting dressed requires a triple-pulley crane. I run like a fat drunk shitting himself, or so everyone tells me. Did you know I might be my grandpa? Crazy, right?"

He can't tell if she understands his Iberian Latin, but the blood gushing from her limb speaks volumes.

Arrows suddenly fly up, past him into hostiles, so Magnus turns around to see the ground floor courtyard cleared of threats and covered in bloody bodies, one of them a uniformed Iberian. Team Franco is now positioned to shoot the hell out of the upper ramp. The boy roars Glorious Victory because this means he won. Without range weapons, the last armed Alamanni hide behind cover or flee to their homes. Many hold furniture like shields, so Iberians prioritize easy victims, who fall, screaming for help. Only the unarmed are spared, but the top floors are getting crowded.

Magnus marches up towards hundreds of defiant tenants defending their homes and families. A thousand residents look down from wooden rails, but their fighters block the ramp at the 3rd floor. Almost half are women, while big boys equal the older men. The prodigy slings pellets into his most immediate threats while dodging pots, pans, vases, furniture, and heavy curses. Some items hit him, but he's hard-headed. Magnus brushes off some things that cling to his chainmail because they make him off-balance. He's aware his skull and face are bleeding, despite his helmet, but he looks forward to the sweet release at the bitter end, which he assumes is soon.

Turning to yell at his cousin. "Franco, I'll lure them down so you can shoot them up."

Once he nears the 3rd floor ramp, Alamanni run down at full speed and he barely

69

has time to escape their greedy hands. A big fucker with an executioner's ax over his head makes Magnus run low into him so his momentum sends him south. He draws swords for other enemies, cutting limbs and thrusting into juicy flesh. Rusty swords smack him and one shatters on impact. Arrows fly past him and some almost hit him. Two big bitches take both his blades in their breasts, but still knock him over as they hit him at a run. The crowd cheers and more hurry down to club him. The young badass rolls away and flings for his life, awaiting the killer blow to his head. A hammer and a few hatchets come close, but Magnus enjoys crazy-fast reflexes. An older man falls on his face from a broken leg and his brave grandson get hits so hard in the shoulder that he goes over the rail to fall to his death with a sickening sound, yet Magnus can't help but grin. Troops throw themselves out of the way, but still get sprayed by blood as the boy's body explodes like a tomato. It looks gross and sounds grosser. In his spare moments, he throws shields over the railing so enemies don't re-use them.

Talking to himself again. "I wish dad could see me now! Great piece of shit, my ass! I'll show you. I'll show everyone!"

He's concentrating on those in front of him when an arrow strikes his back chainmail, just missing the back plate. Magnus arches his back and twirls in pain. After ignoring a hundred hits, he sees a big ugly archer above and behind him on the 6th floor. Not just ugly, but extraordinarily horrible to look at, with a deformed face and burnt hair.

Near-hysterical. "Franco!"

The orphan lunges forward to avoid the next arrow, then slings a lead ball that forces the bowman back. When he comes up with an arrow notched, Magnus is already swinging. His pellet hits the archer in the left shoulder and he twirls away, beyond sight, but not beyond hearing. The ugly man curses and complains. Out of breath, the boy takes a moment to calm his nerves, catch his breath, and organize his shit alphabetically. He tries grabbing the arrow stuck in his back, but can't reach it. He winces and whines because it hurts so much. The Alamanni above him jeer, hoping the injury is fatal.

"Getting fucked in the back is a weird way to lose my virginity. And to think I could have enjoyed Sasa. Without that second layer of chainmail, my goose would be cooked."

The tenants blocking the ramp rush him while his wound distracts him. Pocketing the sling as he retreats, he draws both swords from fat tits and cuts down older men, bigger boys, and a cripple with a cane. He loses a lot of ground as other enemies position themselves to charge him with sickles, shovels, and shoes. A human river flows at him, so he turns and runs down-ramp.

"Fire!" Franco bellows.

Magnus dives down-ramp as 100 arrows slam the folks chasing him. He comes up in a roll, breathless and expecting the worst. His hunters are hurting, so he returns with a vengeance. He stabs and slices the lightly wounded, as he marches to the 3rd floor, humming Girls of Rome. A group with furniture-shields charge him and are too many to stop. That virgin knows he's fucked, so he runs down the ramp again. Though he expects to die within minutes, Magnus smiles in joy at going out as he chooses.

While running scared. "Mama, see you soon."

Then an Iberian volley devastates the enemy, breaking up their charge. A big warrior goes down and another trips over a body, exposing more men to vicious projectiles. A few flee while a dozen charge instead of the 30 that Magnus feared.

70

Turning around, he waves survivors on. All hold furniture or actual shields. He dodges to strike down the fastest with short swords, retreating fast to bleed their momentum. At the last moment, the orphan dives down-ramp, only to come to his feet in a roll while Iberian arrows smash into those sprinting at him. Magnus grabs an enemy shield and crouches as their momentum carries them past. He peaks past his shield, shocked he's alive. He finally hears a thousand wounded Alamanni either moaning and groaning or weeping and sobbing with their last breaths. Franco reaches him and twists the arrow from his chainmail. Magnus removes his helmet and gulps tons of air as his cousin roughly lifts his chainmail vest to inspect, clean, and bandage the worst of his wound.

Franco barks again. "Max, your back is bleeding badly. Hold still while I patch it."

"I might be menstruating; I assume that's why Sasa smelled like fish, but tasted like chicken. Yeah, that arrow sunk deeper than the others. See to it that no one fucks me from behind because I'm saving my virginity for a demon-bitch from hell."

Once dressed with his armor on, Magnus takes stock. With the ramp clear, though covered by bodies, he carefully works his way up, slinging the easiest targets. His bleeding body leaves a red trail of blood that he doesn't notice. Franco's bowmen follow him up, but check for attackers hiding in homes. From the top floor, hundreds of terrified Alamanni stare at Magnus like he's a demon. They're armed with whatever objects are easy to throw. At the 9th floor, Magnus loudly does his breathing exercises to relax because new foes obstruct progress. He looks at them and smiles at Serapio's spawn.

"I might still die tonight after all. I'll win by losing. Top that, father! I'll soon see you in Hell."

The hottie from the Rhine and her three half-brothers stand in his way, several meters up the ramp. Past them, hundreds of horrified residents also block the penthouse entrance, but don't have range weapons. It seems crowded, dangerous, and unnatural to have so much hatred in one place outside Hell. Magnus feels off-balanced; looking down, he sees his iron breastplate swinging free by his crotch. Reaching underneath, the boy tenses up as he concentrates, then finally cuts a string to remove it. Holding it up, he mumbles a curse. Turning it, Magnus shows his four opponents dozens of dents.

"You'll pay for that. I accept bullion, flattery, and huggies."

She gestures to Team Franco, now just a few floors below to protect his back. "Outside, you challenged us to a duel. We accept."

He nods knowingly to buy some precious time. After a swig of water from a sack, Magnus takes a moment to knock arrows, hatchets, and javelins from his twin sets of chainmail armor. The orphan fingers the biggest holes, cuts, and gashes in his outer leather chainmail and grunts angrily when his fingertips come back bloody. He inserts several hatchets into the holes and grunts approvingly when they hang there like God intended. The orphan studies his enemies like a pass-fail exam. They're all gorgeous, with the older boy a little older and the youngest a little younger than himself. All dressed up with over-sized armor and ancient weapons. They look at him with absolute hatred.

But she still stands out. Her tight red dress shows major cleavage, general sexiness, and parts of her privates. Magnus doesn't see the expensive rings she wore in the river to seduce and stab him. They hear fighting and screaming on lower floors, plus distant cries from the city outside, but the five fighters focus on each other. After scanning the upper floor for threats, Magnus draws his custom swords. They're short and straight like the Roman gladius, which are for thrusting, but his are a little lighter and longer due to better iron.

Magnus chuckles. "You ran out of bras and panties? You look good with nothing underneath. Thanks for dressing up in so little for me, but I still haven't reached puberty. Show me your tits again. They're full, fantastic, and unforgettable. Come daylight, I plan to sketch you nude, pubes and all, with your legs open wide – in death, as in life. I painted Sasa's naked corpse and left a copy in my parent's tomb with a fun explanation. I plan on putting a giant statue of my dad, looking fierce, so folks don't think I'm a son of failure. Sculptors will make my mama as beautiful in marble as she was in life. I know I shouldn't care what people think, but I do and it vexes me greatly. I assume it'll be my downfall if I survive this siege." She has never known such rage. Her brothers are terrified, but determined. "Hey, do I have anything in my teeth? Because my mouth tastes like glorious victory.

"Since you're about to die, I saved you a few favorites: My wife loves wine, but hates to go get it, so she gets me to get it for her by paying me a blowjob per bottle. This is genius because now I can't blame her for being drunk every day." They don't even chuckle, for some reason. "I told that joke last week and the entire table was on the floor laughing – with half the chairs. Oh, you're killing me. You know why fucking pussy costs so much? Because it's worth it!" Fucking crickets. "Wow, tough crowd. Love is blind, but lust has great eyesight. You're not gonna even smirk? How about this? When men tell women they're bisexual, women see it as a problem. When women tell men they're bisexual, men see it as an opportunity. No? Nothing? Okay, here's a final farewell: I'm a big pussy; it's why I queff so much."

Iberians laugh from lower levels, but the four siblings are serious as shit.

She's not in the mood. "In the river, I was trying to kill you for wounding my father and grandfather. Mostly for wounding my grandpa."

"I got that impression. You tried too hard. A horny cavalry captain once tried to show me something fascinating in his tent, but instead I kicked his shin and told my daddy, who beat the poo out of that pederast quite literally. The legion nicknamed him the Latrine after that. Not my shit dad; the pedophile. I didn't even know Latin had a word for men fucking boys, besides pedophile. You're a lovely-looking piece of crap for trying to murder a 10-year-old who never did shit to you. I'm gonna enjoy killing you in a not-crazy way. Where's your daddy?"

"Not in Frankfurt. Probably cheating on our mothers again. As a handsome prince, he likes seducing naive girls as soon as they hit puberty. Your wound drove him crazy. He grew up obsessed over Alamannia conquering all of Germania, but now he talks only of you. One centralized government ruling Greater Germania would be more powerful than the Roman Empire."

Magnus reels. "Your dad is my first fan, but not the last. My enemies appreciate me more than my family. I'll try sketching him before removing his balls, his head, and his ambitions. You dress like you want to get laid. You must be a hungrier whore than your nasty mother. Sasa enjoyed my middle finger. Would you like to taste it, too? My fucking stallion can't get enough."

"Over my dead body. Why won't you die?"

Sounding sincerely puzzled. "I honestly don't know. I assume God hates me." He pauses, lost in thought. "It's not for lack of trying. I kissed my ass goodbye 69 times

72

tonight and now I'm wondering if it's sexual." He chuckles to himself. "Dad loved that gem. I should feel bad for stealing his jokes, but I don't. I ran up that ramp expecting the poor death I so richly deserve. I feel twice as old and half as smart. Anger, grief, and bitterness won't let me sleep until I vent it on those who deserve my wrath. I never knew I was so good at killing. Sure, I spent half my life with troops instead of kids, but I've never had to escape certain death so often. I find it thrilling. Sex can't possibly compete." She snorts at that. "I'm bleeding and aching everywhere, but hurting those who have hurt me is so satisfying. Thank you for turning me into a monster. Does Alamannia really have a million people? I look forward to killing or enslaving them all until I find a better way to vent my grief." Magnus turns to address three old warriors by the luxury suite who probably raped a lot of strangers in their youth. "Joko's toddlers are innocent. My men control the city. We'll be more merciful to your kids if you release Joko's mother and twin sons, plus your own kids. I promised Joko I'd try rescuing them, but whether they live or die matters not to me. If your children stay, they'll die with you. Let them leave to live another day. I swear they'll be treated well."

The three argue in East German, but an old elegant lady from within the luxury home impatiently over-rules them. Since she must be a queen, Magnus looks forward to killing her. Non-fighters still carry the last and least of their valuables to the largest home, where they assume it'll be safe. The queen barks a command and a few hundred small kids burst from homes to run down the ramp, past Magnus as if he's not 10.

Serapio's daughter gets ugly. "Flavius, why are you here?"

"You tried murdering me. I take that personally, for some reason. Plus, I don't want to die poor or for my little brother to live poor. Joko says the richest families in Alamannia reside on this floor and I want all their stuff. It took a thousand human mules just to empty the ground floor stores. I saw enough fur to clothe a billion bears; I assume grizzlies shop here. Over the centuries, the Alamanni have stolen Europe's best paintings, portraits, busts, jewelry, gemstones, silverware, furniture, and everything golden. I want all that, plus the notoriety that goes with it. I don't fear death; I fear dying forgotten. Are your pubes golden? You showed them to me before. Sasa made me inspect hers – for flaws, I assume. Until I lost my virginity, I didn't know what I was getting into. You look flawless. Shall I inspect you for quality? I suspect something deep inside you stinks to high heaven before I send you to Hell."

Magnus gets too close on purpose and the oldest boy rushes down the ramp. The orphan knocks aside his long sword and chops into his neck so hard it flips unnaturally to its side, like a chicken with its neck wrung. They were the same size, but otherwise completely different. Flaunting her flesh, the girl looks 16 and slashes at him furiously. The middle son tries flanking Magnus on the ramp, also with a large, heavy sword. They looked surprised that he uses both short swords equally well and unbelievably fast.

While backing up, down the ramp, Magnus manages to nick the girl's underarm. While this distracts her, he focuses on the middle boy. He has an old sword with several gemstones that looks made for a king, but it shatters when the boy blocks a blow. The angry orphan gets a foot of iron in the enemy's throat, so the bastard turns to his sister with a look of horror. That's hilarious, so Magnus laughs like a hyena. Furious, the hot bitch swings her weapon, so Magnus doesn't see the smallest brother leap on him with two daggers of one mind. The boys tumble down the ramp, bouncing on bleeding bodies to the 9th floor entrance. Legit scared, Magnus grabs an arm and whirls the boy about.

73

The courageous cutie flies over the rail and falls nine stories to land on his dead neighbors with an ugly thud. His hot sister shudders upon hearing him loudly splatter. Many Iberians cheer. Magnus has no time to look because the she-bitch runs down to behead him. With amazing instincts, reflexes, and timing, he ducks under the blow to stab her belly even as he throws her on his back and over his head. Her soft body lands hard and bleeds badly. She grunts and groans like she's enjoying sex. Magnus smiles like he just got laid.

Shocked to be alive. "That's it! I'm taking all the huggies."

Alamanni from the penthouse charge, but a volley from Team Franco cuts many down. Bodies fall and flail, then trip companions following too fast. Descending gave them a lot of momentum, so Magnus gets out his sling to hurt the nearest threats while retreating fast. He steps backwards as carefully as he can, but still trips on a corpse and falls on his ass, which motivates men to charge. A second volley hits another dozen and the rest lose their nerve. The terrified residents race back up, with troops sniping them. The orphan advances as he flings deadly lead at unprotected backs until the civilians lock themselves in their penthouse apartments. Dozens die and even more suffer grievous wounds. Humming Girls of Rome, the orphan returns up the ramp. Grabbing the hottie by the hair, Magnus drags her, laughing as she howls in pain and humiliation. This leaves a bloody trail over a field of bleeding bodies, some twitching more than others. The injured, with nothing to lose, try hurting him, so the boy pockets his sling to take out a sword to puncture the most mobile survivors. It looks cruel, brutal, and necessary.

The orphan finally stops, stoops, and stares at her agonized face. "You poisoned my parents, so I'm gonna sketch your nude body as soon as I get my kit from the ship. I'll probably poo on you, then paint you in color so future generations know how shitty you are. Goodbye, you fucking bitch. Say hi to your failure of a father once I kill him."

At the penthouse entrance, the boldest and bravest block the ramp to deny him access. The old folks and small kids look silly in their night clothes, holding furniture-shields, "show" daggers, and not a few cooking pans. They look dumb, desperate, and determined. Magnus sheathes his bloody sword and gets out his sling. He palms a handful of pellets and considers his next move. Outside, they can hear the trawler shelling bowmen on upper balconies.

"Franco, Alamanni archers are on 9th story balconies, if you could please kill them." Iberians hustle to clear that floor while Magnus scans the threat board. "Anyone who surrenders gets to live." No one gives up, so he shrugs. "I assume you all understood my perfect Latin."

The orphan aims for shins and limbs when faces aren't available. Several defenders lower their shields to flinch at their broken bones when the first Iberian volley pierces their confidence. Blood squirts from arrow holes. Men hold shafts in their faces as if that helps. A dozen go down, clutching their legs as if they need clutches. A big boy takes one in the eye and another in the ass. The volley shatters their optimism and their formation. The hero runs up and stabs the most dangerous, then works his way through a tangle of bodies. His blades go deep into flesh, with the horrified expressions of the dying. Survivors flee, limp-running to the roof, where residents wage another war against his artillery trawler. Magnus follows to lock the damn door to the roof with a wooden beam. He returns to smile in awe. He's earned the penthouse!

Talking happily to himself. "Idiots are stuck on the roof!"

The tower's wealth entered a giant home with an iron double-door within an iron doorframe. Three big old men bark commands for everyone to enter the fortress within a fortress. Magnus notices that it opens outwards so it can't be kicked in. A few frightened folks push out a grandma holding the hands of two twin toddlers who run to Magnus like he's their hero. Overwhelmed, Magnus squats to hug them both. He reassures them and kisses their foreheads.

"Boys, you're safe now. I'm sorry you were taken from your parents, but daddy came to get you." They take off down the ramp and Magnus turns on the grandma. "Joko mama?"

She speaks excellent Latin with a terrible tone. "You must be Max." She spat that out like a loogie and looks like she needs to hawk some more mucus. "Did Luca come for me?"

"He's around, but I'm pretty sure Luca came for Luca. That's not a criticism; just human nature. We have time to kill, so maybe I'll murder a minute while you cook breakfast. My men will also be very thirsty, so I'd appreciate your help."

She studies him like a bug she wants to crush, then grandma walks off and disappears into a neighboring home. After the enemy all enter the huge home, an elegant lady wearing a pink silk wrap-around robe holds up a large padlock, which have been around a few centuries, and closes the thick door shut, with the three burly old badasses outside. Magnus hears her lock it with a satisfying click, then flings deadly lead at the opposition. All three have a shield and sword, but the round wooden shields are small to be carried long distance. The teen targets their lower legs and they realize their weakness too late. They try to charge, but only one can limp fast. A pellet catches a foot and that guy groans, then grovels. The next ball pierces his upper forehead and blows his mind. While giving ground, Magnus takes a minute to fling several deadly projectiles at the two survivors until they move no more. Feeling secure, Magnus studies the battle below him. More Iberians have reinforced Franco, who is clearing lower floors to not leave enemies in his rear to fuck up his shit. Yelling through doors, Joko talks enemies into surrendering to speed up securing the skyscraper. Prisoners walk down the ramp, defeated and depressed.

Talking to himself. "Iberia's mercury mine owes me a huge huggie."

Visibly relieved, Magnus and Franco pull several corpses against the double doors so they won't open. They struggle hauling lighter bodies on top, but then seem satisfied by a ton of death. Magnus walks around the open area to inspect each home, slinging the stubborn and pocketing valuables until he finds what he's looking for. He carries several braziers and places them on the corpses against the iron door, then brings back a crate of charcoal. With a captured flint kit, he ignites the fuel, then leaves to get potted plants to lay on top. The green vegetation burns dark smoke that enters through a long narrow space above the iron door. Smiling contently, Magnus ransacks the other penthouse homes, killing all who remain. He surprises some while others surprise him. His armor saves him as he stabs and slings them ruthlessly. Bodies fall and blood spills out as he goes about his business. Each time he exits an apartment, he has more big bags stuffed with valuables, which he stacks by the vault door.

Magnus enters a balcony to check on progress in the city. He's about to roar, when something makes him pause. He turns suddenly and sees a sprinting boy about to tackle him. Grabbing an arm and rotating his upper body, Magnus throws him off the

75

balcony, then roars at the river when the boy bounces. Troops cheer him. His men look up and look happy before going back to work, butchering strangers and kidnapping the saleable. At the opposite side of the cube structure, Magnus sees thousands of horses in a huge, enclosed area between the river and a forest. He smiles at so much wealth.

Talking to himself. "I wish dad stole more horse transports from Constantius."

He piles valuables by the braziers. Heavy furniture he pulls out into the shared circular corridor. He's stuffing sacks when Joko's mother comes with hard bread and harder cheese instead of a good breakfast. She clearly has been crying. Grandma then studies the smoke suspiciously.

"Max, you stupid child, you can't melt the door like that. Iron requires very high sustained temperatures. That storage room was built for security. It doesn't even have windows for thieves to enter from the outside."

The orphan inspects the bread and water for poisonous smells. "I know. I only saw flickering candlelight inside, which means it doesn't even have a balcony. How do they vent the air?"

That upsets her. "What do you mean? It's our kingdom's treasury. This tower houses the Alamanni government – we work where we live. It's not secure if thieves like you can enter from the outside."

He nods thoughtfully. "So they didn't include a way to vent their air? That's just poor engineering. Don't they know that buildings must breathe? Persia has hot adobe cities built to let in air, which circulates most rooms."

The startled lady examines the dark toxic fumes rising above the bodies to enter the gap between the iron door and the doorframe. They can hear coughing within the vault. Someone inside unlocks the padlock and pushes the doors, but too many bodies block them from opening. The elites are trapped.

"Max, you're smoking them out?"

"Just smoking them. The double doors open out, so I piled bodies to trap them in. I'll need a lot more charcoal to finish the job. Oh, and don't touch my barrel of sorghum molasses; it's unnaturally delicious."

She disapproves. "I know those people. Most are decent folks."

"The Alamanni spent the last several centuries killing, robbing, and raping their neighbors, so your people are inhumane. Murder is no way to make a living. I'm not killing decent folks; I'm preventing horrible men from killing, raping, and kidnapping decent folk. Your king stole two toddlers and tried poisoning a 10-year-old. Residents support him, making them accessories to murder. Before I killed him, King Mederic said he approved the plan to poison me, my dad, and my uncle. If you help them in any way, I'll treat you like I treat them. Your people don't create wealth, but instead take it from others. You are little better than professional thieves who profit from the hard work of others. The Alamanni have ruined several million lives, but I've come to fix things over their dead bodies. I just wish there was a better, more permanent way to help decent folks live in peace."

She's scathing in her scorn. "Max, you're a dead boy babbling, so you won't fix anything."

She leaves in a huff and Magnus sticks his tongue at her back. Franco comes up with a team and Magnus sets the rules.

"Cousin, please kill the archers on the roof. They've run out of arrows, but still need to die. Your boys can take what they want from anything in this building except the room I'm smoking and the items I've stockpiled. No, I don't know why I want so much nice furniture. If I knew Alamannia had so many clever craftsmen, I would have invaded a dozen years ago. If Greater Germania ever unites, they'd dominate Europe. The second floor has a buffet-type cafeteria, so I have good news and bad news: the food is inedible, but there's enough for everyone."

Joko arrives with the twins. "I also have good news and bad news. The good news is locals left thousands of their best horses. The bad news is most Alamanni warriors are besieging Julian on the other side of the mountains. On foot or by horse, they're just a few days away. As we're stealing their wealth, I expect most to fight us instead of Julian, who appears stuck in a field camp on this side of the Main River."

Staring at the metalsmith for a minute too long. "Good thing I gave up sleep. Let's work!"

Magnus enters a balcony and scans the city below. The raiders seem victorious, judging by the streams of prisoners flowing toward the harbor for the fleet to deport. A few Alamanni still fight, but Team Magnus surrounds those homes. Thousands of dead Alamanni are visible, many with loved ones wailing in anguish. Raiders are already pocketing plunder and packing sacks, bags, and backpacks. A series of visceral emotions ripple across his bruised face as the enormity of his accomplishment bites him in the ass.

"Dad, Frankfurt is ours. What should I do with it?" The orphan roars to get their attention, then calls his army over. He yells down at his troops. "I just learned the enemy army is just a few days away. I know you're tired, but the more we prepare today, the sounder we'll sleep tomorrow. You know what to do; I'm urging you to do it all faster. But good news: instead of fortifying the entire city, we're gonna fight behind the walls of their tall tower. Sack this city to deny the enemy food and shelter. Take all valuables, deport all survivors, and destroy all buildings after you ransack them."

Several thousand men look at each other anxiously, then hurry off to work their asses off before the Alamanni Army arrives. Suddenly energized after a painless victory, the invaders move with renewed purpose.

Magnus follows Franco into a warehouse, with a squad holding naked blades, and wonders why. A few dozen bearded men are cheering something, but the boy can't see what until Franco elbows his way in, then steps away. With a wave of his hand, Magnus sees a naked West Germani fucking a nude beauty who screams and cries from the pain and humiliation. She yells in heavily accented Latin for him to stop. He's thrice her age and weight. The bearded rapist slaps her again and roars with laughter as she sobs sadly. With her ankles by his ears and her big boobs bouncing, it could have been erotic if consensual.

This disgusts Magnus. "Fucking Saxons. They're as bad as Alamanni. Her family can't be poor if she learned Latin."

Buff Saxon warriors turn to look down at him, but Franco grunts a warning. Magnus pushes his way closer to inspect her bruised and bloody face. Her nose has been broken, her hair pulled out, and welts dot her upper body. Her head turns to look at him, but all he sees are vacant eyes and a tormented soul cover in terrible tears. The rapist suddenly gets louder, as if about to cum. Without thinking, Magnus slits his throat, pushing him back to not gush blood on the girl. The rapist collapses like a pile of shit and the girl curls up in a fetal position. 20 or so shirtless men, however, curse the boy and advance with naked blades and evil intensions. Team Magnus holds up notched arrows while backing up.

"No rape." The words fly out of his mouth like spittle. "My father mentioned no rape when he hired you, so this Saxon got what he deserved."

An angry Saxon speaks with a heavy accent. "Boy, that was my brother. He has 200 Saxon friends here."

"Your brother broke the law; this is what happens to criminals. If you wish to leave Frankfurt, then leave. If you stay, then get rich, but don't rape. If you kept her safe, earned her trust, and compensated her, this Alamanni may have fucked you all, but you got off on beating a defenseless girl. If you kill me, then you lose your bonuses. The sale of our slaves and herds will be divided among survivors. Lose me and you lose all that money. Go back to work and never again look at me with hostility."

"Arrogant boy, this is not over. You'll pay for what you did to Deidrick."

"I recently got my parents killed. I might never see my brother again. Physical pain doesn't compare, so I look forward to oblivion." They angrily scatter, muttering curses in German. He tosses his bear coat to the girl to cover her nudity and holds out his hand. She lets him help her up, sniffling, but coherent. "Franco, I'm sending her to Porto Gordo's orphanage with enough coin and clothes to last her a few years. Please ask your wife to look after her." He pauses, still in shock. "I heard dad rage at his troops for rape, but never understood until now. They beat her long after she quit defending herself. I wouldn't have blinked if they just killed a hostile girl, but tearing off her clothes and gang-banging her just turns my stomach. Slaughtering a hundred strangers on the ramp didn't make me want to vomit like this."

Franco is on edge. "I thought you should know what your workers are doing. At least several Saxons had already enjoyed her. Most Saxons will probably leave us, then kill you if you survive Frankfurt."

"Get them an old boat, then have a gunboat sink it and sink them. Everyone who leaves with Deidrick's brother must die or they'll kill me before Alamanni get a chance."

His cousin nods his head. Holding her hand, the young teens exit the building.

Magnus points at the penthouse escape room. Troops open the double doors and Franco leads the assault, cutting down anybody still standing among the smoke. Wearing cloth masks, troops stab corpses, then use hammers to break openings to vent the smoke that had accumulated all day. A hand-operated bellows blows in fresh air and no one stays long. Also wearing a cloth mask, Magnus enters with two oil lamps and finds himself in a huge warehouse, instead of a home. He kicks the queen as she coughs, then cuts her up with a smile. The size surprises him. It has shelves, boxes, and crates even before residents dumped their loads here. Expensive clothing fills entire rooms. He walks through in a daze. The inner sanctum has the best stuff. Jewelry fills a dresser and it's packed. They watch Joko break open a safe and marvel at all the gems, coins, and bullion bars.

"A few centuries of rich plunder now sits in this room. Frankfurt has more jewelry than all of Iberia. I claim this room and everything in it to pay my people. It'll take me all day and night to fill and nail the special boxes I brought."

The leaders exit to clear their eyes and throats by the open-air courtyard.

78

"Max, you're not gonna share any of this?" Franco demands.

"Cousin, I don't expect to survive Frankfurt, so Maximus Inc gets it. But, to be clear, I earned it all. Without me, you'd still be fighting King Mederic from outside the tower. I got us in and up the ramp. I slew hundreds again. I almost lost my life a thousand times. I saved Joko's mother and sons while executing the bitch who murdered my mama. Did you see my drawing?" He holds out a sketch on a large piece of canvas and she looks great for a nude corpse, though it's unclear she's dead. "Isn't she fucking beautiful? I've never wanted to rape a corpse before. I like her much better now. I feel safer, too. See how her big boobies defy death? For the headshot, her eyes were closed, but I painted them open with a sexy look. Well, I shot for sexy, but got crazy eyes instead. I blame her, for some reason. Boys, this city is loaded with loot. You're all rich because of me, so I don't want to hear any shit, cousin, or I'm gonna tell your mommy. She gave me the best hugs in Iberia, as I always tell her. Pack it up and send it down all night to my uncle's freighter. Honorius can't wait to leave. He prefers counting coin to shooting strangers, for some reason. Joko, there's no way to take the horses overland to Fort Briga?"

"Through Bavaria? Not a chance. Those are the finest horses in Alamannia. Any Germani would kill to steal them."

"Crap! Each transport only carries 300 horses and won't be back until tomorrow. Even crowding the decks of the ships I'm stealing, it'll take a month to move them all! I never knew thievery was such hard work. How is this not taught in school? When the transports return, I'll have them move the best horses to the island and then take the next best to Fort Briga so Theo's legion can ride home to Galicia. I want everyone in the Jovii Legion to get a mount, with centurions earning three and Uncle Theo the rest. Joko, you said Frankfurt had underground tanks to store fish, but failed to mention they have six, each capable of chilling a million fish to separate old from new and anchovies from herring. We found so much that I'm filling the trawler to sell to cities down the Rhine. Thank God some Hanseatic trawlers had not unloaded; Uncle Honorius will sell millions of fish to millions of folks. My family has fished professionally for centuries, so I know those damn fish are worth more than everything else combined. But you didn't tell me about the fish, so you don't get a bite. The Alamanni would have paid the Hanseatic League enough gold, silver, and furs to fill my empty cavernous conscience. You knew a million Alamanni spent all year collecting furs to sell them to Frankfurt for fish during the winter, yet didn't mention it. Hundreds of fresh bear furs, plus thousands of hares, beavers, foxes, and animals I don't recognize. Uncle Joko, no more huggies for you."

The metalsmith walks away disdainfully while the orphan waves over a few dozen trusted Iberians.

"Boys, I've known you all for as long as I can remember, so I trust you to carry my loot to my uncle's freighter. Anything in bags and boxes can slide down their rope to the docks. Don't take anything and don't let anyone else take anything. If you don't steal from me, I'll make sure you're overly compensated."

They follow their boss into the vault. Alone, Magnus fills boxes with gems, jewelry, coins, and bullion, then nails each shut. His boys pass by, grunting under the loads. When done, his trusted troops carry the crates to the roof. Iberians hook up cargo and push it down the rope. The boy's boxes have a white "M" written on their sides.

Magnus watches his loot fly down to the riverport, where Uncle Honorius waves back with a relieved smile.

Whispering to himself from the rooftop edge. "I might be the world's richest orphan. Too bad Europe's largest army is coming to kill me."

CHAPTER 3

From the roof, Magnus watches his uncle leave. From the freighter, Honorius pretend-hugs him and the teen reciprocates until the cargo ship disappears downriver. Horses cover the decks of a dozen ships, with cattle, pigs, goats, and chickens. Only a few prisoners are visible because most are below deck. More plunder and prisoners pile up on the docks for quick loading. Long lines of prisoners carry cargo into dockside warehouses. There's still a mountain of stuff to move.

"Luca, it looks like we're stuck here for another week, until the fleet returns. I hope Honorius finds us alive and I'm surprised he came back. Valencia is the largest city I've ever seen, yet I bet Frankfurt has several times as much clothing because they've stolen so much over the centuries. Nice clothing is absurdly expensive, yet light and compact, making it easy for a raider to stuff into saddlebags. I can't believe the Alamanni have so much silk. I didn't expect to steal so many cups, plates, dishes, utensils, and women's accessories, but I don't want to just let the enemy keep it all. My boys keep finding more fur. I thought stealing a dozen more ships would require more time to fill, but Frankfurt has many valuable things that I don't want to leave behind. Joko was right about their industrial plants – they're the best I've ever seen and I assume I'm an expert. I can't wait to steal their factories, foundries, and mills. Their equipment might be worth more than all the gold we took. Porto Gordo should make a statue of me in thanks."

Luca grunts. Turning, Magnus looks at dense dark smoke rising beyond the city. Distant fires light up the night sky.

"Luca, it feels good to burn so many crops within riding distance. They could build new homes by winter, but can't grow more grain. We might slaughter all their cattle, pigs, and poultry before they attack in force, but there's no way we'll roast it all, much less jerk it, so I'm giving some to Fort Briga and hope they send me salt." Luca grunts. "Are you still mad they duplicated your smelter? Or even angrier that Joko didn't tell you? Hey, they paid him good money before kidnapping his kids."

Luca grunts.

"I'm still mad, but look at all the gold and silver we found! Our raiders won't find many minerals because the Alamanni sent it all here for smelting, refining, and purification. Just the copper from their refinery has paid for this raid, while leaving me a lot of silver as a profitable byproduct. Other than a few mills, the primitives in Rome have almost no heavy industry, for some reason. Romans are stuck, worshipping the past, when the future hits them harder every day. Advance or fall behind – I think that's what Jesus said. If Germani ever got enough engineers, they'd out-produce the Roman Empire. I probably bought Rome another century by sacking the greatest industrial center in Greater Germania. Senator, tell Emperor Constantius to kiss my black boots. Putting a crane within the skyscraper was a great way to deliver heavy cargo faster. I never saw a wind turbine before, though Persia has had them for centuries. It pumps water from the natural spring to give each floor the water it needs. Just ingenious. These are impressive barbarians; I don't care what you say."

He watches the last ship disappear downriver. "Ah, there goes my retirement if my slow suicide fails. If that trawler sinks, I'm broke again and will have to kill for a living like other monsters. I'm sending my share to Amsterdam for my little brother. I pray Dutch never betrays me. Dad says prayer never works or else babies wouldn't die,

81

but Hell may have changed that mean man's mind. I once carried dad's stuff like a beast of burden, but I no longer feel like a burden. A great weight has been lifted and, if infection doesn't kill me, I'm gonna live like a free man until an army of enemies snuffs my candle next week."

The boy laughs and points to the other side of the river. "Look at those impotent Alamanni trying to cross the ford! They mistakenly assume waiting for night helps, and then don't wait until just before dawn. Those fools think numbers matter. Let's see what several thousand fighters with hand weapons do against Franco's range warriors. Admiral Honorius says homes worldwide stink of smoke from cooking fires and, in colder climates, of livestock that would freeze outside at night. Outside of Rome, cleanliness doesn't exist, yet those hovels look especially filthy. We're almost doing them a favor by killing them."

Thousands of locals on horseback wade into the water, armed without looking dangerous. About half are women wielding farm or household tools. They seem determined, so Team Franco waits until they're almost across before running to the river. Just 100 bowmen shoot them up while gunboats sail down to add insult to injury. Several thousand attackers greatly outnumber the 1st Century.

Franco kills their leader, a burly man covered in furs who doesn't duck in time. He falls with a yell, a surprise, and a splash. Hundreds of comrades take shafts, yet thousands try charging through meter-deep water at the foot archers shooting them like fish in a barrel. Any enemy with a bow gets prioritized. From the high rooftop, Magnus laughs at the epic slaughter. A thousand hostiles ride out of the river, but defenders back up while shooting them down. Alamanni swinging swords, throwing javelins, or holding spears die before they ride into range. Those that get close enough throw hatchets, which does some damage. Alamanni archers drop into waist-deep water to fire back, but defenders prioritize them as their only threats. Still, their numbers almost overwhelm Team Franco, when a few hundred reinforcements ride out and slide off to shoot. Even then, the Germani wrongly appear optimistic.

Blood leaks from otherwise good bodies and Magnus laughs at their cries, screams, and falls. Those who ride the farthest die especially hard, leaving Franco with more mounts. Too many die too fast from moving too slow. Another leader goes down and a woman wails in grief, horror, and widowhood. That's when their front line breaks like cheap pottery. Coming to their senses, those in back turn tail before Team Franco can fuck them. Six gunboats race with the current to cut them off and cut them down. Bowmen on the bow shoot these Alamanni with impunity because Europe doesn't have horse archers. Rather confident, sailors throw anchors overboard to fix their position, blocking riders in the river from escaping their dark fate.

The kid finds this hilarious. "It's like killing cattle who give us hatchets and horses. Having predicted this, I asked Franco to only bring a century to give the enemy hope of overwhelming them. Dad's archery competitions identified our best shooters, so I put them in centuries according to their ability. The 2nd, 3rd, and 4th Centuries hid until the last moment to give the enemy hope. Swords and spears – or whatever they're carrying – can't compete against range warriors. Many enemies brought bows, but the water is too deep for them to dismount to shoot back. They're all just targets waiting to die. Ah, the cowards in the back are turning around. Still, I bet we kill a few thousand and wound a few thousand without suffering casualties. We can't deny them the northern half of the city, but we can punish them so they don't try crossing again. Dying is easy; living is hard."

Magnus turns to see his team start fires along the outer edge of the city. This fills the night sky with dark smoke and darker messages. A wooden palisade encircles the city, but won't stop an angry army. Looking down, he watches prisoners and troops carry combustibles into the tall tower. Every structure they empty goes up in flame, starting with the outer ones. Magnus nods as if each is a victory, then turns as the hoist lifts up another Scorpion onto the roof.

"Careful, boys. We're gonna need those soon, though I doubt we'll have enough wooden bolts, even operating their lumbermill day and night. If Germani made catapults, Rome would have fallen centuries ago. Thank God Frankfurt has a million rocks for our Onager trebuchet, assuming we can re-assemble them. Tribune Piso, how'd you get so good at building things? You're hardly older than me, so how are you in charge of our Roman engineers? My father called you a genius, yet you look 18. My abacus can't add you up."

"I've always been smarter than everyone else, so they kept promoting me. I come from a family of master builders, so I grew up with this. Frankfurt fascinates me. I've studied architecture, but never imagined designing an entire city, including stormwater drainage, retention pools, sewers, potable water, and trash disposal. The technical challenges excite me."

Magnus likes Piso. "Calm down, weirdo. You could design an entire city? I'd kill to see that. Get to work on that in case my suicide plans fail again. Luca, dad assumed we'd have more time. Even with 7000 troops and 13,000 prisoners, clearing Frankfurt will take longer than I had hoped." Beside him, Luca grunts louder than the troops moving the *ballistae*. "Luca, do you think Joko will get through to Julian? I gave him the best horse that I didn't want. Having grown up on a horse ranch, I'm pretty picky. Can you believe these barbarians feed oats and apples to their best horses like civilized men? I had assumed they'd all be grass-fed weaklings. And the horsies, too."

Luca grunts louder. "You risk my best son's life."

"Joko owes me for saving his sons, so I punished him by saving his mother. I spent a month with Joko and he never mentioned the three kings built themselves a tower palace. Joko put my dad's life in danger by withholding important information. Good thing I put his twins on my ship so he'd volunteer for this suicidal assignment." Luca grunts again. "Senator, are you feeling gassy again? I told you to lay off the sorghum molasses. I'm upwind if you need to fart."

"Max, you didn't bring enough troops."

"I'm in charge? Senator, I'm gonna need that in writing. What I didn't bring was enough sailors, even though dad brought a few thousand from Porto Gordo. Last month dad asked his pirate uncle for help supporting his invasion, but we haven't heard back. I had no idea the Hanseatic League had so many ships here; they sure were pissed that we're making them work for us. We need warships to control river access because our enemies survive the winter eating fish. I took hundreds of milk cows and their ovens, yet it still feels insufficient. Dumping those corpses into their wells isn't enough. Luca, you should think of better ways to starve your in-laws. Come on, man; what's wrong with you? Get to work!"

"I'll re-phrase: you should all leave because you don't have enough defenders."

The teen dismisses that with a wave of his heavy hand. "Numbers don't count. I think that's what Euclid said. Losing 300 Saxons hurt. I sent word to get more archers, but doubt I'll get enough. The Alamanni have been coming in small groups to burn breaches in Frankfurt's palisade, desperate to rescue loved ones; we need to kill the first before the last arrivals give them overwhelming numbers. When the army shadowing Julian comes here with an ax to grind, they'll assume their superior numbers will win the day when they attack at night. Few Germani are proficient bowmen because hunting in dense forest is hard, whereas I only brought great archers with a million of the world's best arrows, darts, and javelins. On the roof or on the fleet, we have a few hundred *ballistae* to blast them when they besiege us. I bet we have more ammo and archers than they do. We'll take or destroy their factories, forges, and foundries, so they're gonna run short on iron weapons after they lose their lives against our fortified tower. The diversity of their manufacturing shocked me; when re-assembled in Porto Gordo, my family will employ thousands. I'm sure they'll all thank me for their prosperity. Dad was smart to attack like a Germani instead of a Roman. Remind me never to tell him that. The more I succeed at his expense, the prouder I am of him. Is it odd that I talk to dad more now that he's dead? I almost miss him."

"Talking to the dead is normal; the dead talking back is crazy. The island fortress is safer. Why aren't we waiting there?" the senator nervously asks.

Magnus thinks that's obvious. "The Alamanni can't attack the island because we took hundreds of their boats. You and I are bait, so we must be loud and visible; well, I'll be loud and you're quite visible. You look like a target in your bright silk togas. I just wish we found more lamp oil. Do Germani literally spend half their lives in the dark? Millions of olive oil trees cover the North African coast and they produce for centuries, so we should sell lamp oil and cooking oil to northern Europe. We need a canal to connect the Rhine with the Danube to sell crap across Europe's interior. It's bad enough that forests cover Germania, but the leaves they use to wipe their asses are for shit."

The awful orphan chuckles at his joke, but the senator just glares into the future.

"Max, you can't just hold me hostage here."

"Isn't that what I've been doing the last week? I'll let you leave when I don't need you anymore. Your sons, nephews, and cousins are guiding Theo, Pel, Dutch, and Mallobaudes to the valuables you said the Alamanni hid. You'll get the reward you asked for."

Luca looks more sheepish than usual. "They'll find very little because the brother-kings centralized smelting and refining here, where the current helps them automate and mechanize using my technology. I had no idea they stockpiled so much gold to fund their conquest of Greater Germania, so I'm not getting the compensation I deserve."

The boy speaks harshly. "Rain falls on us all. I'm dying at 10 years old, so look elsewhere for sympathy."

The castle looks imposing, with steep sides and multiple walls built three centuries ago. Wearing distinctive uniforms, Batavi lift parts of a catapult onto the roof while others assemble pieces. Prisoners build barriers and improve fortifications. Cattle and horses cover the island, trampling the grass they need. From the rooftop, Magnus watches prisoners dig a ditch and pile a barrier from the log Cube to the nearest dock so they can escape. Others dump furniture and hammer in planks. Troops drag furniture from across the city, leaving the good stuff on the docks while dumping the rest here. He gazes into the river to study the castle on the island.

"Luca, I was smart to get all our engineers. If supplied, the Alamanni will never get Drusus Island back. When we retreat, only our best swimmers can reach it, so we'll use ropes to help them cross the fast current in case we lose our boats. I wonder how soon our herds will eat all our grass, grain, and hay. Not long, sadly."

Someone by the river yells his name, so Magnus tests a rope that extends to a nearby dock. He's 30 meters up, so he looks down and whistles. He takes out a strip of leather with two straps, like a belt, and forces one tiny hand through, tosses the other half over the thick rope, then squeezes his other hand in it. Luca watches with trepidation. The orphan grips the leather like his life depends on it and his eyes follow the rope to a dockside post.

The teen gets a grip. "God, I hope I don't fall to my death unless everyone is watching. Heavy cargo went down okay, so why is my sphincter tighter than usual? I feel like crap, yet talk like I'm full of shit. Luca, I'm the lightest so I'll test it first, but you're probably the heaviest, so you need to test it before I risk the lives of someone I need. You should pee before you fly down to not embarrass yourself more than usual. Oh, and don't scream like a little girl again or we can't hang out anymore." The orphan looks past Luca to his Iberian guards. "Push him off if he refuses to go. Luca, if you don't die, you'll feel very alive. Well, here goes nothing. Living an all-or-nothing life has its uneven moments."

Magnus runs off the roof with a big smile and screams like a little bitch all the way down. He's thrilled and nauseous. Everyone stops to stare at the flying boy who leapt off a skyscraper. The wind in his face surprises him and a tear drips down. His facial expression captures his wild ride. Magnus has never felt more alive. He's literally high as he falls to Earth. His speed slows as the angle levels out. A team waits to receive him. Sad, he slows to a stop far from the post and his guards must run to get him. He hangs in the air, his feet a few feet above ground and he feels ridiculous. Franco hugs him while Magnus twists a wrist free. The Iberian sets him down, then Magnus jumps for joy with excessive energy. Even his moderation is excessive.

Now he's pumped. "That was amazing! And the flight was also memorable. Great hug, Cousin Franco. If we anchor the artillery trawler here, then 6000 of us can defend the tower or the egress route and still escape after they fight their way up. The rest can crowd the fleet." He turns to study the Cube. "Oh, look, we're throwing the senator off the roof. If Caesar the Stallion was here, he'd laugh his huge head off. Now all we need are 5000 straps before they drive us from Frankfurt. Thank God the Alamanni love leather."

They watch Luca as he plummets towards them, screaming his head off and pissing himself in mid-flight. Magnus finds that hilarious and his loud laughter infects the Iberians. Unlike Magnus, the heavy senator goes faster and he reaches the end of the rope, painfully smacking the post. The teen runs over. Luca can stand, but instead drags his feet as if still in the air. Guards lift him up and impatiently wait for him to get his fat fists out. The dark, wet spot by his crotch disgusts them.

"Luca, stand up to help us out. You're safe until the Alamanni attack with overwhelming numbers. Find something to wear that doesn't smell like shit."

Luca stifles a cry. "I felt helpless."

85

Magnus pats his shoulder. "Ah, helplessness. What'ya gonna do? Strive for complacency?"

"Max, I never want to do that again."

The orphan laughs at that. "You only have to fly once more, under fire, after the enemy earns the roof, but now you know what to expect. Luca, dad always advised me to pee before strangers throw me off impossibly tall towers. I think those were his last words. You should heed me more often. I only look 10. I'm actually twice my age. Carriages that travel over rough roads quickly look old. That's me. A carriage going over Rome's smooth roads looks like Cousin Theo, which is why he doesn't squeak as much or fart as loud."

Luca leans against a post to get his shit together. "Your metaphor is wrong. Sasa said you wrote her bad poetry. I believe her."

"You mean my analogy? Seriously, senator: sometimes I don't know if you're being facetious or disingenuous! There's poetry in the world; poets just write it down. Did you know I can play poetry with my flute? Sasa said so before I killed her. I still feel bad for poisoning a beauty who wanted to fuck me, but I feel bad for a lot of things. I'm good at feeling bad. Sasa must get in line, with everyone else. Franco, you're in charge of our escape, so you must go down first because I love you most. Don't let enemy archers line the barriers or they'll shoot us down as we descend. I plan on flying last, so I need you to hoist me up so I can get down. Oh, and make sure Luca boards because I'd like him alive to build Europe's best smelter. Ah, damn! I should have thought about that before I sent Joko off to his death. He's the best iron worker I've ever blackmailed. He must know a lot of shit to smell like that."

"Max, I'll take care of it," Franco says seriously.

This annoys the senator. "Commander Franco, why do you obey a child? The Batavi will escape to the island, but you're risking your life."

He's neither defensive nor apologetic. "Max was never a child. He makes things happen. You're a senator and no one listens to you; the entire army listened to this boy. Magnus plans to roast Alamanni while escaping. Does anyone have a better way of safely killing thousands of armed enemies? I think my friends and I will survive this fight and I bet my life that a lot of Alamanni will lose theirs. Max has made me richer in one day than 20 years serving Rome. He gave us chainmail that actually works and armed us with arrows that penetrate chainmail. Yours, sure, but he gave them to us by stealing them from you. We're all gonna retire rich. Still, I'm open to advice. Shout out if you can improve his plan."

No one speaks, but then Magnus groans. "I'll think of all sorts of lifesaving ideas after they kill me. Franco, we still have 500,000 arrows on the docks. Please position them where we'll need them most. Why do quivers only hold 30 arrows? What genius thought that enough? Luca, your technical skills never cease to amuse and amaze me. Please design a quiver that holds 100 arrows that's easy to carry and leaves our arms free. Wicker might work. And why isn't your wife here to make me sweetmeats and honey cakes? I pay her in golden huggies."

Luca feels afraid. "How safe will I be on the roof?"

The Iberians laugh. Magnus points to troops nailing Alamanni shields to the upper balconies to give them battlements to shoot from cover.

"Luca, our strongest archers shot at the roof and then staked their position. The berm of furniture, rubble, and dirt around the palace tower will put enemy archers just beyond range, unless one is Hercules. We have enough shooters to occupy the top two balconies, but we need the enemy to believe they can hurt us, so I asked for volunteers to fire from the 5th floor balconies. Each will wear extra leather armor under iron plates under two layers of chainmail and hope they don't fall over the balcony railing. They'll shoot from narrow slits between the shields, while planks nailed to the railing protect their lower bodies."

"They'll just burn us out."

Magnus nods. "They might, but they plastered, painted, and varnished the logs to make them harder to ignite. Agenaric is the last of the Alamanni kings until they hold a grand summit. He invested his left nut in this gorgeous tower, so he'll be reluctant to burn it down with all its expensive furnishings. Well, I hate tapestries because they collect dust and breed pests, but his are gorgeous! Instead, he hopes to drive us out. Julian took much of their wealth when he captured Strasbourg last year, on the Rhine's western riverbank. Taking Frankfurt hammers another nail in their stinking coffin. Sure, we face a hard fight, but killing thousands of their fighters will make it that much easier for their families to starve. Their neighbors will exploit their weakness to raid because the Alamanni have grown too numerous. Everyone will fuck the Alamanni like a Roman orgy."

"Max, you blame them for your dad's death."

"I blame them for mama's murder; they did me a favor with my father. I brought a barrel of crappy pellets that I don't plan on taking with me as I fly to safety. Franco, please tell the gunboats to anchor in deep-enough water to drive back the warriors on the other side of the river. I'm very unhappy those pessimists returned to their huts. We'll hit the poorer side of the city tomorrow night, before their army arrives, so we don't have to fight hostiles from both sides. Dad always said the best way to destroy big armies was to destroy them as little armies. We must kill the thousand Alamanni archers on the north side of the river before they start making themselves useful."

That night, Team Magnus loads all their small boats with armed men and rows them across the river. Horsemen follow through the ford. The ships with catapults float down from upriver to give them cover. About 5000 foreigners invade northern Frankfurt. Though well past midnight, an Alamanni sentry wakes up to the danger and blows a conch shell alarm. Warriors stumble from their huts and hovels, armed with bow and spear. They hurry to prevent the invaders from beaching, but six gunboats use Scorpions to snipe them. Hundreds hurry to foxholes with breastworks to shoot from safety. However, some land is too rocky to dig holes and that's where Team Magnus beaches their boats. The orphan stands in the lead craft, looking for targets while steadying himself on bent sea legs because a violent current rocks the boat.

"We should have brought shields. Franco, I didn't know you giants couldn't stand to shoot when crossing on these small, overloaded boats. A warning would have been nice. The river is shallow enough to use poles, so log barges would have served us better."

Franco snaps at him. "You're armed with a big mouth. Use it to buy us some time. You've spent a month learning East German insults. Impress us."

"I *speak* gibberish, but I can't read or write it." His head snaps back. "Oh, look at the size of that old fellow. He's running into range. I'll wait for that big monster to sto – (speaking East German). Sir, have you seen my butt boy? He looks just like you. He limps and cries a lot. Yes, I have a thick accent. No, I don't have thin skin. Are you this ugly on the inside? (Switching to Latin…) Duck!"

The men behind him curl on the floor of the shallow boat. They are helpless until they can stand to shoot back. An arrow strikes their rowboat and audibly quivers in the plank that Magnus is hiding behind. The nearest gunboat nails an enemy, but not the big old dude. Upriver, the big trawler strikes enemies that Magnus can't see, peeking over the side. The riders splash through the river, but need another few minutes to enter the game.

"Was it something I said? Glad I brought extra underwear. I need them to get closer for my sling. Think Your Mama jokes will work?" Magnus stands up and roars like he means it. Yelling in East German. "Where's Serapio? I want to kill him again."

Hundreds of Alamanni bowmen gather to contest the landing. Groups rush the gunboats to drown them in arrows. The big old guy is about to release another arrow at him, so the boy dives into the cold river and swims as far as he can in the other direction. The old warrior waves the others forward to search for the dangerous teen when they should have saturated the boats. The prodigy comes up downriver and loudly splashes to shore. A few dozen warriors run after him. Belly deep, Magnus throws pellets at the ominous shadows coming to kill him, roars again to draw their attention, then dives to swim in very shallow water to shore. A dozen arrows impotently saturate his previous position. Magnus breaks the surface and splash-runs onto land, then sprints for the nearest shelter. The ankle-deep water sounds unnaturally loud in the scary night. After a few moments, he changes direction to run directly away from the archers. Arrows fall where they expected him to go. Magnus screams so they can track him again, but then darts for the nearest hut. The orphan plays a very dangerous version of Tag to occupy the enemy.

He screams in East German. "Where is Serapio?"

This side of the river is less a city and more a bunch of ancient homes thrown up haphazardly. It has no streets, but a light rain left heavy mud. Magnus slings at every noisy shadow; every third pellet earns him a cry or curse. Arrows seek him out, but he ducks or dodges like a rabbit on the run. Two bowmen corner him, so Magnus throws himself into a mud-brick hut, then stabs the first man who steps in. He runs out and around so the other archer lacks line-of-sight, only to find three spearman hunting him. Five pellets hit them hard, cratering a head, breaking bones, and shattering a knee. One warrior looks at a bloody hole in his belly, then curses his killer. Magnus jogs deeper into the settlement while loudly asking for Serapio. Still sprinting, he circles a store, sees too many warriors, then heads for the shoreline while snapping pellets at targets of opportunity. He hears a dozen or more men chasing him through the mud amid screams in panic. The riverbank comes into view and 5000 allies are landing across a wide front. Magnus grunts approvingly.

"I must buy them more time."

Team Franco frantically hurries to shore, wading slowly in cold water while tracking enemies and avoiding incoming. He suddenly moves left while ducking an arching arrow. A thousand troops have landed and another thousand wade out of water. Their leader laughs as if they're not dealing with death.

Franco bellows at his boys. "Max lured hundreds away from us! Having a suicidal boss may save some lives."

The wet troops cheer as if they're winning. The orphan sees his troops in the water, exchanging arrows with Alamanni behind cover. He cringes because Cousin Franco looks very vulnerable. While the first boat fixes their position, others beach themselves downriver. Scorpion catapults from a dozen vessels rain down hell, but the cavalry is taking forever.

Magnus runs behind enemy archers and strikes some while barely pausing. This forces them to turn to deal with the new threat, costing them a valuable minute as invaders earn the northern riverbank. Some Alamanni try shooting Magnus, but he's small, fast, and running unpredictably. The warriors in foxholes can't concentrate on the foreigners by the boats with danger in their rear. Their faces show confusion, doubt, and alarm, but also anger when Magnus laughs like a lunatic. Three warriors sharing a foxhole focus on foreigners in the water when Magnus jumps in with both short swords, stabbing two in the back. The third moves out of the way, escaping a fatal bow. He punches Magnus in the face plate, knocking the boy back to the dirt wall. Magnus rolls away, knowing what's coming, and blindly swipes with a sword, which opens up the Germani's belly. Bloody entrails spill out and he falls to his knees, cursing the kid who killed him. Another victim has bubbles in his blood that loudly pop, startling Magnus. He stares at his work, then shakes it off to look around.

A horde of warriors chase Magnus downriver through the huts. Arrows fly and some hit him, but their shitty iron fails to penetrate his double set of kickass chainmail. Still several arrows and hatchets hang stubbornly to his outfit as he runs for his life. Once enough have exhausted their quiver, Magnus veers towards shore, where his shooters have formed a long skirmish line. He runs through them and catches his breath in the surf while eying the enemy for arrows. Riders are moving in squads to expand their beachhead and the enemy commander blows Retreat. Defenders abandon their homes rather than lose their lives. Franco blows Attack and his men move in.

After dawn, the second-in-command roughly kicks Magnus awake in the lead boat. "Cousin, we're done looting the structures, but they left us little, beyond a mountain of wood. The Batavi began burning those farthest away, but it'll take all day to destroy them all. I can take you across unless you need another nap."

Magnus looks around. "Yes, please. Franco, why did you take my father's bow? I'm not complaining; I just want to know."

"It's bigger because Ger was larger than most men. That's how he could out-shoot everyone in the army. He was accurate at a distance, too, which is harder than it seems. Theo brought him a thousand cedar shafts that are a lot longer than ours. I wanted to practice for the big battle. Shooting farther is only part of the benefit; the arrow flies faster and strikes harder. Last night you shrugged off arrows because hunters use small bows, crappy arrows, and weak iron. Mine would penetrate you."

"We're cousins; don't make this weird. Take me across. I bet there's a million problems I must fix before lunch."

Franco is skeptical. "You still think we'll win?"

"Commander, I still can't see how we lose. Even if they have keys to the gates to get within our compound, plus keys to open the tower's double doors, we'll block those entrances and the ramp. If they invest enough men, they can get past our barriers and drive us from the balconies, but it's gonna cost them more than they can afford. Our command of this river prevents the Hanseatic League for feeding them through the winter, so most will die by spring. Ah, crap, I still talk like a merchant! Damn it."

On the southern riverbank, Joko waits for Magnus to dock. The two horse transports return for more mounts.

"Joko, that was fast. Did you fly to Julian?"

"Dutch came with his best archers to replace the Saxons and Julian is within sight of the upper Main River. I didn't go into the camp to deliver your note, but I swear it's true, so let me go home."

"I don't know. You've fooled me with the truth before. Are you honestly omitting anything important?"

Joko sighs impatiently. "Everyone is coming to kill you. Max, your strategy of starving the Alamanni has made you famous. You killed or enslaved their loved ones. Some may go to Iberia to assassinate you, so please stay away from me and my family."

Sounding sour. "I get that a lot, though usually from relatives. One day I might just feed Alamannia just to see their heads explode. How many is everyone?"

"Hard to say. Word travels fast. In a few days you'll face just the closest ones, but others are coming from across Alamanni. The Bavarians apparently also hate you for killing their fishermen. Your Roman engineers were critical to fixing my factories, so I might miss you."

The iron worker ties the mooring line around a pilon and Magnus gets out. His tired brain has trouble processing the repercussions.

"Then it's goodbye, Joko. Take the next vessel out. I'll write you a note and wish you the best after you give me your master key."

He holds out his hand and, after a long internal debate, Joko shakes it. The valuable key, however, takes longer to hand over.

Joko now feels bad. "Thank you for saving my sons. I don't know why everyone hates you, beyond the obvious." He pauses, almost mumbling to himself, then vomits out more. "The Alamanni have besieged Caesar Julian in a field camp because he didn't get the cavalry that Constantius promised. He's low on food, potable water, and horses. Warriors have been setting up strawmen as they leave and hope Roman sentries don't notice. I doubt Julian knows how few enemies now surround him. Most warriors are crossing the mountains because you're crippling Germania's greatest kingdom. They must kill you because you threaten the existence of Alamannia."

The orphan looks distressed and distraught. "My mentor, thank you for curing my constipation. I hope you never see me again. That's how much I like you."

Upriver from Frankfurt, four sailboats struggle against the current. From the top of the tallest mast, Magnus sees a field camp in the distance and orders the shallow transport boats to beach themselves. The vessels go upriver, turn, then use the current and a strong wind to get far enough on the shoreline to stay there. To be sure, they drop the stern anchor and hope for the best. Horse transports are designed to open from the front, so 600 men walk their loaded-down mounts ashore and set up defensive barriers using picks and shovels. Two gunboats anchor in shallow water to provide fire support with their catapults. An orphan rides into enemy territory, leaving 599 troops as if this is normal.

Romans have dug a standard ditch and piled a defensive berm with anti-cavalry stakes. The Alamanni did the same to trap the invaders and starve them out. Romans organized their tents in neat rows, as always. 30,000 armed uniformed men mill about, slowly doing little and accomplishing less. Beyond the camp, Germani and strawmen occupy the berms fronting the trenches to control access and deny them the river. They talk loudly and make themselves visible. A frantic Roman sentry rides up and gets down to tell a commander something urgent. That guy calls out General Julian, second-in-command and heir to the Roman Empire. He hurries out and looks around, but everything seems calm.

Ceasar Julian studies the messenger. "What is it?"

"Sire, a rider comes from the river."

"Not gonna tell me more? I'm the next Roman emperor, if you plan to keep secrets. One of our riders? Holds a banner? Is naked and fun?"

The commander only knows what he was just told. "A boy is slinging the enemy. Alone."

That's interesting enough for Julian to order men to mount up. "No one can sling from horseback. They'd fall off. Foot slingers from the Balearic Islands fought for Julius Caesar in Britannia. There are no mounted slingers."

Pel hears and shits himself. "Oh, hell! It's Max! When his father wasn't looking, he slung dozens of enemies from the saddle at the Battle of Argentoratum to bring us desperately needed ammo. He saved me and many others; sire, I owe him my life. When Alamanni on foot charged him, Max just avoided them while still slinging his heart out. By fixing their position, he paused their attack, giving you time to rescue us with reinforcements. You wouldn't have won that battle without him."

That startles Julian. "Ger's boy? You fear a child?"

Pel looks around frantically, desperate to escape. "But sir, I shouldn't be here. I should be protecting his uncle's flank. He's very protective of Legate Theodosius."

"You're scared of a mere boy. Why? You did your duty and reported to me, as you should have."

"Sire, that boy invaded Alamannia! The Batavi, Franks, Saxons, his father's legion, and his uncle's Iberians all do what he says. The damn Jutes and Angles listen to him like a grandpa – Jutes, sir! He's not normal!"

"Fascinating. Run if you want, but I need information. Men, mount up! Damn Cousin Constantius for taking my cavalry!"

In shocked disbelief, the general watches a teenager ride around his perimeter, slinging Alamanni warriors like foxes. Most enemies flee, letting the boy hurl lead into their backs in an astonishing display of power. One after another is knocked down and most don't get up, though many wail a lot. Julian and his officers turn as the kid canters around their camp.

Julian is slack-jawed. "I don't understand. He's hit a hundred. Why don't they just kill him? I want to kill him and I assume he's on my side. Why are they so few? Did the Alamanni just leave us? Oh, they see him coming and the great Alamanni are now running away like cowards. I count dozens fleeing. Are we alone in the woods? I didn't hear a tree fall."

91

Magnus circles the perimeter suspiciously alone, hitting hundreds while ducking the occasional arrow or dodging a spearmen on foot. Several attack him alone from horseback, but the boy simply slings them out of the saddle. Roman leaders appear unnerved and unsettled as they mount up and move out.

Julian doesn't get it. "Why don't we have mounted slingers? They'd be a bargain at twice the pay. Oh, Max has finally found time to indulge us. Let's ask him to lunch, if we still have food. Let him in! I'm dying of curiosity."

Now mounted, several hundred officers trot over, but Magnus holds out his palm without entering the camp.

"Stop! Don't come any closer or I'll sling your mounts."

The general gasps, blinks, and shakes his pretty head. "Max, you don't remember me? Caesar Julian, the heir to my cousin's throne? I gave your father an army last month. On a dare, my mother hugged you and still speaks of it. Not that I'm envious."

"Sir, it's good to see you, but someone in the chain-of-command has been sabotaging us. Dad had to execute the quartermaster and his entire logistical team, plus a few messengers. Well, Tribune Pelagius did. My father was too busy complaining about Heaven. He's especially upset with God's No Orgy policy. Heaven would be bliss with sex without consequences. Anyhoo, we didn't receive the pay, food, ammo, and reinforcements we needed, so my father made promises on behalf of the Roman Army. Caesar Julian, tell me true: did you undermine Gerontius?"

That comes out like a threat. Julian is shocked.

"Of course not! Those items don't even go through Reims."

"Then I won't kill you unless I learn you lied, but I probably have a problem with Constantius. Pel, why are you here? Did you pull your troops off their sweep and leave my uncle vulnerable? If he dies by your negligence, your death will be long and painful. Even worse, no more huggies."

Pel pulls his shit together. "I left my legion in the field and reported your father's death to my immediate superior, as is my duty."

The killer teen gives him laser eyes. "No, you came here to shit on me and left my father's legion leaderless to do so. You needed a victory in the field, but were not up to the challenge. I doubt you'll get another military opportunity to shine. You failed in your duties as general. I hereby transfer your share of their loot to Legate Theodosius. Caesar Julian, why are you so far from your plan? You should be hundreds of miles from here."

"Boy, who are you to question me?"

"I'm Europe's only mounted slinger. I'm the boy who rode around your perimeter, pelting Alamanni while your army cowered in fear. I invaded Alamannia to help you. I rode here to help you. I heard you're low on food, drinking water, and horses. I can help you with that, too, but I tire of lies, games, and deceit. Answer my question or I'll leave."

Soooooo confused. "I command here, not you."

The orphan sighs sadly and turns his charger around. "It doesn't look like you command much. All I asked for was honesty. If you can't give me that, then you are not worth following. I thought you'd be different, but this month is full of disappointment. Sir, several thousand infantry wait for you in the woods to hit you when you leave. King

Agenaric cleverly trapped you without drinking water. You can't stay and you can't leave, so welcome to my world. I brought you barrels of potable water, thousands of herring, massive amounts of fresh meat, and loaves of fresh bread, but you don't appreciate me. I killed King Mederic and sacked Frankfurt, so they'll lack warriors, food, and iron weapons for a while. You're welcome. Goodbye, Pel. No hard feelings, you priceless piece of poo."

The general pulls his shit together as Magnus leaves. "Wait! How did you know I was here? Or low on food and water? You were right that the enemy left. How could you possibly know so much?"

"You never answered my question: why are you here, so close to Frankfurt? I assume Pel got you to come here when you should have split up your force to terrorize towns and pillage villages, as planned. You should be burning crops before harvest, slaughtering herds, and deporting the young. The Plan was to starve them, yet here you are, doing nothing slower than usual." Magnus' tone drips disappointment. "I came all this way for nothing, after loading 100,000 stinking fish. Hey, do you have enough bullion to buy 600 horses and all the fresh beef they can carry? I can sell you another 1800 war horses if you've got the coin. Unlike you, we slew their herds to starve them this winter. I'll leave you dozens of water barrels by the river for free, but baking 60,000 loaves was a lot of work. 95% of my horses are better than 95% of the shabby beasts you took to wage war. No, seriously. I just did the math in my head. Why does the second most powerful man in the empire ride a fucking gelding? I thought Pel was also castrated, but turns out he's just religious."

Julian surveys the horizon. "That's a lot of beef. I don't see 600 horses. How did you ride here alone from Frankfurt?"

The orphan looks at him with sad eyes. "Need a designated heir to calm the court, Emperor Constantius pulled you out of an Athens philosophy school to command Gaul. With no military experience, you surpassed all expectations. You beat Frankish armies like they were raw recruits. A few years ago, I mistook you for an inspiring hero. Given my size, I even looked up to you. Now I see you're just another *politico*. Goodbye, Caesar Julian. I'll leave you the water barrels rather than load them again on my fleet, but the fish I'll send to Fort Briga since I already gave Amsterdam a million and my Uncle Honorius sold two million more to Cologne and Dusseldorf. If you did your part, you could have enriched yourself at the enemy's expense."

"Fleet? What fleet? Max, I never gave you permission to attack Frankfurt."

"I heard you approve it when my dad proposed it last month ago. You wanted to hit them hard where it hurt. Those were your words. I see words, though my conscience is deaf and my decency is mute. I thought you'd approve, but why would I need your permission? I'm 10 and you're not my father or employer. I'm not in your army, I'm not yours to command, and I didn't use your troops – as far as you know. It cost you nothing, but benefitted you greatly. I've greatly weakened your enemy, cost them most of their portable wealth, and soon I'll kill most Alamanni warriors. No, don't thank me. I wouldn't know how to respond to honesty, sincerity, or gratitude. Truth is rarer than gold and just as valuable."

"Max, you're louder this month."

"I'm a child-orphan like you were. Did you forget what that feels like? When I heard you were in need, I went out of my way to bring you beef, bread, fish, water, and horses because this morning I admired you. Good mounts, too. Far better than the excuses that your officers ride to work. Maybe I'll open the water barrels and feed the fish with the bread. Sir, 100,000 warriors will soon attack me in Frankfurt, yet I pissed away a precious day trying to help a hopeless hero. I haven't been this disappointed since my parents disowned me. When emperor, you should outlaw Mondays."

"Oh, I see! You need my army!"

The tough teen shakes his head. "No. I have no room. We must leave when out of arrows and my fleet can only carry a few thousand men when we run to the river under fire. By denying them their riverport, the Hanseatic League cannot deliver shiploads of herring and anchovies from the North Sea. The enemy will go hungry this winter, so attacking their towns in early spring will decimate them. Denying them a spring crop will cripple them as a power and Gaul will finally feel secure for a decade."

That makes the officers pensive and optimistic.

"Damn it, Max! What do you want?"

"Fair value. But now the price has doubled to pay for your ill manners. 2400 horses will cost you 4800 gold coins. Your enemies murdered my mother and father, but you've offered no word of consolation. Just because barbarians have become civilized does not mean the civilized must become barbarians. Even Pel managed a kind word, despite envying me my pleasant personality, universal appeal, and enormous cock. Goodbye, you ill-cultured politician."

"I'll buy your horses, bread, and beef, but I brought no bullion. I swear I am good for it."

By his facial expression, the boy doubts that. "For a successful campaign, you offered to pay my father's estate debt. Well, our end of the campaign has been very successful, so you already owe us that. My dad's lawyers wrote the legal documents for your seal, stamp, and signature. I want your officers to sign as witnesses. You also promised Gerontius a good gold coin for every dead Alamanni, paid in coins minted by Constantine the Great. The *solidus* coin that Constantius recently issued barely looks golden while Rome's silver coins hardly have silver. Debasing the currency invites inflation and my Uncle Honorius is hopping mad about it, for reasons I don't yet understand. Taxpayers will fund your government with untrustworthy coinage that suppliers, contactors, and employees will reject. The smartest thing your grandfather ever did was mint a coin that everyone could trust. Constantius is destroying the empire's economy with crappy coins that no one wants. If you can't or won't sign the authorization transferring my family's estate debt to Rome or the gold for the 50,000 Alamanni I've already killed, then just tell me now so I can leave Frankfurt for you to slay 250,000 furious fighters yourself."

Like most politicians, Julian prevaricated. "Max, I'm sorry. Things here have been desperate. News of your father's death upset everything. How did you learn to sling while mounted? I've never even heard of that."

Magnus sounds impatient. "You change the subject when you don't want to answer a simple question with an honest answer. If you get paid for disappointing people, then you must be really rich. My father saved you outside Argentoratum and this is how you repay that life-debt. You were just a philosophy student with a famous grandpa when the Roman Empire fell into your lap after your cousins killed each other, yet you're still an ingrate. It's depressing just to look at you sad men. Or whatever you are."

The orphan adjusts his position in his custom saddle, which have bumps to hold his legs in position to stabilize his shooting platform. "Dad taught me to ride like an expert, then I spent years practicing with a sling. It took a dozen modifications to my saddle before I could sling with power and accuracy. I can gallop or shoot well, but I can't do both at the same time and I can't do either very long because my thighs cramp up like I'm menstruating. I've found a sweet spot between speed and lethality, but accuracy and power still fall with speed. I can fling from a gallop, but without power or accuracy. I can also shoot arrows from the saddle, but not half as well as on foot. I can turn to do a Parthian Shot, just not very far. The trick is stabilizing a bouncing shooting platform. I sling when bumped into the air."

Julian sounds pensive. "The Visigoths, northeast of the Danube, say nomadic horse archers from the steep have invaded their land. Goths fight mounted, but can't shoot when riding. Like all Westerners, their archers dismount to work. No one west of Persia can shoot while riding and Persians rely on saturation volleys because they can't shoot accurately at a gallop. Goths want Romans to get rid of these new threats, but the intruders say they want a safe home in Europe, not more war. Apparently they're fleeing from even more dangerous horse archers from the central steppe that killed most of their warriors. Defending Gaul would be much easier with loyal horse archers."

That fascinates Magnus. "What could horse archers possibly be afraid of on the treeless grasslands of the steppe? Send them an invitation if they learn Latin. You need someone you trust to assess them as a benefit or a threat. Tribune Pelagius has proven himself a loyal leader when not blaming kids for his shortcomings. Pel, if you need help, write my uncle in Valencia because I'd love to learn how they shoot from a gallop." A distant trumpet blows and the kid curses savagely. "They're jacking my meat! The damn thieves are stealing what I've rightfully stolen! Hurry or go hungry."

Magnus gallops off on his stolen horse and hundreds of mounted officers follow. Their facial expressions are all over the map as they race towards the distant river.

Pel, however, has a bad feeling as he tries to keep up. "I pray he's not luring us into an ambush."

Julian laughs at that. "Prayer doesn't work. I might be the Roman Emperor's last non-Christian emperor, but I'm determined to bring back tried-and-true Roman ways. Christianity has made Romans weak and Christ will be the death of us. Max is our ally, not our enemy. Believe what people do, not what they say."

Magnus is at a gallop when he spies an army of Alamanni infantry charging his boys and boats. Something loudly erupts from his bitter soul and it's not Glorious Victory. The atavistic moan sounds sad and haunted, but echoes across the terrain. Magnus gallops ahead because he's lighter and rides a superior horse. He sees several thousand fighters on foot charging his 599 archers, who fire volleys as if their lives depend on it. They can't retreat because they protect 599 horses loaded down with bags of beef – loading them would take too long. The Iberians can't even ride because those animals already carry 250,000 pounds of bloody meat. The land by the river is mostly flat while the Germani attack behind a shield wall with spears.

The sight of an Alamanni army unsettles Team Franco. All 599 line up in two rows so all can fire at the same time. The charging Alamanni clearly think they're gonna take back their horses over the dead bodies of these foreign invaders when an unnatural roar flies over them. That slows them down and makes them look over their shoulders.

Badass warriors suddenly look worried because they know who's coming.

Franco hears his boss and announces his visit. "Max is back! Give'em hell, boys!"

Revitalized, his shooters fire shoulder-to-shoulder. The 599 weighted down mounts ignore the excitement to munch contently on dark green grass. Alamanni warriors look right to see a virgin boy coming fucking fast as if about to explode. He's at the point of no return when he shoots his first load, creaming someone's bearded face with blood that he spits and swallows. Some Alamanni yell warnings as Roman riders gallop near, a day late and a *denarii* short. Many spearmen run to the river to get away from the infamous demon-boy, screaming his name in panic, only to find a few dozen bowmen in two boats sniping them. Everyone notices the mood change.

Julian sounds incredulous. "Max scares them! Tribune, you are not alone in your fears."

Magnus swings behind the enemy and slows to hit them hard from close range. At a few dozen balls per minute, he has the lethality of a cohort. His pellets pierce backs, crater craniums, and break bones with a steady rhythm that music-obsessed Iberians could dance to. Bodies fall or fly, with grown men screaming in agony at the top of their lungs, which dismay the rest. The least athletic Germani in the rear turn around to face the dangerous foreigner while the fastest attackers continue running at the Iberians, apparently unaware of the new threat sodomizing them. This unclenches their tight, packed fist.

Two transports are beached and vulnerable. Two gunboats fire bolts that punch holes in the charging enemies. A herd of horses graze to the north with two lines of Iberians blocking off enemies coming from the south. A thousand Alamanni in the front continue their charge, but hundreds flee towards the river, while a few thousand in the center slow and the last thousand stop to form a shield wall against a mounted slinger. Having induced a thousand of the slowest to stop, Magnus races past them to shoot those running towards his team. Warriors in the center conveniently have their backs to him. The impacts send those men flying forward, which motivates many to stop and turn. Groups rush him, but the teen avoids them without slowing the carnage. It's a deadly dance that he excels at. Grown men get thrown from a tiny pellet at 100 miles per hour.

As Romans charge, Julian ponders his options. For a philosophy student, he's unusually decisive. He sees the horses packed as promised and knows he needs them.

"Follow me!" Julian commands. "Trumpeter, play Attack!"

A burly boy blows a loud brass tuba to tell the unit what to do. About 700 riders holding long, curved cavalry swords adopt an arrow formation for more punching power. Some Alamanni in the lead shout warnings to the rest. The fluid battle gets juicy. The center of the Alamanni must deal with the charging Romans. Most run frantically to get out of their way, but not everyone gets the message. Hundreds plant their spears into the earth, brace themselves, and aim their speartip at a horse's chest. If twice as long, that'd work twice as well. Alamanni veterans, both terrified and determined, stand their ground against a ton of flying flesh. It takes big balls to hold out because their odds of surviving are jack dick.

Team Franco is less lucky. The first and fastest fighters in the front are completely committed. They run at the Iberians at top speed. It's hard for defenders to stop men behind shields, but it can be done because the land is not perfectly flat. As shieldmen run into dips, they expose spearmen behind them. The Iberian archers aim for the lower body and hit bellies, groins, and legs. Others target the spearmen between gaps in the shields as they run over uneven ground. The impacts hurt their morale and momentum. Warriors flop on their faces, fly on their backs, and groan as if they're dead men crawling. But some Germani have several arrows in their shields and continue coming for a colossal clash. Cowards cannot do this. Only the bravest can charge a line of archers, but they don't expect to survive.

Then the Roman cavalry crash into them, with Julian in the lead. At the last moment, Julian changes direction away from the prepared Alamanni center to sodomize the warriors heading for the Iberians. The Romans strike from their blind side. It's an epic fuck by a gorgeous man who never reproduces. At 30 miles an hour, one-ton horses smash into terrified men, knocking them over or aside like a giant arrow carving flesh. Some warriors steady spears to harm horses at the last moment and dozens succeed, sending riders flying. But most horsemen plow through, punching a hole in the ranks of runners about to reach the archers who shot so many comrades. As human obstacles slow the Roman advance, the riders make up for it by slashing down with long swords at spearmen stabbing their mounts. Riders spur horses to speed up to either charge an enemy in front or escape some sodomizer behind them. The Alamanni outnumber them, but the Iberians now have big backs to target at close range. Arrows punch into warriors like a mule's kick, sending them sprawling. Archers roar Glorious Victory as they grin at the gruesome sights. There's nothing like escaping death to make a terrified trooper feel alive. Almost 600 archers face targets instead of threats and send 4000 arrows a minute into the enemy.

Team Julian has decimated their front ranks and spared most Iberians, but not those nearest the river. Many Alamanni had swerved away from the riders, so more warriors reach the riverside Iberians, who back up in a hurry. Two boatloads of bowmen fire as fast as they can with impunity, as they are in too much water for infantry to reach them without range weapons.

On shore, Franco's bowmen can hardly miss as the Germani spearmen and shieldmen run closer. Hundreds are hit every heartbeat, becoming obstacles in the way of those behind them, who trip and tumble. The Roman charge made the Alamanni run to the river. Now they overwhelm the Iberians to reach the beached boats. At the last moment, Franco leads his mobile reserve to cut them with swords. Desperate Germani try knocking down Iberians with their shields to kill them with axes, maces, or clubs. Momentum briefly gives the Alamanni a momentary advantage and they make the most of it to board the nearest boat. The fighting is fierce and hand-to-hand with half the combatants offering no quarter as they take limbs and lives. No Romans have ridden this far, so the beleaguered Iberians retreat under pressure to the transports, eager for distance to shoot the enemy safely. Once shooters fire from boats, Alamanni have a hard time overcoming them. Several defenders get their skulls cracked or their bowels opened as inhumane men unleash their inner beast with atavistic roars and blood-curdling screams. Luca's chainmail saves some, giving them a second chance to avoid the fuck-fest. Iberians give ground and the melee swirls like a ballroom as men mix it up. Any weapon or tactic is allowed in duels to the death as fighters live to their last.

Commander Franco leads a century towards the boats to beat off the breach in their barrier. They fire 1000 arrows a minute, which decimates the brave Alamanni.

These reinforcements protect the Iberian flank from spearmen in ankle-deep water. Alamanni leaders look around and do the math. They shout retreat, but the Romans and Iberians are eating them alive. Someone smart runs to dive in the river to catch the current, and dozens follow, leaving their spears and shields. Franco's bowmen slaughter the slow, the unlucky, and those farthest from safety until the Alamanni front ranks shatter in full retreat.

The Battle of the Main River ends in a rout. Pel finds himself bloody and horrified.

Concentrating intensely, Magnus has more targets than time as warriors run past him or at him. He avoids those trying to kill him to instead fling lead into the easiest targets. His horse charges, turns, pivots, bursts into speed, only to halt suddenly for Magnus to evade death while inflicting the same. Teams of spearmen try driving him off, but his superior speed and maneuverability keeps him within range of enemies without letting enemies reach him. He swaps shoulders as one tires. Many warriors yell curses, but the killer teen doesn't reply because every breath counts – that's just math. Magnus gets as close as he dares and grins as he scores another victory.

"That's for mama. This is for daddy."

It angers Magnus that so many escape into the trees. He doesn't dare follow, so he hits as many as he can, galloping to get within range of those farther away. The obsession on his face is as obvious as he is oblivious to events beyond his micro-world. Some Germani almost spear him or his horse. Distant shouts wake him up to danger from behind and he speeds up before turning around. As the last of the Alamanni disappear into the woods, he frantically scans the treeline for targets and curses when he runs out. Finally emerging from battle-lust, like a sentry waking in mid-shift, Magnus turns to see a thousand distant men silently staring at him in horror-awe. H-awe? A mile away, Franco leads the Iberians in an enthusiastic lion roar and most Romans join in. Confused and distracted, Magnus turns in the saddle to see what they're applauding. When he realizes it's him, he doesn't understand why. His face is as vacant as his conscience.

Magnus is honestly puzzled. "What? They murdered my mama."

From the mouth of babes. Nearby Romans laugh like that's the funniest thing they've ever heard instead of a terrible tragedy. Thousands of groaning, grunting, and gutted Germani soak the soil with their blood and tears, yet no one tends them. In the distance, some good guys treat their own wounded, some wailing loudly from intense pain.

Julian is impressed. "Tribune Pelagius, how many enemies do you think Max hurt?"

"A few hundred, easily. That whistling sound got on their nerves. He slowed and disrupted their charge, saving many lives. That many shieldmen should have overcome 600 shooters. Just having him in their rear messed with their minds. Sir, having mounted archers means the empire would be better defended with fewer defenders. Infantry armies are slow, but nomads ride 100 miles a day to raid. We could multiply our offensive capability while deterring attacks, which saves us time, money, and resources. And you certainly need mounted archers if you attack Persia, as planned."

"Well summarized. I'd like you to find those new nomads on the northern Black Sea, teach them Latin, and report to me on their usefulness. Shapur the Second, the shah of Persia, has taken too much of our territory and I'm determined to get it back. Max, you impress me. I apologize for my callous attitude towards your recent loss. I accept your offer. I'll buy all the horses that you can deliver. You brought enough beef and fish to feed an army if we can cook it before it rots. I'll write you a bank note offering fair value."

"Thank you, sir. You can have it all as soon as you hand me signed and sealed official documents that execute your end of the contract, buying my family's estate debt, what my father's army is owed, and 50,000 gold coins for the Alamanni I've killed."

"Everyone knows my word of honor is as golden as my hair. We saved your men, so we'll be returning with our horses, fish, beef, and bread."

"Over my dead body. Your word is shit. Women don't need to lie because they change their mind so much, but you barely bother to appear convincing. My father didn't receive the troops, food, ammo, coins, and supplies that you promised him. Constantius may have held them up, but he didn't promise them. You didn't even campaign as promised, forcing me to spend precious time saving you. Dad never liked anal; with friends like you, who needs enemas? After a suicidal charge that won last month's battle, dad felt set up to fail. I don't blame you for his death, but your dishonesty dug his grave. You'll deliver the document correctly before you receive a single bite of bread. If you fail to live up to your end of our contract, then I will not take you to court. I'm about to face 100,000 fighters dying to kill me, so I'm not about to take shit from anyone else."

The Heir to the Roman Empire is furious. "And if you die in Frankfurt?"

"Then I'll haunt you from the grave; apparently I've done that before. Frankfurt has six large underground granaries. It's all yours if you complete your word. I know you're not Christian, so swear on all you hold holy so we can leave these corpses for the buzzards."

Julian swears with a solemn face. "Last month you were more respectful. Remember that I'll be emperor after my Cousin Constantius unless his fucking daughters give him a grandson."

Magnus shrugs. "I doubt I'll live so long. I just need to make up for my personality before facing my maker. I've asked for forgiveness, but it turns out I'm unforgiving. I suspect Constantius' campaign against my father was to undermine you. If you ever try taking his throne, please invite me."

"I'm so confused. I don't know whether to hug or hang you."

CHAPTER 4

Vultures circle above or feast on thousands of dead bodies in the blockaded streets. Most bodies form a fleshy berm around the luxury neighborhood. Only a few boulevards allow free passage. Ravens fight dogs for the desserts. Clothing has been torn and pieces of flesh bitten off. There's enough for all, but some dogs still fight for dominance. Chickens, pigs, ducks, sheep, and cattle roam the luxury neighborhood like a poor village. Food waste covers the cobblestones. Team Magnus has burned or broken most buildings to give themselves a killer view and to deny shelter to the enemy. Prisoners push wheelbarrows filled with corpses, wood, or rubble. Teams of two lift logs, planks, or doors. Horses drag logs from the palisade.

Outside the city proper, thousands of camps, tents, and lean-to's are scattered or clumped within and beyond the forests that surround Frankfurt. 250,000 or so Alamanni wander about or work on something. Most are female. Few folks look very old or very young. Large groups of men build things, including a long above-ground tunnel. Others butcher animals or skin them. They don't seem far from the invaders, but live in another world. Carpenters transform wood into shielding. Piles of shields must add up to thousands. Men practice archery, sword fighting, or using the spear, with veterans supervising. They look desperate and dangerous. Alone or in small groups, male and female fighters walk through trails in the woods to join the fight of their lives. They carry what they can. Some drive cattle to feed their friends.

Magnus abandoned most of Frankfurt to defend just a smaller chunk of it, the area around the luxury neighborhood. The best shooters wear extra armor and wait to respond to intrusions. Squads on horseback patrol warily. Outer Frankfurt has been demolished and most logs from the palisade have been removed, though sections remain for viewers to see where it was. The Cube's rooftop now has a few dozen catapults of various sizes and almost as many trebuchets, each with piles of rocks the size of a fist. Bricks form their own cubes, staked high by the trebuchet. The rooftop crane hoists more stones as men push a lever in a circle so the rope lifts the heavy load.

Various kinds of ships load or unload cargo via counter-weight cranes. One has a line of bucket-men sending fish from an underground bunker. Boats sail up or float downriver. Carpenters make big barges out of thick logs. Thousands work hard. Three gunboats face both directions in a staggered formation, each a few hundred meters part. On one end, the gunboat faces downriver while the other faces upriver. The northern half of the city has been burnt or demolished, with roofs collapsed and stone support columns toppled. Sentries from the river now have a clear view of the area.

Drusus Island looks equally occupied. Captives and horses cover the island with cattle walking around as food storage. Men toss bales of hay from a ship deck covered in it. Tribute Piso has a crew with a tripod determine relative elevations. He's studying the edge of the island for the best place to erect a concrete wall. A log palisade is half-complete to make the castle harder to assault. Hundreds of uniformed Batavi remove earth, chisel rock to flatten it, or quarry stone for construction. Collectively they transform Cathedral Hill, which now bristles with catapults and trebuchet. Within the castle, captive men butcher cattle, pig, and poultry while captive women salt and hang it in sunlight. Hundreds of kids, held hostage, run around or help their parents and grandparents.

100

The large riverside grassland by the Cube has a fraction as many horses and they've been corralled against the riverbank, with a ditch-and-berm to pen them in at night. Hundreds of mounts remain, though guarded by men with bows and trumpets. Shadows move in the trees that surround it, but defenders behind barriers keep an eagle eye out.

Max, Luca, Franco, and Dutch visit with a squad of bodyguards. The riverside sawmill is loud, busy, and crowded. Men inspect wood for suitability as bolts. Some skilled Alamanni unhappily work in shackles, with their women and kids watching fearfully as hostages. Within, men saw, plane, or hammer on tables and makeshift workstations, working diligently to get what they need while they can. The men seem tense and determined. None lounge, goof off, or play around.

Satisfied, the leaders move on to prisoners quarrying a rocky hill. Larger stones go to the roof while concrete consumes smaller ones and rock dust. The four leaders check in and nod their heads knowingly. Luca barks an order to an aid who runs out. The ironworks is louder and hotter with lots of hammering. Many men fill it, passing buckets or carrying crates. A line of prisoners dump logs, planks, and branches for burning. Others pour steaming hot liquid metal into molds. No one smiles or jokes around.

An Iberian runs up and leadership follows him to the underground fish tank. Hands on hips, Magnus listens and presses his lips tightly in displeasure. They open the nearby granaries and leaders shake their heads. They arrive at another structure and apparently the place stinks, so they hold their noses and try not to inhale. The tannery and leatherworks bustle with activity. Piles of leather furniture are ripped apart or cut into pieces by men who know what they're doing. Even here the foreign invaders wear two layers of light armor. Helmets hang from belts and quivers are everywhere. Baskets of new shafts with fletches line some shelves.

From downriver, the giant artillery trawler leads a dozen stolen ships and a few dozen big boats into the riverport. From the bow, Uncle Honorius waves happily. Trumpets blow and guards escort thousands of the youngest prisoners to the docks. Teams on the island gather their last herds. Crews run to the cranes and set up counterweights to lift heavy loads, which oxen help move. Archers take defensive positions to repel attempts to rescue captives. The trawler anchors upriver for its catapults to deter attacks. Everyone is tense because the enemy has attempted rescues before. Three leaders jog over and Luca waddles as fast as he can because he hates being left behind. On the first ship, Honorius has news as he lands to give Magnus a fierce hug.

Magnus is happy and relieved. "Uncle Honorius, welcome back. Please take Senator Savelli back to Briga. He's served his purpose here and promises to send me supplies. I hope you now have enough room for the equipment we no longer need. I'm even sending the lumbermill to Porto Gordo, along with the smelter, foundry, and refinery."

"Max, I brought what I could. Iberia's mercury mine is insatiable for disposable labor. Batavia is buying herds cheaply, but paying us in supplies. Your victory here has changed geopolitics. For a virgin, you're fucking famous. Theo is probably alive because he sent more prisoners to Fort Briga. Most returning West Germani have gone back to resume raiding Alamannia, so the hunting must be rich. Instead of big battles, I hear of hundreds of tiny clashes. Our teams have burned so many crops and settlements that I could see the smoke from the Rhine. Wounded Galicians guard our plunder in

Amsterdam. I'll give you a summary in private. The Batavi have traded me a million arrows for twice their usual value because they know you're desperate. I sold the fish from the Hanseatic ships to Cologne and Dusseldorf and that alone makes us rich. I auctioned off the slaves and sold the least desirable to Iberia's mercury mine. You now own a quarter of Maximus Inc, so Marc will be really rich when you die. The Batavi bought the thousand or so wagons that we took from Frankfurt and I sent the oxen to Galicia. I brought a lot more salt while Amsterdam thanks you for the mountain of beef. No word yet from Julian. How are things here?"

"I'm in the same boat, rowing in the wrong direction. We have a few hundred more wounded that I need you to take off our busy hands. I sling a thousand pellets a night at noisy shadows dying to break in, yet we're running out of arrows. The sheep herders who slung as kids are no longer good at it. With a thousand slingers, I could hold Frankfurt forever. I spoke with Julian upriver. He isn't doing much and he's doing it slowly. The ingrate didn't even offer to help me defend Frankfurt. I assume he's waiting for us to kill each other so he can cheaply pick up the pieces. Until last night, most nights were brutal, with thousands attacking. King Agenaric has probably arrived to attack us more effectively. We hear more logging, sawing, and hammering in the woods. He's planning something that we won't see coming if they assault in a nighttime storm. Did you bring more boxes, bags, and sacks? We want to move more grain and vegies to Drusus Island before we lose the city."

"Max, I brought everything I could get my hands on and sent ships to get ammo, bandages, and medicine from Flanders, the Gallic coast, and Britannia. It seems everyone on the Baltic Sea now opposes us and the Hanseatic League has called for a conference at Lubeck to decide whether to wage war."

"Then it's true: Constantine the Great made Sunday the first day of the week because he knew the world will end on a Monday. Well, we have more prisoners, herds, and plunder for you to take off our hands. Sorry for all the nice furniture, but Germani are absurdly good at working wood. I sold the last of our horses to Julian, so we don't need to move more. The Alamanni took most of Frankfurt, but we fortified the inner city. Fear of starvation has really motivated them to repeat frontal assaults. Every night I vent my anger, grief, and regrets on hundreds of armed, angry Alamanni. It's nice of them to help me feel better. I get a few minor injuries a night but, strangely, they don't hurt as much as my mama's last words."

"Max, I don't want you to die here. Most of my kids might miss you."

"They say grief loses its power over time, but I've always been impatient. Before my parents died, I wondered if anyone loved me; now I know no one does. It's terrible and liberating. You lost a big brother, but have a wife and kids to cushion the blow. Uncle, I'll be okay, one way or another."

Watching his uncle's fleet leave, Magnus turns when a trumpet blows. "Who's trying to kill me now?"

Leaders jog where troops gather behind cover. It surprises Magnus to see a crippled girl dressed in a torn woolen tunic. She waits patiently where they could kill her, without trying to get past barriers. Franco shouts questions, but she doesn't answer until Luca finally shows up.

"Oh, that's my oldest granddaughter Basa. She married a local leader. Good

102

man." Luca waves her closer. "What happened to you?"

Basa is bitter. "Rocks rained on us from the tower roof in our sleep. We had no idea they could fly so far. One caved in my husband's head and little Basita can no longer walk."

Magnus shits all over that. "And I'm unexpectedly an orphan, so rain falls on us all. What do you want?"

"Ah, so you're the evil boy who has killed tens of thousands since taking the tower. Uncle Agenaric would like to buy your remaining prisoners for 1000 iron ingots."

"No. The slavers will pay 10x as much. Where's Serapio?"

"Far away, recovering from your wound. Last I heard, he was delirious and couldn't be moved. Our healers say you dipped the lead ball in poop that keeps giving him fever from infections."

Magnus laughs at the memory. "I put those in a special pouch. All my balls are crappy now. He owes me a mama, so I killed his devious daughter and three sons. I didn't even cheat. The little one almost knocked me over the ramp railing. Scared the crap out of me; I filled the Shit Wagon by myself. Do you have gold? If not, then go limp elsewhere."

"Max, you've taken everything of value from Frankfurt. When are you leaving?"

"You cowards haven't given me a real fight. We'll leave after I burn off enough anger, so probably in a year or three. You Alamanni tried assassinating me. I still can't get over it. My mind can't calm down. Every thought is a scream. I was obnoxious last month, but not crazy. I can't live like this, so you'll just have to kill me."

Basa tries reason. "The legionaries can't stay and these Batavi won't fight without them."

"The longer your warriors stay here, the fewer who face my uncle, rampaging through western Alamannia. Given their compensation, we'll stay here until your army battles us. Tell Agenaric that I challenge him to a duel to the death tomorrow morning. No tricks. Just him and me with blades. No sling, arrows, or artillery. If he wins, he gets our remaining prisoners. If I win, you hand over Serapio so I can get on with my life. If you don't want me here forever, then give me my mama's murderer!"

Four men and Magnus gather around a cooking fire that the teen tends with an iron poker. He's roasting something and it smells delicious. He waves his guests to sit and partake.

"Boys, help yourselves. That barrel is the last of our beer because hops help it last longer than ale and mead. I chilled it on the riverbed all day and want to finish it before I die tomorrow. The stew has a bit of everything, so I hope you don't mind old boots and new regrets. We only have two wheeled trebuchets to throw rocks at the enemy tomorrow; the rest are stuck on the roof. We've moved 80,000 dead Alamanni outside the wall that encloses the nice neighborhood. Julian is gonna be pissed when we make him pay up. The slavers paid even more for the prisoners. Iberia's mercury mine sent someone to Fort Briga to buy our older prisoners because workers there never live long. Did you know gaseous mercury kills faster than if you touch solid mercury or drink liquid mercury? Crazy, right? I'm learning how little I've learned. Honestly, I don't know what I've done with my life. I'm gonna use my gold coins to buy me a better mama. If

103

I'm rich enough, someone might love me. If not, I may be forced to attempt normality."

"Max, why are we really here?" Franco asks.

"Cousin, you've known me since birth and still doubt the benefit of giving me the benefit of the doubt? I don't understand your ignorance, I doubt your cynicism, and I question your skepticism. I have half-a-mind to insult your intelligence." He chuckles. "Since the king might win in the morning, I thought I'd spend my last precious time with total strangers because family has disappointed me in the past. You boys can best relate to Alamanni combat veterans, so I want your opinion. Drink up while I break it down:

"Put yourselves in their boots. You're an Alamanni fighter who tends a small field and herd. You hunt a lot and raid for things you can't buy. No one has big farms because this region has too many damn trees and marginal soil. A month ago, you helped defeat one Roman army and almost overwhelmed a second under Caesar Julian. Sadly, a crazy bastard named Gerontius led Batavi traitors in a suicidal charge that denied you victory. But, still, your generals showed good judgment instead of the rash fools you've followed before. You have confidence in leadership and feel powerful, despite that minor setback that cost one of your three brotherly co-kings. Having three kings who actually work together is new and refreshing, rather than the bitter rivalries that usually fragment your folks.

"Then spies report a million cedar shafts coming by land, so Mederic asks for your best archers to burn that shit before Senator Luca attaches his amazing iron arrowheads. You know your impure iron is heavier, weaker, and not as sharp, so you volunteer rather than face a million superior arrows. The ambush site is wisely chosen and starts as expected. You're flanking the Iberian invaders when a single mounted slinger ruins your day, then wounds your king and his charismatic son. Your force fails to burn the shafts, so you fuckers are screwed. Iberians chase you to the Rhine and you swim for your life. You go home bitter and beaten. Leadership holds meetings to get a feel for warrior sentiment. You're not feeling nearly as optimistic, so Mederic kidnaps toddlers to force a brokenhearted girl to poison the slinger, the general, and his legate brother. Only the general dies, but it seems the threat from the west is over. The kings propose massing against Julian and then cleverly trap his army where there's no drinking water. Overjoyed that you don't have to risk your life again, you eagerly dig ditches and pile berms to render that powerful Roman army impotent. You haven't seen your family in a long time but, after the harvest, you promise leadership to return to slaughter the Roman invaders. Sure, Alamannia has challenges, but they seem manageable."

The orphan studies each commander for flaws before resuming. Each barely touches their beer or food.

"You're still besieging Julian or back at your tiny plot when riders claim the dead general's army somehow got bigger and crossed the Rhine. Worst still, that deadly slinger-boy is burning Frankfurt, where the Alamanni keep their portable wealth. Both shock your smelly socks off. You have Julian to the east, lots of raiders to the west, and intruders sacking your only real city. You gather your neighbors and ask, what do we do? What will you do?"

The boy leans back and munches on burnt mutton because he talked too long again. Making faces at his sheep steak, he appears to ignore the Iberian, Roman, and Batavi commanders as they whisper intently.

Dutch speaks first. "As a father, family comes first. I must ensure my kids have

104

food and shelter because winters here are brutal. If their location isn't safe, then I must move them deep into the Black Forest. That's 10,000 square miles of endless trees. Locals get lost because landmarks are few. But the forest has been hunted out, so there's no food there beyond nuts, roots, and berries. My village brought our oxen, dairy cows, cattle, sheep, pigs, and poultry, but the forest can't feed them. We must find a grassy clearing, but thousands of other families seek the same. Plus, I must harvest my crops before raiders burn them."

Magnus nods. "So you've spent the last few weeks traveling. Beyond your village's meager fields, where can you find food?"

"The biggest settlements have the most grain because everyone brings their harvest there to cheaply remove the husks using mechanized mills. Crushing grain by hand to get flour for bread takes too long."

The teen agrees. "So you visit the nearest towns and learn raiders have burned them out and stolen the residents. Three groups of invaders have triggered internal migrations that force thousands of villages to search for safety. A million cattle and horses have no grass or grain. Desperate and starving, you meet with other men to break down the problem. But you can't fight foreigners without food. Where do you get it?"

The commanders sit up and smile.

Dutch knows. "Frankfurt had massive granaries, until you emptied them, and gets enough fish from the Hanseatic League to fill homes. Other men will be there and together we'll find solutions after we harvest our fields and slaughter the livestock that we need the least. Jerking that much meat requires lots of salt, which involves another trip or two."

"Man, you're a busy boy. Where are you now? Outside Frankfurt?"

Dutch looks up. "The weather's been cool, cloudy, and rainy. Grain crops need more sunshine to ripen, so I'm either searching for salt or jerking beef while waiting for the sun to finally shine."

"Unless foreigners have burnt your home, your village, and your fields. They may have slaughtered your animals, so you have no way to feed your family. Your mother, wife, and kids will starve by spring unless you butcher your horses. If so, you'll take your anger out on the enemy. But if you're King Agenaric, your army is scattered across a vast land with no paved roads and bumpy trails. You desperately want to rescue residents, but you don't have enough warriors to make a difference. Until the king finally arrived in Frankfurt, fathers, sons, and brothers threw away their lives against professionals armed with Europe's best arrows. Great archers are, of necessity, champion athletes with superb eye-hand coordination. With no better alternative, you offer your last ingots, which the horrible demon boy rejects. New question: imagine you are King Agenaric. You can send your fighters against the raiders in the west, Julian in the east, or Frankfurt. What do you do?"

Dutch belches it out. "Frankfurt. Julian is doing little harm and must leave soon anyways for lack of supplies. The raiders in the west are tempting, but they're raiders, not conquerors. They have not come to stay. Once some leave, their reduced strength will induce others to flee. By the time most Alamanni harvest their fields and jerk the livestock, the western raiders will be gone. The sackers of Frankfurt should also leave, but that strange kid just claimed he wants a fight. All Alamanni fighters will come here."

Franco punches Magnus hard in the arm. "You knew this morning they were all coming here!"

The traumatized teen takes the punch like a man. "I knew weeks ago. None of you geniuses figured it out? It's all so obvious. Every fighter in Alamannia will want vengeance, even the women, elderly, and big kids. They're all coming here while their non-fighters butcher, roast, salt, and hang-dry their herds before they starve. The Alamanni have several safe strongholds in the mountains that locals go to when threatened by their Germani neighbors. The fighters must come here because there is not enough food for everyone. They must take Frankfurt or starve. They are not risking their lives; they're already dead unless they drive us out and score shiploads of fish. After I kill Agenaric tomorrow, I'll send some Batavi to become pirates. Dutch, my fleet needs sailors who fight, so I need your Batavi on the rivers. Please sink or steal Germani ships, especially from the Hanseatic League. Those are bigger, better, and more seaworthy. I'll split the captured vessels equally with Batavia."

Dutch corrects him. "Max, we prefer to call our country the Batavi Republic or the Netherlands, which means Lowlands."

"Batavia sounds better, but sure. If you don't let me down, I'll ask my great-uncle's shipwrights to share their best designs so you can out-compete your neighbors. We Iberians have greater deep-sea experience than you transplanted East Germani. Imagine having your own fleet of trawlers, netting millions of fish. Dutch, you'll be stinking rich. You'll get all that and more if you don't fuck me."

"What's your evil plan?" Franco asks.

"You think furious fighters will wait for reinforcements once a demon-kid kills their king? No, they'll do what they've been doing every night: attack and hope for the best. There's not enough food for everyone so, if Alamannia really has a million folks, then maybe 250,000 may come to kill me so the rest don't starve by spring. I bet the old, ill, and crippled are the first to face us to leave food for their youngest. Dutch, every week, please send me a thousand of your best archers to replace our casualties, with as many arrows, medical workers, and medical supplies that you can find. Joko is forging more arrowheads, so please send what he has. He might make a million spare shafts before we must flee. After a few weeks of pirating, anchor the fleet downriver and keep a lookout for my signal fire. If you see a dense column of dark smoke coming from Frankfurt, please rescue survivors. I'm keeping the artillery trawler and the next biggest ship to protect the escape route from the tall tower; if we lose that building, we'll need to board those ships in a hurry. Oh, I sent Luca home. He's no longer useful here and promises to get me doctors and bandages. I wish we had remedies for fever because infection may kill more of us than Alamanni. Did you know irony is killer?"

Franco has doubts. "Assaulting that tall tower is suicide. How will you get them to throw their lives away against a massive fortification that gives you a huge height advantage?"

"We are few and they are many." He smiles at them. "If that isn't enough, I'll try to become loud, obnoxious, and intolerable. I must use the gifts that God gave me."

The men chuckle. This kid delights them.

"Max, how will you beat King Agenaric tomorrow?" Franco asks.

"I'll employ advanced technology in unexpected ways." He can tell they don't understand him. "I plan on cheating. In times of crisis, I fall back on my strengths. Boys, are we agreed? I need you to look me in the eye and swear on it instead of abandoning

106

me during this strange siege. If you have better ideas for safely killing Alamanni, now's the time to share them. Our archers will rotate duty between the streets, the balconies, and the roof to share risks equally. Yes, 6000 shooters will face a massive mob, but the enemy can't get into the tall tower or onto our warships. Many of your men won't like spending a month shooting strangers, but we can rotate them. Most won't spend the next month here if Dutch sends us a thousand replacements weekly. Are we agreed?"

"Why are you sending me away when you need me most?" Dutch needs to know.

Magnus meets those hard eyes. "My friend, I've looked into your dark soul and concluded you'll be too tempted to take charge. I'd rather not kill you, but I insist on command. I'll die in a manner I choose. You will not order retreat when I want to stay. You will not send my ships away when I need them here. You will not argue with me in front of our troops. You will not counter my orders or dilute my authority. I'll kill anyone who undermines me, as my father should have done with the pleasant quartermaster. Dutch, I've done well so far while you just arrived with reinforcements. Dad loved to tell me what to do because he knew I hated that. I've spent every night wondering why I let him drink the cider. The best explanation is he held me back. I could not grow up with him holding me down. I didn't want my daddy to die, but I apparently preferred that over living in his cage. He viewed me as a wild beast; well, wild beasts need freedom to hunt and kill. You've heard me roar; I am a lion."

The orphan looks each of them in the eye, man to man. "I'm always open to ideas, advice, and suggestions. Please point out things I may have missed. In the heat of battle, make independent decisions as you think best. We're here to kill, not die. The Plan was always to leave once things get too hot. But do not command me. Keep your tone with me respectful. Talk to me like a dumb child and I might throw a knife at you. I'm in charge. If you want to get rich and kill our common enemies, never forget that. If we don't take the Alamanni down now, they'll just get more powerful. That said, I'll give you one last chance to pussy out. You are all combat veterans who may not feel comfortable obeying a boy. After all, I'm just a kid who's slung several thousand armed enemies this month. I've killed more men than anyone on either side. I'm sure you've known lots of children who've done that. If you don't want me as your leader, then I'll leave; you can either stay to fight or leave as well. No hard feelings, you fucking pussies. Dad said fucking pussies were the best, but the phrase still sounds insulting. You may discuss things in private while I get a good night's sleep to kill the last Alamanni king. It seems like yesterday when I killed the previous Alamanni king; no, Tuesday. Sorry. I'll leave you with a few items: I brought you here, killed a king, and took an impregnable tower before rescuing Julian's army. My uncle has a legion and Julian has agreed in writing to pay Maximus Inc a golden *solidus* for every dead Alamanni – not every warrior or armed fighter, but every Alamanni because he doesn't read carefully. Fight for me and I'll share. Troops who defend Frankfurt will get rich if Julian pays up. When the fleet returns, all quitters can leave because I only work with hungry heroes."

Magnus gets up and walks away, sipping beer while holding a fistful of fish.

Dutch sounds shocked. "Did that boy just give me the boot?"

Magnus sees King Agenaric walk from the woods looking royally pissed. Beyond him, the old log palisade has been burned, broken, or disassembled. He wears

107

Soko's chainmail, has a helmet, and carries both an iron shield and one of Soko's swords. The orphan sighs at seeing them, then studies the dirt for the damn rope.

"I thought he'd never come. Dutch, please begin Phase 1 with all of our West Germani tribes."

Dutch is on horseback, fully armed, within Frankfurt. "Good luck, Max."

"Good commanders don't rely on luck. I rely on advanced technology, I depend on enemies underestimating me, and I count on human nature. Sometimes I also count on numbers. Remember that if you ever turn on me."

The big badass laughs, liking and respecting the little man. "Max, I'll never turn on you."

The kid sounds less certain. "Well, if you shoot and miss, you know I'll come at you with everything I've got."

They meet in No Man's Land, beyond range of the rooftop trebuchets. Defenders have moved a wagon for access. 3000 archers take up positions, but the Alamanni king stays out of range, 350 paces away. The Alamanni also concentrated their bowmen, but they stay in the treeline. Neither side can shoot the other and both enjoy cover. Basa stands between them, nervous and ready to run.

Magnus yells as he walks up. "Sire, on the souls of my parents, I swear my archers won't shoot at you until our duel ends. Basa, I'll sell his corpse for a thousand iron ingots by dusk. If not, we'll all pee and poo on him so he smells like other Alamanni."

"You're a stupid fool who'll soon be dead," Basa retorts.

"I actually hear that a lot, but my damn mirror talks too much. I don't trust you, so leave before I kill you." He watches her march off, then turns to the king. "Sire, welcome to Frankfurt. Have you seen the sights? Your log tower amazes me. I love the symmetry and simplicity, but have suggestions – did you bring pen, ink, and parchment? I hit puberty in the Vault when I saw a room full of virgin papyrus. No one else seems to value Egyptian paper. You must have stolen an entire ship full of it. My Uncle Honorius lost a cantilever as he loaded it all. I'm unhappy that Joko made you a sword, chainmail, and helmet with his killer iron. Joko put the iron in irony. He didn't tell me he armed you. I often wonder if he wants me dead, like everyone else. I thought he didn't like me much, but now I know he doesn't like me at all."

Agenaric waves him closer, looking puzzled. "How did you kill Mederic? I can't find a single witness from the tower."

"He choked to death, sucking my massive cock. Your burly brother had a better beard, but I guess you have a certain something something. Your rich elites died poorly. Serapio's hot daughter and cute sons tried to kill me, while the smallest almost succeeded. It surprised me to survive the tower as I fought my way up the ramp. You Alamanni disappoint me to death. If you give me Serapio, I'll probably leave you alone."

"Sell out my nephew? Mederic named him after me. Only a bastard would kill his namesake."

"My dad named me after his father, then killed him, but he wasn't illegitimate. Dad said he was a son-of-a-bitch, but that motherfucker now rots in Hell. Agenaric, you stink less than your brother. Did you put on perfume? I didn't know you were into boys. I haven't hit puberty, but that's never stopped you before. A pedophile priest once chased me around the musical instruments until he caught me by the organ." He chuckles at his joke. "Well, kneel and let's get this over with. As I told that priest a thousand times – spit or swallow, those are your options."

The teen pretends to pull down his trousers without exposing his hidden knives. The king remains wary and ready to run.

"You're trying to anger me? That's your plan? It's not public embarrassment if my men can't hear you. You have a big mouth for such a small boy, but I'll let you live if you leave."

Magnus finally sees the buried rope, but the king is too far away. "For such a big man, you must have a tiny cock. Is your plan to bore me to death?"

Magnus charges and whacks his big shield. The king swings his heavy sword, but the kid easily avoids it. Even with two short swords, Magnus has trouble turning aside his powerful swipes, so he relies on speed to dart in and lunge out. Staggering from the king's powerful blows, the orphan falls back, cursing angrily. They're now 300 paces from the bowmen hiding behind the Inner Barrier. Both armies watch as if this could settle something. The orphan grunts and groans pathetically, cursing and crying as he reluctantly stumbles back. Near tears, he's evading death-blows, but not coming close to killing the king. Both whack the other's armor, but the terrible teen almost falls from the impacts.

The duelers are now 250 paces away from foreign shooters and loaded trebuchet. One Iberian on a horse has a rope tied to his pommel, for some reason. Some legionaries root for their boy while others chuckle gleefully as if they know something the Alamanni don't. They look eager instead of worried. Magnus is slow, sluggish, and stupid. He spends more time blocking blows than delivering them. He retreats against superior skills, trips, and then crab-walks away. When Agenaric chases him, Magnus turns around and runs a bit, barely avoiding a death-blow.

200 strides from help.

The clash of iron rings louder as size and strength forces the boy back. He's breathing hard and heavy, unable to catch his breath or a break. When given a moment, he gasps and bends over to lean on his knees as if he needs a chair. The king presses his advantage, but Magnus does little more than give ground and dent his shield. The long sword catches his lion helmet and, like being inside a bronze bell, the teen feels that to his bones. Walking backwards while swinging his swords blindly, the Alamanni's iron shield smacks the boy hard and he backs up in a dumb daze. Agenaric laughs as if he has already won. He savors the moment and turns to raise his arms to his warriors hiding in the trees. They roar, happy with their hero. Many show themselves, smiling in anticipation. They clearly can't wait for their king to dismember this annoying boy who slaughtered so many.

Given a momentary reprieve, Magnus studies the dirt around him, spots what he's looking for, then stabs the loose earth with his left sword. His left hand massages his aching back as he arches backwards in an agonizing moan. He sobs for his mama and seems oblivious to the danger. As almost all fighters are right-handed, the king doesn't see the trap from the ambidextrous teen. Sensing victory, Agenaric charges to finally end this charade. A big man, he takes large leaps. Except the orphan's left hand has palmed a knife and now throws it into the top of the king's big foot just as he rests his full weight on it. The clever orphan had faked his pain and tears. The blade burrows deep and it must hurt like hell. His royal face turns to terror and he falls like a tree. He lands with a thump, a curse, and a puff of dust, only to hear his tormentor laugh like he won.

Magnus feels glorious. "Since you're dying to know, that's how I killed your brother."

The tables have turned. Grabbing his second sword, Magnus rushes to slash biceps and calves to cripple him, but the king still moves, so the short swords cut deep, spraying blood as the man screams. Magnus hurries for the rope, buried in the dirt weeks ago at night. Thousands of Alamanni archers watch in disbelief. Most have bows and all freak out at seeing the demon-boy cut their kickass king. They bellow in unison, then pall in horror as they see the boy slip a noose of rope around Agenaric's good ankle, then yell for a distant horseman to burst into a gallop.

The orphan flips them the bird and moons them with his bare booty. When the rope goes tight and drags the big badass, Magnus laughs so hard he hiccups. He yells choice insults and grabs his crotch to provoke them. Hoping to save their king, thousands of irreplaceable archers run out of the forest, just as Magnus had hoped. Several hundred strides separate them, so the savages sprint to save their savior. The delighted orphan chuckles as thousands come to kill him again. He retreats without looking like he's retreating, with smile and guile.

Magnus gets out his sling and starts flinging crappy lead as soon as warriors run into range. He walks backwards so fast he's almost skipping as he carefully avoids incoming arrows. Archers must stop to shoot, which helps him track projectiles. Still, it's a strange sight, several thousand armed men converging on a boy weighted down in armor. Then it gets stranger as thousands of rocks, the size of melons, fall from the sky to split skulls and lacerate limbs. The trebuchets harm a hundred, but don't deter the rest. Magnus laughs loudly so survivors keep entering his Death Trap. The king wails and flails in anger and anguish as an unseen horse slowly drags his sorry ass to apologize for Frankfurt. Near the barriers, but far from the gap, Magnus pulls two full-body Roman shields from under the dirt and hides behind them as Germani arrows saturate his position. Instead of targeting Victores archers, they're shooting at a boy. He's yelling something that's hard to hear over the screaming Alamanni bowmen.

"Wait! Wait, damn you! Wait for my command!" Once a few thousand angry armed Alamanni get close enough to tickle him, he bellows to his boys: "Fire!"

3000 arrows fly at the Alamanni front line, most from point blank range, yet a few stubborn men still stumble into the boy's shields. The horrified hero whacks at them like bees and rolls out of reach because they are desperate to grab him. His face is full of fear that he'll later deny to the death. He's retreating and sword-fighting for real this time, ducking and dodging as multiple warriors try putting him down for good. Magnus loses his smirk and perhaps his shit. He's more interested in fending them off than killing them himself. He gets the best of one after another, but a badass woman is crazy quick and driving him insane. With her own chainmail, she's well built, unusually pretty, and absurdly athletic. Victores archers slay other enemies, but don't risk hitting him. It looks and sounds like when he dueled his father, a lifetime ago, but this time it's life or death. Magnus gives as good as he gets, using his superior armor to nick her neck and cut her calves, but this tall champion doesn't seem to slow. He's getting worried. Despite his lion helmet, his expression looks increasing pessimistic against this fierce fighter. He turns aside her attack and launches his own, but she beats it back like a veteran. He's losing legit and finally acknowledges it with a sad sigh.

Once Magnus stumbles, she thinks she has him.

"This is for my husband and that's for my son! Oh, I wish I could kill you twice."

But the teen used the stumble to covertly palm a knife that flies into her flat stomach when he gets up. As she stares in confusion at the blade in her belly, Magnus backs up and slings her shins to quickly cripple her. The first impact sounds loud and ugly as her lower leg shatters and she falls to her doom, not far from her fucking father. A second pellet sinks into her right shoulder so she can't swing that damn sword anymore. She cries in pain and frustration. The agony in her eyes is deep and dark. She lost a fair fight in an unfair world.

The king screams in trauma. "Helga!"

The teen feels triumphant. "This is for my mama in Heaven and that's for my daddy in Hell. You're the scariest woman I've ever met. Helga, I hope you spend the rest of your life pondering your poor choices. I'll get my blade back later. See you soon in Hell."

The Alamanni resume shooting him, but few are within range, so more run up. 3000 defenders have better range, accuracy, and arrows, but Magnus still must leave. He runs for his life to dive through a hole in the barrier. Several arrows barely miss him and one bounces off his back plate. He comes up in a roll and a smile because winning feels awesome. Magnus yells between huffing and puffing.

"Phase 2!"

Feeling faint, he lays on his back, closes his eyes, and his body shakes uncontrollably like an epileptic. He does not seem okay.

Horrified, Agenaric has slammed into a pile of crappy corpses because Magnus thinks ahead, but the king still grips his damn sword like a throbbing penis. He's trying to get up to take down some enemies, but glimpses his best boys getting blown away by a clever trick that he, ironically, literally stepped into. The Alamanni have run far from the safety of their woods and, ironically, are getting chopped to pieces. Agenaric screams as he loses his best bowmen. The first Victores volley hit hundreds and the second topples a thousand. Given their position behind cover, the Victores and Iberians shoot with impunity. Some laugh as they snipe attackers who left the safety of the forest. While some Alamanni stay to trade arrows with Roman archers behind cover, the rest wisely flee once a second volley of rocks rains on them. Many Alamanni take arrows in the back as they run from Frankfurt. They fly forward to kiss the dirt and eat the grass. Like on the road to Briga, Alamannia pissed away a few thousand irreplaceable elite archers.

With Alamanni fighters a few miles away, 3000 Batavi and West Germani ride double across the pasture to surprise Alamanni in the treeline, driving them back and hacking them hard. The surprised Alamanni do their best while fearing the worst. Invaders cut them down and throw hatchets in broad backs, then stab the wounded. Few use bows because they're less useful in dense forest. Riding minimizes time to target; they dismount when the forest gets too dense and advance across a wide front. Teams target camps and seem to already know where most are located. That's when the fighting gets ferocious.

Hundreds of professional swat down shocked defenders, killing or capturing them. It's like a flood during a drought, overwhelming thousands of Alamanni who never imagined the few foreigners coming out to attack them where they live and breathe. Many brief clashes erupt and herds of locals leave, often carrying kids. They abandon their possessions, including cattle, so the foreigner slaughter the livestock as well. Batavi swordsmen fight spearmen while archers trade projectiles. Women attack with pots, pans, or farm implements. Many give up or get knocked down because Team Dutch is in a hurry. Success depends on speed and surprise, so they must escape before the Alamanni can counter.

Dutch leads a special squad to flank fighters behind barriers within a large clearing. Once in position behind trees, the Batavi open up, forcing locals to abandon their position. Team Dutch jogs into the camp and slaughters the slowest to flee. The clang of iron-on-iron echoes as swordsmen scream in pain. Reinforcements run to help the Alamanni, who never prepared for a counter-attack, but clubs and spears cannot beat bowmen. Dutch rallies his men and leads them through the woods. The attackers flow through the forest like a wave, forcing the old, ill, women, and kids to run for their lives, leaving behind their possessions. Thousands face thousands in the trees, but one side is better armed and armored. Alamanni civilians surrender rather than die, then cry at being taken from their fathers and husbands. Warriors fight back, but only slow the carnage.

Dutch feels glorious. He's shooting when he has clear shots and jogging when he doesn't. He hears his men around him. He barks at women and kids to lay down and they do. He sees something and moves to intercept, maneuvering through trees like a jaguar. He expertly nails several hostiles and laughs at the easy kills. Then something punches his chest. He spots a big Alamanni with a bow walking from behind a nearby tree, laughing at him. Dutch palms a blade and throws it. The warrior doesn't see it coming and examines his side to see what's wrong. Dutch strolls over while unsheathing his sword and chops off his head with all his strength. The commander puts his back to the tree, slumps down in shock, and stares at the arrow in his chest. His friend Lars jogs over with a puzzled frown. Though they were East Germani who moved west to the lower Rhine 400 years ago, their dialect evolved distinctly over centuries of Roman rule. The Netherlands therefore spoke a unique language unintelligible to both East German and West German.

"Dutch, why aren't you dead? He shot you from close range and didn't hit your breast plate."

"Lars, his arrowhead punched through two layers of chainmail and four layers of boiled leather. I'm bleeding bad unless I peed myself."

"You're lucky to be alive. His small hunting bow and crappy arrowhead failed to penetrate the armor that Max gave you. He's gonna demand a public huggie and maybe another blowjob."

The friend finds that funny. "I don't feel lucky. I feel like I almost died. When Max told me to leave Frankfurt to steal boats, I wanted to beat the snot out of him. Now becoming a pirate sounds good."

Lars laughs and wiggles the arrow out as Dutch howls.

Magnus waves them past impatiently. 3000 legionaries leave the inner barrier to jog through the bleeding bodies and into the woods, where they meet resistance. Some pause to stab injured enemies. Oddly, others push empty wheelbarrows with silly smiles. The first several hundred hold shields against enemy archers, forcing them to flee deeper into the woods. Far in the forest, Franco slays strangers with satisfaction. With sword and shield, he mixes it up, slaughtering several before smashing into a small group to scatter them. He's in the Zone, knocking aside spears and clubs to thrust and slice. Bowmen back up and wait for openings, but Iberians and the Victores shooters arrive in numbers. Like the West Germani, 3000 foreign invaders surge into the forest to overwhelm camps and to send thousands of Alamanni running for their lives, terror on their faces.

A thousand Germani bodies, some crawling, are visible after 3000 legionaries have run past. All have been wounded and hundreds look deader than yesterday. Their haunting cries for help stir the soul. Big boys beg for mercy, but legionaries kill those who can't walk. Several hundred survivors are tied up and driven out of the trees, into No Man's Land, head bowed and shoulders slumped. Iberia's mercury mine will kill them all within a few years or give them internal pains that make them long for the sweet release of death. In the trees, professional troops in full kit and heavy armor decimate resistance. When running into barriers, they go around to flank the enemy. Brave boys, wicked women, and old folks with nothing to lose fight back to give others time to escape the slaughter. Legionaries knock them down and knock them out.

Franco bellows at his boys. "Slaves are worth more than corpses!" He pulls down a tent to find 1000 iron ingots and roars Glorious Victory. His men echo it. "To Max!"

An army chants their hero: "Max! Max! Max!"

The teen's two armies have executed a forceps maneuver, meeting in the middle to squeeze the enemy. Caught completely by surprise, Alamanni healers abandon a field of tents and lean-to's full of wounded warriors. Legionaries gleefully end their pain. In all, Team Magnus has killed several thousand, wounded thrice as many, and kidnapped even more. Many Alamanni got away, but they taste bitter defeat after expecting sweet victory. The Lion struck and surprised them all.

An army doctor checks the boy for ouchies. "Boy, be patient while I bandage your wounds."

"I don't have time for patience! You want me to be a patient patient? I'll try, Doctor Doctor!"

"If you stay still, you'll thank me later."

Magnus is impatient. "If I thank you now, then can I go play?"

The boy jogs back into No Man's Land to talk shit to the Alamanni king. He studies the battlefield. Iberians are finishing off the Alamanni wounded in No Man's Land or dragging their bodies to the barriers. All wrap Alamanni quivers over their shoulders. A dozen push wheelbarrows filled with enemy arms and armor. Some Iberians are still going through their pockets for valuables. The boy blocks his nostrils and turns to his captive. On top of old, stinking corpses, the king can't believe his foul position.

"Sire, any last words?"

"You threw a knife! That's cheating!"

"War has winners and losers, but no cheaters. You're just a stupid fool who I tricked. You didn't just lose a duel; you lost several thousand shooters, bows, and armor, plus arrows that we desperately need. I bet we recover twice as many arrows that we spent while I doubt you have many archers left. I win because no one foresees the future better than me."

Ironic, how that turns out.

The knife in one boot and the rope around the other make Agenaric unable to move much. Magnus feints a few times until the long sword falls too far, then the boy cuts into a royal forearm. Now disarmed, Agenaric can't do much while the vile boy slices him. After that, his troops throw that rope over a tree branch and lift the king upside down so his fingers can't touch the bodies he bleeds on. The brave man is in over his head and watches Romans cut throats of injured Alamanni in No Man's Land. His face reveals exquisite anguish as his friends die for his folly. He whispers names of those who fall, his face a mask of misery.

The boy gets in his face. "I lured you to the buried rope and you had no idea. Tonight, every Alamanni here will assault my fortifications, rather than wait for reinforcements, and they'll die by the thousands, so you lost two battles today, not one. Sire, I'm here to steal lives, not wealth. Gaul will never enjoy safety as long as Alamanni exist, so what I do is cruel, but necessary for lasting peace. Your family used poison to make me an orphan. I still can't get over it. There should be a special hell for pagans like you. I was not born a monster; men like you turned me into one. Or so I tell myself. You will hang by your boot until death or rescue. If you really have a thousand iron ingots, I might sell your corpse. If not, I'll dump you in the Main River after we pee on you. For the life of me, I don't understand why Gaul shits themselves whenever Alamanni cross the Rhine. Goodbye, loser. Say hi to your brothers. I'm off to fuck with your dangerous daughter."

"Boy, you'll suffer for this!"

"My parents died in front of me the day I was almost assassinated twice. All my life, my father delighted in making me miserable. Said it builds character or some such shit. I need less personality, not more. Life is suffering. Today was just a momentary respite. I once asked my Uncle Theo if life gets easier. That honest bastard told me no. Life is always hard. The rich enjoy long comfortable lives while peasants tolerate brief, uncomfortable ones. We can't escape frequent suffering. It's built in. The trick is to make life worth the pain that we suffer. If I could devote my life to anything, it'd be minimizing misery. Wouldn't that be something? All of humanity living in peace, never starving or freezing to death. I can't even imagine what such a world would look like. My personal hero, Julius Caesar, wanted to enhance his own *dignitas* and the glory of Rome. I'd rather help folks suffer less. I don't expect happiness for myself, but I'd like everyone else to be less miserable. Hmmm. You're easier to talk to than my dead dad. And you interrupt me less. You even smell good. Do you still want to drink me dry? I've never been horny, but I do have a fucked up sense of humor."

"Boy, all Alamanni are coming to kill you."

"I'm counting on it. I even brought my abacus."

Hundreds of horsemen ride out into the battlefield. They hook up corpses for the horses to drag into Frankfurt. A thousand dead Alamanni create a dust storm.

The teen explains: "Julian signed a contract promising to pay a gold coin for every dead Alamanni. We're stacking them outside the tower's rock wall so their festering prevents living Alamanni from using it as cover. That's right: Alamanni are more useful dead than alive. Scholars have debated this for millennia; I'm just letting you know where I stand. Every time dad gave me directions, I got lost in thought. The irony is

114

you would have been spared all this if you left my father alive. He only planned to steal your vault. I'm more vindicative and less interested in living. But don't worry; I'll sketch you after we shit on you. I have a few dozen drawings of the fools fighting us. Canvas and easel will give me fame and fortune after my death."

"One day you'll die horribly, and probably one day soon."

"Yeah. I expect my family to be the death of me. I deserve nothing less." The boy smiles mischievously. "Sire, when you get to Hell, please tell my father I've surpassed his puny plans and unrealized ambitions."

Helga struggles to regain consciousness and finds herself mostly nude and covered in crap. The stench tickles her nose and makes her gag. Blood keeps dripping on her, so she looks up to see her father, hanging upside down for some reason. The princess yells at him, but he doesn't respond. Hearing hilarity, she exhausts her energy to turn. That annoying boy has somehow set up an easel to draw her. Laughing, he shows her the canvas, which includes her dying dad.

"I peed on you both, but you slept through it. Troops took your armor, then your clothes before shitting on you. Helga, you tried very hard to kill me and I'm getting tired of that. Sorry I exaggerated your fantastic tits and envious curves, but I want this portrait to become famous so my sack of Frankfurt is not forgotten."

"Max, I'll see you in Hell."

"Not if I see you first. I hear that place is crowded."

115

CHAPTER 5

The dark bedroom is scary. Holding a torch to see the cot, Franco kicks Magnus awake. He yells over loud rain, wind, and thunder.

"Max, the storm got worse. I assume they've been waiting for bad weather to use as cover. The enemy is moving into position because we see a lot more shadows than their last attack. They've been building something with all that logging, sawing, and hammering. I've pulled everyone back to the tower. You should have kept the trawler here. All those catapults would have helped us."

The teen sits up. "Guess they harvested the crops that we weren't able to burn. Cousin, I had to send the artillery ship away because it destroyed their last frontal assault. I was hoping they'd rush us again, with the trawler gone, but it should have returned by now." He stands up to study his other commanders, all staring hard at him. "I sent the ships and most West Germani away to give the enemy a tempting target. We need them to piss away more lives before the rest of their warriors arrive. I believe I mentioned this a time or two. I feared they'd burn us out, but not in a storm. They can't reach the gunboats, so they must be after us. You all know the Plan. They only have three entrances through the neighborhood wall. Like last time, pour fire into them as they barge in, then focus fire as they open the tower doors. I assume the king gave them the keys. Concentrate projectiles on the densest mass of men and hope we can recover them whenever the storm breaks. Last week the bastards took our bolts and arrows. We may have to cut open corpses to get our arrowheads back for our surplus shafts. Good thing they don't take our rocks and bricks. The trebuchets can hit them as they pass through the gates with dead reckoning. Don't look so glum! Their last attack cost them a few thousand murderous men and we only lost a single centurion. I don't need an abacus to do the math."

"What if they break in this time?"

Magnus shrugs. "Even better because then we can recover ammo easier! I'd like to think we didn't hoist a million mud bricks for nothing. We already have a dozen catapults on the upper ramp and we may move many more. Remove the weights that prevent the gates from opening so they can hurry to their deaths. 4000 archers can stop a million going up one ramp. Boys, we're not gonna die; we're gonna kill!"

His infectious tone, smile, and body language motivates the men, who yell orders downstairs to troops on the ground floor. The person at the top always sets the tone in any organization.

Magnus runs to the roof to join a line of archers. Stones the size of heads are stacked against the railing. A barrel of crappy pellets makes him smile as he puts on his special gloves. Bowmen line the railing, waiting for enemies to enter the luxury neighborhood. He starts slinging once the gate opens. Iron stakes in the ground prevent the double doors from fully opening. Something similar happens at the other two entrances. Through the rain and darkness, Magnus sees a zillion mobile shadows beyond the wall. Rooftop trebuchet throw rocks at incoming enemies. Catapults on the roof and balconies only shoot at men massed together because missing from this distance is all too easy and bolts all too few. With such poor visibility, the Alamanni feel safe enough to gather in large numbers. Magnus hears his trebuchets throwing bigger rocks that hurt hundreds, but Alamanni sentries shout when it rains rocks, giving warriors a moment to raise shields or find cover. The boy looks disappointed.

Then the shit show shatters his senses.

Magnus turns to bellow. "Crap! They got an Armored Approach Vehicle! Catapults, target it! Trebuchets, throw the biggest rocks at it."

The enemy pushes a wagon through the gate. They must have measured the width because it barely fits. The wagon has hides on top and all around to deter fire. It must have strong supports to tolerate rocks and it looks suspiciously long. The vehicle laughs at the projectiles that bounce off it. On the roof, the legionaries look shocked and afraid as they run out of easy targets.

Magnus can't counter it. "It's a wheeled mantlet! Conserve ammo and move our rocks to the inner rail to throw down at the ramp!"

Indeed, through the hard rain Magnus watches drenched men push a series of structures forming a long tunnel, just tall and wide enough for armored men. The mantlet shields the line of men within from his projectiles to funnel fighters safely to the tall tower. The teen runs to the inner area to yell at his troops:

"Prepare to repel intruders. They'll be coming in all three available doors and will probably break open the walls to flood the ground floor. Good thing our prisoners covered those walls in crap. Let them eat shit. Firemen, prepare to dump incendiaries on their shieldmen, but wait until they commit so the rest of us can slay some strangers."

Chairs, dressers, and other furniture crowd the upper floors, for some reason, with pots, pans, and kettles stacked like ammo.

Too much time passes without the enemy showing themselves on the ground floor. Magnus calls a commander meeting to discuss the problem.

"I hear hammering," Franco says. "They're bringing a lot of materials in. Are they preparing to burn the tower?"

Magnus doubts that. "That wouldn't be the dumbest thing they could do, but we'd just fly to the docks and let gunboats take us to the island. We filled many second story homes with wood. If they don't burn this unnaturally tall tower, then I will. They may be in the mood for revenge. We slaughtered their government, took their treasury, and killed or enslaved their elite, so I'm thinking they want to kill us. The Roman Empire has never threatened the very existence of Alamannia before. Burning this tower doesn't do that. The Alamanni became the most powerful Germani tribe by beating their neighbors for the last century, so they won't take defeat lying down. I told them I wanted a fight. I think they feel the same. If this attack doesn't succeed, then they'll burn us out. Good thing I sent most Batavi to the island or else our evacuation would take too long. Franco, transfer more catapults from the roof to the upper floors and lots of mud bricks. Archers, stockpile your ammo around the upper rails. As we practiced, a thousand bowmen per floor and we'll rotate until the enemy gives up or dies out. Which cohort wants the honor of shooting the enemy from the 3rd floor? I guarantee the first one will suffer fewer casualties than the last one."

Magnus runs to the roof and the rain hits him like a father. He orders catapult operators to use the crane to lower their heavy weapons to the top few floors. He pretends to be calm and professional, but his face looks worried under all that fake innocence. Going to the rooftop edge, he looks out upon a massive army of ants occupying Frankfurt. Their movement makes the city seem alive. Their numbers numb him.

117

"I need more troops, time, and ammo."

Rain still falls hard in the open-air atrium and the wind drowns out speech. The long ramp curves around the perimeter of the open area. If the roof is 100' high, then the ramp is 20x longer. The lightest catapults are on the 4th floor sniping enemies on the ground floor. Alamanni bowmen still trade arrows and insults with a cohort on the 3rd floor. Both sides use metal shields and re-use spent arrows. Germani pull their wounded into ground floor stores for treatment and legionaries carry injured comrades up the ramp to the penthouse clinic. The orphan squats to say goodbye over the loud wind and rain to a seriously wounded Iberian going down the lift.

"Rodrigo, sorry about losing your leg and thanks for shooting so many strangers. Your biggest threat now is fever from infection and then boredom. I know I'd miss me, too. Hide this bullion bar and don't let anyone know you have it. You face a rough period, but your share of the loot should be enough to retire on. Tell Cousin Lorena hi and hug your kids for me. I don't plan on surviving, so I want you to know that I am flattered that warriors of your caliber would fight for me."

"Max, I wish I could stay. We killed thousands, but even more take their place. You are one of a kind. Please don't die on me. I want to see you full grown with the wind in your sails."

Laughing. "I'd fly off the planet!"

On the upper floors, Magnus supervises the elevation of the catapults by lifting their rears onto crates so they point down. It's an odd angle because these heavy weapons naturally point up. They test-shoot one. Loading takes longer and the recoil makes them unstable; this catapult almost falls off the crate. Then it takes many strong men to set it back up. The smaller ones they place on the ramp, but they must push them up when retreating or else damage them so the enemy can't use them.

"Here they come!" someone yells.

Magnus is impatient. "About damn time! The sun's coming up. Today's almost tomorrow and I need my beauty sleep in these ugly times."

From the 5th floor as the sun slowly rises, Magnus watches them assemble a roofed structure to the ramp entrance. It looks like a short metal hallway from the bakery with wooden sides that the rain soaks deep.

Franco freaks. "They detached all three sets of double doors! Thank God we blocked off the door to the docks. Oh, no, they made carts!"

That's bad news. Magnus looks horrified. Even their biggest rocks wouldn't collapse that tank, but what shrivels their sphincters are the carts. Both have four wheels, like a wagon, but each has a steel door in the front and planks on top and on one side covered in hides soaked in water. Two teams push the carts up the ramp, careful not to tip them over. The fighters behind the carts all hold shields. Stunned, Magnus sways like a reed in a river.

"Shoot them as they go up the ramp, but only at easy targets." He blinks in disbelief, then jack-knifes over the rail to squint. His tone says he's lying. "Bears! Fucking bears are shooting us! Oh, man, I shouldn't have drunk beer last week. It's made me as crazy as I pretend!"

Alamanni archers have wrapped themselves in furs, hides, and leather. Some

118

have chainmail or old Roman breastplates, but the thick bear furs stand out. Most still have the bear heads attached because that looks stylish as floor rugs. Almost every Germani family has a bear rug or three, handed down for generations. The Victores stare in puzzlement as bear-ish bowmen step into the courtyard to shoot up, then step back to reload. A ring of shield-women helps protect them.

Franco is frightened. "These are better archers than the hundreds we faced earlier and they're firing our own arrows."

Magnus pops a cork. "Those thieves!"

"They must have used the useless as bait to collect our ammo. Look at all the women and elderly that we wasted our ammo on! I bet thousands of Alamanni, grieving for lost loved ones, prefer dying in battle than slow starvation. We spent over 100,000 cedar arrows on folks hoping to die. Max, we need the javelins and darts to ruin their shields or else they'll advance faster than our lowest cohort can retreat up the ramp."

4000 shooters send 3000 arrows a minute down at the enemy. Most don't pierce flesh, but hundreds a minute do and the toll it takes is terrible. Arrows and rain pour down on the Alamanni, striking helmets, furs, and shields of every sort. Some wounded Germani limp away, crying and cursing, only for others to take their place. The dead and seriously wounded lie where they fall; removing them is a low priority. Executing the demon-boy comes first. Some chant their target's name.

"Verpa Maximus! *Verpa* Maximus (Maximum Dick)."

Magnus chuckles. "If they're bragging about Maximum Dick, they should get in line. Cousin, should I feel insulted? I suddenly want to piss on them. I.P. Standing is my favorite author. I was looking for a great name. It sure beats Flavius."

They watch one cohort jog past the light catapults to replace the lowest cohort, now low on energy, ammo, and nerves. The enemy's wheeled mantlets have advanced past the 2nd floor and hundreds of enemy archers race up to take positions around the rim. 3000 legionaries and 1000 Batavi prioritize them, many now with javelins and darts to get past their layers of leather, fur, and hides.

"They're not reacting to my killer insults, so even their skin is thick."

Franco points. "Those are servants, grandparents, widows, orphans, and limpers holding broken bows. We're killing their non-fighters and giving them our ammo again! I bet most are not actual Alamanni, but Germani that they've conquered recently."

Magnus slings at the most vulnerable targets. The brutal, bloody battle is beautiful as Alamanni fall almost as soon as they get on the 2nd floor. It takes more arrows to get past so many shields and armor, but Team Magnus spends what it takes. The teen's eyes shine as rain falls off his killer baby-face.

On the 2nd floor, the ill, elderly, handicapped, starving, stupid, drunk, grieving, and desperate carry big shields, bad bows, and empty quivers as arrows, darts, and javelins strike them down. Some call out names of lost loved ones while others curse Verpa Maximus. Looking like zombies, the ambulatory continue up the ramp, living to kill the demon-boy. As the two wheeled mantlets circle around, darts, javelins, and arrows hit them hard. Their comrades just step over the injured and kick the dead over the side. The heavy catapults on the upper floors knock men down like gods even as the lighter ones on the 3rd floor back up after shooting their load like a stud. Thousands of dead cover the marble tile. Mobile enemies help out the injured, taking them into the stores or the exits. The Alamanni's best archers still shoot up from the ground floor, moving unpredictably, but defenders target more immediate threats. Eager volunteers huddle in the packed bakery, waiting for their turn to go up the ramp. None have bows because they can't shoot for shit.

Magnus sighs. "They must have 100 non-fighters for every combat veteran. Even a peasant can hold a plank or push a cart. I thought the darts and javelins would slow them down, but they expected to lose a thousand people per floor. I didn't count on their math skills! Damn these barbarians! They're gonna over-run our small catapults. Time for bricks, rocks, and incendiaries. Franco, send down another cohort and tell the artillerymen to quickly retreat two floors while I find my mind. I lost it here somewhere."

As Franco runs off, Magnus bellows a command and the tower's open atrium starts raining rocks, bricks, debris, trash, furniture, furnishings, and clay balls filled with lamp oil, pine sap, and tinder. Bad sofas and heavy chairs do the most good as they fall on horrified strangers. Falling furniture slows the enemy down and pisses them off. The heavier debris injure as many enemies as darts and javelins. Old men and big women burst into flame from incendiaries, but that hardly slows the rest. Some lose eyes and their agony can be heard over the storm. Defenders finally have easy targets and thus shoot gleefully, shouting in joy for every kill.

Flinging with his other arm, Magnus sees artillerymen on the 3rd floor push and pull their wheeled catapults up the ramp, with a century of the new cohort helping. The rest relieve the lowest cohort, now half-a-cohort, many dragging bleeding buddies up. Almost all have arrows sticking out of their armor. They leave behind a bloody mess, but Alamanni replace those pushing the two carts modified into mini-tunnels with an iron door in front.

Magnus whispers to himself. "500 shooters with six quivers equals 90,000 arrows, plus 5 darts and a javelin each. Oooooh, boy."

The Batavi with the clay incendiaries are on higher floors, so Magnus runs up and orders them down. Ironically, they also have carts, though smaller. The boy addresses them like volunteers that he can't command.

"Commander Lars, if we don't burn those wheels, they'll keep climbing. You can either relieve the next cohort or charge the enemy and ignite their carts. Swords and axes will serve you better than bows. Cut up their front ranks and break their carts. Only ten men can stand abreast on the ramp, so form up, with each warrior carrying a clay ball, darts, and a javelin. The last row should hold torches and the front row needs full-body shields to smash into the iron doors at full speed. Succeed, and the rest of your day is easy. Hit them hard and we might even get breakfast. And you boys thought me ridiculous for filling carts with dirt and debris!"

The Batavi take that like a challenge. Lars barks orders like he's looking forward to running down to his death. They arm up, push two carts onto the ramp, and Magnus follows them down, chewing over-salted bacon. A few soldiers slip on the wet floor and the rain soaks them all. Magnus yells at the lowest Iberian cohort to retreat and they happily run up the ramp, moving to the sides so the Batavi can speed up. The Alamanni see them coming and brace themselves for the impact. Filled with earth, those carts are heavy and fast.

The tough teen leans over the rail and bellows: "Target shooters on the ground floor! Reserves, deploy!"

Dirt-filled carts crash into the two enemy carts by the 3rd floor and earth goes flying. The strong men pushing the wheeled mantlets are farmers and loggers, not fighters. The loud impact sends some off the railing, but the Alamanni are pretty packed on the ramp and have nowhere to go, though some carts fly literally off the wooden rails to land on the unlucky below. The Batavi spear the enemy with javelins, throw darts at those farther back, and draw swords to fuck them faster. The screaming is loud, thunderous, and unnerving. Batavi with long-handle war-axes hack the beams and ropes that hold the carts together while guys with buckets of lamp oil soak the wheels for burning. Sadly, other Batavi have so much success against the unarmed and overwhelmed that they keep going, which Magnus didn't foresee. If winning is taking territory, they think they're succeeding.

The orphan howls on a higher floor. "Lars, where are you going? Leave some for the rest of us!"

Lars laughs at the easy kills and splattered blood. He's smacking them around and slicing them up like they've never killed strangers before. He cuts into a neck, pokes an eye, chops a leg, kicks a chest, unarms a bearded farmer, and enjoys it all immensely. But as they stab, spear, and dart Alamanni peasants, servants, and vassals, the Batavi expose themselves to enemy archers on the first two floors. The three-way slaughter eats up hundreds a minute. From above, Team Magnus shoots enemy bowmen on the first few floors, who in turn shoot the Batavi, who only have chainmail and helmets. Franco blows Retreat, then roars down at Team Lars.

The Batavi cut down those on the ramp, trampling their wounded and throwing off their injured. Now reduced to swords, they cut apart those fleeing the crowded ramp, screaming in terror. But now the lowest Batavi are below the 2nd floor, feeling foolish and falling fast. One trooper gets pulled off the rail and folks on the ground floor tear him apart. Another takes an arrow in the eye, right through the socket. A third loses a limb, so he hoses hostiles to blind them. Others ignore impacts as if their armor is awesome. Lars takes a soft blow to his hard head which adjusts his killer attitude. He looks around, seems stunned, and then barks at his boys to back up. Despite holding shields, Alamanni archers are shooting them down as they back up the ramp. Many Iberian bowmen run down the ramp to snipe the enemy while others line the 4th floor railing to provide cover fire. Both sides lose archers rapidly until the Alamanni retreat to their stores, shops, and crap-filled eateries, leaving an army of dead and dying behind. Defenders cheer as if they've won, but Magnus knows better because he can't afford an expensive war of attrition.

Magnus yells from above. "Carry our wounded up before the enemy recovers! Take their bear coats so they can't use them again. I want all the huggies!"

A few thousand miserable troops eat breakfast while many warily watch the Alamanni gather on the ground floor. The number of corpses depresses or elates them. Team Magnus utilizes the kitchen in every home to feed troops quickly before going back to work. Men carry cups or bowls, mad they've thrown so many chairs. Some bowmen on balconies shoot sitting ducks or their Germani equivalent.

The orphan and Franco take the Batavi commander aside. "Lars, how many bear coats did your boys grab?"

He sounds wary. "A few hundred. Didn't know you needed an inventory. Most

121

are very bloody, but we might sell you some if you pay enough."

"This storm might last another day. The Alamanni must win before it ends. They'd rather die killing us than starve this winter. I bet our raiders took a million cattle and half as many horses. Without grain or shiploads of fish, dying here is their best alternative. They literally have nothing to lose. Lars, how close is your Batavi language to East German?"

The leader looks at the dangerous boy like he wants a weapon. "We spoke something very similar 500 years ago, before Caesar settled us at the mouth of the Rhine. There's still overlap, but we can't understand most of what they say. Why?"

"We face a long day and a longer night. At your own discretion, disguise your best bearded bastards in bloody bear coats and get to the 2nd floor via the crane to mingle with the enemy. Most Iberians and Victores legionaries are clean-shaven, while most of your Batavi have beards. The Alamanni may have a million civilians, but they don't have enough archers left after your fearless attack. Winning will be much easier if they can't shoot us. Killing their bowmen saves the rest of us."

The combat veteran now looks at the boy differently. He adjusts his posture and his attitude.

"Sounds dangerous, but smarter than running among them. You haven't called me an idiot for letting my men get carried away on the ramp."

The teen chooses his words carefully. "I wish we had time to pre-position archers to take advantage of that courageous charge. We still shot a few hundred of their last archers, though your boys paid a painful price."

Lars laughs bitterly. "You gonna tell Dutch I'm a fool and a fuck up?"

"But you're not. You took the opportunity to cut down enemies on the ramp, while burning and breaking their carts. The bodies are piled so high that they can't even walk up. I think you're all heroes and plan on telling your leadership if I somehow survive. In case you ask for brave, bearded volunteers to infiltrate the enemy tonight, I'll tell the crane operators to give you access. Any of our killer arrows that you return will be welcome. Come, I want to show you boys something."

They walk to the inner penthouse rail, where Alamanni shield-women protect strong men pulling the bodies down to clear a path. The best Iberian shooters snipe them from the 5th floor. Enemy archers shoot back, but their arrows rarely have the strength to pierce flesh from that distance.

The teen points at an Iberian archer. "That centurion has a dozen arrows hanging from his armor and a hundred spent arrows that hit the wall behind him. He's methodical and cautious, waiting for a decent shot. I bet he's almost out of ammo, despite three wounded men helping recover used arrows. The enemy wears several layers of leather, so even our good arrows don't penetrate deep enough unless fired from close range. However, the darts, weighted down by lead, and the javelins pierce better. Without the brave Batavi assault, they would have recovered our projectiles to our detriment. I propose recovering them before they re-organize."

The other two leaders laugh at that.

"Who do you want going down to the 1st floor?" Franco asks.

"Everyone who can run. They want to hurt me most, so I'll make myself heard and seen more than usual. Overwhelming force will make for a quicker trip. They don't expect us to attack and most aren't even armed. Thousands are treating their wounded and thousands more are crying over their dead. I'd rather kill their injured before they recover. Surprising them today is safer than letting them win by attrition tomorrow. Unless you geniuses have better ideas for surviving the week."

Franco and Lars make eye contact, then reluctantly nod.

The rising sun and falling rain give Magnus, Franco, and the Batavi enough light to see the sad city. Most Alamanni find shelter in the structures that Magnus burned or broke. Some set up tents, but few have cooking fires. They see twice as many women, but few small kids. The numbers surprise them. The orphan looks straight down and sees Alamanni helping the injured out or carrying the dead, often slumped over horses once they get beyond the neighborhood's outer wall. Troops on high balconies or windows snipe the easiest targets. Other drop rocks, bricks, or debris. Magnus sees arrows enter legs and puncture backs. One embeds itself in a head, dropping that woman like a doll. Most corpses they drag outside the building for families to bury because there's so little room inside.

Magnus summarizes. "There might be a million Alamanni after all, if we include tribes they've conquered. A quarter of them are here. I'm thinking their most seriously wounded cover the entire ground floor, despite the crap we smeared on those walls. Their healers must decide who can be moved. Out in the city, we see a lot of limpers. Those with weapons are sleeping off their battle nerves. Some are walking all the way to the woods. I doubt we face 10,000 proficient fighters. Are we under siege? Because they look hungry. Our granaries are full and we have thousands of pigs and poultry on the island. The cold underground bunker is full of fresh steaks. It was so funny last week when they tried to steal the food that we stole from them, only to find our padlocks. Ah, good times."

Lars lights up. "They can't stay! I see them roasting their horses, which horsemen hate doing. That's like a parent who hates kids, so they must be desperate. They left their food with their families. Except for young wives with small kids, they all came here to kill until they die. If not here, they'll simply starve elsewhere. They even lost all three kings within two months. Desperate people are dangerous."

Franco agrees. "They look bitter, but not beaten. They fear winter, but not us because we're too few. We can expect another attack today and definitely tonight. I hate to say it, but Max is right. We need those projectiles. We won't see the next dawn without them. If we must overrun them, then we might as well stab their wounded on the ground floor."

Magnus claps happily. "Let's bring our carts, bags, and boxes to recover ammo quickly. Who wants to use the crane?"

The hoist lowers Magnus and five men in a metal box to the 2nd floor balcony. The boy is the first to get out and sneak inside. He finds a dozen men dozing and a few standing guard, watching the ramp. The wind blows through the balcony, but these warriors have been up all night. Exhaustion has made them look so dead that it's hard to distinguish them from standing corpses. They even smell the same. Team Magnus hides and waits for the next six troops to descend. As the only one in Europe with throwing knives, Magnus leads. He silently jogs past the sleeping to throw five knives into three awake men by the opening to the shared inner balcony. A moment later, he chops a few wrists and cuts three throats before they can sound the alarm. His men murder the sleepers and take their valuables. More Batavi descend to his level and that just amuses him. Magnus smiles at grown men worried they'll die today.

"If you boys worked for me directly, you'd also have throwing knives and a killer disposition. Come on. Let's wipe them out before lunch. I'm starving because revenge gives me an appetite."

Victores bowmen with leg wounds crowd the 3rd floor to snipe enemies, who eventually retreat. 3000 troops form up into rows of 10 and jog down the ramp as if on an odd parade. Many enemies form up to oppose them, but not enough because they're sleeping off the earlier battle. The dozen with Magnus surprise the courtyard from the 2nd floor. They shoot opposition archers and the teen slings runners in the back. When several warriors charge, he throws knives and calls them nasty names. The teen notices piles of arrows, darts, and javelins, which makes recovering them quicker. A hundred Alamanni archers trade shots with shooters coming down the ramp before fleeing. Magnus slides under an arrow and comes up flinging, his pellet destroying a warrior's face and most of his teeth. The next craters a cranium and a third sinks into a big belly. He moves forward, back, and to the side to avoid incoming while slinging for his life. As upper-floor archers catch up, they cut the enemy down and survivors shatter. When Magnus comes up for air, he learns they own the ground floor, covered in crap and corpses. Troops expand into the stores that encircle the courtyard. Women treating their husbands, fathers, and sons are slow to leave, so they get knocked down and tied up. The fastest Batavi cut off three exits while others herd the younger ladies into a corner, crying pitifully like their lives are over. The fourth door leads to the royal docks, but is padlocked. Hundreds of decaying bodies, stacked high, deny access.

The orphan holds up the key as his men stab their wounded. "Take their fuckable women to the boats to move them to Drusus Island. Oh, crap – corpses block the exit to the docks. Well, who wants to scare the crap out of the Alamanni? Let's sweep around the tower and shoot anyone within range of the gates. Come on! War should be fun and games. Grab the ammo they piled and let's work!"

Franco and Lars mass their men to exploit surprise. This is where Magnus had first entered the tall tower, a lifetime ago. Magnus jogs out, forcing troops to follow. The Alamanni already run for the gate in the neighborhood wall, still with the long mantlet, so he hits the easiest targets in the back with crappy pellets. Hundreds limp while helping others. Most pellets don't burrow deep because victims wear so many layers of leather, so he aims for heads or limbs. Though he can't fling while running, he barely has to pause. He sees skulls shatter and then cackles like a hyena to piss them off while scaring them shitless. By cutting off this gate, he traps thousands of poorly armed Alamanni who drops their arms and raise their hands.

"That's for murdering my mama! Where's Serapio? What's taking him so long to get here? My date with destiny has stood me up!"

In the Covered Approach Vehicle, he's first to the gate facing Frankfurt and trades projectiles, counting on his speedy reflexes. He dodges arrows as more enemy archers run up to target him. As his shooters arrive, not many have room to work.

"Destroy this structure so we can shoot them from the balconies. No one brought hammers and axes? What do I pay you people for?"

He turns to watch 3000 troops slaughter several thousand injured enemies within the walled compound and escort several thousand young ladies and small kids to the docks to sell as slaves. Beyond the tower neighborhood, 100,000 Alamanni challenge them in broad daylight, but the three gates are crowded bottlenecks. Team Magnus has more shooters and better shooters, so they win the exchange. The rain has let up, but hatred drenches the combatants.

"Close the other gates and pound stakes to stop them from opening. Drive useful captives to the docks and finish off everyone else. These people came to kill you. Mercy endangers other innocents. Gaul won't know peace until the Alamanni people are defeated, not just their armies."

Around the log Cube, a few thousand troops and prisoners recover ammo, even cutting arrowheads out of enemies. Limpers carry armloads of bolts inside or pile corpses to serve as disgusting barriers. After a long day, time is short. Franco finds Magnus dividing prisoners into those worth deporting and those he kills. The six gunboats are ferrying captives to the island. Dozens of dead defenders go into the cold meat bunker for proper burial later. The boy lights up at seeing his cousin while a guard hits a captive who steps out of line.

"Max, you're killing helpless prisoners?"

"Only if they look at me wrong; our last ships don't have room for them all, so something must give. Franco, we caught six kids! Some fools brought small children to a battle. Can you even imagine a child here? I assume those kids have bad parents. We've moved a few hundred more wounded troops to Drusus Island, our newly deceased, and I'm thinking of asking the least mobile to go there now rather than when we're in a hurry. I'd rather have fewer men who can fully fight than more men that we can't quickly evacuate. The fleet is suspiciously late. What could possibly be keeping Theo and Dutch?"

"A lot of armed enemies are preparing to storm all three gates. I told our teams to fall back. You should get inside."

"Franco, they won't attack until nightfall, so I told the boys to get something to eat and then a nap. Oh, I sent up a few crates of fish for those who tire of beef. All those kitchens have come in handy, but we'll run out of fuel soon. Our biggest catapults have been bolting our besiegers to keep them at a distance. Recovering all that ammo gives us a fighting chance tonight. We probably killed more Alamanni today than in the last week. Easy kills, too. We should pick fights with the unarmed more often. No wonder Germani prefer raiding to war. Cousin, you look uneasy? What's wrong?"

"I don't like tempting fate. I have a wife and kids that need me. Well, I have some kids worth seeing and I miss my mistress. After finally making some money, I don't want to die here. It'd be nice to enjoy life. I want to know what not being poor feels like."

Magnus sighs. "Is that why the boys look scared? But we theoretically get a gold coin from Julian for every dead Alamanni. I love Theory; everything always works in Theory. Well, shit. I probably can't fight them all alone. Ok, tell the boys we'll leave when the fleet returns. I'm hoping to burn the tower with the enemy inside like a funeral pyre. We have enough rope to escape quickly, though not enough gloves. Will it look weird to the Alamanni that we stripped their dead of so many fur coats? I just wish I had a beard to join the Batavi. Infiltrating Frankfurt would be fun."

"I'm going inside. One of us must act like an adult. If we enact Plan B, I've selected 100 Iberians to protect you."

"Thanks, Franco. You must fear Theo as much as I do. Let's give the boys the good news of our imminent departure."

He turns to watch his last boats, full of prisoners, disappear downriver.

The boss has called a commanders meeting and he's not happy. A few thousand troops pack the place.

"Why would the Alamanni not attack? It's been three days! There's no point in staying if they don't do what I want. Whatever they're building should be built by now. Tardy warriors should have arrived by now. Does electing a new leader take this long? If they don't attack us, then I want to attack them at night once our fleet finally returns."

"They're setting up something new," Franco suggests.

Magnus is on edge. "They could have built a rival fleet by now. What could they possibly be doing all this time? Where are their damn fighters? How am I supposed to wage war if they leave me in peace? What's wrong with these warriors?" They hear a trumpet from a gunboat and run to the nearest balconies. Ships sail up from downriver. "Our fleet has finally decided to pick us up. How generous of them. A little late is better than never. Guess you boys don't get to die with me after all. Give my love and my loot to your families. Remember what fun we had when bored to death in retirement or sentry duty. But where's my huge artillery trawler? I need those wicked weapons to do the heavy lifting ever since I hurt my back."

Franco shits himself. "Jesus, Mary, and Joseph! Those ships aren't ours. The Hanseatic League has joined the Alamanni!"

"Watch your language – there's a child present! Well, that complicates our escape. Boys, re-orient our biggest rooftop *ballistae* towards the river. Someone sound retreat so our gunboats evade upriver. Tonight will be the longest of our lives."

Franco is furious. "We're fucked! Max, you've killed us."

"Stop wetting yourself again, cousin. I'm probably a virgin, despite what Sasa says, so I haven't fucked anyone. Our fleet is a week late. How is that my fault? I said long ago that we'd leave once our ride arrives. Those ships can't hit us here. Cathedral Hill doesn't have room for us, anyways, so I say we make our last stand in this Cube."

Franco has a problem with that. "They'll burn us out and prevent us from reaching Drusus Island."

"Unless we piss them off. Boys, let's attack the 50,000 poorly armed hostiles crowding the riverbank, then retreat to the tower and hope they chase us up. Once enough Alamanni occupy this edifice, we'll burn them to Hell so I can visit them after my glorious death."

Instead, the troops argue, criticize, and complain bitterly. To get so rich, only to die before enjoying it, is a cruel fate. Magnus watches them, stunned by this betrayal. He's losing them and, with them, losing everything. He climbs a dinner table and roars defiantly at them. A lifetime of rage flies out like spittle and grabs their attention by the balls.

"You heroes are gonna piss yourselves now? You've killed over 100,000 Alamanni and the rest can't wait to die. You shit yourselves now that several ships show up? What happened to my boys? Where are the badasses that I talked to just moments ago? Those ships carry the same losers that we've been beating for weeks. We have the tallest tower in Europe, with the most artillery, darts, and javelins, plus the world's best arrows. I'm not fucking done! I'm not fucking dead! I'm not fucking defeated when more targets land. I'm gonna kill these bastards just like I killed the last 100,000."

He jumps down and pushes them back, madder than hell and flying high. "You rich bastards have nowhere to go. The river is too fast to swim to the island, which is already overcrowded. The forests are suicide since we killed everyone in them. Our gunboats can't carry 3000 men. To survive tonight, you must kill the fuckers who came here to kill you. You can either wait until their real warriors dock or we can surprise them now. Wanna live? Then tuck in your ballsack cuz we're gonna slaughter the strangers on the riverbank while their reinforcements watch helplessly from their ships. If you give up or give in, you're dead and someone else gets your gold. Those geniuses turned their backs to us to cheer real warriors who need time to land. To live, we must kill. If you want to see your family again, then man up because today will be the most exciting of your life. You'll be telling your grandkids about your heroics because we're gonna defeat and defy them again. Let's hit'em hard while they're helpless!"

The men are now pumped up and eager to fight. 2000 shooters jog down the ramp, then mass on the ground floor. Another thousand limp after them, picking up used ammo on the way. Most have white bandages on their arms or legs. Their fearless leader summarizes the situation and sees the doubt on their faces. Each carries four quivers of 30 arrows, which won't be enough.

"Let's not give them our ammo, so only shoot when you have a sure shot. The fools face the river to greet their reinforcements, so let's sodomize these assholes as painfully as possible like most Mondays. Form a skirmish line to cut off escape. I want the fastest runners to go the farthest. Retreat to the log tower only when they finally start winning, but carry our wounded with you. This is the moment you've trained for all your life. This is the fight you've dreamed of as a boy. This is when you finally measure up to your heroes. Gerontius Maximus watches. Let's make him proud. Or jealous. Why's my tuba man here? Pitsky, I need you on the roof, blowing attack, so the gunboats delay their landing and maybe sink some. Shit, just take a horse and ride as close as you can. Yell across the water to tell them what I want. We need more time and fewer enemies, so sink those ships."

A chubby Iberian with a brass tuba excitedly runs off to the pasture. The prodigy loudly does the math. "2000 archers with 60 arrows is 120,000. Limpers, we need to recover ammo, so bring wheelbarrows, sacks, and backpacks. I brought 1000 pellets, so we can kill them all without even bloodying our swords. Form two firing lines. Oh, I feel soooooooo alive! Franco, lead my 100 guards as a fast-response force. Let's work!"

With pessimistic faces, 2000 men silently jog out of the tower, then through the Armored Approach Vehicle/gate, towards burnt and busted dockside facilities. Franco pauses to look back at 1000 wounded troops limping along to scoop up bolts, arrows, and rocks. A few dozen wheelbarrows fill with stones for the trebuchet while a thousand desperate invaders fill quivers, bags, and backpacks. Those with leg injuries carry while those with other wounds run to recover things that will keep them alive.

Tens of thousands of Alamanni are still in Frankfurt, but all fighters have rushed to the river to receive reinforcements. Some non-fighters, scattered across outer Frankfurt, curse or threaten the foreigners, but most take their wounded, kids, and elderly to flee into the woods. Thousands escape under the canopy. Many Alamanni who stay shout warnings, but the cheering by the river drowns out their horrified screams. Once

127

behind 50,000 poorly armed enemies packing the riverbank, Team Magnus forms up and moves within arrow range. Hundreds of Alamanni yell warnings and thousands turn in shock. Many enemies didn't even bring weapons, but those that do instantly charge the skirmish line.

The rooftop catapults and trebuchets had never targeted this area before, so those artillery boys were pleasantly surprised to land rocks and bolts on the Alamanni mob. Strangers scream as they lose limbs and minds. A bolt spears a man almost in two. The artillery strike stuns most and paralyzes many, leaving too few to charge the invaders. The first Hanseatic League ships veers away to choose a safer dock, downriver. Catapults from the island also try hitting them, but come up short. Upriver, a brass tuba sounds, Attack! That makes enemies turn to look for a new threat, which buys Team Magnus a very valuable minute.

Standing shoulder-to-shoulder in two lines, Team Magnus opens fire with a vengeance. 2000 men occupy 1000 meters, so they're dangerously spread out and very vulnerable from behind. They target the fastest runners, except shieldmen, who are easier to kill with swords. Thousands of Alamanni fall as 2000 professionals shoot 15,000 arrows a minute at point blank range against enemies without metal armor. The closer they get, the deeper the arrows punch through thick furs into warm flesh. It's a spectacular slaughter that no one except Magnus imagined executing.

The Alamanni have some choices: attack, slide down the embankment to hide, swim downriver, run down the riverbank, do nothing, play dead, or flank the foreigners. Some of the unarmed cower or hide, but most armed fighters charge Team Magnus. If more held shields, they might have succeeded. The ambush unfolds beautifully if mass slaughter is art. Behind his lion helmet, the teen's expression lights up in ecstasy as he flings furiously. But then he notices a thousand or so smarter Alamanni run downriver, then circle to screw him from behind.

Magnus curses. "Fucking pederasts! They're flanking us. Guards, with me!"

100 men and a boy leave a 50-meter gap in the center of their skirmish line. The guards sprint, behind their comrades, to reach the flankers fast. Franco is the first to get a clean line-of-fire. That end of the skirmish line turns to face the new threat. Now it's a battle of time. Over a thousand Alamanni, mostly women and older men, sprint with dozens falling to arrows every heartbeat. As more of his guards get clear shots, the odds even, but many Alamanni behind shields are gonna make it. His guards still run to reinforce their skirmish line, which itself is backing up fast, so some legionaries bump into each other.

Then Magnus sprints through his left wing at full speed, right before the first enemies smash into them, and throws himself on a big shield held by an even bigger man. The boy bounces off because he's prepared, but the enemy gets fatally knocked on his ass. The angry orphan has his hands full of knives and begins throwing them while roaring like a lunatic. He's playing for keeps and has nothing to lose. His primal roar captures their attention and breaks their momentum. Hundreds see the fearsome demon-boy who utterly destroyed Germania's finest city and they slow down. Having exhausted his twelve throwing knives, Magnus attacks shieldmen from behind with two short swords and a longing sense of desperation. Even the Alamanni combat veterans clearly fear him and no wonder – he snarls like a beast. As the demon-boy distracts the enemy, his archers are shooting dozens every heartbeat. Several Alamanni crash into the Iberian left wing, but they are too few to engage so many. Some troops draw swords at the last moment and either dodge or brace themselves. Four go down, all knocked on their backs, but their neighbors cut up the Alamanni, who are all old, women, or weak because shooters prioritized young men.

Horrified, Franco sees Magnus dancing with the enemy, who turn to take him. His swords fly while he runs, ducks, and dives. He's giving ground like a coward because dozens try swarming him. The orphan cleverly lures these enemies away from his boys, which is fatal to them, but possibly also lethal to him. He likes to go low to slit legs, then lunge away to fuck over another fighter. But as more catch up, he's not retreating fast enough. Without throwing knives or space to use his sling, that virgin is screwed. Franco watches Magnus plunge a sword into a beefy mother who turns away in agony, taking his blade with her. Magnus loses his grip and, as the woman falls on his sword like Brutus the Backstabber, can't get it back. The terrible teen looks more than just scared. He's blocking blows with his last sword while searching for another moment of life. Three women with shields try corralling him, so Magnus goes low and cuts two calves before an unseen blow dents his helmet and crushes his dreams.

Franco is scared and sprinting in heavy armor. "Max!"

A fat man is bludgeoning him, so the desperate orphan trips him and jumps on top to jab his Adam's Apple. The two roll and several Alamanni beat the boy badly until arrows topple them. While throwing knives, Franco runs up and sees the man viciously punching the boy's balls even as Magnus tearfully smashes his head into the ground until the skull breaks open. Guards finish off their least wounded and then they watch their boss cry in a fetal position. Magnus has never known such pain. Tears fly, but he tries to hide it. He's curled up and unable to do anything but whimper pathetically.

Franco is unsympathetic and impatient. "Max, a blow to the balls is a tearjerker, but we've got to go. They're overwhelming us and we're already running out of arrows. Someone grab his knives and swords. Ah, nuts! They see him and now they're all coming here. Fuuuuuuuck! Max, I need to carry you. I'll walk as quick as I can, but don't piss on me again. You can thank me later, ya big baby."

Team Magnus retreats carefully with hundreds of dead and wounded, saving the last of their ammo for sure shots as they move from debris to rubble over horrifying wreckage. Not many Alamanni have bows and arrows, so they scavenge for whatever used ones they can find. Most natives wait for the ships to land real warriors, but those that pursue the legionaries get shot to hell. A thousand limping legionaries hurry to distribute arrows to retreating troops. A distant cheer goes up as rocks rain on the enemy and bolts blow a few holes in their formation. Franco drops Magnus like rotten fish. They look at the river and watch six gunboats with wind in their sails coming downriver in the center of the current for maximum speed. They pass the island, blow the tuba again, and go for the kill. Despite the pain, the orphan smiles as his gunboats attack.

Magnus uses a loud, commanding voice. "Recover ammo to fill our wheelbarrows. I want the best archers to have the most arrows because our gunboats are giving us a second chance to make a first impression. If you can't fight, retreat to the tower while picking up arrows on the way. Boys, let's shoot the newcomers as they pack the dock, rather than wait for them to kill us in the tower."

The troops thought they were done. The teen faces down those around him, his expression a challenge and a choice. Reluctantly, hundreds limp back with their remaining nerves, some pausing to snipe enemies in their way. Unarmed Alamanni are either ignored or chased because ammo is so limited. Several thousand besiegers wait for reinforcements on a dozen ships to land. Each ship probably has a thousand seasoned warriors, but just a third of them hold bows and most already exhausted their ammo against Team Theo or Julian. The weary warriors had a terrible few months that's visible in their exhausted postures. The first ship docks and mooring lines are quickly tied up to secure the vessel. Those on land welcome them vocally, tears of joy falling from their faces.

In contrast, the total destruction of Frankfurt has shocked these newcomers. That so few ruined so much so fast against so many boggles the mind and empties the anus. That's what Magnus sees as he studies them – empty anuses and fucking assholes. They stand stunned and, when the gangway is laid, they numbly stumble off, not liking what they're getting into. They heard it was bad, but seeing is not always believing.

Someone shouts a warning and everyone turns to see six small gunboats racing at the Hanseatic ships. No one in Europe has catapults on vessels except these bad boys. The Scorpions bolted to their bows wait to fire at point blank range to punch holes in the hulls at the waterline. The Alamanni archers shoot back, then watch their arrows fall into the current. Ger's sailors know how far the enemy can shoot and fire just beyond that before pivoting away. The three enemy ships farthest in the Main River get two holes each. The gunboats turn around to sail upriver for another attack run and now the Hanseatic ships are in a hurry to dump their passengers. There are not enough docks for them all, but the three with holes beach themselves to sink less. Hulls can be repaired above water, but soaked cargo is usually ruined.

Then someone else screams, this time in pain, and the natives by the docks are shocked to see invaders attacking them again. As one, the Germani turn away from the river to fuck the foreigners. The troops get relatively close to hit the new reinforcements, conveniently packed together like sardines on narrow wooden docks. A thousand badasses had hurried to leave the vulnerable ships, only for the intruders to saturate the docks they're standing on. Germani without bows and arrows evade by jumping into the shallow river while archers with ammo return fire. Team Franco is shooting and can't miss the mass of men. Few have shields and fewer defenders are in a position to shoot back because so many crowd the dock. The Alamanni reinforcements look and smell like sardines in a can. Franco, with the biggest bow in Frankfurt, targets their leaders. Ger's policy was the best archers get the best arrows, so Franco is fucking them up and knocking them down. With several times as many bowmen, Team Magnus is raining down hell. While the legionaries and Batavi are spread out to dodge incoming, the dock is a densely packed death trap.

The first Hanseatic ship captain chops the mooring lines to escape the gunboats. His livelihood depends on his ship. Sadly for him, the riverport is crowded. Set adrift, his ship bumps into another, rocking it side to side and tumbling the men on deck. That other ship is now no longer aligned with its dock and now must struggle in weak wind to moor itself to land its fighters.

Magnus introduces himself with a roar and several thousand angry Alamanni charge when they should have retreated downriver to get out of range. Roman and West Germani shooters decimate them. While most archers only carry 60 arrows, Magnus carries a pouch with 1000 pellets, so he's flinging like he has unlimited ammo. Having escaped hot water, fury boils the boy. Magnus looks like he can barely control his explosive emotions as his long sling twirls like helicopter blades above his head. His legs shake from the low blow to the balls and he bends forward as if it still hurts. The orphan switches arms as one palm runs out of lead balls. He's aiming for not just the nearest targets, but for their faces. His beautiful battle has turned ugly, and so has he. The teen grunts every time he tears open an Alamanni face and groans whenever he misses. He sees a nose disappear on a handsome woman in her 30s and a guy in his 40s loses an ear with part of his skull.

Some charging warriors get very close, but he dodges a few that die within reach and kicks a couple who move too much. Hitting someone running is not easy, but Magnus has trained intensely. So many bodies pile up, most still moving, that it slows the rest, giving the orphan more time to deface fewer enemies. An older man loses an eye and the next pellet shatters a hefty lady's jaw. All look at Magnus with absolute hatred and he seems to soak it up, as if anger energizes him. Arrows arc at him, but he keeps moving unpredictably to evade them. With greater range, his archers remain behind him but, as he advances, so must they. Hitting a head, instead of an upper torso, is best done within 100 meters. Most faces he destroys under 30 meters. Any closer and he'd be within blood-splatter range. As the enemy runs out of steam, the terrible orphan advances to hit the rest.

The gunboats punch holes in two more ships, forcing them to beach themselves because they'd sink too much at the docks. Cheers go up from everyone on the island. The back half of the Hanseatic fleet turns to escape because ships are expensive. They take several thousand warriors with them. Legionaries laugh at them leaving because Magnus wins another round in a weird war.

Franco yells over the screaming. "Max, hostiles are circling behind us. Dutch hasn't resupplied us yet and we're almost empty."

The orphan lets a big burly badass get reaaaaal close before transforming his head into fleshy bone fragments. Headless, the Alamanni falls like a tree with a thud. Magnus checks the sky for incoming, then turns.

"You want our gunboats to drown them or to let them land to burn us in our tower? I don't like fair fights; that's why most of you are still alive. We have nowhere to go, but we have time to kill. It must be embarrassing for a boy to have bigger balls, but contesting their landing is smart tactics. Tell me I'm wrong." He stares them down and sees them nod at his logic. "When I'm wrong, tell me. When I'm right, do as I fucking say. Let's finish these fucks and then move on to the next. The more we kill now, the fewer we face later. That is how we survive. Letting them all land is a recipe for roasted Romans."

Unable to counter so many bowmen, the Germani flee downriver.

131

CHAPTER 6

Standing behind an easel, Magnus draws his troops for posterity while sharing the sad news. His innocent baby faces peaks over the canvass intermittently.

"Boys, I hate to shock you, but we're low on ammo. The enemy fleet must have blocked ours. Our gunboats are transferring our dead and wounded to Drusus Island, along with our heavy *ballistae*, though they're a bigger bitch to move than my daddy. Everyone staying should wear extra chainmail tunics. Though it's already tight, I'd like our worst archers to also move there so we can leave this tower that much faster. We don't have projectiles for half as many troops, so we may as well reduce our troop strength to our level of ammo. I have another reason for sending so many of you from the pleasure of my pleasant presence. The enemy has multiplied again and surrounds our neighborhood. Knowing they can't starve us out, their only alternative is to burn us out. We've all seen them collect combustibles in carts and wagons. But what if they see us ship out half our strength? If we look vulnerable enough, they'd be tempted to take us. At least 60,000 of them are armed, though few have bows and fewer have arrows. Sadly, they know we're also out because we foolishly left them in so many corpses. We brought two million arrows here and that wasn't nearly enough. I blame my father."

The orphan stifles a sniffle as if crying. "Boys, I know you all want to fight alongside me to the death, but most of you must leave for the rest to retreat in time. The Batavi have been building barges, but I doubt even a thousand of us can escape in those and the gunboats combined. I've ordered logs from their palisade stockpiled on our sliver of riverbank because I'm pessimistic even when not suicidal. If worse comes to worse, use a log to escape downriver. Our vessels limit how many can stay. Assuming we take horrific casualties, just 1000 able-bodied men can stay with me to defy all of Alamannia. The good news is those who stay with me, to lure those fools into this furnace, will earn a triple bonus, unlike the 300 Spartans at Thermopylae. I'll insist on everyone writing their name so you or your family gets paid for being thrice the hero as the pussies who quit on me in my moment of need. No pressure."

"Max, if you leave, then they might leave us alone," Franco suggests.

"After beating everyone for a few centuries, you think Alamanni will take dying lying down? They have at least 60,000 warriors and another 100,000 armed and angry women, elderly, and big boys seeking revenge. They'll go after Joko. The Hanseatic League might drop off an Alamanni army at Porto Gordo. Luca said they'd hunt me down. Cousin, can you live with yourself if they assassinate me? The more Alamanni we kill, the safer we'll be. Besides, we put a lot of wood on the 2nd floor. I don't know if this log structure will burn completely down, but I'd like to see. I have a deep hole to ride it out and I even made a clamp to hook my rope so I don't fall to my death again. I didn't come here to fart around; I go to Porto Gordo for that. I'm here to fix a problem and profit off the solution, then see Julian's face when I force him to cough up coin. I'll give you until tomorrow to decide, but I assume the boys with the biggest cocks will stay with me in a non-sexual way."

Franco later meets his odd nephew alone. The boy looks up and sighs sadly.

"Do any troops want to stay?"

"Max, some feel obligated. You've done much better than anyone expected. I doubt your dad could have done half as well. You saved us several times. I sure missed some things, despite all my experience. I must stay because Theo told me to not let you die. A few hundred will stay if I remain."

"Franco, you can't stay. I need you to lead the legionaries from the island to surprise the enemy when they try rescuing those burning in the tower. Besides, if it's my fault you die, then Baby Frankito probably won't hug me anymore."

Franco huffs unhappily. "You're just sending me away to not feel guilty for my death. You're a sneaky little shit. I gotta stop seeing a 10-year-old when I look at you. Max, you've always been a step ahead of me. What are you planning now?"

"I didn't exactly send warriors away. Instead, I asked them to rotate duty. Most will stay safe on the island until the last night, when things get hairier than a Saxon whore. Imagine a thousand Batavi infiltrators overwhelming enemy camps at night in the woods when their fighters are burning alive in this tower. The Alamanni won't know which men to trust. Each man who fights with me will earn ten gold coins if Julian actually pays up, which I doubt. They all served my father in that last battle under Julian, so Dutch told them to keep me alive. I can count on strangers more than family. That's just the world I live in. I'll take whatever Iberians will stay, but only if they insist. I don't want quitters or complainers. The Batavi came here because the Alamanni forced them from their homeland five centuries ago. They served Caesar because they were too few to stand on their own. Caesar granting them the northern riverbank of the lower Rhine was a gift from God before Christianity became a thing. But they haven't forgotten who took their homeland. Like me, the Batavi are here to avenge themselves on the Alamanni.

"Julian told dad to get a thousand Batavi warriors, but 4000 volunteered without pay to risk their lives to avenge an ancient insult. But that was west of the Rhine. When dad prepared to invade Alamannia proper, east of the river, 8000 Batavi offered him their service. He didn't even have to pay them. Like other West Germani, they need loot to justify leaving their families for so long, but I settled up with Dutch before I sent him away. Those who remained agreed to fuck'em in the forest whenever this tower lights up. Franco, can you imagine a few thousand bearded bastards surprising a hundred thousand unarmed Alamanni in the forest? Once they get mixed together, it'll be bloody chaos until leaders can sort that shit out at daybreak. Meanwhile, you'll hit outer Frankfurt from Drusus Island when their fighters surround my burning tower. You'll hit unarmed non-fighters from their blind spot and leave before real warriors can counter you. Cousin, that's just a fun stroll through a terrifying park."

Franco gets angry. "You made a deal with the Batavi two weeks ago and didn't tell me? Why?"

"I wanted to see if I could convince you to stay for the final fight. I would have tripled your bonus if you agreed. Instead you said you'd stay because Theo expected you to. You have a wife, kids, a mistress, and some bastards to take care of, so I understand. Just lead our troops from the island to fuck the Alamanni in the ass. Don't do it for me, but for my dad. The barges are really a pontoon bridge; troops from the island will walk across several barges to surprise the enemy. Cousin, can I count on you like an abacus?"

"Theo is my boss."

"But I pay better. Franco, I'm not gonna beg. I need a clear answer and I need it now. The more Alamanni that die, the safer Gaul will be. Will you lead troops into outer Frankfurt to slay unarmed enemies?"

"I'd rather keep you alive."

133

Visibly frustrated. "Sweet Jesus, Franco! Any denser and you'd shrivel. Must I spell it out? I don't want you in the tower because you're old, slow, and weak. When I tell the Batavi to take the rope to the dock, they will fly away. You'd argue because that's your nature or insist I go first. But I'm not going. Depending on how things fall, most Batavi will dress as Alamanni and kill enemy archers in the dark again. Hence, all the smelly bear coats. I'll either join them or hide in my hole, but I'm not going to the island. I've got business with my mama's murderers. I'm still pissed and angry at her death because I can't stop loving her. With luck, you'll see me slinging the clueless after I've roasted thousands of Alamanni warriors. The stench will be epic. I have a plan that requires you to leave the safety of the island to ambush our besiegers. Alamanni raiders rape, kill, or kidnap our women and kids, so justice requires what they've done to others be done to them. An eye for an eye. You'll have total surprise and face few fighters. So, again, can I count on you?"

The orphan seems super upset and unusually aggravated.

"Max, of course you can count on me."

Exasperated, the prodigy tries pulling out his short hair while screaming. "Beloved cousin, if that were true, I would not need to repeat myself! If things go to plan, then we'll control Frankfurt after Alamannia has thrown its best at us. I asked Luca to bring Julian to see the bodies for himself. We're looking at a huge score. You can make it bigger. Stop worrying about Theodosius the Great. I'm making you absurdly rich. You should treat me as such."

"Julian will never pay out so much gold."

The boy pretends to scream to the heavens. His entire body sheds tears. "Why do you think I want Luca to bring Julian here? Where several thousand armed men can detain him until he pays up? We won't let Julian leave until he makes good on his written promise of payment. Romans are the world's most litigious people. Rome has more men in its courts than in its whorehouses; yes, I once checked. Julian's officers witnessed him swearing on all he holds holy. They won't follow someone who breaks their most solemn oath. Luca will also track his treasure chest because Julian separately owes him quite a bit of bullion. Franco, you once said your highest ambition is that your children don't suffer poverty like you did. I'm offering you that. Now look me in the eye and convince me I can count on you. Shake my hand and swear on it because if you fail me, I'll come back from the grave again, just to complain to your wonderful mother."

The cousins shake, then share a comfortable moment of silence as the scale of their task sinks in like a grappling hook.

The boy pulls his palm away. "Why do men shake with the hand they masturbate with? I gotta wash up."

Franco finally commits. "Unless it gets too crazy, I'll lead the men on the island into Frankfurt. I swear it. Max, why do you try roaring like a lion? It sounds scary and absurd."

"In Rome I saw a huge male roar at a tourist who pissed himself in fear. Ever since, I wanted to emulate that. I hear tigers from India are a third larger, but I didn't see a tiger; I saw a beautiful, powerful lion that dominated others. In my next life, I'm coming back as a lion."

Massive numbers of armed Alamanni gather around the outer wall. They have divided themselves into three groups that run through the three gates like water through rock. The last defenders rain down hell at the enormous army coming to kill them. Over half are murderous women who lost husbands, fathers, and sons, but the elderly spearpoint the attack to absorb and exhaust enemy ammo. Locals have grown in number, power, and impatience. They hold a wide variety of weapons, including farm implements. The largest catapults and trebuchet were too difficult to move from the roof, so teams of Batavi send bolts and rocks at the enemy. Batavi bowmen on high balconies fire arrows at the rivers of belligerents, targeting the most worrisome. The orphan naturally roars defiantly and the enemy impatiently can't wait to kill him.

Magnus points. "Here they come – finally! I thought they'd wait until night, but they apparently want to hurt my feelings. They brought pitchforks, but no lit torches. It looks like we're gonna enjoy the stand-up fight we've always wanted until now. Let's throw the kitchen sink at them, then leave them burning in hell – or wherever we are. Positions, everyone, and don't forget to stuff your nostrils. I have unlimited ammo, so I'll begin the festivities. Archers, stay two floors above me unless I fail or fall. Oh, shit, this will be amazing!" He turns to smile at his brave boys. "The Dance of the Lion begins."

With leather gloves on, Magnus slides down a rope to the 3rd floor where the twenty biggest Batavi hold Joko's iron shields. These are heavy, but they'll rotate, with a third resting behind the boy with the doctors, stretchers, and medics. Behind them, the twenty best archers are also wrapped in several layers of armor, including chainmail chaps. All wear thick bear coats, so they resemble bloody bloated beavers.

The troops look doubtfully at their small, big-mouthed boss as he lands in a roll and comes up laughing. The stench of rotting corpses overwhelms Magnus and completely surpasses all the pee and poo that Team Magnus have pumped and dumped here since their arrival. He staggers to the railing, desperately searching for his cotton nose plugs with clumsy gloves. He finds he must take them off to find the tiny cotton balls in his big pocket. Crying with eyes closed, he blocks his nostrils, then splashes perfume over himself like normal soldiers about to face 100,000 hostiles. His shieldmen grunt hard, so he sprays them as well since he stole lots of perfume from the vault. They look absurd with bright-white cotton sticking out of their noses, like pale boogers. Magnus shakes his head to clear his senses, but the stench lingers in his mind and his mood. No bodies rot on the ramp and the blood has dried long ago, but it's now more red than white.

Laughing. "Next time we shit ourselves, no one will know!"

Magnus looks over the railing and almost vomits. Thousands of long-dead bodies completely cover the kickass marble tile. The half-rotten flesh is absolutely disgusting. Dogs, rats, bugs, and birds scavenge them in a fucking orgy doubling as a fantastic feast. They all eat meat like it's wonderful, tasty, and free. Dogs rip open human faces with growls and gusto. Team Magnus piled the corpses like waves of deep ditches and big berms to force the enemy to climb over their tribesmen to reach the ramp. It's disgusting, brutal, and effective. Up the ramp are their relief, two squads each. A few floors up sits another unit waiting to rescue them. Sixty men and a boy block the ramp while the rest of the Batavi circle the 6th, 8th, and 10th floor railings, packed with everything lethal from the entire skyscraper, including several kitchen sinks. On all upper floors, tons of furniture and furnishings join piles of rocks, bricks, and vases filled with earth.

135

"Boys, the first enemies with bows are not their real archers, but their expendables. Prioritize men who actually shoot. They know we're low on arrows, darts, and javelins, but want us to waste our ammo on non-fighters. I expect lots of old and ill Alamanni. Many Alamanni prefer dying here in battle than dying this winter of starvation. I find that selfish, for some reason. Our prisoners filled over a million urns, vases, bottles, bags, bowls, buckets, sacks, and clay pots with dirt, so let's fight dirty. We have every potted plant from Frankfurt and my Uncle Honorius brought thousands of pots, sacks, and bags that are now full. We also have a million rocks, blocks, and mud bricks, plus massive logs the length of my cock. The inner balconies of the upper floors are piled with things for us to drop on them. While we don't have a million arrows, our innovative artillery is still dangerous. Their hatred of me will be the death of them!"

His boys cheer, but don't sound optimistic. Magnus can hear shooters on outside balconies fire down into a river of enemies. The yells of 100,000 deadly attackers drown out the deadly silence. He looks up in the open-air atrium. The interior crane has hoisted a shitty tarp over the center of the open area.

"I want to see their faces when we shit on them! May the better engineer win!"

The orphan grins like it's an ace up his sleeve as his boys laugh loudly while looking up at the tarp.

The enemy pour in through three hallways. Hard Alamanni faces go soft as soon as they sniff a whiff of the decaying corpses. The smell of the above-ground cemetery overwhelms and overcomes them. Some burst into tears while others collapse in horror as the world's worst mortuary comes to life. Expressions blanch and bladders empty. Add sulfur and brimstone and this is what Hell must smell like if Satan never bathes. The dogs, rats, bugs, and birds scatter, quite pissed at the interruption. A German Shepard sniffs a fresh turd and only reluctantly runs away. The shit show begins with a full audience awaiting an encore.

Magnus begins slinging at archers as soon as he sees them. Averaging 20 pellets a minute, he can theoretically hit 1000 bodies an hour until he tires. His archers only have several thousand good arrows and thrice as many shoddy ones that might work at close range. Just a few hundred darts and javelins are left. 100 defenders pour fire into the mass of men on the ground floor. Team Magnus targets Alamanni bowmen. Some arrows fly at him, but Magnus keeps moving, trusting his iron plates between three layers of chainmail, plus a thick bear coat over that. Shieldmen block most arrows, which the Batavi archers then re-use. The old folks hold up shields, pans, and planks, so the killer kid strikes the vulnerable as he backs up the ramp.

All too soon, Team 1 has retreated a floor, giving the enemy a false whiff of victory. He's hitting someone every pellet, but they are too many and too motivated. Magnus hears legs break and shins shatter. Heads explode and metal balls tear off cheeks. The screams are constant, disturbing, and higher than the heavens. Despite moving a lot, arrows hit Magnus, but they've lost force after soaring to the 5th floor. He just grunts and carries on. His chainmail chaps around his legs hurt more than usual, but Magnus looks down and sees he's not bleeding badly yet. Some of his shieldmen and bowmen are down; wounded troopers, acting as medics, carry or drag them to safety. Magnus makes the most of every moment because he expects to die today.

The enemy starts with a lot of archers, but most aren't very good. Defenders see the fear on the faces of their replacements. The other Alamanni expect to die, so they just look gloomy as they walk up the ramp to their doom. On the 5th floor, 20 Batavi with shields and swords run down as they recently trained. Magnus and his shieldmen lean against a railing to get out of their way. In two rows of ten, their shield wall smashes into old enemies and the front half keeps going. The back half slow to stab as they walk over the wounded. None give Magnus the time of day, but then, watches won't be invented for a few decades. Team 1 follows to finish off injured enemies and carry back their own. The Batavi stop the slaughter as they near the ground floor, then back up in a hurry, holding their shields to block arrows. The prodigy sees bent, broken, and bleeding bodies on the lower ramp and summarizes the slaughter.

"Their dregs are consuming our ammo. Killing grandmas isn't as satisfying as I dreamed. Boys, chew on some jerky and drink some water before the real warriors attack us. If ya gotta pee, now's the time."

The orphan digs out his penis to urinate through the railing, upon hostiles below him. Cheering, many troops join the fun. The next assault has younger fighters, but similar results. This time, the Batavi throw lethal obstacles from the upper floors onto enemies on the ramp or packing the ground floor. Thousands of pots, sacks, and clay vases hurt heads and lacerates limbs. That harms far more than it kills, but even a broken bone is lethal now.

"Rotate teams!" the teen yells. Team 2 replaces Team 1 while Team 1 takes Team 3's old position up the ramp. The reserve replaces a dozen wounded. "Eat lunch before the third wave comes."

Around noon, the third assault pushes Team Magnus floor by floor. The Batavi counter-attack with shields at full speed, but they're tired compared to their fresh attackers. Bleeding bodies and debris litter the ramp, making it hard to sprint. Hurting just about everywhere, the boy freaks out. Injured troopers on the upper floors rain down jars, sacks, bags, and clay pots onto enemies. Most just blindly toss items onto the ramp while others throw at specific targets. Teams of two lift furniture to fall onto the lower ramp. Potted plants smack skulls while bags of earth collapse craniums. Those who hold shields over their heads get shot in the chest. Rocks and mud brick fracture faces, smash shoulders, and knock enemies the fuck out. Sofas, chairs, and tables crash and crumble when impacting Germani. Another sink conks a cranium and that bitch drops like a rock. Yet still they come, undaunted.

The terrified teen is desperate and afraid. "Darts and javelins! Whatever we have left! Do we still have toilets?"

The heavier projectiles strike the strongest Alamanni and break their momentum. Team 1 tries plowing over several thousand Alamanni on the ramp and runs out of steam half-way down. Only an infusion of arrows enables them to disengage from furious natives with an ax to grind. The Alamanni almost succeed despite having almost no archers or arrows left. Watching his reserves knock down fleeing fools, Magnus clutches his aching arms and almost cries again from the pain. The combat ends, but neither side has won. The Germani leave, dragging the least wounded with them.

Magnus barks loudly. "Finish eating before they organize another! We need another two teams in order to last until dark. Damn, I'm down to just a million pellets. How is it that no one else slings?"

The tuba guy on the roof blows his top. Sighing again, Magnus jogs up the ramp to see what's up. He looks down at a new enemy fleet, this one composed of small

137

gunboats, each with a catapult on the bow. Behind them sail the same Hanseatic League ships loaded with reinforcements. Appalled, the brutal boy breaks down and almost melts on the spot.

The hero fears failure. "Ah, fuck me! Really? But I was doing so well..."

Commanders, leaders, and veterans join him to see the fleet land thousands of young warriors with real weapons. His gunboats position themselves, but Magnus has the tuba guy blow retreat, so the hostile flotilla dock at the island unopposed. The orphan turns to his troops, suddenly depressed.

Lars gives them all the bad news: "Those are Bavarians from downriver. The three kingly brothers married into elite families. Many of those last archers were probably half-Bavarian. The Alamanni probably offered them control of Frankfurt for their help."

Everyone on the roof collectively groans in despair, but none as hard as their boy-leader, who turns away. With both hands on the railing so others can't see him weep, Magnus implodes psychologically. He can't take any more. His boys have only curses to hurl. They've hit rock bottom and don't have a pile driver to go down any farther. Magnus goes through the Stages of Grief as he realizes he failed, after all. Anger, defiance, and pleading give away to acceptance as our hero deflates in size, strength, and stature. His eyes, face, and body language transform as he looks failure in the face like a merciless mirror. Troops hear him whisper something to his mama, then he visibly pulls his shit together and fortifies his posture before turning around to face his friends.

Magnus puts on a false front. "Those pederasts plan to fuck a 10-year-old? Well, at least I won't die a virgin. Boys, after you move our heavy chairs to the 6th floor, I release you from your vows of chastity and charity. Transfer our dead and wounded to Drusus Island and, if there's time and room, please join them. Anyone stuck with me will die in good company. I plan to burn this bitch to the ground and then hide in my hole or disguise myself until caught. I thank you heroes for giving a bad boy such a good time. I couldn't have asked for a better or sooner death. Life is precious, but lives are cheap. When you get to Heaven, please yell down to let me know you're eternally bored. Now, if you'll excuse me, I need to finish sabotaging the lower ramp. Tribune Piso taught me what to do."

The remaining men silently watch him go, knowing he'll die soon. They look like total badasses, but all get sad and some openly weep.

Lars breaks the deadly silence. "I'm spending the rest of my life here, but not for the boy. I welcome anyone able. It's been an honor to serve with real warriors. Our ancestors would be shocked and ecstatic at our success. I'd say we've avenged them, but I'm still angry. I don't want to die angry, so I'll unload my remaining bitterness on these Bavarians. Life is cheap, but I plan to die expensive. I might take 100 enemies before I go. This is my goodbye. Don't bother me with further farewells because I need to focus on my last hours on Earth."

The men mumble among themselves.

On the roof, Lars roughly kicks the orphan awake. "Max, it's almost dawn and a lot more enemies have come to kill you. The number of good warriors has doubled in just a few days, so you are very unpopular, for some reason. They're moving into position, but we only have a few hundred men. The enemy saw most of our troops leave, so they know how few we are. I tire of their insults and am dying to kill them. I don't understand

138

why they didn't attack last night or even yesterday. Sleep well?"

Not sure how he feels. "I slept like the dead. Lars, why are you still here?"

"I lost my son in a raid, so I joined your father because he wanted to fight. My only son would have been your age, though twice as cute and half as loud. I like you because you want to fight to the death, like me."

"Not me. I just want to make the world a safer place while I vent my anger on those who took my favorite parent. But, hey, close enough. Oh, and I want to surpass my dad. Does that make me a bad boy? Because I'm pretty sure I'm a bad boy."

Lars doesn't care. "How many enemies do you think we'll take down with us?"

"As many as we trap in the tower before we burn it. Thousands, hopefully. If Franco keeps his word, then we'll also surprise the rest. The Batavi will fuck them in the forest. Have you heard any fighting?"

"Max, I slept for the last time, so I don't know. Our remaining men are gearing up to repeat yesterday in case there's no tomorrow. Max, I've enjoyed serving with you. Gerontius would be proud."

Shaking his head scornfully. "He'd be pissed. He never liked me excelling at anything except silence, but he was an odd man who loved getting even. Mom once had to pass for a man to fool bandits. Dad later got mad because he wanted her to look good, but not better. If she had a cock, I think he would have sucked it dry. If all fairness, mom was the hottest man I've ever seen."

"Max, you are deeply disturbed and probably crazy. You make inappropriate sex jokes when frightened, so you must be scared to death. You make your father sound like a brute for beating you, but I understand him; if my son talked like you, I would also have beaten him."

"Dad wasn't trying to punish me; he wanted to change me and I didn't want to change. You think I'm not aware of my flaws? Everyone reminds me of them daily. Mama often told me that she wished I was more like my father, but I think that was the problem – I inherited his good looks and bad attitude. Dad saw himself in me and desperately tried to turn me into his brother. Why couldn't my parents accept me as I am? Lars, you would not have beaten your boy if he talked like me. You would have talked to him instead to figure out why he's weird. No one's normal and everyone is odd. Dad never tried understanding me and I've never understood why. I bet you loved your son too much to ever beat him. Tell me I'm wrong."

The Batavi meets those bright blue eyes until he loudly exhales in defeat. "I had the best son ever, so I never raised my voice to him, much less my hand. He gave hugs worth killing for. No one has ever loved anyone like my son loved me. Fathers should not hit kids unless they are disrespectful or disobedient, but don't act surprised that your father hurt you. You're a wicked kid designed to rub folks raw. You should have held your tongue and behaved as he asked until old enough to leave home or defend yourself. Ger hardly ever would have hit you if you kept quiet and followed orders like any other trooper. You'd rather be beaten than ignored. Tell me I'm wrong."

His orphan's eyes glaze over as he looks into his past and blanches at his future. "That bastard abused me! You saying I should apologize to my tormentor?"

"If you could bring your dad back, would you?" The boy's mind fights with itself, which makes his cheeks twitch and his eyes blink. "Yeah. Thought so. Whatever evil Gerontius Maximus did in life, he paid in full by dying young, so you should stop being angry with him. You sad, angry boy, please stop making me look forward to death. I deserve better for my final day. For centuries, the Alamanni have had a policy of kidnapping young women and children to turn them into Alamanni. By killing their men, you have crippled their ability to kidnap. For that I thank you. The Bavarians joined our enemy to assimilate their women without husbands and their children without fathers. That is both good and bad. The Gepids, Marcomanni, and Burgundians will retake territory and raid the Alamanni while they're weak. The Alamanni will recover, but their boys need a decade to grow into warriors. By massacring so many, you've done a great thing. You reduced misery for tens of thousands."

The boy is livid. "You couldn't say that with troops around? I live for public applause, in case I didn't privately make that clear. Kissing my ass only works in public. I thank you for thanking me, but please praise me in public from now on." He looks over the edge of the roof to a ground entrance. "They haven't moved the carts that we left to block the exits. I hope those fools don't wise up." He tests the thick rope. "That's a long drop. I hope you don't sprain an ankle when landing. Are the other two volunteers equally suicidal?"

The Batavi grins. "I know them well. We are all highly motivated to burn Alamanni and Bavarians to death. A fluent friend has been teaching us useful phrases in East German. I look forward to learning how well I learned them."

"I memorized a list of 100 insults. I'm just glad they didn't attack last night. My hands still hurt like I masturbated all day. Now that I face death, I have so many questions. Hey, I knew a girl who smelled like tuna, yet tasted like chicken. Is that normal? Did you ever look at your wife and wonder if you could do better? Because that's how my dick looks at me." The suicidal stranger laughs. "Troops have told me thousands of jokes."

Lars likes the boy. "You truly do not fear death."

"Oh, I look forward to death. Dying, no. Dying is often painful, but death is a release from pain. I'm not scared of death; it's life that I fear. I don't want to spend the next ten years as miserable as the last ten. Death isn't a problem; it's a solution."

"Goodbye, Max."

The sun peaks over the eastern horizon and thousands of enemies across Frankfurt sing Happy Birthday. Looking over the railing, they're both confused until Magnus puts 1 and 10 together.

Shocked. "Those bastards know it's my birthday! How dare they?"

"Happy birthday, Max."

Furious. "Oh, fuck that! They planned their big push for my birthday. That's why they waited! I hate patient enemies! Serapio is telling me he's behind it all. He wants me to know he lives when I die. He must hold a grudge, just because I killed his parents and children. Well, that's just typical of barbarians. I need to survive so I can kill him, but good this time. Last time I wasn't bad enough. Man, mercy bites me in the ass every time, which would explain the butt-cheek scars. Wait! I'm 11 years old? Are you sure? I never thought I'd live so long. I wonder what I could do with another 11. Well, too late to start dreaming now. I should roar. I haven't roared since I was 10."

"Live it up while you can. I'm gonna trigger the trebuchet."

"All righty. I'm gonna throw away pellets until my fingers freeze when I need them most."

With white cotton in his nostrils, Magnus slides down a rope to the 6th floor. He looks over the rail and sees the enemy on the ground floor, filling it up for a mass charge. The piles of bodies are taller and wider now, with more dogs and rats until Bavarians shoe them off with their boots. Thousands of stinking bodies and thousands of pieces of debris cover the ramp, making walking difficult and running impossible. Broken chairs, tables, vases, rocks, and bricks completely cover corpses. Magnus jogs up to barriers that block off the wooden ramp. The Cube's biggest and heaviest furniture present rows of tall obstacles between the 5th and 6th floors, with many sofas and oak bedframes. These have been nailed and screwed to stay in place, with ropes and chains to frustrate attackers. The enemy will need axes, saws, and patience to get past them, though the nimble can climb over.

The birthday boy looks up from his chest-high inner barrier to see twenty Batavi troops sitting on wide-backed chairs, facing forward, on the 6th, 8th, and 10th floors, plus four doctors and medics, dressed in white with red crosses. Each group has a water barrel, freshly baked bread, and various edibles on a clean table. The half holding shields either limp or have odd injuries. All have bandages under the triple sets of chainmail that covers their iron plates. Their facial expressions suggest they don't plan to survive. Magnus sees it, too. Before they put on their helmets, their boy-boss marches up to them as if inflamed. If matches existed outside China, just one could detonate him.

Magnus addresses his troops for the last time. "I wish you badasses could see yourselves in the mirror, wearing bear-coat pajamas. Your fathers would be so proud. My dad watches us from Heaven, pissing himself in envy. I've never seen anything more beautiful than you ugly heroes. If you haven't noticed, my micro-penis is rock hard. I have an honest face, but my cock is a damn liar. Just 200 men defying 100,000! They'll make theatrical plays like they did for the 300 Spartans at Thermopylae, who actually had 6000 troops – that's why I personally wrote all your names on a list. The heroes of Frankfurt! You're all going down in history and, more importantly, so am I. You warriors are making the Rhineland safer, though I find it funny that they name land after a river. Every Alamanni you slay is a woman not raped and kids not kidnapped, which makes you heroes. I thank you for staying with me. I know you have your own selfish reasons, but I love you despite your fatal flaws because true love accepts people as they are – or so I told my parents. Well, I've never been loved, except by my horse and a puppy named Maximo, but poetry says it's wonderful, everlasting, and unnaturally sexual. Every love is unique. What I feel for you will never see this world again unless reincarnation is a thing. For those of you making mental notes, I'm not crazy; I just miss my mama and I might massacre her murderers.

"Remember the Plan. We thin them out until we can't anymore. Then we escape into the vault, down our ropes to the docks, or into our hiding places until this bitch burns. Unless you see me inert or headless, don't worry about me. I've got enough plans to fill an itinerary. If you hear a lunatic laughing, it's either me or my killer. If you hear a lion roar, it's probably a lion. I'd talk longer and louder, but the enemy is impatient and you boys are drowning in more expensive perfume than my cotton balls and nut sack can tolerate. Oh, live or die, your families are getting a huge bonus because you chose me over the island. That was so flattering that I nearly undressed. I'm sorry, but I'll never apologize for silly sentences. If you never see me again, you're welcome."

141

Magnus puts his helmet on and his troops do the same. But then they lay heavy planks across rows of chairs to enjoy breastworks. This protects their lower bodies from flying projectiles. Team Magnus has not just nailed planks against the inner railing to protect their legs, but raised planks above and behind them to collect enemy ammo. Though chest high, the shieldmen rest their shields on the chairs, giving archers narrow openings to shoot through, like crenellations. As they stand to pee, drink, or eat the last loaf, nine huge chairs are nailed together, with just enough room for one person to pass along the inner railing. The next row of chairs allows only enough space for a single guy at the outer railing. Very big chairs and couches have been placed on the ramp between the 6th and 7th floors to slow the enemy.

Angry enemies fill the ground floor with new archers and the game resumes. Each attacker has a shieldman who looks surprised by dozens of catapults on the upper ramp pointing down at ugly angles. The Batavi fire iron-tipped bolts that could pass as spears. The first volley smashes into shieldmen with enough force to throw them back onto others. Shock deforms Bavarian faces as they lose limbs, heads, and minds. Those indifferent to life are the first up the ramp, holding shields or their equivalent. A line of thousands carefully navigate the corpses and rubble as they scramble up past a corridor of corpses. The attacking Bavarians have more archers than the defending Batavi. Their arrows can reach the 6th floor, but lose half their strength, unlike arrows flying down, which pick up speed to penetrate deeper. Batavi shields block the death-blows. While Magnus flings his unlimited pellets, most of his men actually sit, with the back of their chairs in front, while waiting for work. Some even lay down to avoid arrows. Hundreds of arrows stick to the planks above them and even more bounce off to be recovered quickly. Tall vases hold arrows upright for easy access. The Batavi bowmen want to wait until closer enemies give them easier shots at more dangerous targets. Instead of the nearest, Magnus targets those on the spiral ramp who show him their backs. The ramp circles around a few hundred paces, so he has plenty of vulnerable targets. He doesn't need to kill them to kill them; almost any debilitating injury will do. Magnus aims for limbs and heads because many layers of clothing protect their upper bodies. He is so much higher that there's little they can do to him. Once the enemy is across from them, his archers open up at close range. Many Alamanni hold shielding, but many more do not because stomping up six flights of gentle ramp takes a while, exhausting their arms.

But eventually the Alamanni bump into the first fortification. Some brought tools, but too many hammers and not enough hatchets. Ironically, Bavarians stuck across from the Batavi get hammered by projectiles. Leaders yell down for the tools they need, plus archers for cover, but that delay kills another hour. Bavarian bowmen then face Batavi bowmen and both must recycle arrows. Most Bavarians have smaller bows for hunting in dense forest, while the Batavi enjoy three layers of metal armor sandwiched between boiled leather. As they suffer wounds, usually to a limb, troops from the 10th floor replace them. A few get knocked out from arrows hitting helmets, but few die right away, despite thousands of arrows sent at them. It must infuriate the enemy to lose thousands of fighters to just 100 or so shooters.

The teen turns to cock his head to hear *ballistae* on the roof hurl rocks and bricks at those outside and glimpse shooters on the outside balcony sniping strangers. A familiar voice screams on the balcony, holding up half an arm, but Magnus can't help him. He can't help anyone anymore. The second barrier takes half as long to break through, but the Bavarians lose many of their remaining archers. They trade shots, but the Batavi are better shielded, higher up, and can recover more ammo thanks to the high plank wall behind them. A dozen light catapults between the 8th and 10th floors hurtle spears and their equivalent. A few have broken down and no bolts have metal tips, but they still knock down and fuck up enemy archers on the 5th floor. Limpers dump more pieces of sharpened wood that the lumber mill made weeks ago. Teams concentrate as they bark orders and move away from the recoil. The more time they have, the more Bavarians they take out.

Thousands of Alamanni, mostly women and older men, crowd the homes and the inner balcony on the 5th floor. Most rest and all stay away from the railing to deny Batavi a clear line-of-sight. Few look like fighters and most seem exhausted by this ordeal. Once others break or breach the barriers, they'll flood the ramp and overwhelm foreigners. Magnus continues slinging but, even rotating arms, he's in a world of pain. He strikes the easiest targets, which are often the closest. Pellets explode heads and bullets sink deep into chests, limbs, and last hopes.

Talking to himself again. "Giving my muscles the day off, yesterday, was a fatal mistake."

Magnus whirls his sling over his head for power, so his personal shieldmen maintain a safe distance in front of him. He tells them to move left or right as he tracks targets. For once, he doesn't seem angry or offended; just busy and professional, like a butcher with a mountain of meat to turn into steaks. Magnus looks neither happy nor sad behind that iron mask. He's just working, destroying a few dozen men a minute as if that's normal for a birthday celebration.

With reinforcements to help carry the wounded, Team Magnus retreats up another floor.

Once the enemy tears a hole in the third barrier, they find caltrops. A heavy man steps on the first and he goes down hard, landing on more. Others pick up pieces of sharp metal, welded together so something points up regardless how they land. Even as Magnus pelts them hard from point blank range, an older man struggles to pull up a spike because it was hammered into the wood. Unlike the rest of the ramp, Team Magnus removed the plaster to expose wooden beams. The first fighters through the breach yell for hammers and hatchets, then get on their knees behind the shield wall to knock the spikes from the wood. This gives defenders more time to kill. Once enough tools have been handed up, Magnus' men move to massacre them.

Troops start by throwing darts and javelins at 30 or so attackers past the barrier. The iron tips stick to the shields, weighing them down to expose terrified shieldmen. Then, slipping through a narrow gap in their wooden chairs, defenders carefully charge the enemies to finish them off, recover their projectiles, and steal tools. Hammers and hatchers get thrown at enemies within spitting distance and often fall off the rail to the ground floor. The Alamanni go crazy, but too few can get through the narrow gap in the big barrier, which is too high for most to shoot over. Batavi on the 10th floor focus fire here to delay the inevitable.

Both sides pull back, but one clearly lost again. The enemy regroups and moves forward, but has lost hundreds of heroes during the delay. If time is money, then a slow assault gets expensive. Behind more shielding, the enemy advances through the gap in the big barrier, then waits for enough fighters. Defenders can't easily hit them, so instead they pulverize attackers farther down the ramp. Fighters fall, dying or cursing their wounds, because the injured become obstacles in the way. Slowly the assault team clears the floor spikes and reaches the narrow entrance left in the chair-barrier. A big Batavi shieldman denies them entry while other shieldmen stand over the chairs. The Alamanni must climb over the chairs while taking pellets to pull down shields for comrades to hit the defiant Batavi. Both sides throw rocks and bricks, which hurt enough defenders for Magnus to finally signal retreat.

He's been whacking men and women within spitting distance and the blood splatters have been epic. With the enemy massed where Magnus wants them, Batavi on the 10th floor dump the last of the skyscraper's furniture and furnishings. Expensive tapestries fall to cover the mess. Entire doors and dining tables fly down to fuck them up with ugly sounds and beautiful blows. Once his big shieldmen back up to the next line of chairs, enemies pour through the gap, only to find four hidden swordsmen who spring up and cut them down. Instead of lethal wounds, they create cripples, cutting arms and legs, then throwing Alamanni shields over the chairs to other troops to deny them to the Germani. Wounded troops nail three wooden shields together, then toss the giant disks at enemies far below. They land with a crash and a cry. The task done, the swordsmen crouch or crawl through the tiny gap behind the second line of chairs while injured Alamanni obstruct their able-bodied comrades. Magnus and his range warriors decimate the most lethal-looking opponents. Hatchets, hammers, darts, javelins, and pellets tear them apart to create more obstacles. His men rush forward to recover weapons and stab the least injured enemies during this momentary advantage.

Still behind the chairs, Magnus yells and the Batavi on the 10th floor walk down to relieve Team 2. The next wave they fight with sword and, ironically, spears until pushed past the second and third line of chairs. It takes the enemy an hour to rise one floor, but Team 2 is finished. Magnus yells and Team 4 from the roof comes down to replace them since they ran out of projectiles, time, and luck. Now neither side has much ammo and both look exhausted. Defenders have defied and delayed the determined enemy far longer than either expected, but now the shit gets real. Team 4 is battered beyond belief, so Magnus calls down the Batavi from the penthouse to form a defensive line as the able-bodied carry and drag the wounded away to the vault. Magnus shakes his arms to get some feeling back, then slings some more before fumbling to get his gloves off. He has pellets, but his arms don't work anymore. Both hands have cramped up, looking ready to masturbate. The orphan seems more suicidal than usual.

Furious Alamanni pour past the chairs, shocked by their losses, but seeing light at the end of their dark tunnel. Then they spot Team 3 carrying 20 long spears and they pause to ponder their options. Those nearest the gap try to retreat, but too many bodies literally stand in their way. Over 100 Alamanni have passed the last barrier, but the Batavi spearmen speed up into a full sprint while yelling. Defenders hold up shields and throw a few projectiles, but the crunch is brutal, bloody, and badass. Team 3 breaks most of their spears on the enemy, but expected this. They draw swords and continue working before new enemies interfere. Team 4 had hurried to either railing to get out of the way, but they are in no condition to fight, much less defend themselves. They've already moved the dead, dying, and grievously wounded to the roof to be ziplined to the gunboats, but many more can't move without help. They flee up the ramp as fast as they can limp, with Magnus urging them on. As they slash strangers, the orphan greets the backs of Team 3 in a horrified tone:

Yelling frantically. "My hands cramped! I couldn't wipe my own ass even if I wanted to. I'm gonna start some fires. Retreat as slowly as you can."

Over all the screaming, it's not obvious if any hear him. They're too busy slaughtering strangers. Though his arms are useless, his legs carry him quickly up the ramp. He massages one arm on the run, looking and feeling horrified. He wanted to go out fighting, not defenseless.

"Lars! I need help."

The badass Batavi jogs down from the roof, eyes wild. "We ran out of projectiles and debris. Why are you holding your hands like that? Have you been masturbating?"

"No, but I wiggle it a lot after peeing. My hands don't work. I never anticipated cramps, so I need help igniting the tower."

They run to the communal toilets on the 10th floor, where they've stored shit-tons of lamp oil. Only one toilet remains because they threw the rest at the enemy. Males and females have separate sections, entrances, and pipes. It looks like an outhouse built for 20 shitters. Magnus massages his other hand with clumsy fingers and angry impatience. He thinks he's about to die and now doesn't find that funny. Lars works as if he'll happily die soon.

"Lars, drop the clay pots of lamp oil down the shit tube because I can't feel my fingers or find my conscience. It was genius to pipe everyone's pee and poo to a wagon in a special room on the ground floor with an outside entrance. I laughed so hard when we dumped the Shit Wagon into that tarp. The kingly brothers put outhouses on all nine upper floors. Every night they'd replace a wagon covered in dirt, then mix it with animal and vegetative waste to fertilize fields. Joko said they'd add mulch or soil additives like ash, potash, or crushed fish bones. Building vertically makes it sooooo much easier to collect human and vegetative waste. Ordinary homes need crappy servants to shovel their shit or haul pails of poo for miles onto fields. Very inefficient and labor intensive; much better to truck that crap out and shovel it from wagons onto fields.

"Residents shit about 150% of their body weight a year, though I do that daily. That's a massive amount of crap. Imagine being able to grow grain in the same fields every year without declining yields. That changes everything. Farmers also ranch so that herds fertilize fallow fields for a year. What if farmers could use all three fields instead of leaving one dormant? Their income increases a third. 90% of our economy is agricultural. The world would be a third richer with no one losing. Imagine the human waste from millions of people enriching soil instead of polluting drinking water by dumping it in the river. That's brilliant and I'm envious. Everyone says I always claim to be smarter than everyone, but apparently everyone is wrong. It's too bad I must die because I'd like to give folks more food, cheaper food, and more reliable food so no one starves. Instead of one tower, what if all of humanity lived in tall towers to simplify the fertilization of fields? I could spend my life giving people food, shelter, and security behind walled port mega-cities. Lars, I think my cock tickled my toes again so, yeah, I'm terrified of my imminent death more than usual." He cocks his head to remember. "Troops talk shit right before battle and I must have picked that up from them, along with herpes. I started masturbating when I sleepwalk – and my neighbors are pissed. Oh, what other gems should I tell before I die? My wife made me wait a month for sex. When I insisted, she

145

said, you cruel bastard. Once she got her first orgasm, she said, you made me wait a month for that? You cruel bastard!"

Lars laughs while working.

"Wait, wait – I got more! My wife must love anal, given all the assholes she fucks." They both chuckle. "My wife smokes after sex. After all these years, it's still strange to see puffs of cloud float out of her vagina." Lars loves that one. "When my wife wants sex, she smiles. When I want sex, I breathe." Magnus chuckles to himself. "I treat my wife like a queen: I kiss her ass and beg her for favors. What else? Oh! Until I married, I did not know it was possible to be a dumb ass, smart ass, and jackass in the same sentence. I like having sex with my wife wearing nothing but high heels, but it's hard to find high heels that fit me. My wife and I are actually monogamous; just not with each other. My wife told me that I'd be the perfect lover if only I had a big dick. Wait, sorry. That's what I told her. Wanna know how spouses get so good at lying to each other? Practice. All right, last one: I often wake up with a boner, so my wife no longer lets me sleep in church."

The Batavi is impressed and impatient.

Lars pours oil. "You could save humanity from hunger. I've changed my mind. You should not die."

The prodigy laughs with real bitterness as he ignites a torch and drops it into the shit pipe. They take turns watching the fire spread ten floors down.

"Slinging all day has disarmed me. No way I survive. Too bad, really; I still have bitterness to burn. I could fuel a blast furnace with it. They varnished the logs, so it'll take a lot of heat to ignite them. I'm not even sure the entire tower will go up in flames, but I'm dying to find out."

The Batavi dumps the last of the jars down the pipe and watches flames multiply.

"Max, I must reach the roof before my companions lock it or the enemy blocks it. Goodbye, my friend."

"I'll go soon. I must say goodbye to the severely injured in the vault."

Lars runs in one direction while Magnus takes another. Batavi with notched arrows and bad legs guard the entrance. The orphan jogs in and sees it filled with wounded instead of treasure. The last doctor waves goodbye to the boy before flying down a new zipline to the docks. The most able-bodied help send comrades down the rope head-first, like corpses. These brave heroes look closer to death than the river, but one dying trooper waves a hand goodbye to Magnus before he flies down like a missile. The terrible teen looks through the hole they made in the log wall and sees a bandaged cripple hanging horizontally from a harness until Batavi on the dock stand him up and transfer him to a gunboat. Only those incapable of being moved will stay in this tinderbox. He turns and makes eye contact with men who assume they'll die soon and badly.

He's more emotional than usual. "Boys, I started the fire, but doubt the tower will topple. You have enough food, water, and medicine to last weeks. The fleet should come soon. Take the rope tonight if you can because it may get hot in here. I doubt the enemy can get in with a padlock on the inside. Ride this out and go home heroes. I'll try distracting them with my good looks and bad jokes. Goodbye, boys. See ya on the other side."

His rearguard is running for the roof, limpers helping the lame. The teen needs to buy them time, so he runs to the railing and vents a raw roar that makes the enemy pause and piss themselves. Magnus easily has several thousand soft targets for his hard pellets, but can't hold shit due to cramps. After venting his favorite insults, he sprints for the rooftop entrance, hopping stairs as stoic Batavi wave him to hurry. Once through, they lock the door and pile heavy stuff against it so the enemy can't open it. Trebuchet and catapults still cover the roof, along with scattered stones and bitter memories.

"Everyone notch fire-arrows, then fly to the dock. Please get away while you can."

Jogging to the best spot to hit the oil-soaked tinder below the first floor ramp, a dozen of their best bowmen dip their arrows onto his torch. They fire carefully, hitting the mass of wood, weeds, and leaves below the ramp. The tinder ignites and quickly consumes the lamp oil. What starts small grows into a monster inferno. This horrifies hundreds of hostiles who hurry to extinguish the flames.

Magnus smiles at his die-hards. "You boys ever see shit fall?"

He has one last surprise and this is where the shit gets real. He holds his nose at the tarp full of crap and hanging from the crane in the center of the open atrium. Leaning over the inner railing, the last troops grin in anticipation. Laughing, he releases a mechanism and a tarp full of poo falls to earth. A few tons of old crap fall onto the ground floor to splatter disgusted enemies. The weight crushes several and injures others. Human waste flies in all directions, covering the ground floor in doo-doo. His boys shat up a storm. His loud laughter haunts the interior, then Magnus roars Glorious Victory.

Thousands of Germani fighters on the upper floors look down as the lower ramp burns up and breaks down. They have no escape because the 2nd floor is bursting with flames. 20,000 warriors can't escape the towering inferno. Their horrified faces realize they've been outsmarted again. Some attackers jump to the ground floor, but slip, covering themselves in shit instead of glory. The stench overwhelms and paralyzes, so they cry out. The strongest crawl to freedom, ignoring the pee and poo to escape this hell on Earth.

Most Batavi run to the rope and zipline down to the dock. Magnus jogs to Lars and helps him fit the rope through his harness.

Lars sounds skeptical. "I expected to do this at night and now wish I practiced more. Enemies surround the tower. I doubt I'll have enough time to push the cart of lamp oil into the entrance to block it. Hammering stakes to immobilize it will be noticed. I bet they cut me down before I finish, so I'm thinking of just slaying them instead to leave a berm of bodies to slow their escape. Maybe dump that oil."

"Lars, I'd go with you but my hands can't slow my descent. Maybe another trooper would help, but that mob could cut down two men as easily as one. With surprise, you could ignite the cart, then push it to the entrance before they tear you apart. I'll roar to distract them a moment. I'm a bad boy, but a good distraction."

The suicidal veteran nods in agreement, then looks the boy in the eyes. "Dutch was furious you sent him away. Please tell me your real reason."

"Because sacking Frankfurt is my project; I want credit and doubt anyone could do it better. Lars, tell me true: could Dutch have killed more enemies than I have? What about my father or Julian? We slew 150,000, including the grandmas."

Proud of his boss. "I say this as a warrior with no charity: no one could have done better. Dutch is very good, but you somehow see farther into the future. You have a gift, so I hope you don't throw away your life like I'm about to do. Oh, the fuckers took my daughter Elia. Please find her for me and take care of her."

Looking like someone peed in his face, the angry teen tries grabbing Lars' coat, but fumbles because his fingers won't function.

"Are you fucking with me? Elia? Seriously?"

That surprises Lars. "What? I named Elia after my grandma. Unlike my ma, a real nice lady."

Close enough to rub noses, Magnus studies his face like a pass-fail exam. As his face softens, it's obvious the orphan believes him.

"My mama's name was Elia and I got her killed. If I survive, I'll look for your Elia because I can't imagine a more appropriate penance."

Shocked, Lars nods, then concentrates on the next moment as he drops down the skyscraper like a rolling rock. Magnus looks over the edge as the Batavi commander rappels down ten floors using ropes. Of thousands of people below, none look up to see this unnatural sight. Instead, they babble something about shit everywhere. Fighters flee, covered in crap to everyone's horror. The sight and smell monopolizes attention. Dressed like a Bavarian with a fur coat, Lars lands hard and needs help getting up. Two ladies lift him and he thanks them with a kind smile. Excusing himself, he asks their help in pushing the cart into the entrance. Inexplicably, others help, but look puzzled as Lars strikes the flintlock to ignite the lamp oil underneath the cart full of branches. Lacking the energy to hammer in stakes, he strolls off like this is a Monday in the park. A few fighters stop him, but then Magnus roars from the rooftop and everyone looks up except Lars, who walks away unhurried, blending in with the frightened mob just before the cart explodes in flame, trapping those inside.

Magnus looks around and sees he's alone with his fears; all other troops escaped down the rope to the docks. He runs to the open center and looks down. A column of dark smoke rises to the heavens, but down below he sees Panic, Hysteria, and Chaos – the three gods of war. The packed skyscraper is burning to a boil and Alamanni are trampling each other to avoid a roast. Doing a shit job of escaping, they flounder in crap and corpses. The lion roars, but few faces look up. Disappointed at being ignored, Magnus goes around the rim of the square rooftop and roars from each corner. The Iberians on the island roar back, happy he's alive. Everyone, including the enemy, knows where he is. Hungry flames consume the defenseless tower filled with rapists, kidnappers, and thieves. Smoke from the skyscraper has multiplied with the screaming. The world's largest apartment building is lighting up Frankfurt. The intense heat forces folks back. The towering inferno is awesome, amazing, and appalling.

Needing a rest, and perhaps a new life, Magnus sits on the crates blocking the rooftop entrance. He hears fruitless pounding from the interior and smiles sadly. Then, looking at his useless hands, he slowly starts to cry. The poor orphan looks like he's lost everything. For all his boasts, he's a broken boy eager to end his suffering.

"I'm sorry, mama. I'm so sorry I took the love of your life from you. I was selfish, cruel, and gleeful. I knew how much and how deeply you love him. I wasn't thinking. I'm coming to see you soon. I'd really like a huggie. My first memory is you hugging me while singing a lullaby. When my thoughts get too loud, I re-live that moment and then sleep like a baby. Mama, will you please sing me another lullaby? I promise to be a better boy. Dad, I'm sorry I didn't save you like I saved Theo. You just make me so mad. I honestly didn't think you'd die. Why couldn't you just accept me as I am? If you really regretted murdering your father, then you would have treated me better. Theo accepted me long ago, when I chased down and killed that horse thief – my first kill with a sling. Theo didn't like me, but he accepted me like a pet snake. Why did you insist on changing me into something I'm not? If you only loved me for me, then I would have been the best son ever. I always dreamed of us fighting barbarians together, like these disgusting barbarians somehow living in the world's most sophisticated tower."

Having lived too many years in the last month, Magnus breaks down and curls into a fetus position. Tears, anguish, and guilt plaster his baby face even as the shouts and curses from the other side of the iron door get louder and more desperate. Trapped in his own world, Magnus doesn't seem to hear them. Waves of emotion bitch-slap him as flames burn holes in the rooftop and several sections loudly collapse with grunts and groans. The entire tower moans like an old man getting out of bed at night to pee again. The orphan expects no mercy and welcomes the end of his misery. He looks up and sees dark smoke floating in long columns into the beautiful sky like shit scattered across a clean canvass. Magnus sighs and accepts his demise.

"Goodbye, cruel cosmos. You can't torture and torment me anymore, so I win!"

Then an old voice from the past gives the prodigy a new future. "Flavius! You still there, Flavius?"

The boy shakes in rage, like a sleepy baby-epileptic desperate for titty. His eyes need forever to focus, but then he puts his mind into gear.

"Who's trying to kill me now?"

He gets up with a vengeance and runs up to where Lars went down. Down there, on a kickass white stallion sits Serapio, his nemesis, with a dozen richly dressed elite Alamanni. They seem both happy and unhappy to see him. With explosive fury, Magnus roars defiance as the sun sets.

With a burning building lighting up the night, the Alamanni prince turns to his companions.

"Yeah, that's him," Serapio says. "I wanted to build a better tower anyways."

Magnus backs from the edge to be alone with his thoughts and fears. His mind churns as if a waterwheel powers it and then, an epiphany hits him hard. He searches a pocket until he turns up Joko's master key. Flames engulf a quarter of the rooftop and eagerly eat the rest. The killer kid holds up the key and smiles as if it's lifesaving.

"There you are."

CHAPTER 7

Hostile vessels attack Drusus Island. Batavi badasses manning their biggest catapults watch the enemy fleet sail upriver to stop the foreigners in Frankfurt from reaching the island. Weak winds force them to tack back and forth. The burning tower lights up the river and casts ominous shadows that dance in the dark. All the Batavi on the island limp, hold an arm, or wear a bandage because the able-bodied went hunting in the forest or already infiltrated the enemy.

A Batavi warrior yells out. "They're sailing against the wind and the current. I doubt they can even reach the gunboats rescuing our soldiers. If Captain Gari farts, that might send them downriver!"

The guys laugh nervously at that. The Hanseatic League fleet is intimidating, but the warships sail slowly.

Gari walks over. "Karl, your mother didn't feed me enough beans this morning to fart, so we might have to actually work for once. I hope they don't know our able-bodied troops already invaded their forest. Let's try delaying them by sending bolts into their sails. Maximum elevation. Load practice bolts and fire when confident."

The first few bolts from the catapults miss the first ship, but then they get their range and load real bolts, which punch holes in the main square sail. The first ship fights the river, but then another bolt adds another hole. The ship looks like it's station keeping. Sister ships catch up, but get the same treatment. The enemy fleet lines up, but makes little headway.

Gari claps. "I'll take that as a win." He sniffs uncomfortably. "Max sure roasted a lot of Germani."

At the island's dock, lightly wounded Batavi on the island help heavily injured comrades from a gunboat. Most lay down in travois, which horses pull to the infirmary. Once they unload that boat, another sails up with even more victims. One badass turns to the others.

One Batavi to another. "Max was right. No way could we have evacuated more troops. He saved hundreds by sending them away." A defiant roar from the burning tower makes them all turn. The bright flames contrast with the darkening sky. "I'm gonna miss that monster. Julius Caesar couldn't have done better. At just 10 years old, imagine what Max could do at 20!"

In the castle's plaza, troops pack the open space to hear their fearful leaders speak from a raised dais.

Franco sounds unsure. "Max wants us to attack Frankfurt after midnight, but they recently received thousands of Bavarian bowmen. He expected us to fight armed women, big boys, and old people as they sleep off an exhausting battle. The Alamanni are celebrating, but don't have alcohol to get drunk. We malted the last of their barley and drank it cold from the river. Max made me promise to go, but none of you agreed to attack an army of enemies that can't threaten you. Legate Theodosius needs us and Max is almost certainly dead. The enemy will sift through the embers and ashes to find his corpse, so we cannot save him. I'd like to save the seriously wounded stuck in the iron vault, but don't see how we can do that, even if some survive the building after it collapses.

150

"The wise course of action is to do nothing. After all, since getting ambushed on the road to Fort Briga, we've done enough. On the other hand, we lost many good men – and Fernando, damn him to Hell. Max never wanted us to fight to the death; he just wanted a killer visit that took them by surprise. I therefore propose a lightning strike. We hurt as many as we safely can, then retreat back across our bridge of barges. The more we kill, the safer we'll be. By burning that beautiful building, Max killed thousands of their most aggressive fighters. Again. The able-bodied Batavi already entered that dark forest to slay enemies, so they probably drew off the fiercest fighters, leaving us with civilians. Plus, let's not forget that we earn a good gold coin for every bad Alamanni slain. Without Max to take the general's share, I propose we put that in the general fund. However, the fighting has hurt some of us harder than others, so I'd like to see a division. Those who just want to wait for someone to rescue us, go to my left. Those who'd prefer to hurt the bastards who killed Max, gather to my right."

They all move to his right, most eagerly with stern expressions. Even those who can barely limp.

Franco sighs in disappointment. "We're all in agreement then. It'll take a few hours to tie up and anchor the barges to cross the river. The smoke should give us cover. A little before dawn, we'll hit 'em hard. Those who can't move fast will become our rearguard. I'll ask the gunboat crews to support us. Those who can walk, but not run, should try stealing their ships. Most are moored not far away, so cut the mooring lines and become a pirate. Anyone who can stand, but can't walk without help, should shoot from the gunboats. Come back before the sun rises. Are we agreed?"

The angry men roar their support.

"Then eat, drink, and get some sleep. Bring all our ammo and pray it's enough."

Franco didn't think he could sleep, so it surprises him to feel a boot kick him awake. After gearing up, he stumbles through dark corridors to the kitchen for a hot breakfast with a thousand other sleepy soldiers. Drusus built a stone fort, so the galley is huge. After gulping down warm porridge, Franco takes a loaf of bread and a water sack with him because this might be another long day. Reaching the river, people pee because there might not be time later. Engineering teams assemble the bridge. Franco inspects it for sturdiness and seems convinced. It'll soon connect to a dock with wooden step stools to help the troops up. Returning, he calls over his unit commanders.

"Sailors hear fighting in the forest, so the Batavi and our West Germani have lured them away. Avoid the tower. Stab the sleeping as fast as you can because once enough of them get their feet, we're in trouble. They vastly outnumber us, so let's hurt them in their huts and hovels. The faster we do this, the safer. Retreat when they fight back effectively; don't wait for my signal. The smoke has gotten worse, so listen as much as you look."

A few thousand optimists walk across, then start jogging downriver to form a long skirmish line. With that, they advance into Frankfurt at a brisk pace into thousands of humble camps, tents, and lean-to's. The enemy are easier to kill than cattle. A soldier's job is like a butcher: it's ugly, bloody, and doesn't pay enough, but folks gotta eat. 2000 rested troops seek out 80,000 sleeping locals.

Franco lets the young bucks jog ahead. They stab the sleeping without pausing. Some enter ruined buildings because they provide some protection from the cold, wind,

151

and drizzle. All too soon, a warning horn blows, so leadership must have set sentries. Franco wonders whether to recall the team, but thinks it premature. Left behind, Franco jogs to keep up with the younger troops and manages to slay the sleepy and slaughter the standing. The surprise attack has put the enemy in a panic. Most are women and the elderly. He sees his half-legion hurry to catch up and cut the enemy down. Thousands of targets are just out of reach, so he speeds up, a smile lighting up his face as he cuts strangers down. He thrusts into another back and chuckles as she falls with a cry and a curse. Non-warriors try defending themselves with sickles, fish gaffs, and reefing hooks, but don't last long against properly kitted professionals. Happy as a dung beetle in shit, Franco chases unarmed enemies and kills them with a wild smile. He's having a great time until he hears horses. A lot of galloping horses. Franco flinches and freaks out, then blows Retreat. The horsemen hear and divert to get him.

"I fatally fucked up!"

He runs to the river, but hears riders catching up. At that moment, the tall tower topples with an awful sound, like a giant monster fainting while farting. Both sides look at the edifice swarmed by flames and crackling like whips. It's painful to hear and strange to see. The middle bulges like a fat guy, which takes the top down with it. The impact by the luxury docks is loud, impressive, and terrifying. It looks like Hell designed by architects, just like a camel looks like a horse designed by a clueless committee of bored bureaucrats. Scared to death, Franco runs, only for a horseman to emerge from the dark smoke to hack into him just as he chopped into so many others. The commander goes down and knows it's fatal. A hundred horses slash other Iberians. That so few can slay so many is bloody ironic.

Screams of pain and curses of anger rip through the darkness. Smoke fills Frankfurt like fog. Iberians desperately look for the damn river as Bavarians come at them from every direction. Most are men and all are pissed. Some legionaries defend themselves against superior numbers from wrecked homes and eateries, but too many attack. Team Franco takes down several times their number, but they die, nevertheless.

A stunning champion dances among frustrated Bavarians, never letting them box him in. The hero yells at comrades to escape. He's running from some to attack others, bouncing off shields to overwhelm the weak, the under-armed, and the untrained. The enemy around him fall like wheat. This Iberian badass seems to sense danger, the way he ducks and dodges, lunges and leaps. Spears, arrows, and blunt instruments seem not to affect him. Finally, an arrow pierces his leg and then a horseman knocks him down. A dozen enemies gleefully hack him to pieces, but his heroism helped hundreds escape.

The sun rises on another bloody day. Serapio and other leaders finally find the barges tied to their dock and charge, but enemy limpers have cut loose a barge. Neither side has any more arrows, so the foreign invaders retreat to their island with only half their number, but leave thousands of enemies dead or wounded. The Alamanni and Bavarians stumble around Frankfurt, shocked at the slaughter, with thousands of moaning men and wailing women. They thought they had won a costly battle, only to get surprised in their sleep. A few thousand ambushers killed 10x their number and half escaped justice. Ravens pluck out eyeballs, dog rip out flesh, and vultures feast on the buffet. Everyone alive is in anguish and the dead are too numerous to count.

As the morning mist clears, a new fleet arrives, but flying the Roman flag. It assaults ships of the Hanseatic League before they can raise anchor or cut mooring lines. A dozen ships can't even turn to defend themselves. Troops board these vessels in overwhelming numbers to take out sleeping sailors below deck. As planned, Caesar Julian brought his army after Magnus won the war.

Alamanni elites ride over and see a foreign fleet packed with legionaries. They scatter to warn their people, who leave as quickly as they can with all that they can carry. The Alamanni abandon their capital after spending 200,000 lives to keep it. Two transports bring 600 West Germani horsemen who gleefully hunt the harried. Vessels dock and troops pour out, each with a backpack to stay longer in the field. Many injured legionaries from the bridge of barges jump in the river and swim to the riverbank to check on friends.

Someone finds Franco and demands a doctor.

After the legions deploy, Julian, Pelagius, Dutch, Luca, Joko, Marc, and several senators land to walk through the smoldering battlefield. Theo, his Uncle Honorius, his brother Honorius, his cousin Honorius, his wife, sons Theo and Honorius, and daughter follow. Theo's son Honorius is a little smaller than Theo the Younger, less cute, and less impressive. Theo hears his name and jogs to a small group to find Franco breathing his last. Someone gives him a sip of water and a final prayer. Franco looks and sounds sad.

"Theo, Max saved us several times, but I got carried away. Serapio himself got me. Max wouldn't have mucked it up. Please take care of my wife, mistresses, and kids. Frankito wants a military career, but I hope his talents lie elsewhere."

"I'll take care of your family. You did well. Where's Max?"

"On the roof, last time we saw or heard him. He burned the building, got most of us out, then stayed. He trapped 20,000 enemies inside, plus at least that many corpses. Some immobile Batavi might have survived in the vault. Cousin, I'm sorry about Max. He's too headstrong. After what happened to his parents, he didn't want to live."

They all turn to look. Among the tower's wreckage, Dutch sees his men rescuing others from the vault. Most look dead, but apparently are not because rescuers carry several on stretchers to the docks while screaming for doctors. Dutch and doctors hurry over. The other leaders stay with Franco until his eyes grow dim and lose their light. His body slouches and grief buries Theo.

"I've known Franco all my life. I attended his wedding and saw Frankito born. This trip has seen too much death. I only wanted to repay my brother in his moment of need."

Someone yells from a distance. "Sire, should we pursue the enemy into the woods?"

Julian yells back. "Hunt down the cowards, but be back tomorrow."

While senators wander the battlefield with their own bodyguards, the leaders head for the collapsed tower. It fell towards the river and left a big smoldering mess. Legionaries and Batavi check on compatriots while Roman doctors do triage. Joko brought his puppy, who expertly searches the wreckage and barks happily. The men find the dog pawing something and help remove rubble.

Theo yells tearfully. "Max, are you under there?"

Marc screams frantically. "Max, come out, come out, wherever you are! I'm sorry I denied you a hug from mama and daddy before they died."

Looking conflicted, Cousin Theo says nothing. They quiet down, then hear a flute playing Girls of Rome. They all scream, but the heir to the Roman Empire screams the loudest.

"Fuuuuuuuuuck!" After his peak rage passes, Julian notices everyone studying him. "I hoped to save some coin."

Admiral Honorius is equally furious. "That damn bastard refuses to die!"

Theo looks puzzled as he notices their horror. "Sire, you thought Max's death would save you money? Did you not read the contract that you signed, stamped, and sealed with your imperial ring? You agreed to pay our family's parent corporation, Maximus Inc, a gold coin for every dead Alamanni. Max didn't expect to survive, but wanted to fund the family. You save nothing from his death. Is that why you delayed the rescue?"

That shocks the gorgeous heir to the throne. Furious, Theo orders his Iberians to clear the wreckage. They toss piles of debris until they come to a stanky broken wagon that smells like shit from Hell's sewer. They see nothing more, despite the flute somehow playing. Six troopers then lift the collapsed wagon and a brilliant boy crawls into the daylight like a lizard from a grave. He pulls out several heavy backpacks like they're full of bullion. Several coin sacks hang around his neck to match bulging pockets that make him look bloated. The doggy licks his face and asks how he is.

The teen answers, "Maximo, you're the best doggy ever! I love you so much. Let's play catch later."

Magnus laughs as he struggles to get his last leg beyond the wagon. The legionaries drop it like a bad habit and Marc helps his hero to his feet. The 8-year-old hugs him until it hurts.

Marc cries. "I thought I lost my brother, after losing my parents. Max, please don't ever die again."

"I promise. I was planning on immortality anyways. I really needed that huggie, but you'll need to burn those crappy clothes. For what it's worth, I apologized to mama and daddy. Uncle Theo, did you fart or did I hide in the enemy's Shit Room?" He laughs hysterically and looks at the sun as if he has never seen it before. "Cousins, I'd happily hug you if you hate your outfits. Aunt Flavia, every year you look younger and prettier; please sell me your secret. I blame diet and exercise, but I haven't ruled out dark magic. Cousin Honora, I'd like to donate a thousand dolls to your collection; well, 1012 dolls and stuffed animals. You can repay me in smiles.

"Uncle Honorius, did you leave your cute kids in school? Having audited their books, I calculate they owe me several huggies. Will you, Aunt Flavia, and Uncle Theo please carry a backpack and sack for me? They're full of huggies. Brother, if you and Cousin Theo help, then I'll love you both forever. Pel, please carry the last one. Admiral, grab that weapon and I'll kill you. You won't get another warning." They all hear the clinking of bullion as he makes them put on the backpacks. "Admiral Honorius, I didn't expect you to come after I won. We could have used you yesterday. I hope you didn't come to fuck me like you fucked your brother, my father, and our family."

The old pirate freaks because that's exactly why he's there. Magnus scans the battlefield and sees too many of the wrong corpses. His expression turns to sadness and horror as he spots more dead Iberians.

Joko does the math. "You used my master key to hide in the Shit Room? They didn't look inside?"

"They did, but not hard because it smelled like poo. They found the door locked and so didn't get on their knees to search for a boy hidden under a dirty blanket in a hole under the Shit Wagon. My hands were still so cramped from slinging a million pellets that I could barely hold my breath, so I slept instead. Uncle Theo, please ask your legion to drag enemy corpses out into the open so Roman clerks can verify our count. The Batavi probably left tens of thousands in the woods and about 50,000 are buried in this tower. Over half are women, but the contract specified Alamanni, not males of fighting age. They sacrificed their elderly to exhaust our ammo, so they count, too." He shakes his head to clear it and finally reads the room. "Crap. Who died? Don't tell me Franco died."

Theo spills the beans. "Franco died. Serapio killed him. He then died in my arms. We would have been here yesterday morning, but Caesar Julian mistakenly thought your death would save him money. A thousand brave men from the Jovii and Victores legions died because of that."

Angrily turning on Dutch. "I told you to bring everything you had when you saw the smoke. Franco needed your reinforcements. I sent you away to induce the enemy to piss away their strength against a fortified position, but we still required rescue. We could have killed them all if you came as planned."

Dutch is already in a rage. "Caesar Julian forbid it and Admiral Honorius prevented it. Theo and I argued with them all night, but neither would budge. I lost a thousand Batavi in the woods. They killed many times their number, but most would have survived if reinforced. I told Julian days ago that this may cost us lives, but he didn't care. Admiral Honorius even parked his giant warship in the river so my boats couldn't pass. In return, Julian awarded him any ships he captured, plus all of yours."

Ripples of emotion roll across the orphan's face until they crash on a reef. He looks at a dozen Germani vessels docked at the riverport and understands. The boy buries a moment of honesty under a mountain of deceit.

"Well, good thing we found the gold bullion that the Alamanni stockpiled to buy fish from the Hanseatic League. It's right over here."

Excited, the prodigy runs to the river, uses the master key that Joko gave him to unlock the padlock, and flips over a wooden lid to expose an underground bunker. The men follow, but Julian runs the fastest. Expecting a battle, he wears an iron breastplate. Magnus grabs the top and pulls Julian over him. As the teen falls on his back, his feet rest on Julian's tummy and send him flying with their combined momentum. A few gold bullion bars slip out of his backpack and several spill from his sack. The second-in-command of the Roman Empire lands on his back in the big bunker on top of corpses awaiting burial after the battle, along with the last of the cold, dead fish. He's in literally over his head and can't get out because the bunker is morbidly deep. The concrete hold is bigger than a luxury home. River water flows around it to chill the fish and dead bodies. The orphan walks around to mostly close the lid and trap Julian inside.

Magnus looks murderous. "Uncle Theo, don't let the Admiral leave. I want my ships back. Boys, Julian cost us a few thousand heroes. I say we kill him and blame it on a berserker faking death. Dutch, he let your men die. What are your thoughts?"

"Caesar Julian deserves worse than death, but he brought an army."

"But they're getting lost in the woods. By the time his commanders return, we can make up anything we want, as long as we're all in agreement." Holding the lid to his

155

waist, the vengeful boy looks down on his betrayer. "Julian, if you wish to buy your life, you should say so now. I bet we killed 200,000 Alamanni, but your treachery doubles the price. You must authorize 400,000 good gold coins or its equivalent in bullion. Luca, how much did Julian bring?"

"Not much and he left little in Reims, though my contacts say Gaul's capital, Triers, has a bunch of bullion. Julian tried taking our loot in Fort Briga, but you cleverly sent yours to Amsterdam, so he came here to take what he could. I'm offended by your distrust, but I'll probably get over it."

Magnus takes a tone. "Dutch, Franco, and I agreed that the dead should earn as much as the living. I promised more to the Batavi who stayed in the tower with me, but that comes out of my share, as the supreme commander. I propose we distribute 30,000 gold coins to the widows or children, on top of the death benefits and loot distribution that they're already owed. Dutch, you oppose this?"

Dutch laughs harshly. His people would get rich off this proposal. He couldn't bring back the dead, so this was the next best thing.

Stinking of fish, Julian calls their bluff. "You wouldn't dare kill me."

The males all stared down at him without pity.

Magnus takes a swing. "That's what 200,000 Alamanni said before I killed them. They even said it in perfect Latin. Some days I wonder who the real barbarians are."

"Well, you can't argue with success," Julian says.

"I argue with success all the time, unprofitably, out of either spite or habit. Julian, all you had to do was not interfere. Instead of offering to help me kill your enemies, you denied me the help I counted on. Ergo, you fucked things up and should pay the ultimate price. Pel, you've sided with Julian over me in the past. Will you share in our secret or must I throw a knife in your dick? I know a dozen of your bastards; they will not be safe if you betray me again."

"I'd rather live, but his death will destabilize the empire again."

"Like Constantius, Julian doesn't have sons and doesn't look like he ever will, so letting him live doesn't buy much time. Our borders stretch several thousand miles – that's too much to secure. I'd rather protect the Iberian Peninsula by fortifying the coastal plains between the Pyrenees Mountains and the Med. My grandfather's grandfather dreamed of building barriers to control access, just north of Barcelona. The Iberian Peninsula could be safe even if Germani pour across Gaul and Italy."

Honorius and Theo nod in agreement. Their victim tries reason.

"Pay their widows out of the loot you took or out of the 200,000 gold coins."

"No, because you wanted me dead. I'm taking that personally. According to the contract that you didn't apparently read, whatever is unpaid on the Alamanni dead converts into a loan that the Roman Treasury pays 12% interest on. Once army accountants count the dead or agree with our count, then you have 30 days to pay up. Whatever isn't paid becomes a loan. Uncle Honorius, thank you for teaching me finance. I think I'd be a killer banker."

Julian laughs bitterly at his sudden change in fortune. "Constantius will never agree to that, even if the Senate does."

"If Emperor Constantius doesn't pay what he owes us, then I'll kill him. Caesar Julian, if you ever become emperor of the Roman Empire, would you immediately pay off that loan?"

That silences the men. Julian looks at the boy in a new light. "Constantius is only 40 years old and might marry his mistress if she gets pregnant. He could live another 40 years while his two daughters give him grandsons to succeed him. If you kill him within five years, I'll not only make good on the rest of the 400,000, but I'll double it."

The males above the bunker share a silent conversation.

That startles Magnus. "I did not see that coming. I thought we'd have to let you stew overnight before you came to your senses. Julian, if you authorize 400,000 from your imperial treasury at Triers, then we'll probably let you live." Given the stench in the bunker, Julian nods in eager agreement. "But you deserve nothing from Frankfurt because you didn't help sack it. Last month you thought a gold coin was a fair price for a dead Alamanni, so you're getting fair value. Alamanni boys will need another decade before they can threaten Gaul. Armies are expensive and decisive victories rare. You can take the credit as long as we receive what we have earned. Agreed?

"Uncle Honorius, please get papyrus so Caesar Julian can authorize 400,000 gold coins or its equivalent, plus whatever my father's army is owed and something for Uncle Theo's legion. Ah, crap! Where's the admiral? That pirate is running for his flagship! A man that old should not be able to run that fast. Uncle Theo, please take me to Cousin Franco so I can say goodbye. He was a good man and a great cousin. I owe Serapio another death. Please tell Frankito that his father's demise was not my fault. As Franco was the second-highest ranking officer, his family will get enough to retire on. I'm so tired. I was never this tired when I was 10. Aging is horrible; someone should stop it."

They walk through a minefield of decaying bodies when Magnus sees one he must inspect. The sword got stuck in Lars' chainmail, so it sticks out of his back like a throbbing erection. The orphan turns the body over and sees Lars choking a man to death. The boy bursts into tears.

"Oh, Lars! You almost made it, man. Uncle Theo, Lars was the best. The Alamanni killed his son. I need to find a girl named Elia. I know we haven't recovered her because we ask kids if they can speak other languages. Uncle Theo, please take care of things while I search for her."

The orphan jogs to thousands of terrified young women and small kids herded against the river so they can't escape. Most will be sold as slaves. The teen belts out the girl's name until a woman holding her daughter walks over.

"Do you understand Latin?" Magnus asks the mother.

"Of course. All Batavi learn Latin except peasant farmers. Why do you yell my daughter's name?"

Elia looks 6, shy, and terrified.

"What's the name of your Batavi husband?"

"Lars refused to marry me. When Alamanni killed our son in a raid, grief overcame me, so we left to stay with friends upriver. I met a good Bavarian who eagerly married me, despite having a daughter, but you foreigners killed him yesterday. Now I don't know what will happen to us."

"I think I found them both. This is something you should see." The lady and the girl follow him into Frankfurt, where two good men died in the dirt. "I think Lars choked your husband to death, then others stabbed him. I am sorry for your losses. They both

157

loved you very much and Elia will receive what her father earned."

Towering over Lars, the grieving woman sheds silent tears, looking at both men, covered in blood and hatred. Luca walks up, sensing something.

Mama is in tears. "Why is God such a sadist? God delights in making us suffer. Elia, your father killed the man who loved and supported us. We live in a cruel and capricious world that plays with our sentiments. Tragedy strikes whenever I get too happy. Life is a penalty that God inflicts on the innocent. Nothing else makes sense. It's better never to have been born than to suffer so much."

Magnus disagrees. "It's not all bad – I could be dead. Luca, I'll pay you Lars' bonus if you take care of them until they move on. I'm really good at a few things, but this is not one of them."

Feeling helpless, Magnus listens as Luca introduces himself, then invites mother and daughter to live in Briga Town. They gratefully accept their least-worst option. Something in the river distracts the prodigy, who points at the Sea Horse.

"Luca, why is there a giant wooden horse head in the water?"

"You didn't know? Admiral Honorius built himself a massive flagship called the Sea Horse. It's the largest vessel I've ever seen."

"Luca, tell me true: does the old pirate jogging to that ship look like an honest man? Because Admiral Honorius looks like my survival has terrified him."

"He's no worse than most senators, but something about him is sleezy. He's good at sales, flattery, and bullshit, yet walks like he's wicked with weapons. Even Julian fears him, and rightly so. His reputation is as unsavory as my wife's cooking."

Incredulous, Magnus watches his great-uncle yell for the ship to cast off before he even boards. His crew scrambles to obey. The Sea Horse drifts into the current to escape downriver as soon as the pirate climbs in.

Magnus deflates. "That man is guilty of something serious. I assume he has stolen from me, thinking I was dead. He was the best fighter in the family when his profitable piracy business grew into merchant shipping. He says he's personally killed a thousand armed men, but I assume that includes the competitors that he sank."

"Ah. That explains why he claims your ships. You took a dozen here and offered them to Dutch to steal even more, to be split evenly. The Batavi are good sailors, so they replaced or complimented the crews that they captured and Iberians did the same with the other half. Good luck getting those ships back. The Admiral seemed to think of them as his."

The orphan feels himself burn up inside. "Any idea how many ships he confiscated?"

"Dutch added 24 to the Batavi fleet. They took Hamburg's port by surprise and almost attacked the city. Your great-uncle probably added fewer because he wanted bigger ships to cross the Med while the Batavi prefer smaller ones with lesser drafts for shallow rivers. Wow! Look at him go. He didn't even turn to wave goodbye. Look at Theo! He also suspects foul play from that chicken. What will you do?"

"I'll ask Dutch for help returning what I rightfully stole."

Across the river, on Drusus Island, Magnus, Theo, and Julian watch the last of the enemy dead be dragged by horse into the Main River.

Magnus doesn't sound like a kid. "Caesar Julian, this is your lucky day. Because

Alamanni families took their dead loved ones for proper burial, we've only recovered 147,832 enemy corpses, though I feel like I've personally killed a million more. Add those that I slew outside your camp and let's call it, 150,000. I said your penalty is double, so your total due is 300,000 gold coins instead of 400,000. Your part in this campaign cost several times that, not including my father's army and all the good they did. All in all, you're getting off cheap and I believe all 11-year-olds would agree with me. War is expensive, but you failed to bankrupt Rome. Congratulations. Batavi will get proper burials back home, but that's on me; you, however, should bury the legionaries that you abandoned.

"Sadly, breaking the Alamanni will make the empire look at you as a huge hero while I get no credit for being awesome. Constantius is a jealous bastard who will resent Luca leading the Senate in offering you a triumph through the roads of Rome. You'll be feasted and feted while I run and hide from my implacable enemies. Some of your centurions want to elevate you to Augustus. We've had co-emperors before. Constantine the Great let his army elevate him, then treated the real emperors, Maxentius and Licinus, like usurpers. I advise you to resist that impulse because Constantius has beaten everyone for 20 years. A civil war will cost millions of gold coins that you claim the empire does not have. Please wait until I'm older. I have my own score to settle with Constantius for depriving my father of what he was promised. Dad should have enjoyed a day in the sun before I buried him under my giant shadow."

Julian dismisses the boy. "Theo, if I let the army elevate me to Augustus, would you vocally support me?"

"After you let my nephew die? I have a big family, not including the branch that stayed in Rome. We cannot afford to back losers. Constantius is probably a better general than his famous father, Constantine the Great. He'd wipe out my clan if he beat us in battle. Constantius let me raise a local legion on the condition it never fight outside of Iberia. Before I left Barcelona, I sent him a message saying we were just escorting supplies and did not plan to take part in the Alamanni campaign beyond escorting prisoners to the slave markets. The ambush was naturally unexpected and the shocking poisoning of my brother justifies letting my legion raid Alamannia. But we need to go home now and I need to tell Constantius the moment we leave the Rhine. I will reassure him that my legion will not leave Iberia again. I cannot let him think I oppose him. That said, I can't join his army because he undermined my brother's one shot at glorious victory. He set Ger up to fail at his first independent command. And you let my troops die, so no, I can't support you, either. Sire, you've beaten the most powerful Germani. I'd advise you to take a victory tour of Gaul, Iberia, and Italy. Win people over before you challenge your clever cousin. Savor your victory while winning over powerful players. Luca says the Senate doesn't know you. Charm the togas off them before you reach for the world's highest throne and maybe take time to beget a legitimate son. I, for one, will be a secret supporter rooting for your success while silently seeking invisibility. Please mention me, Max, and my legion as little as possible while claiming all credit for crippling Alamannia."

"Ah. You plan to wait until Constantius dies and I become emperor. I may not have your patience. Max, I authorized payment, so you should release me. Holding me hostage here is horrible. It's beneath even you."

"But I look forward to killing you if your treasury does not pay up. You were smart to send Pelagius to the Black Sea using a ship on the Danube, and even smarter of Pel to leave while he could. I bet he plans to stay far away until the political dust settles in these dangerous times. Constantius never dreamed you'd do so well and now he's having third thoughts. My family doesn't want to get caught in the middle, so we're returning to Iberia while you test the political waters for swells and reefs. I wish there was a faster way to send messages, but the speed of horsemen is our communication limit."

"Max, I hear rumors that you're incredibly wealthy, even after generously rewarding your boys. It doesn't seem fair that you blackmail me and hold me hostage when you're so rich."

"I killed over 200,000 of your enemies. My army was cheaper than yours, more effective, and won an actual victory that you get to claim. I gutted, crippled, and depopulated Alamannia, yet I haven't heard you thank me, so don't ask me for a loan. The Batavi will spend theirs on more dikes, waterwheels, and water pumps. Farming the Lowlands requires a massive investment. They talk about digging thousands of miles of irrigation while erecting thousands of miles of dikes. Crazy right?" Still wearing chainmail, two swords, and a knife belt, the boy looks tightly wound and somewhat explosive. "Julian, is your offer of 400,000 gold coins for killing Constantius still good for five years?"

The ambitious upstart feels a chill flow down his spine. "Yes. How would you do it?"

"Apple cider. I found the recipe in Serapio's papers, along with the design for the tall log tower. When you want it done, leave half the bullion at my Amsterdam warehouse and then send me a red rose. You must first pay because you can't be trusted."

The next Augustus mentally postpones his plans to assassinate the boy. He holds out his hand as if they are equals. Magnus shakes it to everyone's relief.

"Thank you, Max. You're expensive, but worth it."

"That's what all my lovers tell me instead of tipping. I had to quit prostitution because my regulars kept fucking me."

Theo laughs loudly. "Ah, Ger loved that line. He told it a thousand times."

On the large stinking artillery trawler, Magnus sails past an even bigger ship with a stunning stallion on the extended bow. The Sea Horse is big, beautiful, and brand new, with large catapults and teams that look like they know how to use them. It's a pirate ship dressed as a freighter, but five Batavi gunboats anchor around it. Those sailors give Magnus a thumbs-up, which he gratefully returns. On the Sea Horse, the head of the family and four kids run to the starboard rail and most applaud the new hero of the family. Marc is suspiciously happy, while Theo's three small children look bored or envious. Admiral Honorius wants the gunboats to let him leave, but the angry look on the orphan's face makes him check his violent temper.

Magnus yells across the water. "Brother, I hope you like the clothes I sent in that oak chest. Admiral Honorius, I love your Sea Horse. I've never seen a more beautiful ship. Can I buy one?"

"We'll talk after you settle your affairs. I'm in a hurry, yet Dutch won't let me leave; he says I must compensate him for a thousand dead Batavi. Perhaps you could talk to him. In Amsterdam, your Uncle Honorius has cataloged your loot from the vault and

160

considers it considerable, but he refused me entry, for some reason. The gold coins from Triers are the new debased currency, but we can pay taxes with them."

"Admiral, if you replaced your debased coins with my good ones, I'll kill you."

Astonished, the old man cocks his head like a chicken as the smaller ship moves past. "What was that?"

"Admiral, I said if you cheat me like you cheated my grandfather, I'll gut you like a fresh fish. Your family in Iberia are hostages to your honesty, so you better take better care of my little brother than you did your own little brother. You look at me like a dumb child while I look at you like a lying thief. You saw what I did to Frankfurt, so think thrice before fucking me. If you betray me, I'll hunt you down. If you happen to have anything of mine, then meet me ashore with a full list and all will be forgiven, if not forgotten."

The old man suddenly looks older as he realizes Magnus trapped his flagship, not Dutch.

The trawler sails into the crowded riverport, where Magnus lands with a bang. It seems everyone came to greet the hero of Frankfurt. Franks, Saxons, Batavi, Jutes, Angles, Frisi, and Romanized locals cheer him and chant his name until he roars happily as the ship docks. His uncle meets him mounted with a century of armed Iberians who are mostly family or family friends. Theo kept dangerous men that he trusts because his war hasn't been won. Magnus knows them all and gratefully greets several by name. Wearing a backpack and a pouch over his chainmail, he blows kisses to the crowd, then hugs Caesar the Stallion like a prized possession. His pockets are still full and bulges don't quite hide several coin purses hanging from his neck. Loading Caesar with sacks full of bullion does not go unnoticed.

"Uncle, they act like I'm running for mayor, but I'll be assassinated if I stay here. 750,000 Alamanni probably want to kill me and the rest are even angrier, down in Hell's basement. Marc and your kids need to leave."

"Little Man, the rabble want you to share your loot. All your backpacks and sacks from your shitty hole in Frankfurt are now in Amsterdam. I sent my legion home, half by land with our new herds and half by ship with our plunder. The West Germani seemed surprised I did not come out of this rich. We found little gold in western Alamanni, whereas you sent mountains of ore here; Joko is still smelting it all. The thousand iron ingots that you traded for the king's corpse have become arrowheads, throwing knives, and a few dozen special swords with gemstones taken from Alamanni elites. Without risking anything, Admiral Honorius did better than I did, buying very cheap herds of horses, cattle, prisoners, and slaves, so I should learn to sail. The mercury agent paid more than the slavers, so he bought a bunch. My brother Honorius wants to know if you're interested in buying neighboring land in Galicia. My legion is herding 100,000 horses and a million cattle to our province, where land prices are dirt cheap."

The orphan looks serious as he mounts up and rides out.

"Uncle, buy all the productive land that we can afford." He waves and the crowd goes wild. "I have a talent for tactics and theater. I blame dad, along with my looks. Let's settle up so I can leave for Amsterdam to see all the crap I stole before someone steals it." With a sling in one hand and a shield in the other, Magnus rides through the crowd with guards forming a wary perimeter. He can't wait to get into the castle-fort. He looks relieved once they leave the crowd behind. "Uncle, I bet Alamanni were in that crowd,

161

hoping for an opportunity to take me down. I'm more scared now than when I waited until the last moment to rappel down the tall tower, with most of it already in flames. I couldn't feel my fingers, so inserting the master key into the lock took forever. It was like jacking off drunk with a palsied hand in freezing weather – or so Luca tells me. Once buried in that shit hole, I felt like a blind quadriplegic in a dark basement at night seeking a black cat that isn't there. It took terror to new depths."

Uncle and nephew ride through the castle gate just as they did a lifetime ago, after the Alamanni ambush, where Magnus realized he had a talent for tactics. The fort looks the same, but feels different because it's basically theirs. Troops greet Magnus like best buds, but none say shit to Theo. Magnus knows some by name and jokes with them until they tie up their horses at a stone complex and load his loot into the castle vault. Then they go into a large conference room where clerks organize paperwork. Magnus recognizes some from Theo's legion and greets a few by name, including another cousin, but the leaders are new.

Theo clears the air with a fart. "Max, I don't want accusations of favoritism, so I asked the accounting team at Maximus Inc to divide the spoils according to our agreements. What you sent to Amsterdam is beyond their reach. The legion's clerks are either keeping them honest or looking for ways to profit. You stayed so long at Drusus Island that most of the payments have already been distributed. Briga's whorehouse made a mint. Their screams of ecstasy could be heard all night. The population has tripled and muggings have multiplied, so please don't wander alone. Everyone knows you're rich, so they assume you jingle coins as you walk."

"Nope. Just losing most of my marbles."

They sit down and the accountants go through the numbers. Magnus works an abacus like a pro, but nods in agreement at discrepancies. Finally, they sign off and both Theo and Magnus take some documents with them to the boy's old room. It's plain and small, with just a bed and a wash bowl on a milking stool. The orphan checks the lock he installed a few months ago.

Theo is worried. "Marc sleeps on the flagship now. You two are still small enough to share a cot. He'd love to have you."

Magnus waves that away. "I'm missing a massive amount of cargo. I assume the Admiral took it. He'd throw me over the rail if it meant taking the bullion I earned off Hanseatic fish. Uncle, I need your help to take back what's mine while you deserve greater compensation for the risks you took. I sent my loot on ships that I stole from the Hanseatic League, but he somehow got his dirty paws on some. I've never trusted that slippery weasel, so I won't put myself in his power or control. I might actually be your father because I've never liked Admiral Honorius. I like his sons, but they're not great men. You and dad, sure. I'll be great. I think Marc and Cousin Theo have great potential, but the rest are common men who will never shape the world. Dad planned to invade Alamannia and he planned to win. Despite his shitty luck, he radiated confidence. The only thing he worried about was you not showing up with what he needed. Without Joko's master key, he wouldn't have emptied the vault, but that crazy Galician fully expected to raid Europe's most powerful people and get away with it.

"When he died, you didn't blink at crossing the Rhine into Alamannia, where Roman armies fear to tread. You maximized your time to take what you could and destroy what you could not, while Julian had a better army and slowly didn't do much.

Dad was right: I'll never be half the man you are. I'd love to visit Persia and India, but I'd rather serve as your assistant than make a fortune with Honorius. Uncle, you didn't take one *denarii* more than your fair share, though the Admiral came here to clear us out. Why are you so honest?"

"Max, I'm not rich, but I've never been wealthier. I'm a simple man with simple tastes. What I hate is owing others. Uncle Honorius calls himself the head of the family, but he's always gone and rarely interested in family affairs that don't profit him. We never told you, but he refused to help us with our estate loan because he wanted to acquire our inheritance for himself on the cheap. Thanks to you, he can't lord it over me anymore. You paid off my father's debt, which my brothers, uncles, and I could not do. When I get home, I'll add your name to the estate to replace your father's."

"Please add Marc's name to that, plus your kids in case something happens to you. Your daughter, too, to give her some security. Both Julian and Constantius might take a shot at us, while Serapio is dying to kill us. Dad always claimed the Admiral tricked grandpa out of our best ranchland. If you want it back, now's the time. I think we should gobble up Galicia as aggressively as possible."

Smiling. "Little Man, I'm finally getting to like you."

"Well, don't get carried away just because I made you rich. Uncle, what's your favorite color?"

Warily. "Green. Why?"

The prodigy takes out a few dozen gorgeous emeralds from pouches around his waist or coin sacks hanging from leather threads.

"I've always liked how you answer a simple question with an honest answer. The evasive are untrustworthy. Please pick a rock." Theo grabs a green beauty. "I wanted to thank you for being a great brother and a good uncle. You should be the head of the family. Many are older, but none are wiser. I need to tell you a secret in case I don't last long. I gave Marc several hundred gemstones that we pried off Alamanni cups, weapons, and furniture, plus several thousand rings and Frankfurt's best jewelry. I sent it all with the silk to our warehouse in Porto Gordo. I asked Marc to sell his at rich ports and we'd split the profit evenly, but not to let the Admiral know because he'd just steal them. I asked the pirate here because he acquired most of his fleet through piracy. I just didn't foresee him stealing mine."

"Max, why give me a priceless emerald that I don't deserve?"

"I gave you a priceless emerald that you do deserve. It's your priceless huggies that I don't deserve. But, if you want to pay me back, then find great archers for Marc who like sailing. I'll contribute a dozen throwing knives to each. I want him to run the fleet one day. We might find someone better, but we won't find anyone more honest."

"Why not sell the gemstones yourself and keep the cash?"

"Because I love my brother as much as you love both of yours, even though Honorius has an abacus for a heart. With all the money from those rings, jewelry, and gems, Marc will buy things in one port and trade them in another. He needs valuables to buy silk, spices, and sugar from the East. I want the shipwrights in Porto Gordo to build vessels with iron hulls that last forever. Uncle, imagine our family with the world's only iron fleet. No one can sink them and no one can stop them. The Admiral is old and his ships won't survive him long, but his contacts and trading posts will endure after his death. We have dozens of cousins serving his fleet; in time they'll serve ours."

His uncle looks at him with new hope and old fears. "Little Man, you never cease to surprise me. You have a deal. Let's get our land and your cargo back from my uncle without killing him. Max, you're a good boy. I don't care what everyone says."

The hill overlooks the river. Holding a scroll, Magnus is gesturing dramatically to Joko and several other experts on a hilltop when Theo rides up with Luca and a squad of Iberian guards. Someone barks, presumably the dog that found Magnus. They all seem super excited, which makes Luca super suspicious.

"Why do I suddenly feel poorer than usual?"

The orphan runs over and points to the roaring river. "Folks ford the river at Briga because the bend in the Rhine slows the current while the shallow riverbed widens the river to make it easier to cross on horseback. For over 100 miles upriver and downriver, the Rhine is too fast, deep, and cold from snowmelt. 370 years ago, Caesar Drusus built his stone *castra* to control access. Fort Briga therefore stands in the middle of the ford with catapults and sentries. The town grew here to supply the garrison, so you built your forge, foundry, and factories here. But the iron mine is several Roman miles away because your grandfather wasn't me. Crazy, right?"

The orphan laughs like he's insane and stomps his boot like someone told a joke. He has enough personality to create a crowd.

"One of your books explains how Thales of Miletus, around 600 BC, was the first to show how to calculate distance despite mountains in the way. Aristotle regarded him as the West's first philosopher, its first major mathematician, and many now regard him as the Father of Science because he started the Greek tradition of explaining things in natural terms, instead of supernational phenomena. He calculated the heights of pyramids and the distance of ships offshore. The Thales Theorem is the first math discovery attributed to a historical figure."

Theo looks around. "Is anyone else lost?"

"Uncle, you're on a hill, but I'm on a roll! Thales began what others developed into the profession of surveying. Rome couldn't have built 50,000 miles of roads without it. Romans burrowed through hills, bridged ravines, and put pile drivers across marshes to get a direct route from here to there. They engineered solutions rather than bypass problems. I played around with this over a month ago, but partial ownership of this valley motivated me to get it right. I needed a little help before bothering you with the good news. Luca, our iron mine is just a mile from the river. It's far from the Bend, but just a mile from a bottleneck where the current is fast and deep. Waterwheels there will spin thrice as fast. Using a vacuum through airtight terracotta tubes, we're pretty confident we can pump river water into tanks on this hilltop. From there, gravity will send it down pipes to a series of top-spun waterwheels to power our stamp mills. They could even pump water from the mine shafts that today you foolishly fight with buckets. With that power, a mechanical scooper could lift more earth than 100 men. We believe this mine could produce 1000x as much iron with the same payroll through automation and mechanization."

Luca looks at Joko, who smiles like he just got laid. Even the dog is pumped.

"Max, you expect me to build a new road and another riverport? Docks, cranes, and warehouses also aren't cheap."

The prodigy looks sadly at Theo, next to Luca.

"Yeah, umm, Luca, I got some bad news. Your wooden docks can't hold enough weight, so the cranes are too far from cargo holds and therefore slower and weaker. We need concrete docks, quays, or wharves so floods don't wash them away, wider and longer than yours, with heavy-duty long-neck cranes cemented in the concrete to hold them in place. The family fleet has been improving them for decades. The faster that a ship can load and unload, the less time it spends in port and the more time it's making money. The water in the Bend is only deep enough for the Sea Horse at peak river levels, but our bottleneck should stay deep enough even during droughts. That means ocean-going vessels can deliver and receive heavy loads. That reliability will save us time and money, while improving logistics."

The clever boy points inland at a distant hole in the ground surrounded by shack structures.

"From this tall summit, it's literally all downhill from here. The new road will follow a game trail to the docks. Luca, your grandfather's road is several times farther, so it takes several times longer, making transporting supplies and cargo expensive. Our road is much shorter, but must be built better than what your grandpa did because I want cast-iron wagon frames that carry 10x the normal weight. One wagon team will transport 10x more ore, which means we need 10x fewer wagons and drivers. The Alamanni have a word for how much a wagon can carry: ton. Except they pronounce it angrily, for some reason. I assume because the German language has too many consonants and not enough vowels. If an ordinary supply wagon can carry one ton of cargo, then we'll design iron-framed wagons that transport ten tons. The pavement must therefore rest on solid bedrock instead of compacted dirt. Water expands, when it freezes, so cracks have destroyed your road. Dad was quite the engineer who helped construct some impressive structures across Iberia. I love building almost as much as destroying, plus I know who would be ideal for this project."

He points. "Luca, that's Tribune Piso. He's a young construction genius who will oversee it all. You can trust him. I can't, but you can. Out of boredom during the siege, he surveyed Drusus Island to optimize its terrain. Crazy, right? Did I mention your ancient stamp mill is little better than pestle and stone? Piso literally laughed when he saw it. More waterpower means a heavy block of iron to crush the ore into tiny pieces, with rollers to reduce those into a powder. We'll multiply the volume it produces. The fewer impurities, the cheaper that iron costs to produce. Luca, your mine will not just be profitable, but will become Europe's most profitable iron mine by an order of magnitude."

"Max, there's no world where I can afford this."

"For 70% of Briga Inc, Maximus Inc will build it all. You won't spend a single *sesterius*. Furthermore, you'll pay our profits in iron ingots instead of cash. Again, we're buying all that you produce on an exclusive basis. The company will need to adopt our 2-book accounting system that the Admiral borrowed from Persia and every year will involve an audit, but your financial records will be the best in your family.

The senator seems skeptical. "Max, with all due respect, I can't help but feel that you are profiting off my ignorance. How could you possibly recover your costs?"

"Water can power scoopers, excavators, giant chisels, massive hammers, and huge shovels to extract 100x faster. Having stamp mills by the entrance saves having to haul it to the river. High-pressure water hoses can knock a prepared man on his back.

With proper drainage, we'll wash the dirt off the rock and divert it to our fields. The Midlands in Britannia has enormous amounts of coal near the surface that they sell for near-nothing. We'll burn that coal on your hardest bedrock to super-heat it, then soak it in cold water for the extreme temperature changes to break it up. Your richest iron is also deepest, but we can pump water from those shafts to make extracting ore easier. Have you ever seen a pile driver, when they build bridges or docks? We need a huge iron chisel that works the same way to break up bedrock. Volume makes mining profitable. Iberia and Britannia are years ahead of you primitives in the Rhineland."

Luca inhales deeply and slowly to think clearly. "You're trying to overwhelm me so that you don't have to tell me what I really need to know. Boy, spit it out or we won't do any business."

Theo turns in the saddle. "Luca, you agreed to sell us your iron at cost-plus 10%. Your margins remain the same, but volume justifies our huge investment. You'll make more by selling more, but we'll acquire your iron cheaper because mechanization will drop your costs tenfold. Our investment will make your mining operations a low-cost, high-volume competitor, which is why we insist on monopolizing your output. We will spend a fortune, but in return we will get an incredible flow of extremely cheap iron. In several years, you'll look at market prices and realize you're selling to us dirt cheap. Then you'll want to sell to others, which is why we need our folks in administration and accounting. Luca, I like you, but if you steal from us, I'll kill your family and make you watch. That's the Catch. You'll still make a lot of money, but only because we mechanized and automated operations. We'll return in the spring with most of my legion to start construction. Doing everything will take several trips because most of the equipment is custom-made in Porto Gordo. If we add a mercury smelter for the region's gold and silver, everyone will use us because we'll be the cheapest, most dependable, and most professional. We could serve all of central Europe. Luca, you'll make more with us than you can with competitors."

That leaves them pensive. All except the foresightful orphan.

"Luca, you have several thousand miners and twice as many family members living in ancient, unsanitary mud-and-thatch hovels. Your own doctor says dozens die every winter. That seems unnecessary, unethical, and unsustainable. We can deliver wheat and fish while they garden and tend fruit trees, fruit vines, and berry bushes, but what bothers them most are kidnappers. The Alamanni ruled this side of the river for a century and did what they pleased. We'll have less employee turnover if we give miners physical security and reliable food.

"I found the design for Frankfurt's log Cube tower, but want to make it 3x bigger. I'd like to build one for our miners by the main mine entrance to minimize their walk to work, except I want underground concrete bunkers for cold storage and to withstand a siege. To reduce turnover, we should reward the best workers with beer and sex. What folks want most is guaranteed safety, shelter, and food. Frankfurt's tower had a cafeteria like those used by legions, but I've thought of improvements. A squad of Iberians will provide security, which is cheaper than replacing and training hundreds of new workers every year. We can fit more folks by sharing entire floors and leaving just the penthouse for private homes for guards and managers."

Looking exhausted, Luca holds out both palms. "Max, please. The more you talk, the poorer I feel. I'll agree to whatever Theo proposes as long as no one screws me.

166

Dictator Gaius Marius made his nephew, Julius Caesar, Rome's high priest when Caesar was just 7 years old to prevent him from entering the military. Max, Caesar must have been like you for so powerful a man like Marius to fear a child. You have been generous with your uncle, your troops, and with me, so I'll trust you with everything except more granddaughters. The mine costs me money to operate. I doubt you can ruin me faster than that monstrosity. Theo, your uncle has been taking advantage of my hospitality. He's running up bills in your name while his thugs take what they want as if they never plan to return. You gonna do something about that?"

The legate looks at Magnus, then meets Luca's eyes. "Yep. And I'm gonna need your help. Here's what we're thinking..."

The senator leans in and grins deliciously at Theo.

CHAPTER 8

Hiding in trees on horseback, Theo waits for Uncle Honorius to go ashore with four guards to trade more stolen goods for fresh fruit, vegies, and grain. Once out of sight, Team Magnus rides to the Sea Horse, chatting as if they don't plan violent theft. They hid most of their weapons, but none of their charms. The four small kids run to greet them. Theo dismounts to stroll up the gangway to hug his kids, which the Admiral had been holding as hostages. Magnus follows, yelling at Marc about inconsequential things, but stops to admire a catapult railgun. Theo drops a green rock and his sons pick it up in awe. The orphan yells at Theo's guards, armed to the teeth.

"Boys, come check this out!"

"I thought we were riding for the iron mine," a trooper yells back.

"Later. I want to show you something first."

Complaining too loudly, 50 Iberians get off their high horses and walk up the gangway to see what all the fuss is about. A dozen sailors also want to see, but Theo takes them all to the other side, where the superstructure blocks the view from town. Soon they're mixed together as if some aren't enemies. The ship captain runs over, looking wary and worried. He carries a sword and a bow as if he expects hostile boarders.

Theo greets him with a smile. "Cousin Honorius, where's your father? He said to meet him here."

"He ran an errand. He'll be back soon."

"Your entire crew is fully armed. Are you expecting trouble?"

The captain keeps an eye on Magnus. "Better safe than sorry. Theo, please wait ashore for the Admiral and take your men with you. He won't be long. Max, I'm afraid I must ask you to leave. Threatening the head of the clan means you are banned from our fleet. I won't ask you twice."

Positioned past the superstructure, Magnus is looking ashore when he suddenly points. "Rules apply to me? That's not what dad said before I killed him." In a pleasant voice. "Oh, there's the Admiral." When the captain turns, Magnus throws a knife into his right shoulder, then runs over to take his weapons before the captain regains his senses. "Call everyone over or I'll start stabbing you. Your wife was nice to me, so don't make me cut off your cock. I just want the stuff you stole."

Angry and bleeding. "You stupid boy! He'll kill you."

Magnus thrust a knife into a thigh, then searches him for the keys.

"Cousin, I'll stab you every time you make me repeat myself. Tell your crew to drop their weapons and come here now. Even the cooks, cleaners, whores, and servants."

The captain caves and obeys. The crew comes over carefully and only releases their weapons when Honorius insists. Theo's Iberians tie them up and lock them in the storeroom. A dozen are family and they feel betrayed.

"Uncle Theo, have a team sweep the ship while we take a long look at the cargo hold. I'm anxious to see my stuff."

They hurry below, unlock the largest cargo hold that they have ever seen, and marvel at the sights. Holding oil lamps, they separately explore long rows, piled high. Each opens crates, boxes, and bags. Theo whispers in wonder while the orphan gets louder by the minute. He can't believe it.

Magnus yells over stacks of stuff. "The Admiral stored the most valuable cargo here to sell across the Med. That bastard took thousands of my furs! If I don't get lost in here, I could probably pinpoint the day he started stealing the ships I stole. I see products meant for Amsterdam; no wonder the Batavi are pissed. Only the ore reached Fort Briga and only because a giant pile of rock yields a spoonful of gold. Luca posted guards at the smelter and now I understand why. The fleet I captured only got a few trips before the Admiral started taking what he wanted while I was still alive and kicking. This flagship is richer than the rest of the Rhine. Did anyone in our family warn you of this massive theft?"

Magnus hears his uncle yell back and he sounds deathly cold. "Not a word, and some I've known all my life. He knows you'll find out. Why didn't the Admiral leave while you were stuck on Drusus Island?"

"He knew he had to kill me. Though a virgin, I've been fucked before. After seeing what I did to Frankfurt, the Admiral can't afford letting me surprise him. I might be a lot more like him than my own father, the next time you want to insult me. The Admiral must kill me to sleep at night. Uncle, can you think of a better explanation?"

"That old bastard cares for loyalty, not family. He says the only good enemy is a dead enemy, so I doubt he'd let you live."

They meet in the dark cargo hold, between rows of riches. Each holds a lamp like they're spies sharing secrets. They lower their voices as if God listens, but sound carries far.

"Uncle, are you also a threat? You command the only legion in Iberia and made it mobile to respond anywhere. The governor admires you while the Admiral owns a big chunk of Iberia's farmland. You could jeopardize all that the Admiral has built or else hold his family hostage. Theo, if he kills me, can he afford to let you live? What will happen to your beloved wife and kids if you let him kill you?"

The cool commander suddenly feels colder than the Rhine. "He refused me a tour of this fantastic flagship until my legion left; now he repeats the invitation often and urgently. But he only wants me, not my centurions, so I assume he wanted me dead before you arrived. Max, not all this stuff is yours, but he has been trading your cargo for things he wants to trade elsewhere. However, I'm thinking my life has a price that equals a quarter of this cargo."

The orphan smiles up at his uncle. "Agreed. Dad always called you a modest badass. Theo, you're Iberia's *Magister Militum* – the government's top commander. The Admiral has tried killing you, which makes him a criminal. I'm just 11, but I believe the governor should confiscate the Admiral's property, including his ownership in those ships. The family owns more than he does, so our share should increase. I've contributed about 30 ships taken from the Hanseatic League, which might give me majority ownership. The Admiral's last two sons can keep the ships they command, but the governor must brand the Admiral a criminal to confiscate his estate."

"Crap. We must kill him."

"And his oldest, who's also a dangerous pirate, but I'll take care of that. The crew is very loyal to him and may seek vengeance. The family serving him have the most to lose. As head of the family, you must decide their fates."

Theo hesitates. "Only a summit of family leaders can choose me as their head."

"The Admiral has been calling himself the head of the family ever since his

169

father died. He wasn't elected, but I think you should call for a reunion to choose a new leader – after I kill the Admiral. He owns most of the land around Porto Gordo's harbor. We'll upgrade the container-handling facilities and build us the world's only iron fleet. Today is cloudy, but the future looks sunny. Agreed?"

"The governor is greedy. He'll confiscate everything for himself. I have no leverage over him."

"Then we'll just say the Admiral and his son died in the fighting, along with everyone else you think will be a problem. Aren't you tired of being poor and powerless? Iberia pays you a pittance for risking your life. You deserve this. If you won't take what is yours, then stand aside and I'll man up. Oh, I saved several beautiful dresses for your wife, but feel sad that your kids will remain peasants scratching dirt for a living while I roam the seven seas with Marc as my admiral. Since you spurned Julian, you'll never get a chance for advancement, so you might as well retire like other 29-year-olds."

"Boy, don't push me. And I turn 30 soon."

"I know. Your birthday present is here somewhere if you still like silk-laced bear coats. I collected several thousand without blood stains, but this one was special, so I thought of you. Uncle, you know what needs to be done, but don't like killing family. Well, I'll do that for you. If you deal with the crew, I'll take care of the captain and admiral, but then I get the flagship, free and clear. I paid off your father's debt and loaded your legion with riches. As their commander, you could have demanded a share, but you failed to step up because you think you're a good man and there's the rub. 400 years ago, when Paullus Maximus conquered Galicia, he said good men are rarely great and great men are rarely good. Each of us must choose. I decided to become great, so I'll do the dirty deeds that you are incapable of. Just stay out of my way and protect my back. I want to make you the head of our family. I think you'll be good at it because you honestly care, but I also know you crave higher status. You don't want glory, fame, wealth, or women, but respect. Our clan will become the most respected in Iberia once folks appreciate the usefulness of our iron fleet. If you lied better and learned to talk out of your ass, you could even become a senator, but I'd prefer you as Iberia's governor. Oh, yeah, you didn't think I'd see your eyes light up, but I hooked a whopper with that one!" Theo chuckles. "I got my leverage over you now, boy! You'd like to become governor and I'd like to help you. Uncle, you never treated me like a child, so let's shake on our partnership as equals. I swear I'll never fuck you if you swear the same."

"Partner, there's something you should know. Admiral Honorius, as head of the family, refused to let me marry the love of my life. As a beautiful baby, I had been holding you as you played with my hair when you suddenly reached out for Admiral Honorius while screaming bloody murder. Flattered, he let you leap into his arms, only for you to shit on him literally and figuratively. That's when we started wondering if you were our dead dad. My Uncle Honorius has hated you ever since, less for the crap and more the public humiliation. Once your mother cleaned you up, you crawled back to me, holding up your arms for me to lift you. You ignored your father to smile at me instead. I proposed to Flavia once you fell asleep on me because she saw me as a great daddy. I didn't have a ring, job, or prospects, but the world's most beautiful girl fell in love with me because of you.

"Who you spend your life with determines your happiness more than money or material possessions. I've always had a soft spot for you because you got me her. You never made your parents happy, but you made me happy by inducing Flavia to marry a poor, awkward boy who didn't want to farm or ranch. With her looks, vitality, and connections, she could have done better, but she insisted on me over her family's better judgment. Despite being buried under the world's tallest tower and literally left for dead, the first thing that crossed your mind upon seeing her was a compliment so dishonest that I wish I had said it. Honora believes you have a thousand dolls for her and Flavia believes you think she's prettier than ever. My girls love you with an intensity that your mother could never relate to and it pains me to give you more leverage over me, but there it is. I owe you for a decade of happiness and I love you like a son. I want us to be partners for life and I want you to become partners with my sons for life. Are we agreed?"

The two shake on it, feeling on solid ground as the current shakes the ship.

"Uncle, the Admiral kept Julian's gold from Triers and swapped it for worthless coins that we must reserve for taxes and tariffs. I bet Honorius has a private vault that Joko can break into. Oh. Marc mentioned the Admiral called me a bastard at the tower. He's done that before. Years ago I told him he was there when my parents married and he laughed at me. Does he know something I do not?"

Theo speaks reluctantly. "Your mother only had you to trap Ger. He refused to marry her out of principal and cheated as often as opportunities allowed. He had your bad-boy looks, so he fucked around, but he liked her taking care of him. She devoted herself to him and that sucked out the bitterness. Right before Marc's birth, they married so Marc would not be a bastard. Ger claimed they married back in Britannia, but I was there and knew that they did not. She ran off with him, which infuriated her family, though Ger's rise in the Roman military helped them reconcile later. Rome appoints Londinium's mayor and Britannia's governor, so Ger bragged he'd come back to rule with their support. It was a good lie, but the emperor didn't like that peacock. Still, he was bold, brave, and charismatic, so it seemed plausible to your mother's family until you literally shat on his luck and the governor. Ger was persona non grata after that."

The boy takes that like a load of crap.

"I knew I was a bastard, but not literally. Good to know, probably. It certainly puts me in a murderous mood. Let's get out of here while we still have light. Something is getting dark and it might be me."

They leave, partners in crime.

Back ashore, Magnus mounts Caesar on the grass nearest the ship. Locals gather and soon swell into a crowd expecting a circus. They have no idea why their celebrity hero is in a killer mood, but the 4th century is boring, so they seek excitement. Each holding supplies, Admiral Honorius returns with his four guards and two bows, but stops at yelling distance because he's on foot while Magnus sits a saddle.

"Great uncle, you have stolen from me. Your ledgers give me no credit for the ships and cargo that you took. The ship captain confessed everything before his long, ugly death. I might miss that miserable man, but your oldest son deserved the hard death I gave him."

The old badass is pissed. "Where are my crew? Who are those men on my railguns? Where's Theo?"

"You did not return my property after you learned I lived. Instead, you fled Frankfurt and hid my cargo in your ship. That marks you as a thief and so I plan on shitting on you again. I'm here to arrest you. Surrender or resist arrest like your dead son and dumb crew."

The pirate turns on his men. "Kill him!"

His two bowmen are not prepared for battle because only a boy faces them. All must drop their heavy luggage first. As they unsling bows from their shoulders, Magnus kills them both with head shots at 30 paces. When their brains splatter, the mob loses its mind and wildly applaud. The other two guards have swords and shields. Magnus cripples the first and then gets a lucky shot at the other, tearing off an ear. The old pirate falls to his knees to grab the nearest bow and Magnus inserts a pellet into his back as soon as he stands. The Admiral is a warrior, so he still turns to shoot an arrow, but Magnus simply rides to avoid it while returning fire. This lead ball blows off his jaw and kicks in some teeth. The third pellet hits center-of-mass and the next three are probably superfluous, redundant, and unnecessary. The orphan rides for a better angle to sling survivors.

From nearby trees, Theo, Luca, and a uniformed watchman ride down in relief. The audience parts, still cheerful. The senator turns to his son, the Watch Captain, and loudly yells:

"*Praefectus Vigilum*, I saw the whole thing. That innocent boy was pasturing his horse when one of those five heavily armed men ordered the others to kill him. That rider defended himself from an unprovoked attack. Legate Theodosius, what will you testify to?"

"Mayor Savelli, I saw and heard the same. That man was my uncle. I'll take his body and possessions back to his family in Iberia. He'll trouble your town no more. Watch Commander, we planned to sail soon. Can we give you our written statements now to settle this matter?"

While Iberians from the ship load bags and bodies, the crowd disperses, content at scoring some action. Magnus rides with the men to town to celebrate his first piracy. They speak indistinctly. In his office, Luca's son puts down their statements on parchment and then writes his own, ending it all. Laughing at their good fortune, they raise their wine glasses in a toast, drink up, then shake on it.

On the Sea Horse, the ex-captain looks glum and gloomy. "No, Max, your other left. Yes, that painting. Just push the bottom aside and insert the key you took from my father. Remember, you must let me go. I wish we did this back in port. We've been sailing downriver since sunset. Why didn't you stop at Dusseldorf or Cologne? I won't find a safe landing until Amsterdam."

Magnus inserts the key as if losing his virginity and hears the primitive levers click. Springs and tumblers don't yet exist. The vault opens and Theo hands the orphan a lamp to illuminate the darkness. They moan as one, except Captain Honorius, who almost cries at the wealth taken from him. His wrists are tied together and twine digs painfully into his skin.

Magnus loves it. "It's big enough for several horses. I doubt Triers has this much bullion. Dangerous storing it on a ship, though."

The pirate captain explains: "Dad didn't like leaving it in Porto Gordo or Valencia ever since Theo stationed troops there. My brothers will be very angry unless you leave them a lot. Most of that is ours, not yours."

172

"Your brothers will get what they deserve. Theo, let's count and categorize it together after taking our cousin back to his new cabin."

The Sea Horse travels fast in the current. Magnus looks back and sees the trawler and the gunboats following him. Theo and Magnus push the injured captain along the superstructure when one of them calls a halt.

"Little Man, I change my mind." Theo is almost as big as his big brother, so he barely strains in throwing his cousin over the railing and into the lower Rhine. That hard man sinks like a rock because his hands are tied. Theo's angry and unapologetic. "My brothers and I exhausted our savings, income, and patience to pay just the interest on the mortgage. The Admiral claimed he was broke when he had enough bullion to fill a vault. You're right; I'm barely paid and my wife grew up living well, so I'd like a taste of the fortune you just inherited from my uncle."

Happy for him. "Uncle, half the wealth in that vault is yours because we're partners. Together we'll buy a majority of Maximus Inc and put ourselves in charge. We'll need massive wealth to forge iron hulls, but then we'll have a fleet to make us money. Some men muddle along, but boys like us make things work. Few folks inspire confidence, but we're two of them. You studied engineering like dad and you invaded Alamanni without permission. You're a modest badass. Tell me I'm wrong."

His uncle sheds tears like no one's business. "I have thrice my weight in gold? It makes me wonder where they store their silver. Thank you, Max. You're a lifesaver."

"That's not what the Alamanni say. Appreciation is nice, but I'm just paying down a moral debt. You've been a fabulous father to me. Men like you are rare, invaluable, and irreplaceable. I can't put a price on your head. If I outlive you, I'll cry the tears I couldn't shed for my dad. I should stop feeling like an orphan. My parents cared little for me when living. You're my real daddy, so I'm not just an awful orphan. Dutch should be trapping our Hanseatic ships outside Amsterdam. The Admiral brought eight freighters that I need you to command. We should rehearse the story we tell them so the Admiral's crews welcome their new owners. Now's also a good time to dump this crew overboard. I'll kill them first so none survive. I feel bad about our crooked cousins, but they wanted me to die and I draw the line around there. Not one came to you, so they're dead to me."

"Max, how rich are we?"

"We're not rich at all. We're starving sailors struggling in rough seas. Our plunder will fund iron ships and tall towers. Don't think of us as rich because we'll blow through that bullion in no time. We'll struggle just like other beautiful businessmen from fine families until we control a fleet that operates profitably. The Admiral was a criminal, but a competent one. He knew every port on the Med like the bottom of his booty. Knowing who buys what is half the trick. I like Marc's idea of trading with East Africa, Arabia Felix, Persia, India, the spice islands, and eventually China. Sailors say sugar, spice, and silk sell here for 100x what it costs in Asia. Imagine turning a thousand bullion bars into a million. Pirate Honorius didn't dare because wooden ships sink too often with their expensive cargos. Bigger iron ships, however, should survive, but developing them will cost us that entire vault and then some."

"We should diversify into farming and mining. Waterpower saves all kinds of labor. You're young and smart. Learn to make us better waterwheels, Archimedes Screws, pumps, and vacuum systems. Mills have been around several centuries, but look

173

the same. I bet you could hire experts who design something better. Partner, let's do what we can, as fast as we can, for as long as we can."

They shake on it.

A warning horn blows on the Sea Horse and Magnus scrambles onto deck with everyone else crowding the passageways. Sailors are dropping anchors and cutting sails. The sentry on the bow is losing his shit and it's getting messy, so Magnus sprints over to see for himself. The sight makes him roar. Eyes wide and vomit in his throat, he roars again before Dutch destroys his new flagship. A fleet blocks the river. They positioned themselves to punch holes in the hull. A chain crosses the river at a bottleneck, but the warships beyond shock them. Gunboats pour out of hidden inlets to fuck them from the rear. It's an ingenious ambush. Magnus waves wildly and yells his friend's name. A brass tuba blows and the Batavi ambushers stand down. Well, in their boats they're already sitting, but they abort their attack runs.

The terrified teen turns to his crew and he's near tears. "Aren't you glad I'm here? You all thought it was silly for me to roar, but that just saved your asses, didn't it? I'll graciously accept your apologies later." The orphan leans over the rail as a Batavi boat sails up. "Dutch, old friend, you cured my constipation, but gave me hiccups. Have you been collecting the ships we stole?"

"We? My sailors started with the ten we took from Frankfurt, plus a few dozen more from home. We sank a dozen and captured almost 40 when that big ship started taking them back in your name. Some old man said you were dead, that he was your uncle's uncle, and that he brought the Iberian sailors you asked for. You and I agreed to split the vessels evenly, so that's what we did. But, once our warships were out of sight, that damn pirate started attacking everyone, including us. Plus, the Hanseatic League wants to wage war on us. They're a business confederation from many cities and tribes, not a political entity, but they're adding catapults to counter ours. The Batavi are at war with everyone in the rivers and our leaders are furious that so many of our warriors died."

"I'm angry to. If reinforcements came as planned, they'd be alive. You're Rome's allies, not vassals. You should not have let Caesar Julian stop you."

"Julius gave the order, but that old man blocked the river until your birthday."

"That bastard! Now I'm even gladder I killed him and stole his ship. I'm sorry for your losses, but I lost too many Iberians and almost died myself half-a-hundred times. All Alamanni want to personally mutilate me. It's been a tough month all around. All we can do is pick up the pieces and prepare for tomorrow. Julian's treasury in Triers paid, but half in new debased coin because it was meant for troops, who have no choice. I also have a chest full of coins for your surviving troops and the widows, but your leaders must let me go through the numbers with them so they know I'm a thorough boy who doesn't cheat his friends. Artwork, heirlooms, and precious stones must be sold to determine value, but I swear the Batavi will get their share. I am not generous because I'm generous; I'm absurdly generous because not everyone loves me, for some reason. I need a life-long partnership with you and the Batavi. My uncle and I plan to make iron hulled ships, so you will want us as partners. I also brought you a great bear coat and some odd weapons to wield as conversation pieces as you fight boredom with your wife's friends."

Theo, his wife, and his kids join Marc at the railing. Dutch's face softens.

"Legate Theo, I'm relieved to see you alive. We had our doubts. Please tell me what happened to that old man who attacked our shipping with the biggest naval catapults

I've ever imagined. He had us out-ranged, which is a terrifying feeling. That ship is a menace to shipping."

The legate stands tall, stern, and unbending even as he leans over to yell down. "Not to our shipping; not anymore. In Briga, in front of thousands of witnesses, Max removed his head with lead pellets. The senator and I saw it. Well, arranged it. By blocking the river, my uncle tried killing my nephew. He also stole everything he could, which also justified his execution. The original crew of this ship was killed; you'll see their bodies float down once bloated enough. Commander Dutch, I thought we were friends and partners united against common enemies. Is that still so? Amsterdam has my brother, our wounded, and several clerks. Are they well?"

The Batavi tires of looking up to foreigners. "Your brother's relationship with you saved him. We're very vulnerable to warships and the Baltic has many of those. We must win, negotiate a peace, or fight to our last breaths. As a Roman legate, you could broker peace between the Batavi and the Hanseatic League."

"Who do I need to talk to?" Theo asks.

"The Hanseatic League is a decentralized trade alliance, but the group summoned leaders to a conference in Lubeck to levy fighters. As the southwestern-most city on the Baltic Sea, it ices over the least in winter. Most of the Baltic's coastline freezes deep enough for wagons, so sailing is seasonal."

The boy jumps so abruptly that everyone stares at him as if he'll explode. "I've always wanted to see the Baltic! Uncle, tell Flavia it's a second honeymoon, even more dangerous than the first."

"Second? I was never able to give her a first honeymoon."

"But that's cuz you were poor. Uncle, you're not poor anymore and you command Europe's largest pirate ship." He leans over the rail and shouts. "Dutch, if we get you peace, will you forever be my friend? I sent a lot of loot to Amsterdam. If none is missing, then we'll probably help you."

Amsterdam, the Netherlands/Batavia

So many armed vessels sail up that the population freaks out. Covered in catapults, the trawler is obviously a warship and no one knows what the hell the Sea Horse can be. The city is in chaos. The militia mobilizes and men rush to the river to repel hostiles. Batavi gunboats dock first to calm folks down, but Magnus is not far behind in the largest ship to ever unsettle the Rhine. He lands with a bang, well-armed with weaponized charm and a few dozen Iberian guards. An anxious mob approaches and he greets them like a pro:

"Relax, everyone – the hero of Frankfurt is here! Have you already eaten the million free fish I gave you? You're welcome, by the way. I bet you sold them for an unforgiveable profit, but I'll try to pardon you."

A well-dressed merchant with several guards walks up and throws down: "Who are you?"

That offends Magnus. "Sir, that's the most insulting thing ever said to me. I am Max the Lion, killer of 200,000 Alamanni and Bavarians. Some heroic friends may have helped."

"Are you related to Henry the Lion of Saxony?"

175

Legit shocked. "Sir, what you first said is the second most insulting thing ever said to me. You're insufferable, if you're anything like me. No, not all lions are related and apparently I need a better name. I don't know how I'll compete with a lion, but I imagine I'll dream of something great to end this nightmare. Most men must get to know me before I disappoint them. How have I failed your expectations?"

As hundreds gather around, the big man looks down on the boy, unhappy and disappointed.

"Henry's bold grandson is even more impressive, though not as loud. Your clothing blinds me."

"Sir, I'm not gonna stand here for your insults! Got a chair? Your tongue is sharper than my blades, so your whetstone must be killer. I'll send for quill and paper while you vent your best material. I have a precocious cousin who's hard to offend. Wha' do ya got?"

"Child, where are your parents?"

"Buried upriver last month. My arrogance and foolishness killed them. Kids aren't responsible for their actions, yet everyone blames me anyways. I gave you a million fish, yet no one thanks me. Just typical. If you treat me any worse, I'll consider you family. If our audience gets any bigger, I may sing. Sir, you have a proportional mouth for someone your size. You got a name?"

"I am President Dutch of the Batavi Republic and thanks for the fish. You must be my son's dead friend. At his stubborn insistence, we've sequestered your enviable wealth into a dedicated warehouse that your uncle monopolizes. Some Iberian family members guard it, if you can trust family. I'm an honest man, but that's a lot of loot."

"As it happens, I just killed twelve family members who preferred me dead, if you can imagine that. You may see their bodies float by soon. I don't know what sequester means, but I must warn you that I have uncles who read, for some reason. President Dutch, war with your neighbors will ruin you because the Batavi live off trade. My other uncle, the legate, can broker peace, but I want a portside trading center with a dedicated dock and warehouse here, in Rotterdam, and on Frankfurt's island-fort. I had Drusus Island surveyed to make it impregnable, but your trading vessels, raiders, and garrison can share it with me. Denying Frankfurt to the Alamanni takes your biggest competitor off the market. My sacking of Frankfurt included a few dozen ships that the Hanseatic League used to aid my enemies. The League can have them back if they have a better navy, better aim, and better luck. If not, I'll blockade the Baltic and let them starve. I'm confident they'd prefer peace. Forgive me if I'm overly feisty; I get like this every time the sudden death of my parents makes me kill a few hundred thousand strangers. It seems the Alamanni are better at kidnapping kids than killing them. I've urged them to add that to their flag, banners, and anthem, but they stopped listening to me once I slaughtered them all. Their terrifying reputation now barely scares their neighbors."

Dutch Senior is wary and unnerved. "I see what my son sees in you, but some of our Christian soldiers think you're the devil."

"Is that why I'm sexy as hell? I've become a bit bossier since I bagged so much bullion, but I'm a generous ally and a killer enemy. Devil seems an over-reaction. Even the Alamanni only called me a demon-boy. My flaws are louder than my virtues, so try to look past the obvious to squint at what makes me special. Someone in Frankfurt mentioned a possible canal between the Main and Danube rivers. It'd be a little over 100

Roman miles long, but imagine enjoying access to the Black Sea and the Med. My family will soon manage Iberia's largest and most profitable trading company. We'll split the cost with the Batavi Republic while charging everyone else as much as the market can afford. We can invite Rome and the Hanseatic League if they each pay a quarter. Perhaps the Baltic tribes, the Scandians, Flanders, and the Finns will join, but we need the Hanseatic League to broker deals with local tribes. That offer will do more to create peace than anything else we can offer. Having a fort, naval base, and port on Drusus Island would multiply its value and usefulness, so I'm offering value for value for a little land by your harbors."

The proposal seems to stun the man and wows the crowd, who suddenly chat excitedly. His eyes go vacant as the President of Batavia stares into the future while swaying like a log tower before it collapses on a boy.

"I'll need to summon leaders to a summit, but I'd rather stick it to Flanders. They're just down the Atlantic coast and are annoyingly competent fishermen. Access to the Danube, the Black Sea, and the Med could multiply our customer base. Mr. Lion, I was hasty in judging you by your age, height, and volume. Welcome to Amsterdam. Rotterdam does twice the trade and the Hague is prettier, but we're on the Rhine."

Magnus feels on sturdier ground now. "I'd also like land for a dock and trading post in the Hague for the million fish I sent you. If I get you peace with your neighbors, then maybe you'll stop clenching your fists. Just because I've slaughtered 200,000 armed adults doesn't mean you should fear me."

Theo jogs over, yelling at them to wait. He arrives out of breath and full of fury. He smacks Magnus on the back of the head and dares him to do something.

Angry. "I told you to wait!"

"And I told you to visit your brother later. We might as well be married. Legate Theodosius, this is the boss of the Batavi, President Dutch of the Netherlands. The canal nearly made him shit himself. Again."

The president winces at those words. "I like sausages, called sauerkraut and bratwurst, more than they like me. But, afterwards, things can get messy. Legate Theodosius, how serious is this proposal? 100 miles would take years. The Marcomanni and the Alamanni must agree, but everyone here would love to sell things to Constantinople. In comparison, Rome's a shitty dump living off the glory of past centuries."

"Sir, we can't know the cost or time frame until we have it professionally surveyed. I know an experienced Roman who can help. You and the Hanseatic League should hire someone you trust. My family will pay our share of the survey. Once we know the expected cost, we'll discuss financing the actual construction."

Magnus chuckles. "Theo, look at him shake. I think his sphincter just beheaded a bratwurst. At his age and bulk, he wants to run to tell his friends. This man appreciates the canal's value better than we do. Batavi trawlers could sell millions of anchovies across Central Europe, the Black Sea, and the eastern Med. A canal linking the Rhine with the Danube would expand and transform the regional economy. Tired of small, dark, oily fish, folks in the Med would love large, light dry fish from the North Sea. The Batavi would grow their market, power, and influence while becoming richer than their neighbors. Rome would love to reach the Rhine from the Danube. Their gunboats and supply ships would instantly become twice as useful, so they might even partner with us if we provide a solid survey. Connecting the Black and Baltic seas would be like discovering a new world. Uncle, Maximus Inc must find the best locations for fortified trading centers on the Danube and Rhine river systems before their value becomes obvious with the canal's completion. A network of riverports won't come cheap, but our vessels will need safe supply bases to operate profitably. Munich, Vienna, Budapest, Belgrade, and Bucharest would be obvious priorities. President Dutch, we could halve the cost by sharing construction. Our fleets could dump all the fish, grain, and goods that those cities can afford, storing them in underground concrete bunkers that the river keeps cold. The more land we wall in, the more residents working for us."

The president and the legate exchange knowing looks, then smile in agreement.

At the warehouse entrance, Uncle Honorius opens his arms for the huggie that Magnus always demands. The gunboats, the artillery trawler, and the Sea Horse anchor nearby. The newcomers nod at family members as they enter a log storage facility that would take axes to break into. High windows let in light. The quantity and quality of luxury furniture surprises the boy. The furs alone monopolize a corner and the expensive clothing another. After food, textiles account for most economies. Magnus stops and stares. His tone drips awe.

"Uncle Honorius, it's more than I remember because the vault was so dark. Please show me the gold. I wrote down every item and counted every coin. Uncle, if you've spent any, best let me know now."

"I've itemized it all, you paranoid bastard. They had chests full of nearly worthless bronze and copper coins that I suspect have zinc, lead, and tin. I've been paying for food, drink, and rent with that whenever possible. Even with Frankfurt's purification refinery, it's probably cheaper to turn that coin into tools and utensils than separate out the base metals. I offered our guards good pay and a bear coat because a lot of locals have been snooping around; I'm afraid to go out, so we always eat in. I'm curious what I'm earning out of all this."

"My huggies are priceless, but tell me what you want as a bonus."

The banker hands over a few documents with seals and wax like they're wet teenage pussy. "The fish netted you several hundred talents of silver, paid via check that you can cash at the Bank of Batavi. You have over 100,000 gold coins and thrice as many silver ones. I want 100 *solidus*, plus 1000 *denarii* because I'm cash poor." He leads them to a box with clothing, toys, tools, art, silverware, furs, and fine porcelain. The number of paintings surprises Magnus. "I'd love to give my family these things. I'm simple, but I hate seeing my wife and kids dress in rags. It's bad enough that everyone lords it over us petty peasants, but it seems I now work for you, of all people. I'm sorry that I need so many outfits, but bankers must dress up and you killed elites with terrific taste. I wish all savages had such sophisticated sartorial taste."

"Uncle, if you'll spend the rest of your life working for me, then please accept 1000 gold coins, 10,000 silver ones, and a million huge huggies. I have enough nice clothes on the Sea Horse to fill your old house. You, Theo, and your wives should take the best stuff before I offer it to the rest of the family. Ditto for tools, toys, utensils, weapons, art, furniture, and furnishings, but only if you flaunt it all in Iberia. Everyone will kiss our boots if they think cleaning out Alamannia made us filthy rich. That will make electing Theo head of our clan easier, plus buying a majority stake in Maximus Inc.

I plan an even bigger log tower at Porto Gordo's harbor, another as far up the Mino River as boats can reach, and on Arosa Island since Admiral Honorius no longer needs it. I want you and Theo to each own a floor while I occupy the penthouse. Building vertically is genius because it provides the cheapest housing per land area. Imagine capturing everyone's pee and poo for fertilizer. We'd triple yields, use all fields, and may even get another harvest per year. With enough buried crap, the sky's the limit. The more people we shelter, the more shit we'll enjoy. Galicia has rich soil; now we know how to replenish it economically. Imagine if a million tall towers housed all of humanity – no more starvation. The rest of Iberia is rather dry, so they'll need us to avoid starving."

The banker seems skeptical. "Sounds expensive."

"Once we take the Admiral's fleet, we'll own 68 ships and countless boats. At the next family reunion, we'll update ownership. We need to hire Iberian crews, which will give our family more clout in Iberian port cities. What we will soon need is our own governor. Uncle Theo, being a legate doesn't keep you busy. Julian could appoint you governor if we force him to. Get started on that."

Honorius looks scared: "Beloved nephew, why would you give me 10x more than I asked?"

"We succeed or fail as a team. Not as a family – fuck those bastards. You're a banker. The family owns a bank and I just got really rich. I might need your services, so learn all you can because I want you to run our bank someday, except I'd like to change the name to Bank of Iberia."

"Little Man, I thought you preferred death."

"Oh, uncle. That was ages ago, when I was only 10. I'm older, wiser, and less patient now. I have a new purpose in life: guaranteeing humanity food, shelter, and safety. Keep up or I'll leave you behind. We need to send everything to Porto Gordo, except trade goods meant for Londinium. I must tell mama's family of her passing and recruit her brilliant brother. Before visiting Lubeck to end hostilities with the Hanseatic League, we must prepare for a naval battle. I hope the Batavi fleet joins us. Let's park our wealth here in case our ships sink."

Lubeck, Germania, Southwestern Baltic Sea

The Sea Horse approaches land. Theo, Magnus, and Dutch go on deck to see the city as it appears over the horizon.

Dutch gives them the low down: "Traders only recently started calling this commercial alliance the Hanseatic League. They trade a lot of grains, timber, wax, resin, amber, furs, and fish. Germani cities from various kingdoms seek markets and raw materials across the Baltic – Ostrogoths on the southeastern shore, Finns to the northeast, Scandians on the rest of the north, and scattered Baltic tribes along the south, trying to retain their ethnic identities amidst so many northern Germani. The Batavi language evolved into something distinct, so no one understands us. Scandians speak something different from Finns, though outsiders equate them. Ostrogoths are East Germani, but are western Goths, having separated from Visigoths, now nomadic herders northeast of the Danube. Several languages, cultures, and competing polities make commerce, communication, and peace more difficult and less economical. The farming season is short, winters brutal, and hunting can't support many people, so they all developed a

179

raiding tradition. Trading reduces that by offering folks an alternative method of getting goods. Kingdoms and borders are ineffective, so the League provides mutual protection against piracy and banditry. Duty-free treatment fosters trade and profits, along with diplomatic privileges and a shared maritime law. Fewer trade barriers increase interdependence. Trading posts, mercantile branches, and factories arise where they make the most sense instead of a particular kingdom. The League has already prevented many petty wars. Even kings must respect Hanseatic Law. They have a legislative body called a Diet. In time, the Hanseatic League could become the world's most successful trade alliance."

Magnus points at something piercing the sky. "Henry the Lion must know we're coming because he's sporting an enormous erection. God, I'm so glad I gave up masturbation. Men say quitting is hard, but I've quit masturbating thousands of times."

Dutch doesn't want to touch any part of that, so Theo explains.

"He's nervous. Max overheard his dad tell sex jokes to the troops before battle. Surviving death has left him terrified. Max, tell our friend your father's favorite."

"Do all women fake orgasm?" Dutch thinks he's done and is not sure if he should answer, but the boy continues with a smile. "Or am I just doing it wrong?"

The Batavi laughs, wishing he knew Ger better.

"Lubeck says that lighthouse is the world's tallest, even bigger than Alexandria's old one. The brickwork church is behind the Holsten Gate, one of seven. That's the Trave River and so Hamburg isn't far. The Scandians joined the alliance with the cities of Birka, Konisberg, Mecklenburg, Schleswig, and Haithabu, plus Visby on Gotland Island, but none of their best port cities, who view the Hanseatic League as trade competitors. Because the Batavi have Roman support, our factories and craftsmen enjoy access to the West's largest market, though the voyage is long. The League grew to counter us since Rome would not let them simply destroy us. They need economies-of-scale to survive dark winters and long droughts. If they continue to grow, the League will become far more powerful than any northern kingdom."

Magnus knows enough. "Bring the leaders that we captured on deck and let's see how badly the League wants peace."

Tied up, captured captains crowd the railing as the harbor mobilizes for defense. Lubeck had never been attacked by sea and the sight of so many hostile ships unsettles them. The foreign fleet could easily sink them, but instead waits patiently, flying a white parley flag. Every vessel in the harbor raises anchor with armed men to counter the foreign fleet. Their biggest warships sail up, crowded with shooters, and anchors just within yelling distance. Nose to nose, both parties shout from the bow.

An expensively dressed man yells from the other ship. "I am Henry III of Saxony. Are you the demon-boy who destroyed our greatest city?"

The prodigy explodes in a mad rage by the rail. "Why do so many barbarians speak better Latin? Sir, how long did you live in Rome?"

"Five years in my youth, plus another in Athens, though I've forgotten most of my Greek. I like their word for general, *stratego*, better than the Latin, *magister militum*."

"Sir, I've never spent a day in school, though I often hid there at night. What kind of ignorant barbarians are you? A year in Athens studying philosophy, geometry, and rhetoric? Who has the time when the world needs fixing? I bet Rome was still beautiful, clean, and efficient in your day. Now they can't even fix their weights and measures, much less clear the sewers. Rome's Cloaca Maxima sewer system caught fire when I was there. Residents don't drain the marshes, so plague swept the city just months after I left. The wealthy spend their lives on rural villa estates where an army of serfs works for free to produce wealth for the few. A few hundred families own everything worth owning in Italy because they use the government to take from the less powerful. Oh, yes, I'm the demon-boy who sacked Frankfurt. How was Athens?"

He sounds tired and confused. "Athens has always been a dangerous cesspool. Their streets have rails for wagons and carts, but no drainage or trash removal. Pericles, who led in their Golden Age, lost his family to a plague that their crap created. Greeks hate arched doorways, straight streets, and each other. Even in Caesar's day, Greeks lived off the greatness of their ancestors while doing nothing to improve their living conditions. Every year Greece gets poorer. The single city of Constantinople enjoys a greater economy than all of Greece. They started the first written alphabet with vowels, which Jews still don't have. It must hurt to start Western Civilization, then become permanently irrelevant. Demon-boy, have you come to return our ships?"

"No. They were helping my enemy, so I confiscated them as prizes of war. You backed the losing side and so you get what losers always get. That said, shit got out of hand, and not just in Rome's exploding sewers. As I expected to die, I didn't see it as my concern but, having survived, I now need to clean it up. One family killed my parents, but the Alamanni are not our enemy, nor the Hanseatic League. War is expensive and benefits no one except worms and vultures. I'd like peace between the League and the Batavi."

"The ships you took are very expensive and some had cargo of even greater value. We appreciate the return of our sailors, but they worked hard to harvest millions of fish. You are a thief to keep them from their rightful owners."

"Nope. I'm a general with the right to take from the enemy. As King Brennus told Rome after sacking the city in 390 BC, woe to the vanquished (*Vae victis*). You should not have helped the Alamanni. Two Roman armies prepared to invade, yet your ships delivered fish to feed the folks we were trying to starve. You aided and abetted Rome's enemies and got what you deserved. Don't pretend you didn't know the risks you took. You expected the Alamanni to win, so take your punishment from a boy like a man. If you don't make peace, warships will blockade the Strait to bottle you up in the Baltic and deny you the North Sea's fishing grounds. Then we'll shell port cities every summer until folks kill the stubborn men who insist on a war they cannot win."

That goes over like a turd.

"Boy, I can see why your family wanted you dead. Did you come to negotiate or just to tell us to take our lumps?"

"I hear you have an impressive grandson about my age. Is he the short one with the tail? I'd like to challenge him to a roaring contest."

A boy younger than Magnus yells across the water. "Grandfather is Henry the Lion. I'm just Henry and lions rarely roar."

Magnus is loudly exasperated. "Even the boy speaks like a Roman elite! Sirs, it's not right that barbarians speak better Latin than those who wrongly call themselves Roman. I doubt you'd understand half the legionaries in my father's legion. Well, armed with my big mouth, I was looking forward to roaring, but I guess we can finally get down to business. Gentlemen, I apologize for any sailors that we've killed and understand

181

you've taken debilitating losses that have crippled your economy. I've also had a bad month. I'd like to make things right: would the Hanseatic League like a canal that links the Main River to the Danube so you can sell logs, fish, and furs to Constantinople and the Med? Maybe metals, charcoal, and coal? You could make a fortune by selling food and fuel to southerners. Maybe you'd buy olive oil rather than spend half your life in the dark like filthy animals who speak excellent Latin."

The offer throws them like a whirlwind. Hundreds of expensively dressed men whisper-shout while others bellow to poorer bastards in the back. The deck comes alive with rapid chatter that answers the question better than a contract. The Lion lets them settle down before asking the obvious.

"Demon-boy, your thick accent is hard to understand. What did you just offer us?"

"I propose that my family's company, Rome, the Batavi, Baltic tribes, the Hanseatic League, and hopefully the Scandians to share the cost of a canal that links the Rhine and Main rivers. Flanders, Finns, Franks, and the Ostrogoths may also be interested and I know Jutes, Angles, and Frisi would love access to Central Europe and the Med. We divide the cost equally among major investors to earn free sailing forever. Everyone else pays tolls to use our canal.

"Getting the relative elevations right alone may take a year, plus deep core sample to excavate soft earth instead of hard bedrock. Local tribes would need to provide security, so we need you to deal with them. Europeans have dug hundreds of canals; this would just be longer and deeper for oceangoing ships. A professional survey would not cost much because we're splitting the price while the canal itself would be funded over many years. We know surveyors, but can't send them until we have peace, plus protection guarantees. I'd bet our investment will pay for itself within just a few years, then fund prosperity eternally. Linking the North Sea to the Black Sea would give cold northerners a lot of leverage at the expense of rich southerners. As a bonus, our fishing fleet will sell you millions of fish on credit for half the retail price. Distribution, warehousing, and sales would be your responsibility."

On the Hanseatic warship, the prospect glazes eyes and empties bladders. Access to the Med would transform Central European economies.

"Boy, how do you benefit from this canal?"

"Oh, it doesn't affect me, one way or the other. I'm just paying back the Batavi, who don't want war. We Iberians prefer the western Med. You won't be seeing me or your old ships in these waters. I had nothing against the Alamanni until their royal family poisoned my parents, but I've balanced those scales, so I no longer need to punish the Alamanni."

The Lion studies Theo. "Sir, you must be the silent uncle we never see. You look like a serious man. How serious is this proposal?"

"Completely serious. Since my nephew killed my pirate uncle, I've become head of the Maximus family, Iberia's largest. I can have experts here in the spring if you guarantee their safety. Just agree to end this weird war. My side and the Batavi will release any remaining prisoners that aren't Alamanni or Bavarians so everyone can get back to business. You can't get your ships back; they're already in the Med, but that's the price you pay for backing the loser in a killer war. Next time, bet on us winning."

The Lion takes the temperature of his colleagues with a glance and knows he has no choice. "Agreed. Please tell the Batavi to stand down, release our men, and we'll expect your surveyors here in the spring."

THE NORTH SEA

Using nets in calm sea states, the trawler catches zillions of fish. Magnus hops up and down as another net full of fish descends into the vast cargo hold. Even Uncle Theo looks stunned at the catch.

"Uncle Theo, Amsterdam is the closest good port to North Sea fishing grounds, except for Aberdeen in northern Britannia, which Picts control. Stationing that trawler in Batavia will make us a fortune off fish. If we dig concrete bunkers at several cities that rivers can chill at night, then the trawler can just dump their catch and return to the North Sea while our trading port sells seafood at its leisure. The deeper we dig, the colder the fish and the longer they last. Cold storage means our managers are not forced to quickly sell."

Theo catches on and catches up with a sigh. "Oh. You want to build our own docks, cranes, and warehouses in Amsterdam to reduce the commute. That won't be cheap."

"Plus a brothel-casino-tavern on the top floor of their Cube so our sailors spend their salaries at our businesses. Tribune Piso wants to replace logs by cementing concrete around an iron frame to make it harder to break into and easier to defend, with catapults and trebuchets to deter attacks. The first time that it survives attack will pay for the extra construction costs. The ground floor could be just for storage. Locals will mess with us less if we have a mini-fort within their port city. Bank of Iberia could even open a branch, giving us a vast network as we build Cubes in every naturally sheltered, deep-water port."

Theo doesn't like it, but he also doesn't argue with success, so he nods agreement.

Londinium, Britannia, 357 AD

After the trawler docks, Theo deals with purchasing agents. Fishing vessels have their own wharves with brokers who buy entire hauls. The trawler is huge, so locals gather to check it out. A crane fills a wagon with fish, which leaves with an armed escort. They ride in a defensive perimeter northeast into empty countryside. Magnus leads the vanguard.

Uncle Honorius is pumped. "We just made more money than Maximus Inc earned last year. Fishing the North Sea is good business. We need our own fish bunkers, underground granaries, cranes, and a Cube in Londinium. Max, I've never been to Britannia. What's your mother's tribe like?"

"They were fierce fighters, long ago. They fought Caesar when called the Iceni; they fought Governor Aulus Plautius when he invaded three centuries ago; and Queen Boudica slaughtered 200,000 Roman supporters. Romans now call them the Icelinga, if they bother to call them anything but Britons. Most folks in southern Britannia are Romanized, but the raids never end: West Germani from the mainland, Picts from the north, plus Hiberni and Scotti from Ireland. This island is a Roman vanity project. Britannia never provided more revenue to the empire than it cost, making it a lousy investment. Rome is too far and far too disinterested. This island needs a strong leader to punish the raiders and centralize the government. It's been a few years since I visited. Most of mama's family lives in or around Colchester. We should reach the town tonight and find my uncle in the morning."

Colchester, Britannia

The guests sit on benches outside a clinic when a young man shows up to unlock the door.

Magnus looks up. "Doctor, I'm in great pain. Can you help end my suffering?"

The young man glances at the boy, but ignores Theo, his wife, their kids, Honorius, and Marc.

"I'm just an assistant. What ails you?"

"I'm sick of annoying everyone and not having anyone love me. Is it true your huggies are lifesavers?"

The healer opens the door, then loses his shit. "Max!" Instead of hugging him, Bede looks around. "Where's my big sister? I miss her terribly."

The orphan gets suddenly sad and lowers his arms when his uncle doesn't hug him. "I have bad news. You should sit down for it. Can you skip work today? I'd like to address the family."

"Oh, I can't afford to miss even a day of work. I work sick, which is ironic, given my profession. My boss gets very mad at me when I'm late or take breaks. Hey, Theo. Long time. And Flavia, right? What's happening?"

"Uncle Bede, I'll double your salary if you work for me."

"Theo, you're hiring doctors?"

Suddenly tired, Magnus exhales loudly. "No, Bede. He's just a poor legate; he can't afford doctors, but I'm incredibly rich. He barely pays his troops, but I need a personal physician who travels with me. Did you finish school and pass their test?"

"Sure, but the government doubled the internship requirement, so I must work for a public clinic or hospital before they'll recognize me as a real doctor. You know how much I've always wanted to be a physician."

Suddenly sounding suspicious. "Bede, you're no longer clean-shaven and you wear a knitted robe instead of a woven tunic. You wear a linen head-warmer under a straw hat instead of a brimmed travel hat or that fun felt cone. What's going on?"

"Oh, things are bad and getting worse. Rome can't provide security, so their officials are increasingly disliked. You'll still see togas in Londinium, but a fraction as many as a decade ago. Romans often wear things on their heads, but rarely hats, so Britons use hats to show we are not Roman. Tunics were popular because they're basically upside-down linen or hemp bags with three holes for a head and arms. Now you'll see costly trousers, which require more fitting. Get old or fat and tunics still fit, but not trousers, so looking unlike a Roman is costly. Locals have also turned to ancient clothing or mainland sartorial fashions. The Franks are more popular here than Romans. Folks still speak Latin so tribes can communicate, but local governments have pushed the Briton tongue up to Hadrian's Wall. Standardizing a language helps us replace Latin. Most books published here are written in Brittonic, using the Latin alphabet, though that limits their market."

184

The orphan had no idea. He looks at his other uncles, perplexed, then shows Bede a gold coin.

"Uncle, I'll pay you monthly in advance if you agree to work for me from now on. My parents died of poison in the Rhineland, so I need someone I trust. I came all the way here to tell you because you loved Elia as much as I did."

Bede slouches on the bench besides Magnus and looks at Theo for confirmation. The Iberian grimly nods and they share a look of sadness.

Theo sounds sadder than usual. "I'm so sorry, Bede. My brother was lucky to have your sister. They died in each other's arms and we dug their grave personally, overlooking the middle Rhine. She was happy until the end. Are your parents alive?"

Bede shakes his pretty head. "Papa died when they chose a different chief. Mother passed soon after. I'll lock up and take you to the family farm."

The family ride to a large estate by a river. It looks like it was once prosperous with about 100 workers tending the fields. Despite recognizing Bede, many farm hands hurry inside or run into the woods. Bede calls out names and the family assembles outside the large home, mostly armed. A huge athletic teenager lowers his bow and steps forward upon seeing his cousin.

"Max? I didn't think you'd ever return. It's good to see you."

Smiling. "Cousin Wynstan, I was hoping to find you. You've grown into a giant. How old are you now?"

"17 and I go by Winston now to sound less Roman. I won a local archery contest, but still use your sling to hunt rabbits and rodents. That gift kept me fed when we was starving. My mama is alive because of your sling. I'm glad you're back. No one here can keep up with me."

"I can't stay, but we need ambidextrous giants. I brought a horse for you, so go get your stuff. I guarantee you'll make far more with us than staying here."

The big teen lights up and takes off.

An old man bellows. "Bede, who are your guests?"

"Some of you remember Theo, who is now a legate. He has sad news of my sister."

"My brother, General Gerontius, was preparing to invade Alamanni with a Roman army when an Alamanni named Serapio poisoned him. Elia also drank the poisoned apple cider because she literally couldn't live without him. They died that night without much pain. Max and Marc are now orphans."

The old man doesn't hesitate. "We'll take the young one, but not the loud one. That bastard killed my dog with a sling when it bit him."

Magnus is furious. "You told that bitch to bite me, you cranky geezer! You're lucky I didn't sling you, too."

Marc tries to help. "Max, please don't start anything. Give them time to grieve."

"Grieve? Do they look sad? They all said mama could have married better. I want you poor farmers to know that Gerontius died a general in command of 50,000 troops that plundered Alamannia. Yes, the same Alamanni who beat the Franks, Saxons, and Marcomanni. I just got rich by sacking Frankfurt. One of my ships just sold a million anchovies in Londinium. I brought a wagon full for the family, but you never appreciated me. Never mind. This visit was a waste of my busy time. I'll just dump the fish by the

185

road instead of giving it to you ingrates."

A woman with a scowl laughs at the orphan. "Ah, Flavius, don't leave mad. Just leave now."

"Are you getting my name wrong on purpose? My name is Max until I think of something better. One day I'll have a great name that no one else has. Something unique to go down the ages. Uncle Bede, please wait for Winston if you can tolerate these folks."

Magnus makes Caesar stand on his back feet, punching the air while one of them roars angrily, then they ride off, best friends against the world. Theo, looking sadder than normal, signals his riders to leave.

Bede holds up a gold coin to his family. "You geniuses just ran off the richest person you've ever met. He showed me a sack with 100 gold coins and Theo says they have 100,000 in various banks. Unless Theo is a remarkable liar, Max got the better of Caesar Julian, the Alamanni, and the Hanseatic League. He has 68 ships, an attitude, and plenty of bullion. Oh, and he wasn't kidding about a wagon full of fresh fish. You better hurry before your neighbors grab them all. Max hired me at twice a doctor's salary, so this is goodbye."

Bede rides off when Winston mounts up. Enough of the family are curious enough to saddle up and chase them down the road. Bede sits his horse beside a pile of anchovies, watching poor people stuff big pockets with small fish. In utter awe, Winston looks like he's never seen fish before. The family rides up and gets down, shocked at the sight. The astonished look on their faces at all this free food is priceless.

Bede isn't sympathetic. "I told you he brought you a wagon full of fish. Your neighbors are taking what was meant to be all yours. Just being polite would have enriched you. Did none of you geniuses bring sacks, bags, or boxes?"

Chuckling sadly, Bede and Winston gallop down the road to catch up to their new boss.

CHAPTER 9

Port Bata on the Black Sea, 361 AD

A Roman fort on a hilltop overlooks the rich grassy steppe and the harbor. It has a suspiciously tall stone wall around an even taller log tower within it loaded with catapults and trebuchets. A small garrison works calmly as if the world is not very dangerous. A warning horn blows and Commander Pelagius reaches the balcony in time to greet a dozen visitors. He yells down rather than allow them within his outer wall.

"Good afternoon, King Naulobatus. Hello, Naulo." He smiles with longing at the young hottie and sighs, as if in love. "Greetings, Fauna. You look lovelier every day. Sire, have the Visigoths stolen more cattle?"

The Heruli king looks like an impatient grandfather responsible for many people. He speaks with a heavy accent. "We must talk. The Heruli people face a difficult decision. Will you open the gate? I promise not to threaten you again unless you touch my granddaughter."

Pel orders the iron gate open and a dozen of the world's most dangerous men ride in. Wary troops surround the intruders, all carrying bows. None notch arrows, but they act anxious. The riders face Pel, who doesn't get down from his high balcony. He has put on a breastplate and looks fearful.

"Sire, I'm not responsible when someone steals your strays. However, your Latin is excellent when you want it to."

The king barks something to his beautiful, blond granddaughter, who nods nervously. Fauna has a soft, sexy accent.

"Father wants me to explain because I'm more comfortable speaking Latin. We heard the Alans just submitted to the Huns. Like the Sarmatians, they speak an old version of Persian. Slavs have moved north to avoid the Hun's wrath, so there is no one between them and the steppe's deadliest horse archers. If Huns ride between the two great seas, they could reach us within ten days. We defied them five years ago and lost most of our warriors. They will pursue us to the edge of the Earth. With 50,000 women, elders, and children, we cannot stay here. If you wish to help us, it must be now. To wait is to die."

"I only have 30 troops left, so there's nothing I can do. This is not Roman territory. If Huns show up, I'll probably leave. I only stayed here in case your 6000 mounted archers would agree to fight for Rome."

The king angrily yells. "You only stayed to enjoy my granddaughter! You said your superior would grant us a home with autonomy if we fought for him, but that promise has not been met. With the Huns coming, we have no time for patience. If you cannot find us a home, then we must find one without you. I only promised you Fauna in marriage if you found us a good homeland. This is your last opportunity to have the girl you love. What say you?"

Exhaling loudly in defeat. "Sire, I told you that things got complicated. Julian has declared himself emperor, so both emperors are raising huge armies. Nowhere is safe until one cousin vanquishes the other. That's another reason I stayed away. If one emperor thinks we support his enemy, then he will attack you; Europe's only mounted archers can't stay neutral. You'd have to pick sides and since I've been teaching you

Latin the last four years, I'd share your fate. Europe is not safe for us."

The king doesn't buy it. "You cannot or will not help us. Huns will enslave or exterminate us. We must go as far west as we can ride."

A distant trumpet blows and Pel turns to look at the harbor. The Sea Horse enters Tsemes Bay like Magnus owns it, with four big passenger ships and 24 empty horse transports following. Once the harbor master in a fast skiff moves to intercept, Magnus roars from the topmast while several of his crew blow trumpets like God wants them to tear down the walls of Jericho. On the balcony, Pel farts and shrieks like a virgin getting an anal poke.

"Oh, Hell – it's Max! Fuuuuuuck!"

Shocked at his transformation, Fauna measures the Roman and finds him faulty, but this new guy interests her.

"Who? An enemy comes?" the king of the Heruli asks. "We will kill him for you if you escort us to a safe home."

Expert riders, the Heruli race out of the fort. The dozen riders gallop down an old road to the bay, but slow at the largest ship they have ever seen, with a giant wooden horse overlooking its bow. Nomads literally worship horses, so attacking such a ship feels wrong. As they get closer, the upper half of an oak horse rearing on its back legs gets bigger and more beautiful. The warriors point and shout, clearly awed by its beautiful majesty. Huge catapults line the railing, manned by serious women who track them. On the strange ship, a 15-year-old slides down a rope from the topmast as if that's normal.

The Heruli slow to a canter as the king summarizes. "We worship horses, so how are we to kill someone who built a horse boat? It's the most beautiful thing I've ever seen! Fauna, whoever owns these ships might be rich and powerful enough to help us. Win him over and we won't need Commander Pelagius."

She nods obediently. "Yes, grandpa. I just hope he's not too old, fat, and ugly. I was hoping for a great warrior, though I would have settled for Commander Pelagius."

Naulo speaks with lisp from a cut lip. "Whoever built this ship loves horses. Sister, please fuck him for us."

By the time the riders arrive, townsfolk crowd dockside facilities and men on deck play musical instruments. The teenager starts singing and his angelic voice is beautiful. Something smells delicious and the king is shocked to find the biggest fish he has ever seen on a very long grill dominating the foredeck. The teen plays the flute between stanzas and the audience applauds when they finish Girls of Rome. The teen athletically hops onto a crate for the height and waves happily at the Heruli. Though young, Magnus clearly is an alpha male before his prime. The ship is so tall that the newcomer towers over them all.

Magnus weaponizes his killer smile. "Hello! Are you King Naulobatus? I'm Commander Max and this is part of my fleet." He looks at Naulo. "Sir, you must be his grandson, Prince Naulo, and I assume the beauty is your sister, Princess Fauna." His eyes linger on her, getting softer by the minute. "Wow. Pel said she was the world's prettiest girl and now I see why. Welcome aboard with your warriors." He waves at locals. "Folks, please make way for my guests. You have all week to enjoy me. I'm best savored in small bites – or so everyone tells me. However, I don't bite, though I've been known to nibble."

The riders dismount and walk through the crowd, leaving a warrior to protect the horses. The teen shields the sun from his eyes to look for someone coming from the fort, giving Fauna time to visually inspect him. The longer she looks, the hornier she becomes. The Heruli walk up the ramp, but look uncomfortable on the deck because the ship gently rocks and rolls. Staring at a magnificent man with bulging biceps, Fauna boards in a daze.

The king speaks with a heavy accent and points to his knife belt. "Sir, why carry so many blades? No man can use more than two."

Magnus whirls and begins throwing 22 knives into a crate, including from his boots, then laughs as if this deadly skill is funny. He could have killed 22 men before they notched an arrow. Being ambidextrous, it only takes a minute and is impressive as hell. It shocks the warriors, who now gaze at him with respect, envy, and admiration. Unnerved, Naulo suddenly looks like he wants to leave.

"Cousin Winston, please kill a different plank for their amusement."

The ambidextrous Briton repeats the feat, throwing 22 knives at defenseless wood. The Heruli applaud.

The king is not sure how to feel. "I'm learning a lot today."

Magnus looks past them, disappointed. "The Queefer isn't coming? But I brought Pel's books and a bunch of crap from his mother. I paid an absurd sum for an early Gospel written in Coptic. Oh. Pel isn't still afraid of me, is he? I haven't threatened him in four years, as far as he knows. I wrote him as often as he wrote me. Did he forget he invited me to his wedding?" The big Iberian sighs sadly. "Sire, please make yourself at home or else we've cooked too much food. I hope you're hungry. Sit at my table because I get served first. Uncle Bede, are the presents ready? Great, but first let me present my Cousin Jaki. Prince Naulo, she's from a peninsula called Iberia while my Cousin Winston is from my mother's side, on an island called Britannia. We can trance our ancestry back a thousand years." He gestures theatrically. "Prince Naulo, she's a virgin, unpromised to anyone, but very picky. Before she births a bastard, her mother begged me to marry her off while her skeptical father dared me." He smiles at Naulo's reaction. "You should put your eyes back in their sockets or she might keep them."

As planned, Jaki dresses sexy without looking slutty and has been checking out the husband that Magnus wants her to have. Magnus promised the moon and other expensive bonuses if she got Naulo to marry her. They make eye contact and the hot vixen lights up when she sees his expression. Jaki has olive skin, black hair, and black eyes, so she's shocked that her target is sandy blond with pale skin like a Scandian. The two stare at each other, lost in their vision, and in no hurry to break eye contact. Everyone feels the electricity between the two and most step back to get beyond the heat. The giant Iberian approaches the athletic teen with the friendliest smile that he can fake.

"Prince Naulo, besides Jaki, I have gifts if you'll be my friend."

"Why bring me gifts?"

He speaks with a lisp, and so speaks as little as possible. Pel had warned Magnus, who doesn't seem to notice. They make comfortable eye contact, one champion athlete recognizing another.

"Pel says you're the best Heruli mounted archer. You win every contest, so you are very valuable. Let's start with armor." He receives a chainmail vest and tunic. "Thanks, Winston. Naulo, this is the world's strongest chainmail between two layers of boiled leather soaked in brine – salty water. Very hard for an arrow to penetrate. Having

189

both a chainmail vest and a tunic protects your upper body as well as plate armor, though we have those, too. Let me help you with that – it's a little loose, but you'll gain weight traveling with me. Now strap on these chainmail chaps to protect your legs. If you wear a helmet into battle, then only your forearms, eyes, and boots are exposed on horseback. What do you think?"

In awe. "How good is it?"

"You tell me. We nailed a suit against the superstructure for target practice. You carry a bow. Start from the front rail."

The lean teen marches to the ship's bow, lets loose, and easily hits a stationary target, except his arrow bounces off and falls to the deck. Everyone laughs, but his sister Fauna laughs the loudest. That's incredibly embarrassing, like a guy who can't get it up on his honeymoon. Armed Iberians stay silent, but Magnus covers like a pro.

Magnus sounds impatient. "Stop playing around, Naulo. This is serious business."

Naulo snaps at a friend. "Taleg, can you do better?"

A buff warrior, Taleg tries, but does no better. The prince fires again, pulling back the bowstring completely, and this time the arrow sticks, but hangs like a limp dick. Some Heruli run over, but the king can't feel the sharp tip from the inside.

"It might have tickled the enemy, but probably didn't draw blood. Naulo, try from a little closer." The teen comes ten paces closer and shoots again, but disappoints grandpa. "You bled him, but now the enemy is mad. Do it again." They watch Naulo walk ten paces nearer and fire like his reputation is at stake. Dad feels inside and announces his judgment. "The enemy felt it, but the arrow didn't kill him. Metal plates are too heavy for light horsemen and I've never seen chainmail before." He turns on Magnus, his tone far more respectful now. "Sir, I didn't catch your name. Who are you, again?"

The enormous orphan strolls over and holds out his hand. They shake firmly.

"My name is Max. I'm the richest man in Europe, I own a bank, and I command a fleet. Pelagius was my father's second-in-command. Dad was a Roman general so feared that the enemy poisoned him and my mother. I was so mad that I killed 200,000 of their fighters and got rich sacking their capital. You won't believe any of that, but Pel knows it's all true."

Hiding behind warriors, Fauna stares and studies him, her throat dry and her loincloth wet. She feels cold chills down her spine and hot flashes that pinken her cheeks. This makes her shake and sweat. Her skin feels on fire. She loves how her father and brother respect this man. Taleg takes down the armor from the superstructure and feels the inside, impressed and appalled. The musicians continue with another catchy tune.

Naulo is uncomfortable. "I like the suit, but we don't have money because there are no stores on the steppe. We can pay in horses, cattle, hide, meat, leather, and furs."

Magnus measures the athletic teen and likes what he sees. Grinning, he nods approvingly to Jaki, who literally jumps on her tip toes so her big boobs bounce. Everyone knows Magnus just gave her the go-ahead. Naulo not only passes the test, but she can't wait to claim the prize. The Heruli prince looks her up and down and smiles like he just found a wife. She's got curves and enough cleavage to form a valley. After making delicious eye contact with Naulo, she pulls her chemise apart to show an indecent amount of booby. The warriors cheer, so she slowly twirls like a dancer on the ball of her

190

foot while smiling hungrily. Jaki didn't hit puberty, but smashed it instead.

Magnus adds some caution. "Naulo, Jaki is young, so please take it slow because she is not used to living slowly. She's a great rider, a natural athlete, and loves weapons. She likes sports, dancing, and telling boys what to do. If you break her heart, I advise you to run. Prince Naulo, you're more likely to survive combat with that suit. How much is your life worth?"

Grandpa loudly interrupts because Naulo is cheap. "10 horses! 100, if the Huns come. They just defeated the last group in their way. Alans were a powerful tribe, but they submitted like a slave and moved their entire people to the other side of the Caspian Sea. Now there's nothing but empty space between us and the deadliest tribe on the steppe. We must leave before Huns arrive. I will not witness the slaughter of my family again. Please, sir. How much for the armor?"

"I said it was a gift. You get one, too. Keep your horses. I already co-own a million, including some of the world's best warhorses. I want a relationship, not a transaction."

They laugh at the million horses and the king asks Fauna to translate to make sure he heard it right. They briefly exchange gibberish, then the king snaps his head back. She looks at Magnus like she's hungry.

The king is unamused. "Sir, you are a funny man, but I am in no mood for jokes. The Huns seek to assimilate or exterminate us."

"I was not joking. Our ranches have over a million horses, a million cattle, and almost as many sheep. We also farm and mine a lot. Winston, let's help the Heruli king with his chainmail vest, tunic, and chaps, plus his helmet." The old man puts it all on and instantly feels safer. "Oh, I almost forgot the bear coat. Sir, the inside of this coat also has chainmail that the enemy can't see. Jaki, please give Naulo his bear coat. Taleg, I'll also find you something."

She helps her new boyfriend put it on and smooths it out to touch him all over. They make eye contact and sparks fly. The gifts overwhelm the Heruli. The king and his grandson look kickass and they know it. Fauna likes how the warriors treat Magnus and is ready to explode. Feeling her heat, Magnus walks up to Fauna, studying her like a jewel. She looks up at him like no girl has ever looked at him and caresses the scar by his eye as if he belongs to her. Her big green eyes shine like emeralds. He can't stop looking at her and it goes on far too long. Finally he sighs and takes her to a table with her stuff, feeling empty inside. He opens a jewelry box, a perfume chest, a makeup organizer, and lays out a variety of gorgeous silk dresses with bright colors that no Heruli has ever seen before.

Magnus speaks with intense bitterness. "Pel is a lucky fucker. He bragged you are ambidextrous because he knows I want ambidextrous children. I haven't had kids yet because I'm waiting to meet someone special." Looking into her eyes, he sighs in deep despair. "Princess Fauna, you also get armor and a tailored bear coat because Pel wrote that you are the best female mounted archer. But he also stressed your beauty, so I brought you clothes, footwear, headwear, jewelry, perfume, incense, and makeup. Jaki can help you with it all for a late honeymoon." He leans in and sighs with longing. "How long have you two been wed?" She doesn't understand, so he asks differently. "Pel said you were promised to him. He invited me to the wedding. Am I early or late?"

The king roars angrily. "That liar will never marry Fauna, though I know he

191

loves her deeply."

With a dozen badass warriors as witnesses, the Iberian orphan staggers back as if a giant pushed him. He looks about to fall. As if struck by lightning, his eyes glaze, his face glitches, and his voice sounds unnaturally shrill.

"Princess, you're single? You are not ready for marriage or Pel just isn't the right man for you?"

"She'll marry whoever I need her to marry," grandpa says, "but Fauna hasn't flowered yet."

She looks impossibly young and beautiful, except the old eyes and sexy smile. She dresses as a child, wrapping herself in layers of furs to cover her curves, but now she has an itch that needs a scratch.

"Oh, I flowered last year, but hid it to avoid marrying Pelagius. He is rich, handsome, and loves me, but I won't be happy with him."

Grandpa is furious. "Girl, you lied to me?"

"Of course, grandpa. Mama told me to, before dying to save me. She said, who I spend my life with is the most important decision I'll ever make. I'll marry a man I choose." They turn toward land to see someone screaming like a little bitch. "Ah, here comes Commander Pelagius. What is a queefer? I never knew anyone called him Pel. You Westerners are so informal. Commander Max, I believe you still scare him. Look at how he rides that poor horse. I've tried teaching him, but he doesn't have the right instincts for horses or for girls. Pelagius should become a monk." Then she studies the luxuries on the table and totally glitches. "Wait! What? These are mine? How?"

Magnus twirls like a dancer to beseech Cousin Jaki with a knowing look. Everyone sees him silently ask the obvious before words fly from his mouth like arrows.

Magnus throws his future at her. "Princess Fauna, these are yours if you'll be mine. My love will be your dowry. Jaki, please help Fauna try out her new things."

Feeling richer, Jaki starts closing the containers and gestures for Fauna to scoop up the clothes. The two girls look like kids in a candy store about to get laid. On the way below deck, they chat excitedly like sisters about to bag billionaires. Everyone studies Magnus, who only has eyes for Fauna until she disappears into the bowels of the Sea Horse. The Roman rides up, scared for many reasons. He runs onto the ship to manage the damage.

"No, Max. You can't have her! You don't deserve her! You can't be faithful to anyone but your urges. I've gone four long years without sex – she was promised to me."

"Pel, you planned to throw your sexy wife in my face – I'm still not sure how to complain. I brought you a bunch of theology books and a load of crap from your parents, yet this is how you repay the favor? Your father found a cache of early Christian manuscripts, some written in Coptic, if you can decipher Egyptian. He claims our Gospels are poorly translated and have stuff not found in the originals, so I partnered with your parents to find Christianity's oldest texts. Apparently almost everything known is from the 3rd century. Our oldest texts are copies of copies of copies of copies. Papyrus dries quickly and never lasts long, so we're sending agents to offer absurd sums to monopolize anything ancient, then varnish it under glass. Our specialists visit the oldest churches. Oh, your mother wants to know when you'll return. I told her whenever the civil war ends."

The king jumps on that. "There's really a civil war? Commander Pelagius says

192

it's too dangerous for the Heruli to go to Europe. Each side will demand we fight for them for free. Yet we cannot stay. The Huns have beaten everyone and I can't figure out why."

"Roman emperors don't call themselves emperors; they call themselves Augustus, after our first emperor. The second-in-line and/or the heir is named Caesar. Because the emperor's pregnant wife might give Augustus Constantius a heir, Caesar Julian recently declared himself emperor by renaming himself Augustus Julian before a baby boy supplants him. Constantius also has two fucking daughters who also might give him a heir, so Julian must force the issue now or be executed later as a rival to a royal son or grandson. Pel mentioned the Heruli seek a safe home out west. You are why I came and built a few dozen large horse transports. I can offer you the westernmost grasslands in all of mainland Europe. Further west is only endless ocean. If you pledge your arms to me personally, all Heruli can live there safely."

That excites the Heruli warriors. They're saved! They look relieved and giddy.

The king tears up. "We'll be safe from Huns? How long would it take to ride there?"

"Over a year, but we're not gonna ride because that's too dangerous. We're going by ship to avoid the fighting. Sorry about your horses, but we can only bring the best several thousand mounts per voyage. I brought someone from Constantinople to buy the rest of your livestock."

Pel attacks. "Your tiny fleet can't move 50,000 homeless refugees!"

"50? Your last letter said 30,000, half of them kids."

The king explains. "Our numbers have increased because roving bands that didn't join us earlier now see the wisdom of leaving the eastern steppe. We've also mated with many Slavs, over the generations, who have accepted my strong leadership. Most of our young grew up bilingual – well, now they also speak Latin, thanks to Commander Pelagius. Huns have captured thousands of Heruli, but many more simply moved west or north. The steppe has never faced a threat like the Huns before. They are organized as a nation with a centralized authority that can field large numbers of the world's best mounted archers. The Slavs vastly outnumber them, but they fight each other too much to unite against a common enemy."

"Sire, you don't look like a man who scares easily. What is it about the Huns that makes your toes curl?"

The old man holds up a double-curved composite bow, about 5 feet long. "Huns were not the first to develop a composite, double-curved recursive bow, but theirs shoot farther and hit harder. We have since duplicated them. What bothers me now is their ability to fire accurately at a gallop. They shot my horse at the beginning of the battle, so I watched all five of my sons and most of my cousins get out-shot. As I was wounded, I led our people away while the able warriors slowed them down. The Heruli came from the northern shore of a cold, icy sea many generations ago that Commander Pelagius calls the Baltic, so we had to become better than locals when we entered the steppe. Unlike Slavs, we needed a centralized authority instead of a Council of Chiefs. Like Naulo now, I was the best mounted archer in my day, but an average Hun defeated me fairly. They organize in units of 10, 100, 1000, and 10,000 to simplify maneuvering, so we now do the same with our best 10,000 shooters. Every winter we test everyone to put the best shooters in the first units, so the 1st Squad of the 1st Platoon of the 1st Battalion have the best and the 10th Squad of the 10th Platoon of the 10th Battalion have the worst. The worst units can lure away enemies while the best engage. This division trains as if the extinction of all Heruli is at stake."

"Sire, I'd like a Hun bow."

The Heruli laugh at that.

"It takes our veterans a year to make one. Maintaining them also takes time and patience. We made one for Commander Pelagius, but he still can't hit grass at anything faster than a trot."

The big Iberian turns to look inland; grasslands fill the visual horizon.

"But I can offer value for value."

He walks to the front of the ship with a bow taller than himself to shoot exactly where Naulo fired from. His biceps bulge from pulling the taunt bowstring back. The Heruli are impressed and appalled. The cedar arrow lands loudly and penetrates deeply into the wooden superstructure. Heruli hurry to inspect it. Magnus used a longer arrow that pierced both sides of the light chainmail. The fletches quiver like they're horny. The Heruli struggle to pull the armor from the wooden superstructure. They tug and tug with increasing frustration. That's when they notice thousands of dents from blunt blows. The king can't believe his lying eyes as Magnus strolls to the superstructure as if he re-invented the wheel.

"Sir, how did you do that?"

The orphan smiles. "Practice. I'm already bigger than my father and I'll be even larger in another year. He used a bigger bow, so I made myself the world's longest bow. Stabilizing it requires stepping on the bottom to pin it to the ground. I liked it so much that we're making longbows for our strongest warriors. We organize them into dedicated units called Tall Archers and call them longbowmen. Everyone who qualifies earns a higher salary. In between laps around the deck, I shot hundreds of times a day on this boring voyage to build up my biceps. I can't do that from horseback, but I probably have better range than anyone on Earth because I use expensive, machined cedar shafts and the world's best arrowheads." He hands every warrior an arrow and smiles as they cut themselves on Joko's iron tips. "My partners and I make the world's best arrowtips – stronger, sharper, and lighter. Advanced technology compensates for my primitive persona. Try them. Winston, give them some pointers."

Warriors line up to shoot the superstructure with their arrows and the cedar ones, amazed how deep they penetrate wood. They chat excitedly in a foreign language, relieved at finally scoring some good news. Sailors and servants offer lunch. Seated across for Magnus, the old man has new hopes.

"Sire, that cutlery is called a fork. We melt debased coin into utensils. Though not used in the West, Persians have utilized forks since Darius the Great around 500 BC. Constantinople is the only city in Europe where table forks are common. Using utensils is much safer than dirty hands."

The huge Iberian digs into his fish, so they follow his lead. Naulo skeptically picks at his plate.

The king discusses business. "Even with our female horse archers, 10,000 are too few to challenge Huns and their new vassals, but using their bows and these arrows while wearing new armor gives us a fighting chance."

Pel tries being useful. "Max, Huns apparently came from a dry, windy plateau

194

on the far northern steppe, with China on the other side of a long mountain chain. Several decades ago, they conquered Bactria from Persia. Alexander the Great settled Bactria with Greeks who gave locals a written language that Huns adopted. They've invaded the Indus River valley, expanded southwest into Persia, and northwest into the steppe. The land they rule is probably bigger than the Roman Empire, though with just a few million folks. They conquer and assimilate their neighbors. Their artillery is now as good as Persia's or Rome's. Most of their engineers, carpenters, and mathematicians are foreign, but Huns know how to deploy them. I think the Heruli are right to expect Huns to come here one day and, eventually, to Europe. I can't imagine what could stop 250,000 horse archers until they reach the massive forests of Greater Germania."

The orphan takes that like a right cross. "250,000 horse archers? As a mounted slinger, I hurt more enemies than a thousand troops. A mounted archer will have much greater range and penetrating power. Sire, what can stop 250,000 horse archers?"

"Only horse archers can contest horse archers on open ground, but Huns are the best. No one has beaten them. Not nomads from the steppe, Indians, or Persians. Huns are unstoppable and unbeatable. They are the greatest warriors the world has ever known and they will conquer the Roman Empire as they are conquering the Persian and Indian empires."

Magnus sinks into a stunned stupor. "If Huns threaten civilization, then we must stop them." The warriors laugh at that and the king laughs so hard it hurts. "I'm serious. If Heruli breed with my people in Galicia, I'll reward the mother with a home for each baby so she enjoys financial security. With 10 kids, a Heruli or Galician mom would own 10 homes, selling or renting out some. 50,000 mothers having the usual 10 kids that survive the birth would yield 500,000 youngsters; if half are female and half the males are athletic, then we could have over 100,000 great mounted archers wearing the world's best armor in 25 years. With that, we could get the Roman, Persian, and Indian empires to help us wipe them all out."

After a deadly moment of silence, the warriors burst into tears, completely blown away, but the king falls apart on another level. Eyes closed, tears fly off his face. He just absolutely loses his shit. Their halibut gets cold as the mood heats up.

"Max, you'd really do that for us?" Naulo asks. "I feel bad for using you to eliminate our enemies."

"Prince Naulo, I've dedicated my life to walling off the world's most naturally sheltered harbors, in the best climates, to build pre-planned port mega-cities to provide humanity with guaranteed food, shelter, and security. Huns threaten that mission so, no, I won't exterminate Huns for you. Instead, I'll use the Heruli to eliminate a threat to humanity. And I won't feel bad about it." Seated in his folding chair, he sizes up the warriors ignoring their kickass halibut. "I'm sorry it's come to this, but I need you fuckers to breed an army of horse archers to end the Hun threat, once and for all. Jaki has beautiful sisters, aunts, and cousins, if you like her look. Heruli must mate with Iberians and raise enough horse archers to exterminate Huns so they cannot threaten all that I've built. I hope you fuckers are up for it because Iberians are famous for their passion."

They take that like gold thrown at beggars. Warriors stare at each other as if in a dream. The big Iberian leans back and the Heruli stand up to applaud him like they've found a new leader, with the tearful king yelling the loudest. Taleg swats Magnus happily on the shoulder.

The girls come on deck like dragon slayers. They dress sexy as hell. Jaki only has eyes for Naulo and Fauna monopolizes Magnus' mind. Both are tall teenagers showing all the cleavage they dare. Freed from a ponytail, Jaki brushed Fauna's blond hair, painted her nails, and added makeup, perfume, and jewelry to someone hot enough to cook her clothes. Pel gasps and curses because she no longer passes for a child. The transformation stuns even grandpa. Fauna twirls on the ball of one foot so her dress flies up, then adopts a pose that Jaki taught her. When Magnus looks her up and down, she gets wet and covered in goose bumps. Fauna looks at her arms and rubs them, embarrassed at displaying her inner desires so visibly. Magnus and Fauna stare at each other uncomfortably long, as if time paused. Even the blind can tell they desperately need to fuck each other. Magnus gets up and invades her personal space as if he intends to stay.

Jaki smiles like she just pocketed a paycheck. "I bathed her and almost turned lesbian. She's taller than me, with bigger breasts, but I probably won't resent her for it. I told her she can't let her tits hang out, but she says she wants you really bad. Sorry if one bounces out of her new sexy silk bra, but she doesn't know how a slut dresses."

He leans in as if to kiss her. "Fauna, even if you wear my armor, I could still penetrate you."

Her delighted smile lights up her face as her grandfather waves the others away, leaving the lovers alone.

"Why are your trumpets so loud?" she asks.

He loves her sexy accent. The haunted orphan grabs a brass instrument, bent twice into a rectangular shape.

"I came across an ingenious Persian design made from a single sheet of metal that makes it lighter and louder. Brass trumpets have been used for millennia for military signaling, but are heavy, requiring two hands. Horsemen need something that only requires one hand. My family has invested heavily in metalworking, so we worked out the cast-iron process. We call it, a bugle. Blow into it. It's fun and so am I."

The beauty does and blows herself away. She laughs, liking the tall stranger too much.

"Max, you are very clever."

"That's just one of my many flaws. I'm also loud, vain, and a disobedient rulebreaker. The world revolves around me – or so the Sun says."

The warriors press the Roman out of earshot of their host and corner him against the far rail. A dozen senior warriors study Pel like a dangerous snake.

"Commander Pelagius, does Max really own a million horses?" the king needs to know.

"Probably. Max and his uncle took a million mounts, cattle, and other livestock from a neighboring kingdom. The Maximus family has ranched in Galicia for centuries. They own a lot of land and have probably bought much more since becoming really rich. The Heruli should be safe there; it's far from the fighting, but you'll need to pledge loyalty to Rome to get citizenship."

"But can we trust Max?"

"You can't trust Max with Fauna, but he invested a lot to sail you to his home."

The king blows that off. "I don't trust Fauna with him. Why does he want us?"

"For the same reason Rome wants you: Europe has no mounted archers. You'd be the only ones. That doesn't help in mountains, forests, swamps, and besieging walled cities, but much of eastern Europe is wide open plains like your grassy steppe. Commanding Europe's only horse archers would give Max enormous leverage over Rome."

"Who will he use us against? How strong are his enemies? What neighbors threaten him?"

Puzzled. "Sire, Galicia is a small part of the Iberian Peninsula and his Uncle Theo commands the province's mobile response unit. The Pyrenees Mountains cut off the peninsula, except on the eastern coast, but Galicia is on the western end. Rome rules Iberia and the area to its north, so there are no hostile neighbors. There is no one for Max to attack and no kingdom that can attack Galicia."

"What of Rome? Could Max attack Rome?"

Pel laughs so hard that spittle flies from his mouth like lies and some sprinkle the king's stern face. The old man backs up and angrily wipes his face with his furry sleeve.

"Sorry, sire. The Maximus family has saved Rome from foreign invaders for centuries. Max considers himself a Roman. In time he might be tempted to become emperor, but he'd never harm Rome."

"Damn it, man! Who does he want us to kill?"

Pel looks at Magnus making Fauna laugh and his desire to destroy his rival becomes palpable. "If Max wanted someone dead, he'd take great pride in publicly killing him. I can't think of anyone that Max would need the Heruli to attack. You are leverage over whichever emperor wins, but he wants no part of a civil war. The victor can only get mounted archers through Max. That gives him political, economic, and military leverage. Max wants his uncle to govern Iberia. He might get that in exchange for your services against the Persians or Germani. His family owns a merchant fleet, a fishing fleet, and a bank. Commanding mounted archers helps the family exploit economic opportunities. He has no interest in fighting Rome, but governors might pay through the nose for your services. Slow infantry armies on open ground would probably just concede rather than challenge you."

Pel can't help but show his envy, jealousy, and pain as Fauna's carefree laughter washes over them. She puts her palm on Magnus' chest and gets nearly nose to nose with the fantastic looking megalomaniac. The blond hottie stares at him like a wolf eyes a full moon. Pel can see that his dark bad-boy looks spin her gears. She's horny for the first time and Pel almost bursts into tears.

"The one thing that Max wants above all else is to be loved, admired, and remembered. He wants to stand out; commanding horse archers does that. Rich and powerful people will seek his help. Max wants to be a great man; he needs to be remembered down the ages as the greatest man who has ever lived. That obsesses him and that will be his downfall." The thought hits Pel like a shin to the balls, yet the Roman smiles as if serving his comeuppance. He yells just a little too loudly. "Max, I just thought of a great name for you. Great. You should just call yourself great. Pompey started calling himself Magnus Pompey at 15 years old, before winning his first battle at 17 when helping Sulla take back Rome 500 years ago. Magnus is a great name for you."

The Iberian laughs that off, already in love with a stranger. "Magnus Max?

Great Max is the worst name ever."

"No, my friend: Magnus Maximus – Maximum Great. If you want posterity to remember you, then calling yourself Maximum Great is the best way to do so."

Fauna instantly loves the name and jumps for joy. "Magnus! From this moment on, I'll only call you Magnus." She turns on the Heruli and roars a foreign command with authority. "You want a safe home for your families? You want distance from the hated Hun hordes? You want vengeance on our enemies? Then hail our new leader, Magnus Maximus!"

Her voice is a whip that makes the Heruli jump to comply. Even grandpa wakes up to look at her with fresh eyes. The Iberians on the ship join in, chanting the new name. The traumatized orphan's ego flies into the heavens. He doesn't just like the name; he loves it. He hugs Fauna and she kisses him passionately. He's so damn tall that she's practically climbing up him.

The king whispers in Heruli. "Naulo, you have a problem stepping aside for him?"

"No. Since Huns cut my lip, I cannot even speak without feeling foolish and sounding stupid. Let him have his fame and glory. I just want my people safe. Fauna will soon have him wrapped around her manipulative fingers, just as she conquered Pelagius with suggestive smiles. Praise Max highly and often and he'll be our little bitch. We need to tell the elders, the warriors, and the veterans so they know what to expect. Max – no, Magnus – needs careful handling, but he can't sincerely call himself Maximum Great and also regard Huns as the best. We can use him to beat them. He must prove himself the best to adopt the name, Magnus Maximus. With his armor, we could rescue the Heruli that Huns captured."

The Heruli warriors light up at that idea. Hope infecting their faces, they smile at each other.

The king looks at his senior warriors. "We need Magnus to deal with outsiders, but you will be king of the Heruli after me. If clever, you might one day convince Magnus to exterminate the Huns and avenge your parents, our family, and our people."

Nodding their heads, all the Heruli grin in agreement.

The Sea Horse slows towards an old fishing village. From the topmast, Magnus and Fauna see portable yurt huts, huge wagons, riders, and herds in distant grassy hills.

"Magnus, this is the closest dock to our new home. The steppe is so vast that you can ride a year without seeing it end. Commander Pelagius says it extends 5000 miles from Pannonia in Europe to the North China Plain. Most of our surviving horse archers are old, female, or teenagers too young to fight Huns five years ago. Like thousands of other kids, my brother and I grew up seeking vengeance for the deaths of our parents. That obsession makes us train constantly. We have regular contests and the worst shooters are vilified. I'll get our leaders."

The ship docks and crews land to set up grills to cook fish and stews. Others roll out barrels of booze or pushcarts full of freshly baked bread. Magnus stands on Caesar and plays the flute while 15,000 dangerous illiterates from Central Asia ride up to see their new patron. Fauna gallops up as horny as a bitch in heat. Few folks can stand long on a horse, but Magnus makes it look easy. He waits until most warriors ride within yelling distance before bellowing:

198

"My family's factory makes a metal cup, plate, and bowl with a fork, knife, and spoon modified so they fit together in a leather kit to stay clean. Within a leather pouch, the ingeniously compact design makes them hang from a clip so you don't lose any at a gallop. They are light, quick to pack, and easy to wash. Please take a set as a gift if you accept me as your commander, then eat what you want. I brought a lot of salt so your ladies can jerk your oldest cattle for the trip. I did some fishing in the Med, so we need to eat all that up before it spoils. After breakfast I'd like to see how good your warriors are to group them from the best to the worst. Pel says you shoot better at a gallop than Slavs and that the neighboring Visigoths can't shoot from a saddle at all, which puzzles me. I brought wine, ale, mead, and beer to find out which of you can't handle alcohol. Just as you are measuring me, so am I testing you to see if I should invite all Heruli to my beautiful, safe homeland."

Fauna grumbles possessively like a bear clawing trees to mark her territory as attractive ladies look up as they ride by. He's a handsome devil, all agree, with a killer smile to die for. Magnus notices their saddles are similar to his own to stabilize riders when shooting. Sailors serve the Heruli on their brand new cups, bowls, and plates. They take big bites of small loaves as they sit down in the grass or munch while mounted. Some try every form of liquor and like them all. The happy warriors smile at Magnus and nod when they make eye contact.

A few hundred elites dine on deck, with folding tables and folding chairs that impress the nomads with their ingenuity. Loud laughter and pleasant chatter in a foreign language animate the meal as Magnus charms nomadic leaders with limited Latin. Iberian sailors, servants, and soldiers serve them a variety of simple foods to win them over. Magnus and Fauna greet guests at tables on the ship, then walk ashore to chat with warriors. Fauna holds his hand like he might fly away. He answers questions, asks some himself, and roars upon demand. Dozens of kids follow him because he is unlike any man they have ever met. In the middle of nowhere, Magnus finally feels at home.

The contest attracts their best riders and shooters, eager to make a favorable impression on their new boss. Magnus watches with the king and Fauna, all mounted, while horsemen target trees. Naulo is very good, but not necessarily better than some veterans, but now Magnus must show his stuff. When Naulo misses, Fauna laughs and Naulo gestures for Magnus to come out. He rides out and shows off, doing his trick riding, like gracefully turning around in the saddle. Magnus manages gymnastic on Caesar, who slows or speeds up as if mind-reading. He stands, jumps down, then pops back up to sit his saddle facing backwards. After some twirling, he's hanging low enough to grab weapons off the ground. Standard shit, really, for nomads from the steppe, but the Heruli applaud because Pel is not a natural horseman. He can't shoot from the saddle, so Magnus slings pellets that smack the tree audibly. Folks enjoy the whistling sound and cheer him on.

On foot, Magnus holds up arrows painted white for all to see before shooting them with his giant bow when a breeze blows hardest. The audience claps at the unbelievable distance. Winston steps up and fires almost as far. Magnus gestures to the strongest Heruli who each take a few shots with arrows of different colors. None shoot as far because none have spent months on a boring voyage training all day. Magnus curls his big biceps for Fauna to fondle and all can see she's about to explode in her kickass clothes. She wears something different every outing to piss off old rivals with new outfits. Magnus beats up the defenseless tree with pellets that whistle. Bark flies off with an angry sound. Then he attacks with thrown knives. Warriors gather around to fondle his weapons with envy, then the orphan rides to a hilltop and asks men to hear him out as they look up.

"10,000 warriors, including the ladies, are too few to protect 40,000. On the steppe, hostiles can attack with surprise anytime and from any direction. You usually break into small nomadic bands, moving as your livestock eats out the grass, but scattered groups leave you even more vulnerable. You defied the Huns and they cannot tolerate defiance. You must submit so they can rape your women and slaughter your men while rearing your kids like Huns to repeat these atrocities on your next generation. Or you must move very far away, where Huns can never reach you. What if you rode west? Even with guides and permission, it'd take you a year to reach my home. As homeless refugees, locals would demand your valuables and then your pretty women as the price for passage. After throwing away your daughters, you'd lose your horses, cattle, and respect, becoming increasingly impoverished and unable to feed yourself long before you got near my homeland. Local militia and trained armies would attack you and sell survivors as slaves. The Roman Empire now has two emperors fighting to the death with huge armies; either would compel you to die for them without compensation. Unlike the steppe, Europe is not empty. You would have to defeat a tribe and deport them, then beat off their neighbors who naturally see you as a threat. Rome employs 300,000 troops and Germani many more.

"I offer the best alternative, but it comes at a price: you must all accept me as your patron. Swear fealty and I'll provide 10,000 warriors with a sword, throwing knives, armor, and iron helmet. Becoming my clients is an ancient Roman idea that involves reciprocal obligations. You'll still have your own king, but your warriors cannot fight anyone if I oppose it. Settling you on my family's lands is very expensive and will anger many locals. The head of our family agreed only conditionally; anyone who causes trouble must leave. You must also work to earn back my investment, which means warriors must fight under my command. Powerful people will bypass me to offer you the moon to fight their battles; you must refuse them. Beyond some ungrateful cousins and a stubborn gopher, I don't have enemies, but I do plan to make a career in the military. Rome employs non-Romans in units called *foederati*. Mounted archers who prefer war over ranching will serve under me as part of a larger Roman force, but only against enemies I choose. I don't want to spend years in Persia because I can't leave Iberia for so long. That said, there are a few rival families in Iberia who complain too much as my family grows in power, wealth, and influence. We may visit them to induce them to keep their complaints to themselves. The new governor threatened to replace my uncle as commander of Iberia's mobile legion, so I need to replace that governor.

"You warriors would therefore serve under me as a semi-independent force that fights for Rome when I agree. In return, Caesar Julian – Augustus Julian if he kills his cousin – has agreed to grant you Roman citizenship under this arrangement. That means you can travel or live anywhere in the empire with rights that only citizens enjoy. Your loved ones would be safe while you travel. The future is bright and Galicia is beautiful. But everyone must swear a holy oath to accept me as your patron. Even kids. As my clients, I'll take care of you but, as your patron, you owe me loyalty, hard work, and

200

service. You must provide value for value. My fleet can only carry 10,000 of you at a time, so warriors should stay for defense while mothers of young children go first to Galicia. Older women can turn herds into jerky. Any questions, problems, or complaints?"

The king has a problem, so he rides up and speaks out. "Huns captured thousands of Heruli and we'd hate to leave without trying to rescue them. Each of us has lost a loved one still living. Most are young women and children that Huns will turn into more Huns. We now have Hunnic bows. With your armor and arrows, we can rescue family if we enjoy surprise. Magnus, imagine never trying to rescue people you love; how could we live with ourselves? The risk is great, but so is the reward. If we try and fail, at least we tried, but warriors cannot respect themselves if they just give up. I hate quitters. We have been training hard every day to improve our skills with our new Hun bows, and even organized our war parties into units of 10 like the enemy. 4000 of our women are as good as most of the men. With your arms and armor, we might recover our dignity, if not our people. The mother of Fauna and Naulo might still be alive. Magnus, we will eagerly pledge our loyalty to you if you give us one moon to attempt a rescue. You can have Fauna and as many other women as you want if you'll supply us with arrows because we ran out of goose feathers. Sadly, Huns are the world's best warriors. I know we are not better than them, but you can't call yourself Maximum Great until you prove yourself superior. If you help us rescue our loved ones, I'll be forever grateful. In all, 10,000 horse archers can go. What say you?"

Sitting his gorgeous white stallion, Magnus stares down at his new clients, feeling delicious. How could he say no?

"My friends, there is something I couldn't share with you until the Heruli agreed to our arrangement. A year ago, Pel told me of the plight of your friends, so I prepared accordingly. Please wait; I'll return soon with a surprise."

He gallops away and returns with something white and bulging covering Caesar. No one can figure it out. He stands on his stallion so more warriors can hear him. Not everyone can see and those who do see still cannot believe their lying eyes. Hard-ass combat veterans burst into tears and scream joy in the Heruli language, which evolved from Old North German. Few understand the sudden excitement until their new patron breaks the news like a priceless porcelain vase.

"Previous battles frustrated me because my archers could only carry two quivers of 30 arrows each. Who faces just 60 targets? I helped design a reed basket for foot archers that carries 100 on their back, but even that is not enough. Over four years, we've modified these arrow sacks several times until they could carry 1000 arrows without pissing off the rider. They are bulky, but weigh little. We also optimized them to cover the horse to protect them from projectiles. Your legs are less vulnerable and my chainmail has detachable sleeves to protect your arms. Imagine: enemy arrows impotently striking our ammo sacks!"

They cheer because this will be a lifesaver. "I also took 10,000 bear coats from dead enemies and tried getting the blood out. The best shooters get the best horses, armor, and bear coat." Magnus smiles at Fauna, who looks up at him adoringly. She is deep in love and that scares the shit out of her, curing her constipation. "My fleet should take your young and your best horses to my home. It's a long trip, but my Cousin Jaki grew up sailing. Those capable of butchering and salting jerky should stay to exhaust our salt. Jaki

201

can get more salt on the return voyage. Uncle Bede, your trip to Constantinople must wait in case I need you in the field. With you and my personal bodyguards, I have about 100 Tall Archers, though not all can ride all day. As for rescuing my future mother-in-law, I brought 10 million of the world's best arrows, 10,000 sets of arrow sacks, plus 10,000 sets of chainmail armor, 10,000 swords, and 10,000 iron helmets. Huns didn't beat you because they are stronger, smarter, or braver, but because they employed superior technology. Now you do. Lastly, I brought a million rusty spikes that our rearguard can throw behind them to slow pursuers. Romans call them caltrops; no matter how they land, they point up. But I don't have time for a war. If you agree to a simple rescue operation, then I propose we hit Huns, then leave before they organize an effective response that costs us lives. Oh!" He's suddenly excited. "Oh, there's something else you must see."

Magnus blows a bugle and his fleet shells a nearby hill. Rocks the size of heads land hard with a thud while bolts pierce the slope, killing it instantly. The distance impresses the warriors, who suddenly want to learn more about *ballistae*. The 15-year-old does not look his age.

"My friends: what do you think?"

The Heruli answer by mobbing him with shrieks of joy and tears of happiness. Fauna is the only one unhappy because horsemen push her from her fiancée. When he finally frees himself, she's looking at him like a god.

"Magnus, you're the most impressive man I've ever met."

Startled, he speaks without thinking. "Marry me!"

"Magnus, I need you now and I need you forever. Take me before I go crazy!"

Pel watches all this from his balcony and knows the Heruli give Magnus what he so desperately needs: love, attention, and fealty. They eagerly accept him as he is and will never try changing him, which flatters him to his tippy toes. 50,000 strangers fill the cavernous hole left by his parent's bitter rejection.

"Careful what you wish for, Magnus Maximus, because I've planted the seeds to sow your self-destruction."

In the distance, 10,000 Heruli ride in formation, 4000 of them female, wearing armor and helmets. Commanders carry signal flags attached to their saddles, with Magnus wielding a red flag snapping loudly in the breeze; battalion commanders use yellow, platoons green, and squads blue. Magnus pulls his flagpole to signal a change in direction, holds up his hand in a fist to signal Attack, then blows his bugle for them to execute their maneuver. The ten battalions spread out to engulf the enemy, with the wings riding faster while the center slows to form a C shape to fuck a forest. They charge an isolated group of trees. The wings extend and the center spreads out so more riders have a clear field of fire. By the time the center gets within range of the trees, the wings flank the forest, racing to get within range, then slowing for a more stable shooting platform. 10,000 shoot at almost the same time and continue until they've unleashed 100 arrows that will be a bitch to recover. A bugle blow signals the end of the training exercise and again to call for a Commanders Meeting. While most dismount to retrieve their ammo, unit commanders leave to confer with Magnus and the king. All commanders have a bugle hanging from a string around their neck and a stick secured to the saddle holding up a flag for military signaling.

Magnus snaps at the king. "Sire, that second bugle was for all commanders to gather around me. You're a commander. If you won't follow orders, then no one else will." The king recoils at being reprimanded. "Mobs of savages won't beat disciplined Huns. You said they attack in formations, with units organized in teams of 10, 100, 1000, and 10,000. They wave flags and blow conch seashells for military signaling beyond yelling distance. Commands must convey clear orders that's heard over the screams of battle while units must coordinate. Infantry prefers drums because they can be heard over long distances, but riders are stuck with brass instruments and flags. Commanders, please pair hand signals with waving your flag and blowing your bugle. Some of you suck at blowing; if it's not clear, your units won't know what to do or what you want. Only we have the bugle, but you must learn to blow Attack, Retreat, Encircle, Stop, and Scatter. We'll try more sophisticated sounds if we survive the Huns. We must scatter across a huge area to hunt roving bands of nomadic pastoralists, so sentries will use their bugles to inform you if you can decipher their intent. When I blow a command, I expect you to obey; otherwise, you're useless.

"This practice was much better. Taleg, I'm making you my second-in-command even though you barely understand me; you instinctively understand what I want done. Commanders, putting the best shooters in the first battalion and the worst in the last has worked out well. Treating women the same as men was also useful because a quarter of them are better than most males. Your veterans were great a decade ago and your teens have potential, but hundreds of ladies earned their places in higher battalions. I'm very pleased.

"Even Uncle Bede can sling from a trot now; I wish he had Heruli lovers to encourage him long ago. Cousin Winston, slinging from the saddle won't be enough against Huns, so let's practice more archery from a canter. Fauna, you got too close again. Wait for us to get into position. I know many of you don't understand my Latin, but I'm learning your language as fast as I can. Remember to either pull back for saturation volleys or close the distance because they are more accurate than we are, for some reason. Our armor gives us an advantage from close range, but Huns are experts at dodging arrows, so we must target their mounts when not saturation-bombing them. Take their horses and they're just stinky pedestrians. Your job is not to kill Huns, but to rescue Heruli; don't risk your warriors. We must get in and get out before they can counter us. We recover who we can and then we leave fast. Kill as many Huns as you can, but include women and children because they are all enemies. Slay their herds so they starve, but focus on the mission. We're here to rescue, not for revenge. That said, I think we're finally ready. If things get bad, then break off and fight independently to support other units."

The king feels offended. "I'm the most experienced veteran here. I've fought a thousand battles, so why are you in charge?"

"Because I have a gift that senses what needs to be done in fluid situations. You lost most of your warriors, so you should not command. Before I got here, your training minimized formation maneuvers, though that's how the enemy beat you, so I don't know what the hell you have been doing the last four years. Your units could not even communicate even with signal flags like Huns use. Courage is not enough. Fighting smarter takes preparation and training. Failure is easy; success takes planning. In just a few weeks, you've come a long way. I'm proud of you, but we are still not their equal in a fair fight, so let's cheat. We will break into 100-rider platoons to hit more bands faster, but we must come together when they gather an army. Huns won because they are organized. You lost because you fight like raiders."

Naulo is next. "Magnus, you still can't shoot for shit at a canter. I should be in overall command."

"Brother, being a great shooter does not quality you to command. Fauna can shoot accurately, but is too aggressive to compensate for her sex, youth, and inexperience. Naulo, you still question yourself against a copse of trees. The enemy will move and they will move quickly. All of you have raided or have countered raids, but that is not war. That's surprising or being surprised in small numbers. A lengthy battle changes suddenly in unexpected ways. Each commander must foresee it and quickly counter. Huns are better shooters and dodgers; we counter that by trusting our armor, firing a lot more arrows, and by shielding our horses. Again: our goal is to avoid a pitched battle against a superior foe. Your orders are to ride away when out-numbered or out-maneuvered. If you can't obey me, then I can't effectively use you. I don't need raiders; I need troops.

"Oh, and not enough of your healers will let Bede teach them. He knows more about medicine than anyone west of Asia. He has eastern medicines, tools, and treatments that can save lives if only your ladies listen. He'd prefer studying in Constantinople; a little appreciation would keep him with us when we ride a thousand miles into the steppe. Fewer of our injured will die if your healers learn from him. The ladies and elders have packed 10,000 sets of non-perishable food for a month. 20,000 follow-up riders will escort prisoners and herds back to the Black Sea. Each of you must make sure you have 1000 arrows, enough water, and four extra mounts for the rescued. I assume the enemy will chase us, so we must ride farther and faster. It hasn't been long, but I think your horses are stronger since we started feeding them grain, apples, and enriched hay. We'll bring as much as we can to keep their strength up. We need to pasture enough horses somewhere so we can enjoy fresh mounts while the Huns exhaust theirs. If they do chase us, then pause on higher ground or when you enjoy wind to loose saturation volleys. I'd rather spend twice as many arrows to lose half as many riders. Pack wisely. Our armor and ammo sacks cost us in weight, so each rider needs an extra remount to ride farther and faster."

King Naulobatus sits straight in the saddle and pulls out something wrapped in a blanket. "Magnus, the Heruli people would like to gift you something special. Our best craftsmen have been working on it day and night. I hope you like it."

Magnus accepts it, unwraps the gift, and then bursts into tears like a total bitch. "A very long, composite, double-curved recursive longbow? Oh, sire, you get me; you really get me."

"We trade value for value. Since Hun bows are more powerful than ordinary ones, your new longbow probably gives you the most range of any archer, anywhere."

Magnus begins laughing and soon they all join him.

The flat grasslands seem endless. When he sees a bump in the landscape, Magnus rides up with his battalion. Looking left, he sees other Heruli in a wide skirmish line. Turning right, there's more. Behind them, Magnus sees 20,000 young, female, or old Heruli, all armed with remounts to flee hostiles.

"Fauna, I expected more roving nomadic bands between the Caspian and Aral

204

seas. It's gotta be several hundred miles between them. The Alans abandoned their territory without a fight. We've only killed a few thousand and captured several thousand. We've taken more herds than captives."

"Huns moved Alans to their homeland of Bactria to pair each band with Huns they trust. Single Alans must mate with a Hun for higher status. Their kids will be Huns, not Alans. They'll return soon, but with Huns in each band."

"After riding 100 miles a day for a week, I never imagined so much empty grassland. It seems endless. No wonder everyone rides all day, every day. They only left the old and very young behind to guard livestock, wagons, and yurt homes with several Huns in charge."

She points excitedly. "Magnus, look! Another band, and the largest yet. Most roving bands have fewer than 100 folks, but this has a few thousand so Huns need fewer managers to keep their new vassals in line. I hope this one has more Huns; the last ones died too easily. Killing Alans doesn't feel as satisfying. My love, please let me have them; they might run if they see men, but are less likely to shoot girls to rape us instead."

It seems to take him forever to spot a tiny shadow moving on the horizon. "My love, you have great eyes. Your eyesight is also excellent. All right. Take your pink platoon, but lure them west, away from their band, while the rest of us circle around."

Grinning, she takes off while taking out her pink silk wrap-around robe. Her ladies see this and get out their own, knowing Magnus is using them at bait again.

The Huns and Alans see 100 women, all dressed in bright pink, for some reason. All fighters gather up and gallop over. About 150 approach cautiously, but don't see any other enemies. Fauna holds the high ground and waits until Huns and their vassals charge to envelop them. Against expectations, Team Fauna saturates the Hun center while slowly advancing downslope while half the Hun force waste time circling around and climbing up. The volume seems to surprise the Hun leader when he goes down with a cry and a curse. The pink ladies ride through the hole they carved and ride away, forcing the surviving 70 or so mounted archers to chase them. At a gallop, Fauna closes her eyes and moves her face left and right to feel the wind. Smiling, she holds up her hand, pointing left, and they follow her like birds in flight, except in a dense square rather than a long V shape. 70 hostiles hurry to catch up before these pink bitches slaughter their civilians, so they, too, are densely packed when the first saturation volleys fall on them like hail from Hell. The brave men shrug off the first hundred arrows, but the second lands with great impact from closer distance and the third fucks them up. Survivors either scatter or continue to return fire, but the odds are against them. 100 ladies trot closer to finish them off. Those that fled return angrily because blood can only be paid with blood. Squads chase each straggler to overwhelm them. All too soon, the good guys win and, for some reason, they're all women.

Team Magnus surrounds the roving village and only see scared kids under 6 years old, crippled veterans, and elderly folks who can't work a weapon. Everyone but kids are killed, except two males holding hands and expecting death.

Magnus rides up to them and sees their fear. "Fauna, please ask these two homosexuals if they'd like to live. I can't hate anyone who loves sucking cock. The more gays, the less competition for beauties. Men should be encouraged to suck cock, not punished, at least if they swallow. For some reason, spitters piss me off. If men could suck their own cocks, they'd do nothing else."

Both gay Alans nod vigorously. Alani children seem to accept them, so they mount up and ride with Heruli escorts back to Bata.

She smiles. "Magnus, have you ever sucked your own cock?"

"Oh, for years. At first I thought I was getting free blowjobs. I quit when I realized I was *giving* free blowjobs. Man, those were the most confusing 50 years of my life."

Laughing, she swats the 15-year-old, then can't stop touching him. "My love, I need more. Sorry I'm greedy."

"That's why I'm marrying you. Let's first send our captives off."

Captured kids ride double with their follow-up forces. Others herd their livestock to the Black Sea. They move slowly to the western horizon.

Magnus calls a leadership meeting. "We need to break up into smaller units to cover more area faster. That means each platoon must fight Huns instead of me having all the fun. I'm more comfortable now, though. Huns are easier to kill after shooting their horses."

The night sky seems limitless. Topless and indifferent to her audience, Fauna rides Magnus like a stallion, grunting and groaning loudly. Her big boobs bounce in the moonlight, her shoulder-length blond hair dancing as she finally cums. The explosion shakes Fana to her core. Her eyes glaze over, as if faint. She collapses on Magnus, who rolls them over to pound her. Beyond them, Winston bangs a beauty from behind, her big tits begging for two hands. Completely naked, she's smiling like he's huge and barks at him happily. A buff, handsome 21-year-old, the big Brit clearly loves this and nails her with an increasing intensity. Magnus doesn't seem to see them. Fauna's ankles bounce against his ears when a sentry whisper-shouts a warning. Cursing, the big Iberian concentrates as if Huns come to kill them. Horses gallop up around him, but riders don't get down, which makes it harder for him to focus. His muscular upper body stands out over the furs around them. Her breasts bounce in every direction as she urges him on in Heruli, eager for his seed. Finally, he blows past the point of no return and empties himself into her. He opens his eyes and sees her looking at him like a god, easily the sexiest thing he's ever witnessed. Still inside her, Winston and the Heruli hottie still go at it, as if combat is not imminent. Neither want it to end.

A Heruli scout speaks up. "Magnus, splitting up into squads worked. We hit a roving band of Alans and heard Huns barking orders. Their languages are very different, so they have trouble communicating. Targeting their horses really angered them. About 30 men chase my unit. They should arrive before dawn. Without a campfire, I doubt the enemy will detect us in time."

The warriors grin nervously. Payback feels good. Winston and his latest Heruli lover get dressed and arm up. Bede is bent over an injured Heruli, saving another stranger. Magnus shouts orders and the fighters get into position.

Sure enough, 35 hunters chase 9 Heruli into their ambush. Team Magnus pounces in the dark, surprising them from all sides. While those in front stop the enemy advance, others race into their blind spot to shoot them in the back. 100 against 35 is not fair and that's how Magnus likes it. From the front, the devious Iberian ducks so an arrow bounces off his helmet, giving him time and space to get into range. He rides slow with Fauna, Winston, and Bede who target their mounts and laugh when horses collapse, slide, or tumble. With enemies riding in their rear, these Heruli and their vassals charge into invaders in front of them, who throw knives at close range, then unsheathe swords to reach out and cut them down. With two big blades, Magnus veers into one after another, counting on his luck and armor. An arrow to his chest plate almost topples him, but he lifts himself back into the saddle to find another combat victory. The Heruli eagerly slit throats and rob corpses. Their boss turns to his warriors.

"I hope the other platoons are this lucky. Boys, hit their camp, but don't kill until you can clearly identify the women and kids."

A thousand Heruli escort several thousand liberated women and kids when a distant Heruli rider blows a bugle and points. Magnus frantically looks around for cover. There is none. Everything is green, flat, and treeless. The orphan blows Commanders Meeting.

Magnus complains. "It's like being in a green ocean! It looks like we must offer them a fair fight. #10 Platoon, take the civilians away in the opposite direction with Dr. Bede and the longbowmen. Fauna, please put on your pink silk dress with the frilly laces and hope the enemy mistakes your ladies for harmless girls instead of dangerous horse archers. Ride without helmets so the enemy can see that all 100 of you are women. My love, gallop north as if running for reinforcements, then circle behind them after they commit to their attack. I'm hoping they dismiss you ladies as a threat. Boys, prepare to panic hysterically, like we practiced. Wait for me to lose my shit before caving our center and fleeing like screaming cowards. Wing commanders, retreat cowardly until they dive into the middle of us, then hurry to their blind spot to hurt'em hard. Don't worry when I roar; I want them to focus on me instead of looking over their shoulders. I won't wear my helmet so they can see that I'm not from around here; my signal flag will identify me as a leader. If my plan works, they'll be dying to kill me. My squad of longbowmen will teaching these old dogs new tricks."

Nine Heruli gallop towards them and, a minute later, Team Magnus sees several hundred enemy archers, but not riding in formation. Magnus looks at his own team, who all wear bear coats over leather-chainmail.

"A lot more Huns than Alans this time. I wish our entire battalion was here. With equal numbers, we'll have to cheat. All righty, form up and let's see if they fall for our fake-panic like the last fools. My squad has the best shooters on the best horses wearing the best armor, so I'll lure some enemies away from the real battle. Remember that our best archers are on our left wing and the weakest are on our right wing to give ground."

Without high ground, trees, or other cover, Team Magnus waits in a skirmish line. The enemy charges down the middle, then a Hun commander blows a horn and then attackers split into three equal groups, with two pivoting to flank Magnus. The Heruli wings extend to block them. Those fights should get interesting because Magnus put his best shooters in one wing and the worst in the other, just like Thebes did to beat Sparta in 371 BC. Though even in numbers, the weak wing gave way while the strong wing advanced, enabling Thebes to displace the Spartans and then finish them as a military power. As in training, the battalion shatters after launching a blind saturation volley. Though Magnus roars like a lion to distract them, most enemies swerve to avoid arrows fired from long distance. He signals by pulling or swishing his flagpole, which marks him as a top target. Screaming like anal virgins, the Heruli center flees at top speed and a third of the Huns give chase with wicked grins and high hopes. As Magnus hoped, the enemy ignores the long-haired, silk-and-lace beauty running away with 99 other cowards, not realizing Fauna would gladly die for Magnus.

Screeching like a fucking nun, Magnus rides away with just a squad, turning often to make sure they hunt him. His antics and ostentatious outfit make him stand out, so most enemies chase him. He can't shoot well, so he needs to get close to hit horses in the head with pellets, which usually topples them. Riders fall in spectacular fashion, often with other horses stomping them. Finally putting on his bright red lion helmet with long feathers, Magnus lures a few hundred enemies away, stretching them out in a long line. The ten men repeatedly pivot left to shoot, as they are all right-handed. Every volley takes out several Hun horses or horsemen. Once the hunters get too close, Magnus blows a signal and his squad scatter caltrops behind them. Enemy mounts step on them and howl in pain. Riders fly and scared mounts collide, while all slow. That breaks their momentum and gives Team Magnus time to fire free volleys at close range that takes down dozens of enemies and even more mounts. With furious faces, these Heruli slow to snipe as long as possible while dodging incoming fire. Magnus is just as aggressive, though he must get closer for his lead pellets to hit horses hard enough. Thrice as many mounts go down, infuriating the enemy.

Once enough hostile horsemen threaten to overwhelm them, the big Iberian signals for them to retreat at a gallop into the wind, which strings the enemy out. The fastest Huns leave behind the slowest, stretching them out in a long line. When winds blow strong, the Heruli squad slows to fire saturation volleys that the enemy can't evade, then race ahead on rested mounts to repeat this. As the enemy gets close, Team Magnus turns to hit horses, which rear up or fall down, stranding riders in an empty sea of grass. A whistling metal ball enters a horse's head and the mare falls on her side at top speed, crushing the Hun and frightening his friends. Others get shafted to strand shocked pedestrians with dick to fight with. The enemy, wearing conical and comical hats, are furious at being forced to walk to work. They dearly want to kill the odd screamer who roars. In exploiting his ability to annoy, Magnus turns a vice into a virtue. The foolish enemy mistook Magnus for bright red bait. The few hundred Huns and Alans chasing Magnus can't see what's going on behind them.

He yells at his squad while slinging. "It doesn't matter how many shooters they have; it only matters how many shooters can hit us. Usually we outnumber them; if not, we ride away. Look how tired their horses are! They've been riding all night! Boys, killing Huns is easy!"

His laughter energizes his team and infuriates the world's deadliest warriors.

Riding away fast, the Heruli left wing pauses periodically to send saturation volleys that get harder to avoid as Team Hun gallops closer. This leaves a trail of wounded men and mounts stretching over a mile. Hun arrows bounce off or stick limply in Heruli armor as the fast hunt strings out hostiles. Instead of following Magnus, the Heruli center races to join their weaker wing to fight off flankers. The left wing leaves the area, so Huns must chase them, which conveniently puts the Heruli center behind the enemy. The center races to shoot unprotected backs. After losing dozens of dudes, Huns pull up to fight back. The center slows and their weaker wing turns around. Together, they sandwich their hunters with almost twice as many shooters when Fana shows up with a hundred ladies to add pain to their misery. The Killer Triangle works wonders because Huns have nowhere safe to go; no matter their direction, hostiles will attack them from behind, so they fight a losing battle as best they can. Mostly immobilized, Huns trade arrows at close range against superior numbers. The difference in armor grows ever more obvious because locals wear none. Huns are horrified as their horses go down, taking riders with them. Team Fauna increases their numerical superiority, which is good because they're needed elsewhere.

About even in numbers, the Heruli right wing shoots-and-scoots while luring the enemy in a wide circle to buy time at a deep discount. Instead of trading shots, they race away, slow to turn and fire a saturation volley, then resume galloping. The fastest Huns and Alans get hit often, losing their mounts and their minds. Assuming they'll win, their comrades blow past them to catch up. But they can't catch up because virtually unlimited ammo rains down on them. Once they get close, Heruli target their horses to strand them. Only a rare Hun arrow impotently hits a Heruli while dozens of locals get shafted every volley. Several miles later, Hun horses, who have ridden hard all night, can't keep up, so the hunters become the prey. Strung out as planned, Huns lack numbers as Heruli gang up on isolated groups to destroy them piecemeal. Other Huns hurry to help, but rarely arrive in time to save their comrades. Alans take more time and scan the bigger battle more carefully; smarter ones leave while they can while the rest end up dying for nothing.

Magnus' squad has Winston and ten other Tall Archers from his flagship. They gallop in a wide U-turn that returns them to the battalion. He keeps his squad just out of range of the fastest enemies, pausing periodically to send volleys when he enjoys wind or height. While most horse archers carry just 60 arrows, his squad has almost 10,000, so they shoot as if they enjoy unlimited ammo. Huns can avoid a few arrows at a time, but not dozens. Those ten riders take down several enemies a minute because Huns don't wear metal armor. Maintaining an ideal distance with 10 riders is much easier than with 100, though it looks suicidal for just a squad to defy a few hundred Huns. Magnus yells for Squad 1 to slow down or speed up, going from a trot into a gallop, then slowing to shoot again. Changing speed while zig-zagging avoids most enemy arrows. Huns are now sensitive to his bugle sounds and watch him signal with his flag.

Once they've lost most pursuers, Team Magnus stops upwind, on a bump in the land, because his hunters are spread out in a long line. About 100 belligerents jog to catch up, which Magnus finds hilarious. Only about 60 mounted hostiles still pursue Magnus, so he does the absurd and dismounts. The twelve men step on the bottom of their bows after resting a meter-long quiver basket at their feet. With wind at their backs on higher ground, they aim high to saturate in long arcs using their brand new, giant, double-curved composite bows. Three of five hunters avoid the first volley, but only one survives the second. His pony crashes and the rider gets crushed in the impact. Magnus is still laughing loudly when the next group comes, slower and more carefully. Two Huns and three horses take shafts, but the rest race to get close enough to return effective fire. Five more go down, but the remaining six gallop uphill to shoot these damn intruders. The Tall Archers target mounts, which go down hard, spilling riders all over the ground. They get up, dead men limping to exchange arrows with strangers with more powerful weapons. More Huns and Alans charge, but go down as fast as they ride up. Seeing this, riders go around, but face the same fate from a different direction. The last 30 hunters wait so they can all attack at the same time but, instead of riding over heavily armored infantry, they dart in to fire back. Not surprisingly, they lose. Team Magnus has a 50-meter range advantage, thanks to their bigger bows and bigger biceps, something Huns have never encountered before. The last dozen stare at Magnus as he takes off his lion helmet to roar at them playfully. They have even numbers, but the Hun leader evens the odds by attacking with the wind at their back, something earlier attackers should have tried. Huns now have about the same range, but learn, to their horror, that their iron arrowheads don't sink into the strange newcomers. Giant bear coats cover armor plates and two sets of chainmail, sandwiched in leather, so locals die of ignorance. Magnus' squad checks each other for injuries, then laugh at their good fortune.

Magnus walks to the nearest survivor to question a dying Hun, pinned under his horse. The Iberian holds up a piece of leather that Huns stood on while shooting. "What is this?" Surprised and confused, the Hun blurts something out in a foreign tongue. "Stirrups? The hell is a stirrup?" He swallows that and the worm that came with it. "What a weird war; we need to steal Hun saddles."

Just over 100 hostiles who lost their horses walk over, feeling furious and optimistic. The first don't wait, so they die before they can do any good. The last pedestrians charge as one, but Team Magnus has greater range and better armor. Huns and Alans lose again, so survivor scatter, only for Heruli horse archers to gleefully shoot them down with a vengeance.

Corpses cover a wide area, some still screaming. Team Naulo has vanquished another roving band of enemies when Team Magnus rides up to admire his work. The victors are taking everything of value and helping freed Heruli onto horses. Hundreds of young Alans opt to join them rather than die. Cattle, sheep, and goats lie dead and flames burn their huge wagons, sending dark columns of smoke into the sky.

The Heruli prince gallops over. "Magnus, my battalion has rescued almost a thousand Heruli, twice as many Slavs, and have captured thrice as many young Alans, plus quite a few who speak Turkish. Umm, why do you look odder than usual?"

The 15-year-old gestures to the stolen saddle he's riding. "Brother, Huns can shoot better because they stand on something called stirrups. Their knees absorb the shock to give them a more stable shooting platform, whereas we bounce up and down in the saddle. I can't believe no one ever thought of this before. Everyone needs to replace their saddles with a Hun version to stand while shooting. That can mean the difference between life and death. My cock already feels twice as big and your fucking sister is thrilled. I also have bad news. Your grandfather says a Hun army is returning from a campaign against the Slavs that fled northwest, so we need to go before they cut us off. Messengers went to collect our division. Where are the rest of your men?"

"Freed Heruli said most of our people are to the south, where we used to rule. We can't leave before seeing who we can rescue."

"Well, that turns a problem into a predicament delivering a dilemma swallowing a conundrum. Unless we leave now, the enemy will block off our escape. We'll be trapped between the two great inland seas with several thousand non-fighters and tens of thousands of stolen horses."

210

"Not if we ride south of the Caspian Sea, then north along the Black Sea's eastern shoreline to Bata. It's about the same distance from here. The southern shore of the Caspian is Persian territory, but Huns have been launching raids deep into Persia, so the Persian army should be elsewhere. Persians built a wall there, centuries ago, but it has fallen apart. Crossing the Karakum Desert will be the bigger challenge."

The giant Iberian looks at the older Heruli around them and they nod eagerly. "Avoiding an enemy army sounds good, but a rearguard will need to slow them down by luring them away. Brother, you lead rescue operations along our escape route, but I'll need all the Hun saddles you have and our best shooters. I want to get a better look at Hun leaders to understand why they scare me."

The Lion is not sitting on Caesar and all have two remounts. The orphan surveys his commanders and likes what he sees. The Heruli clearly appreciate the possibility that they may soon die, but they look resolved instead of terrified. Everyone who volunteered seeks vengeance, even if it means their death. Half his force are women and most of the males are orphaned teens. Magnus, 11 guards, and about 5000 Heruli watch a far bigger army fill the skyline. In the distance, an old crippled Heruli who speaks Hunnic passes a mound with a white flag to greet them. From far away, Magnus sees him address his Hun overlords.

Magnus smiles at his fiancée. "Whenever I do something special for my wife, she rewards me sexually, so I try to do something special for her, like, every hour!"

She laughs. "Another of your dad's jokes?"

"Nope. I just made it up, which means I'm anxious. Took them long enough. These patient Huns must have waited weeks for us to return the way we came. I'm guessing 60,000, but half are not Huns. Sure wish we could have stolen more Hun saddles, but I'm glad we're running away. 5000 troops is not enough. We've never fought more than a thousand before, so I hope my plan still works. All right, then – let's see if they'll surrender peacefully."

"I'll die fighting those who murdered my family," the old king says with great confidence.

"Only if my optimism fools me again," Magnus says. "You must hug our firstborn a thousand times before you leave us. Commander Taleg, your expression never changes. Challenging 60,000 horse archers doesn't bother you?"

Everyone turns to look.

"Huns killed my parents and stole two sisters. I live to hurt them and your plan should work."

Three on each side ride without bows to the mound in the middle. They stop within talking distance, with Magnus facing an impressive old man who looks like he has his shit together. He resonates charisma, authority, and what Romans call *dignitas*. In front, a physically impressive warrior sits his horse besides a clever advisor. Like other Central Asians, Huns have little facial hair and none have beards, yet the advisor does, marking him as non-Hunnish. The unarmed, crippled Heruli interpreter dismounts and kneels to the side to translate. The strong warrior wears a beautiful diadem with a golden image of a ram's head set in precious stones on his head. His silk cloak, bejeweled sword, and rich furs make him stand out. He looks majestic, like a misplaced Greek god.

He speaks through the kneeling interpreter. "Greetings. I am Kushansha Peroz."

211

Even illiterate Central Asian barbarians are big on manners.

Fauna translates from Heruli into Latin. "Kushansha means king of the Kushans, who ruled Bactria before Huns vanquished them. It's their word for king."

"I am Naulobatus, king of the Heruli. Kushansha Peroz, are you related to King Kirada, who conquered Bactria before my birth?"

Magnus laughs at that. "That's not Peroz. Just look at him." He waits for Fauna to translate that and sees the anger on the warrior's face before addressing the old man. "Honored Elder, please tell me the name of the genius who thought of stirrups."

The old man hesitates, but sees the eagerness on the teen's face. "As a child, Kirada the Great visited China and saw the elderly, the sick, the injured, the weak, and small kids mount horses using paired stirrups instead of stepping on a stump, steps, or a rock. His father made one for him, then for his friends, who grew up hunting at a gallop using stirrups. Accuracy was so much greater that all our hunters started using them. We beat our neighbors until we faced mounted archers like us – mostly Xiongnu and Xianbei, who would go on to invade China. We represented a dangerous threat, so they united against us, forcing us to move south, where Kirada defeated a mixed group of peoples that included Greek-speakers, who gave us a written language, metalworkers, and craftsmen. I am one of his grandsons. Now that I answered your question, please answer mine. Who are you, who are your people, and why are you here?"

"Those are three questions. My name is Magnus Maximus. What is yours?"

"Kidara. I am too old to use a bow, so I came here to meet our new enemy. You have slaughtered women, children, and elders, plus entire herds. What sort of horseman kills horses?"

"You took what we value most, the Heruli, so we took what you value most. To answer your second question, I am Roman."

"What is that?"

That shocks Magnus. "Sir, are you serious? You have not heard of Rome? What about the Roman Empire? Go west and you can't miss it." The old veteran looks at him blankly, so he shrugs and continues. "Naulobatus wants to rescue his people, including my wife's mother, but we learned she died of her wounds. If you return your Heruli captives, we will probably leave you alone."

The old man speaks for them. "We'd rather kill all Heruli than release them. Why do you say our man is not Peroz?"

"It's obvious. He's a strong warrior, but he's not clever enough to rule an empire like you did before you grew too old to fight. You once wielded great power. I was always afraid of losing my mother's love, but I've never feared any man until I met you, old as you are. My father beat me, but I don't fear beatings. In your prime, you must have been the most impressive man alive. I'm shocked you passed your power to another. Few have the strength to do that. I am honored to meet you and will include our conversation in my next memoirs. Sadly, you are too dangerous to let live."

With that, Magnus throws a knife into his chest and then another, to be sure. Both fly true and sink deep, surprise on everyone's faces. As the Hun badass turns to attack, he gets a knife in the right shoulder and Magnus gallops off, laughing hysterically to piss off the warriors watching from a great distance. Fauna, her grandfather, and the crippled interpreter follow fast, terrified of 240,000 hooves pounding the earth behind them. It sounds and feels like an earthquake. Dust from the stampede rises like a storm behind them.

A mile away, 60,000 mounted archers charge at full speed because that pale foreigner just killed their previous leader, the genius responsible for their empire after Kirada founded it. Emperor Peroz and other leaders stop to attend Kidara the Great. The wounded warrior and the merchant advisor have removed the blades and now bandage the wounds, but his death is inevitable. The buff badass is in tears, the emperor's expensive diadem falling off his head into the mud.

The burly warrior cries like a little bitch over the dying old man. "I'm sorry, grandfather. I'm so sorry."

The real Hun emperor radiates power, authority, and badassery as he dismounts to hear his grandfather's last words. "Grandfather! Why would they kill an old man instead of a young warrior? That was the whole point! And, cousin, you dropped my crown in the mud!"

The Persian merchant explains: "Their leader is not Heruli and saw through us. He addressed Emperor Kidara with great respect, but said he was too dangerous to live."

Kidara whispers weakly. "Peroz, you must kill that Roman, Magnus Maximus. He's a greater foe than I ever faced. It's more important to kill him than all the Heruli combined because he is unnaturally clever. He comes from the west, a place called Rome. It is he who steals our saddles for the stirrups and slays our herds. Huns cannot enjoy security as long as he lives. But don't kill our Heruli captives – make their warriors return to fight for them on our turf."

The emperor grunts agreement and comforts his hero until light fades from his eyes. Though a hard man, the Hun leader lets his anguish fill his face, then turns on the Persian merchant.

"Learn all you can about this Roman, Magnus Maximus. Send a team to Rome and deduct it from what you owe us. The more you learn, the safer your family will be." He then picks up the three knives. "The Roman threw these? He has knives that can be thrown? Kidara the Great is right, as always: Magnus Maximus must die."

Team Magnus rides abreast in 50 platoons, one of them pink, with each commander flying a green flag. They pause upwind on high ground to send saturation volleys before moving on. The Huns chase in 60 battalions, also with a leader with a flag flying from a pole, some trying to cut ahead or flank them. It's impressive and terrifying. It rains thousands of arrows where Huns ride too close together to avoid. Most miss, but hundreds of riders get shafted in each volley. As the chase continues, the aerial view shows a trail of dead and wounded men and horses.

The king and his companions catch up to their army and watch in dread as the enemy stops on higher ground to send 40,000 arrows that his fighters must evade. The sight stuns as the shafts arc in the air, then land with cries and curses. Hundreds die and thousands suffer injuries. The emperor rides by many bodies. Once Team Magnus returns to a gallop, Peroz catches up to his teenage son, who doesn't slow.

"Father, the enemy knows what he's doing, but I'm shocked the Heruli follow a fucking foreigner. His horses are rested while ours rode far to get here. All their riders have our stirrups, which means they've killed 5000 warriors. Whenever he enjoys higher ground or strong wind, they pause to shoot us. Their leader uses a metal device to blow several distinct signals, so the loud one has organized the Heruli into formations like ours. As we start flanking them from the left or right, they turn to open the distance so we can't get too close. They tend to quickly shoot five arrows, the comfortable amount that a hand can hold, before moving on to avoid return fire. If they enjoy a good breeze, they'll pause to toss another five at wherever Huns concentrate the most, while ignoring our vassals. I put our vassals in the center and Huns on either wing to flank him, but they still target Huns, so we should mix up our units. He rides upwind to extend his range and the power of the impacts, so he's going northeast, away from safety. There's nothing in front of him except distant mountains that riders can't climb, so I don't understand his plan."

"Magnus plans to kill Huns. He's here to help the Heruli avenge their families. They are not here to steal women, horses, or cattle. He threw knives to kill Emperor Kidara the Great, but didn't bother to slay my slow cousin. I've heard of knives that can be thrown, but have never seen any until today."

His son looks serious and competent. "They're from the West, yet ride east, so they can't escape. We'll slaughter them once they run out of ammo."

Peroz points excitedly. "We killed a horse! I need to see what's on it because our arrows don't seem to work." Father and son divert to a bloody mare complaining of an arrow in her ass. The emperor dismounts to open the system of sacks that hold 1000 arrows. He looks up at his son, deeply disturbed. "The Heruli may not exhaust their ammo and they put chainmail between blankets to protect their mounts. They've had five years to plan vengeance, so let's keep our distance and herd them against the mountains." He pulls out a nosebag. "Oh, no. They've been feeding their horses grain to give them extra strength. This foe plans ahead."

"The Heruli know we can field 250,000 mounted archers, yet they raid this far into our land? What's his name?"

Peroz locks eyes with his son. "Octar, we face a new threat from some place called Rome and his name is Magnus Maximus. I sure hope he can't ride all day."

The Hun Army rides long after dusk before camping at the foothills of a mountain chain, visible in the background. Sweat and fatigue cover their weary faces. They all look exhausted, frustrated, and miserable. The emperor calls a leadership meeting to puzzle this out.

Peroz raises his voice: "We've already lost 10,000 warriors, while I doubt the Heruli lost 10. The enemy only has two remounts per rider, just like us, but for twenty days has been riding them to death. The Heruli eat in the saddle rather than stop long enough for a cooking fire. Magnus must study the sun and stars because he has consistently traveled northeast, past the Smaller Sea. Uldin, what is he doing and why?"

"Father," a different son says, "we are not chasing him; he is luring us away from our homeland. It'll take us a moon to return. Why else would he ride so far in the wrong direction? China is just over those mountains."

Uldin looks 10 years older than his half-brother, Octar.

Peroz nods. "I sent messengers to warn our people, but doubt Heruli will go into Bactria. Other Heruli are trying to rescue their people, but we scattered them across our empire so they'd assimilate faster. Kidara said it's more important to kill Magnus Maximus than the Heruli, so here we are."

Octar speaks up. "Father, our horses will die if we ride them tomorrow and we have no food. We must think of another way to win."

214

"After 20 days of riding all day, we're too tired to think clearly. Rest and we'll dream of something in the morning."

In their vast camp, Huns sleep on blankets, dead to the world. Few sentries stand guard because Huns think they stand on top of the food chain. Team Magnus creeps up as silently as hooves allow on soft grass, but charge when someone detects them. Iron horseshoes won't be invented for another few centuries. 5000 riders shoot 40,000 arrows a minute into the Hun camp. Most miss, but thousands of Huns get hit. The night sky looks full of shafts. Men scream in rage and cry in pain. Warriors scramble to their feet, notching arrows and searching the darkness for enemies when it starts raining arrows. Huns don't wear armor because weight slows them down, yet there is no cover to hide behind.

The monarch fires blindly at a massive shadow. "They're riding around us! Protect the horses."

40,000 men run for their mounts, but 5000 attackers target them. The Heruli move aggressively to exploit surprise. Mounted archers enjoy a mobility advantage, so they slay Huns stuck on foot. The instinct of horse archers is to mount up, but saddling a horse takes precious time. Team Magnus shoots them up until too many mounted Huns fire back. A bugle blows and Team Magnus melts away in the dark. Peroz rides around his camp, fury building with every corpse, then dismounts to hold a friend gasping his last breath. The king tears up as his friend dies in his arms. He scans his camp. Bleeding bodies are everywhere. Corpses call for help as they stumble or crawl. Many won't live to see the sun.

Peroz is beside himself with rage. "Magnus just took another 10,000 warriors from me."

Octar wants to kill Magnus so bad it hurts. Several thousand Huns chase the Heruli. Their grim determination is written on their faces as they gallop in the dark. The rising sun illuminates an empty land devoid of trees. Huns see Magnus, standing out in red, walk into a dry riverbed with 11 other foreigners. He roars defiantly to announce his presence. The Hun riders are stretched out over a mile instead of massed together, so the fastest give chase. Octar follows hundreds of fighters to the dry riverbed, but he wisely doesn't go in. At the far end of a curve stands Magnus in a bottleneck, firing the biggest bow that anyone has ever seen. He looks absurd in his red cloak, peacock helmet, and long feathers; he also sounds absurd, singing Girls of Rome in a beautiful voice. 11 other large men with recursive longbows shoot behind him at a narrow stream of Huns riding to their doom. Dozens of dead and dying horses create an obstruction, forcing survivors to exchange projectiles, using corpses as cover. Just 12 foreign invaders decimate Huns, usually before they even get near enough to shoot back.

Something's off, so Octar pulls up to study the situation, though another thousand Huns descend to pack the crowded riverbed. The enemy wears bear coats with arrows clinging to them like lint. Their quiver baskets are tall and their arrows long, but their bows are taller than the men. Without horses at hand, they can't even escape a successful charge, yet don't seem worried. More and more Huns add their firepower, but few arrows seem to do any good, hitting the enemy from maximum distance. But plenty of Huns go down every moment. Though greatly outnumbered, Magnus is inflicting killer casualties. Octar puzzles over this when ladies ride up either side to shoot down into the dumb Huns, packed like sand on a beach. Huns can't ride up and can't ride out, so they trade arrows with armored women wearing bear coats, chainmail, and iron helmets. Warriors around him snort at the prospect of fighting females, but Octar grows alarmed by how many Huns they knock off horses. Shocked, he blows retreat.

"Flank those bitches! Magnus chose women to mislead us."

He leads horse archers out of the riverbed and then circles around to fuck those ladies from behind, only for a few thousand Heruli to suddenly ride out to confront him. Octar turns and sees his brother Uldin try flanking the opposite side, just to meet the other Heruli blocking force. Octar curses under his breath.

"It's an obvious ambush! Ride around!"

The two armies exchange arrows, but only one side wears armor. Incredulous, Octar blows Retreat before they become outnumbered. Only then do the badass women retreat, their mission accomplished. Octar stares stupidly at these fearless females as they get off their final shots before fleeing. Octar rides to the edge of the riverbed and sees a dozen longbowmen advancing to shoot the most mobile survivors as they scurry out. The sunken riverbed has as many dead horses as horsemen and Oscar can't trust his own eyes. How can so few slay so many?

Riding closer, he tries sniping Magnus, only for the Iberian to turn and shoot Octar's kickass stallion. The long cedar arrow sinks deep below the horse's shoulder. The Hun leaps off, comes up in a roll, and rushes closer to strike that red demon down. His comrades crowd the high embankment, enjoying height and a stationary shooting platform, but the enemy on foot, with unnaturally tall bows, are fucking them up fast. Octar dodges an arrow and backs up because Magnus is targeting him. He hurries behind a horse and its rider flies out of the saddle, in front of Octar, who finally looks scared.

"Get away from the riverbank! He wears iron armor."

The Huns retreat to lick their wounds and eat shit again. Team Octar chases the enemy across a ford with a few thousand riders and gets the shock of his life. Without a command, the Huns pull up and stop to stare at something disgusting. They all look sad, stunned, and horrified.

In awful pain, Uldin yells angrily. "What sort of beast would do such a thing?"

Octar looks across the river to see 5000 enemies galloping west on rested horses.

"His name is Magnus Maximus and we must kill him if it's the last thing we do."

The monarch is still staring at dead friends when his young son rides up.

Pissed and puzzled. "Octar, they shot almost a million arrows before leaving! How is that possible? They even tracked where Huns slept and barely bothered with our vassals. We lost another 10,000 Huns! Many more suffered wounds." Then he sees his son's face. "What else is wrong?"

"Father, there's something you must see. Words are not enough."

They ride to a river ford where they find 15,000 dead horses without saddles. Some warriors moan and groan as if this physically hurts. It's a strange sight. The king must blink a few times before his brain accepts what his lying eyes are plainly telling him.

Octar sums it up. "How does Magnus beat 60,000? He sent his best 15,000

216

horses here, then rode stolen ones for 20 days to exhaust us. He wanted us to know he could ride horses to death. These horsemen slew their mounts with blades. Few men can think that far ahead, so we must kill him before he returns. I'll send assassins to Rome."

"Magnus got away and will never return. None of us will ever see him again."

"Dad, you might never see him again, but I'm pretty sure I will."

The 5000 Heruli dismount to water their horses. They've captured thousands of ponies, so each leads about a dozen extra mounts. Fauna, as always, is by her man when grandpa rides up and gets down.

Magnus smiles like the world is his oyster. "Sire, this is the best honeymoon ever! I bet we killed, crippled, or captured 50,000 hostiles. The horses we took from our enemy alone made this worth the few hundred lives we lost. Did you see Fauna at the riverbed? I got so hard I almost started masturbating, which requires three hands."

Sobbing, the Heruli king hugs Magnus hard enough to nearly tackle him and embraces him long enough to make the Iberian uncomfortable. After kissing his forehead, the old man finally stands back to floor him across the wet grass.

Shaking with a burning intensity that unnerves the Iberian. "Thank you, Magnus. This last month has been a dream come true. You helped me avenge my sons, brothers, cousins, uncles, and nephews. The Heruli have regained their honor. You've asked us for loyalty and service while exchanging value for value. All I have left to give is my life, so it is yours. Magnus Maximus, I am King Naulobatus of the Heruli and I am your man to the death."

CHAPTER 10

Between the Black and Caspian Seas

Magnus and Fauna take a team south to find his future brother-in-law with Heruli and Slavic riders. Several thousand young Alans and Sarmatians walk. The herds surprise him, but not as much as a few thousand wagons filled with bulk goods and little children. Naulo rides up looking pissed and relieved.

Magnus waves happily. "Brother, we expected you weeks ago, but now I understand the delay. How many cattle and horses have you stolen?"

"I don't count like you Romans. Oxen slow us down, but we hate not taking them. Locals can't counter horse archers. For five years I felt inferior, but now I know I just needed stirrups, armor, a better bow, and better arrows. Your arrows fly much more accurately, especially at a distance. The Shah of Persia sent his army to Merv to deter Huns from raiding, so only tiny local militias contested our travel. They hit us at night or at bottlenecks, so we take what we want and pile it on their wagons. It's funny: we took wagons because they are valuable, then later find stuff to fill them. We demanded the wealth of every town to spare them from a pillage; most coughed it all up because they mistook us for Huns, who slaughter cities that defy them. The amount of gold, silver, jewelry, and gemstones shocked me. The Armenians slowed us down until I paid them with oxen to escort us north to the Bantu Peninsula on the western Caspian. Once past the mountains, no one has challenged us. I'm glad to see you and Fauna alive. How did you escape the Huns?"

"By riding a lot. Your success as a thief gives me an idea. I auctioned off your old cattle, sheep, and horses to agents from Constantinople, but they want more. With the Alans to our northeast and Slavs to our north gone, there are no horse archers around except some Sarmatians, along the lower Danube River. After we drive these herds to Bata, let's sweep the area. The Visigoths and Bulgars have big herds while Slavs must move theirs south for the winter. Grass sprouts in the south months before the north. Constantinople has almost a million people, including recent refugees, so they always need beef. I hear Greece and coastal cities in Anatolia get hungry, too. Best of all, Emperor Constantius is in Tarsus, near Cyprus, raising a huge army to kill Julian. I hope to visit him after selling him all the food he can afford."

Fauna looks well laid. "Naulo, I'm already pregnant. I feel delicious!"

"Magnus, you gonna marry my sister or let her breed bastards? She's a pearl beyond price. I'm ready to marry Jaki whenever you man up."

He hesitates and is lost. "I've promised to marry Fauna a few thousand times, but the head of my family told me not to marry without his consent. I'm impulsive and he's stubborn. I need him for my military career, so I planned to marry her under Heruli customs and tell him whatever he needs to hear. I gave her an expensive wedding ring which she will happily show you long after you want to sleep. Most Heruli around Bata have left for Iberia. Jaki says she misses you. If you marry her, I'll provide the ring and dowry. The more we mix our blood, the more we become family, so I told our clan to breed with Heruli. Bede took two ladies to Constantinople and Winston has countless lovers, the last time I did the math. Fauna and I need to sail to Tarsus to murder an emperor, but we'll rejoin the Sea Horse when it passes through Constantinople. I can't

218

wait to show you that enormous city. It's preplanned with excellent sewage, storm drainage, and trash disposal."

Naulo laughs at that. "Magnus, you're so odd."

"That stuff is critical while doing it at scale is truly tricky. My family is optimizing Porto Gordo harbor to build a planned port mega-city. It's harder than it sounds. You'll see soon. Oh, the horse transports just took their sixth set of mounts up the Danube instead of the Med. Pel's troops help escort them from a riverport on the Sava River, near northeastern Italy, to his uncle's ranch, where his family will send them on a highway to Porto Gordo. It only costs you every tenth mount, yet helps us move several times more horses, several times faster. We're selling about half of your herd locally to reduce the burden. I thought we could only make three trips through the Med, but Pel may help us move 100,000 horses via the Danube. Some Heruli and lots of locals are grazing your herds on Thurvingi land, at the mouth of the Danube to save on traveling time. 60 years ago, some Thurvingi settled in central Germania, but hostiles surrounded them. I had assumed we'd have to kill them, but Pel knows a chief who needs help driving off Sarmatians. Brother, I thought I'd have to spend a fortune on the Heruli, but you collectively may arrive rich. Divided by 50,000 people, it won't be much, so we should steal as much as we can since we're never coming back."

"Magnus, are you really going to take care of 50,000 Heruli, plus 10,000 young Slavs, Alans, and Persians?"

"Yes. I'll set you all up with food and shelter in Galicia, then most adults must work, like everywhere else."

Naulo sounds skeptical. "You have homes for 60,000 people?"

"Yes. Jaki owns enough homes for several thousand folks as compensation for her help. She will be rich, so you should marry her. A double marriage might be more memorable."

The Kingdom of Bulgaria, north of the Black Sea

The Heruli ride up quietly until they see their target by starlight. The town has dozens of buildings.

Magnus squints at the town. "Not having a palisade seems optimistic. King Kubrat rules the Bulgars, who speak Turkic and hate Alans. The fewer we kill, the more warriors to get in the way of the Huns when they invade Europe. Let's trap them inside while our non-warriors drive their herds south. Having 20,000 riders helping 10,000 cavalry will clear thrice the area. I'd bet on our worst horse archers over their mounted spearmen. They're scattered across a huge area, but keeping their king here will help us. Try not to trample their crops."

A guard dog does his duty, alerting the men within. This is the headquarters for the Bulgar monarch, so the Heruli barely have enough time to open corrals, stables, and liveries to drive off their horses. The Heruli exchange arrows with the Bulgars, but try not to kill. Once they have taken their horses, Team Magnus leaves. Magnus rides with Fauna as they herd thousands of horses, cattle, and sheep south. Oxen pull stolen wagons carrying chickens, pigs, and goats. Heruli kids, elders, and women keep the animals in line while warriors ride a wide perimeter. He looks over at her and smiles.

"If the other nine battalions capture as many animals, then the Heruli will be

219

rather rich ranchers in Galicia."

A bugle blows, so the Rapid Response Team gallops north. Upon cresting a rolling hill, they stop to study the problem: a small army of riders want their herds back.

"I hoped it'd take them longer to find horses. Boys, there's several thousand of them and only 100 of us, but they can't shoot from the saddle. Let's hit their horses until they go away."

The Bulgars slow upon seeing 100 enemies ride to intercept them. They look behind them, assuming there's more. Seeing no other threats, they spread out to envelop the 1st Platoon. Magnus turns into the nearest horsemen and several hundred arrows a minute slaughters their mounts. A mob of men try swarming Team Magnus, who escapes to circle around. The platoon changes direction to approach the closest riders to hit their horses, then opens the distance to repeat that. The king leads a courageous charge. Magnus flees, screaming in a panic. When the fastest Bulgars have left behind the slowest, he turns to cut down their rides. It's no contest. The Bulgar king feels stupid, holding a sword against bowmen who can shoot at a gallop. After getting thrown, a Heruli uses a hoop of rope to snag the king's ankle and drag his royal ass to the river. The big Iberian holds out his hand and roars like a maniac at the Bulgar warriors.

"Stop or we'll kill King Kubrat!"

The Bulgars pause, not sure what to do. Many turn towards the herds, but several hundred new Heruli now form a skirmish line to block them. The orphan rides to the king and literally talks down to him. Every time the monarch tries standing, the horseman advances to drag him more.

"Sire, do you understand me? Then stop interfering. Yes, we're taking most of your herds, but that's because we can shoot accurately from the saddle. Please don't make us kill you. A thousand horses died. You'll need to jerk them all to eat this winter. If you don't have enough salt, we can sell you some."

"Who are you and what do you want?"

"I'm nobody, so nobody was better than you. We're just passing through, and we want to sell your herds so we can leave this area. A tribe from the steppe are conquering their neighbors. One day they'll come here and you stand no chance against them. I'd advise you to move to Anatolia because that dry mountainous peninsula doesn't offer enough grass to satisfy nomadic horsemen like the Huns. I'll even let you live if you hand me your jewelry."

"I swear I'll find and kill you."

Magnus' tone gets darker. "Then I guess I won't let you live. If I must kill you, I might as well kill your men. Your young women and kids can't survive on their own, so we might as well take them, too. Your neighbors will finish you off, exterminating Bulgars as a people. I like your belt. Give me it. Your boots, too; they might fit my brother. Would you like a moment to pray before we drag you to death?"

King Kubrat reconsiders. "I misspoke. I won't look for you. If you don't return, we'll never see each other again."

"Then I won't kill you, but I still want your belt and boots. Keep your ugly rings; I shit better jewelry. They look too cheap to sell."

"You attacked several thousand warriors with just 100 fighters, some of them women. I've heard reports of other thieves stealing our herds. How many riders do you command?"

"10,000 good horse archers and another 20,000 riders. Sorry to impoverish you. I'll send a wagon full of salt here so a thousand tons of horse meat doesn't go bad. But, in return, I want all your good jewelry, coin, and bullion."

"Sir, without oxen we can't plow this spring. Without dairy cows, some will starve this winter. We are not enemies. Any help will be appreciated."

Magnus nods agreeably. "I'm a terrible thief. Sire, I'll see what I can do if your men let us leave. If harassed, we'll slaughter men and steal fuckable women. Or, if you really anger me, we'll slaughter the fuckable women and steal the men. If you make me kill you, I'll write on your gravestone: Nobody was greater."

"I could field 30,000 fighters, but it worries me that this doesn't worry you. I've seen what just 100 horse archers can do. My ranchers are furious to lose so much livestock, but I'll try to calm them down. That's all I can promise."

The king removes the rope around his boot, takes them off, with his belt, and then strolls to his riders. The big orphan watches the humbled king ride away with his warriors. Winston rides up, worried.

Magnus sighs. "Winston, I'm losing my monstrosity. I'm barely a beast now."

Team Naulo bursts out of the dark to drive away hundreds of horses. 30 Bulgar warriors give chase on foot. Naulo takes a platoon to greet them. Five Bulgar bowmen try shooting them, so the Heruli kill them, but let the rest live.

Naulo hates his lisp. "We are taking your herds, except the oxen to pull your huge wagons. If you interfere, we will slaughter everyone. You cannot compete with horse archers, so do not tempt fate."

Team Naulo rides away, unsure if they understood.

A Heruli warrior doesn't understand. "Why are we not killing them? They will come after us."

"Magnus wants to minimize death because Bulgars are not our enemies. They raid others, so he feels justified in raiding them. With them in hiding, we can go after Slavic herds if we dress like Huns. I find it hard to believe that we can sell so many cattle and horses, but Magnus wants to send thousands up the Danube to feed some canal project, rather than pay them cash. It'll take much longer to drive them to Port Bata than to steal them all."

"But why don't we sell these people as slaves? Every pretty girl is worth a dozen horses."

The prince smiles sadly. "Something ugly happened to make Magnus oppose slavery. He's quite fanatic about it. That mass murderer and extraordinary thief says slavery is against his moral principles."

He snorts derisively. "Weirdo."

Naulo nods in agreement.

Port Odesa on the Black Sea, 361 AD

The burly Iberian leads them to a hilltop to see a distant city on the Black Sea.

"Boys, we rode all night to surprise them. The bigger the surprise, the fewer of us that die. I can see the Sea Horse, which means Pel's Romans have infiltrated the city to learn what's valuable and who's important. I hope they have a lot of grain because

221

we're low. Pel has probably rented a big building and set up a cafeteria. He says Constantinople doesn't want to buy any more cattle, horses, or sheep. We've saturated that market, so some ships are selling livestock to Greece – Thessaloniki, Larisa, and Athens. Odesa is the biggest city in this area. We need its port facilities to load herds onto ships, boats, and barges to go up the Danube. Pel hired a team to build huge sailing barges, so we should have dozens by now. Our fleet will sell livestock at hundreds of settlements along that river system. Unsold animals will be sent up a tributary just northeast of Italy rather than risk storms in the Med. From there, we'll sell them in the Po Valley. Pel has been loading them in Bata, on the other side of the Black Sea. Odesa saves us months. Driving a million animals around the northern shore takes too long and leaves us vulnerable to raiders. Let's break up into platoons to secure dockside facilities and to trap them behind their palisade. We've ridden through thousands of sheep, cattle, and horses, but I bet they have many more that we haven't seen, grazing outside the city. The grass here is darker because Odesa gets more rain than Bata, so more tribes fight over it. I hear the farming along the Dniester and Dnieper rivers is great, with rich black earth. I'd love to build a huge wall around this port one day."

"We're not sacking Odesa?" Taleg asks for them all.

"Not if they hand over their portable valuables. Don't destroy their farms and fields. No rape and only kill when necessary because Huns must get through these fighters to reach the Roman Empire. Pel says the market for livestock is insatiable. As a high-status Roman, he's been an ideal salesman to local leaders. He earns 10% of sales, so he sold over a million beasts while we were east, killing Huns."

"I find it hard to trust a young man who doesn't want sex."

"Pel wants sex; just not with you. He fell in love with Fauna. I can't blame him for that. He can't unlove her or desire anyone else, so he must find something else to fulfill him. He has bastards across Europe. I met some. He's a good man going through a bad time. Plus, he's useful, well connected, and good with elites, so please be nice to him."

The Heruli fan out in platoons to position themselves by their targets. The wooden gate is locked, but they sweep structures outside the city, rousing sleepy peasants. Riding Caesar, Magnus hears screaming and cursing, but no one needs his Rapid Reaction force. Arriving at the docks, he finds Pel with a smile. The Roman leads Magnus to a huge warehouse, opens it, and looks within. Magnus yells something and his troops divert their captives here. Heruli in heavy armor and shields gallop to the front gate, slide down, and hammer stakes into the ground so the gates can't open. While some hammer, others hold up shields because angry sentries on the wall are yelling down at them. Once done, they mount up and ride away. A horn blows within Odesa and armed men pop up over the wooden outer wall. Residents mobilize for combat. Outside the outer wall, an old merchant walks to the main gate and city leaders are dying to know what's going on.

The mayor looks down at him. "Chief Merchant Andino, what can you tell us?"

"Mayor, the Heruli from the steppe are robbing us with the help of some rogue Romans who claim they have 10,000 fighters. Just a few thousand attacked us. One Roman speaks better Greek than I do and seems to know every classic. They're taking our boats and ships, but will return the older ones. They demand all our herds, grain, coin, bullion, gems, and jewelry. Their leader threatens to burn Odesa and everyone

222

within if not paid. But, if we do, they'll leave without harming anyone or destroying anything. The Heruli could kill us just by burning our crops. The new ships that docked yesterday are theirs, so they planned this long ago. I would have been here sooner, but they insisted I eat breakfast. They set up something that Roman legions use to feed vast quantities of troops. They will release their hostages if we don't cause problems or kill them if we do. Oh, they'll let us harvest our crops if they get half. The big Roman fixing the waterwheel criticized our grist meal in minute detail and says he'll leave us a design that's 10x more efficient."

The men on the wall murmur and whisper to each other.

"Chief Merchant Andino, these are odd besiegers, but you don't sound optimistic. Should we not fight?"

"If they break into Odesa, sure, but spearmen stand no chance against horse archers on open ground. We can't harvest if Heruli oppose us. They have my family, but will release them if I pay them all my valuables, so I'd appreciate you opening a sally door to let me in."

The mayor nods and disappears below the log wall.

Volga River Valley

With 25,000 Heruli, including kids and elderly, Magnus rides to another huge herd by the Volga River and blows his bugle to call his commanders.

"Platoon leaders, 30,000 of us swept Bulgaria and then the Visigoths, but Slavs are more dangerous because they can shoot from the saddle, though without stirrups. We'll raid isolated bands across a wide front on both sides of the Don, Dnieper, and the Volga to get in and get out before too many Slavs get organized. We'll dress like Huns. Every group should have someone who speaks basic Slavic. Your old Slavic neighbors must send their herds south for the winter or else they'll freeze. If we ride from dawn to dusk, we should catch them unprepared like the Bulgars, except these Slavs have much bigger herds. The more we take, the fewer that Huns will eat. Minimize killing and destruction. Slavic horse archers can't compete with you, no more than you could compete with Huns five years ago. I'd rather you kill their mounts than their men. I must return to Odesa to manage sales and shipping, but Naulo will probably stick around. Previous captains have told others, so livestock sales have become a feeding frenzy. Vessels from across the Danube River system are descending on Odesa for cheap beef, sheep, and horses. This is great because our stolen herds have eaten out the grass around the port, so we must graze them farther away, which makes us tempting targets for Bulgar raiders. We must leave before winter, so take what you can and leave as fast as possible."

The Sea Horse in Odesa Harbor

Doggy style, Magnus makes Fauna come again as her big boobs bounce. Her scream wakes the crew again. They cuddle afterwards, content with their life mates. Both are topless, with a blanket covering the rest.

"Fauna, I want to kill Emperor Constantius for undermining my father's first chance at an independent command and because Emperor Julian promised me 400,000

223

gold coins to avoid a war that he will probably lose. I want Constantius to drink poisoned apple cider like my parents. I found the roots, leaves, and flowers, then practiced on violent prisoners, but I don't know how to get access to him, though Pel could get me into his command center."

"Ah. You need me. Don't be shy; that doesn't become you. I like you bold and brave. Tell me what you want and I'll do it for you if you'll actually man up and marry me. I'm pregnant, yet you keep making excuses. If you fail me, Pel will marry me in a moment."

"I need you to get the emperor to drink the poisoned cider. The only way to do that is by pretending you're an expensive whore. He may not let you in unless you take off your clothes and he may not drink the cider unless you have sex with him.

Initially shocked, she quickly recovers. "If you want him dead that badly, then I'll suck him dry, which will also make him sleepy. I am comfortable nude. Many have seen me bathe naked because nomadic bands do that at the same time for safety. I'll kill this king if you'll be with me to the death, but you must marry me first."

Hesitating. "There's more: I need Pel's help getting in. I am too young, unknown, and have a provincial accent. He looks like a legate and speaks like a Roman elite. Money isn't enough because he just made a huge fortune selling herds for me. I don't know how to compel him to help us."

Backing away from him in disgust. "Lies turn me off. You know exactly how to get him to do what you want, but you want me to propose it. You must be a man and tell me boldly or I'll lose respect for you."

Pissed off, conflicted, and desperate. "I want you to fuck him. Well. Not just a quickie. He's gone four years without sex. Masturbation is for relief, not satisfaction. I want you to satisfy him because I feel terrible for taking you from him. I'm bad at being horrible. I don't understand why my conscience keeps returning, but I blame my father."

She sits up and lets her breasts sway. "For four years I assumed I'd have sex with him, as his wife, so that is no problem for me. He is handsome, kind, and loving. I'll promise him the best night of his life if does this and suck him off first to show I am serious, but you must watch your wife fuck him and enjoy herself. Because I will enjoy it. I'll drink his juice and sit on his face and lick his ass and beg him to cum up my butt – but you must watch. You cannot look away and you can't interfere. If you want me to poison Constantius, then this is the price you must pay. To be clear – I'll enjoy myself with both men. I'll seduce them as I seduced Jaki; if I knew girls taste so good, I would have ravaged them years ago. I am very young and very horny. You are barely enough for me when you're here, but you are often away and my fingers can only do so much, damn them to hell."

Magnus picks his jaw off the floor. "You want to fuck Pel?"

"I want to punish you for wanting me to fuck other men to get what you want. You are using your wife for sex and that must come with a cost. We will only do this in Tarsus and you will owe me forever. I know you cannot be faithful because you are gone for lengthy times, but I won't fuck any other men, unless your life is at stake. That said, I'll drink every man on Earth if it will save you."

Her fiancé begins crying like a little bitch. "You love me, Fauna. You really love me. Yes, I'll fucking marry you."

224

Port Odesa

Naulo rides up, shocked at what he sees. Magnus trots out to greet him.

"Welcome back, brother. Your grandfather and cousins are well, so we can finally schedule our joint wedding. Jaki won't lose her virginity so much as throw it away. Things here are under control. How are things up north?"

"We had to kill quite a few stubborn Slavs, but we captured a million livestock. We dressed as Alans, but I don't know how convincingly. However, a few thousand more Heruli joined us with several thousand young Slavs, eager to escape the Hun invasion." He gestures to the city. "Why are locals outside the wall? They're walking around like this is normal."

"Their leaders agreed to not attack us if we let them go about their business. They must harvest their fields, stockpile firewood, and operate their shops. I don't want to hurt them; I just want to sell their herds, although I left them some dairy cows. I even warned them about the Huns, not that I expect them to master horse archery in time. I didn't tell them about stirrups, but that wouldn't help them because they don't grow up hunting from horseback like pastoral nomads from the steppe. After the wedding, Fauna, Pel, and I must sail for Tarsus. I must spend my honeymoon fucking the emperor who undermined my father. Winston will stay here to manage things. Our fleet will transport the rest of the Heruli to Galicia. In a few decades, when we have enough horse archers, we'll wipe out all Huns, then grow old together with grandkids to spoil."

"Magnus, you and I are orphans, so you should understand that I need to avenge my parents, uncles, and cousins. Shake my hand, look me in the eye, and swear on it." Magnus does. "Brother, if your word is true, then I am your man to the death."

The intensity of his tone shocks the Iberian.

"Naulo, you've never called me brother before."

"Because you were not my brother until now. Marrying my sister doesn't make you my brother. Committing ourselves to a cause does that. You must never waver because I will not."

Magnus watches him ride off and squirms as a freezing chill flows down his spine.

Tarsus Harbor in the Eastern Mediterranean Sea

The fishing ship stinks. Below deck, three fuckers look out a port hole to remain unseen.

Magnus sounds conflicted. "Julian's letter says Emperor Constantius finally has a baby on the way, via his third wife, Faustina. If a boy, Julian will never rule shit."

Pelagius points. "Mark Anthony met Cleopatra here. Tarsus minted coins with the image of Hercules after a legend where the local god, Sandon, held him prisoner. The Tarsus Mountains are beautiful. St. Paul was born here, near the Berdan River. Fauna, I love your short hair, but I don't understand how you made it so sexy."

Smiling at Pel like she's horny. "I trimmed my pubes, too. Do you like my tits? Until Jaki gave me bras, I've never had cleavage. I'm so tired of dressing in loose tunics and wrap-around robes. I wish I could walk through the city nude so everyone stares at me."

225

Resting a palm on his shoulder, Fauna leans a tit onto Pel instead of Magnus as she stretches for a view out the port hole. She makes Pel uncomfortable, soft-headed, and rock hard because Fauna is really looking forward to sucking off her ex-fiancé.

Magnus breaks the moment. "Business before pleasure, my love."

Pel is clearly uncomfortable. "Magnus, are you finally ready to tell me how you plan to get in? I've already refused many times without you ever asking. I still can't figure out why you brought me on your honeymoon."

"You can get us into the command compound, probably without even identifying yourself. We'll escort Fauna as an expensive prostitute sent by a senator who needs a favor. Constantius has a habit of staying up late and a history of enjoying young girls, so Fauna will strip and then touch him with hungry hands. While she sucks him off or has sex, she gets him to drink the fresh apple cider, then leaves when he falls asleep. Everyone will assume he died of natural causes. She'll wear a long dark wig and we'll have civilian clothes hidden in case they chase us."

Laughing. "Why would I ever help you, of all people? You fuck the woman I love! I had planned to spend the rest of my monogamous life with her. Dick move, man!"

"Constantius knows Julian sent you to get him horse archers from the steppe. As soon as the Heruli arrive in Iberia, Rome will hear of it and Constantius will assume you are his enemy because the timing is suspicious: Julian declares himself emperor and then your horse archers show up. You even taught them Latin. If Constantius can't find you, your parents live in Rome. He will hold them hostage, probably in prison, and liquidate your family's fortune. Your parents, siblings, uncles, and cousins will be destitute because of you and through no fault of mine. Surely this has crossed your mind; why else would you delay so long to bring the Heruli to Julian? Constantius will avenge himself on you and your family before he clashes with Julian because he is competent, ruthless, and thorough. Even if Julian wins, it will be without the Heruli, so he'll also destroy you. Julian sent you to get horse archers not to fight Germani or Persians, but to beat Constantius before his fucking wife or daughters breed heirs to the realm. Unless Constantius dies before their armies clash, you'll be ruined. You might risk your life, but are you willing to jeopardize the lives and property of your entire family?"

Pel is suddenly unsure. "I just get us in? Well, if I can't have her, then at least the man who undermined your father will enjoy your wife. I thought we were friends."

"Pel, I'd like us to be friends for life. I've always respected you and, like my dad said, you're the smartest man I know. To be clear, you've agreed to help us murder the emperor?"

"Yes. He never liked me, so what choice do I have?"

The hot blond steps up and bitch-slaps the innocence off Pel's face. "You were supposed to demand sex with me as the price he pays!"

Pel backs up warily, unable to hit her back. "Wait! What? You're so beautiful that it's hard to hear you."

"My genius husband assumed you'd demand sex with me to do this deed, so I've already counted it in my abacus. Our plan was for me to suck you off now, then fuck you all night while Magnus watches. I might pleasure him, too; we'll see if he behaves. Heruli ladies often enjoy two men at a time and such fantasies now obsess me. It's weird to wake up wet. Whoever invented puberty is a fucking dick."

Magnus pops a cork. "What? Fauna!"

226

"Don't give me any shit, Magnus. Jaki says you've fucked every gorgeous girl in Iberia."

"Only the un-related! I just turned 15! I was almost a virgin when we met. Wait! You still plan on fucking him?"

The hottie turns on Pel, licks her lips, and then starts taking off her clothes. Fauna caresses her tits and pushes them together in her red silk bra.

"Oh, I've been dreaming of giving him a night he'll never forget."

The Iberian fully freaks out. He can't believe this is happening. "You're not wearing underwear!"

She's dancing now for Pel, not her husband, with a sexy smile and killer moves. Pel is hard under his tunic and Fauna purrs when she grabs it.

"Riding a million miles from the Huns has really strengthened my thighs. Being so close to death for so long left me drenching wet for weeks at a time. When both Magnus and Jaki were gone, I did nothing but masturbate – thank God I'm ambidextrous. Pel, Magnus needs hours to recover when I'm ravenous for more. He assumes sex eight times a day is enough, but I need twelve. Pregnancy has taken the edge off, so I'm not clawing the tent as much, but puberty is a fucking bitch. After the first time I came, I thought I wasted my life. I started looking at everything differently. The world turned upside down and inside out. If I knew then what I know now, I would have ravaged you and probably your troops. I'm loud in bed *and* I snore. Four years now I've assumed I'd be fucking you. I'm too wild and you're too religious for marriage to work out. I've never wanted to marry you, but always looked forward to fucking you. Before I hit puberty, I imagined us together naked in bed. Since I hit puberty last year, it was all I thought about alone in bed. I've soaked my saddle blanket, fantasizing about you."

Magnus shrieks. "Fauna!"

"You popped this cork, so I get to drink deep. You asked me to fuck Pel to get him to do what you wanted, so this is on you. You're lucky he didn't demand half of the 400,000 gold coins that Julian promised you. Pel, I told you not to fuck anyone else and you didn't. I spied on you. I hired whores to report to me. Four years you went without sex because you loved me so much. Can you imagine how flattering that is? You made me feel sexy while other men ignored me. Give me your finger so I can show you how horny that makes me."

She puts a foot on a chair, then she guides Pel's finger inside of her. "I'm so wet that I can hear the squishing. Pel, my love, I want to suck you off and drain you dry. Not to pay you for murdering a man, but for me. I think you deserve this and more, but I'm doing this for me. Please sit on the sofa and look at me as I wrap your cock in my mouth. Oh, God, I'm so hot! If you recover before it's time to kill Constantius, please fuck me. Don't try making love to me. Magnus says making love is what women do when men are fucking them. No, I need a relentless, brutal pounding. I like it rough and I love it savage. You're too civilized for me, so I'm asking you to tap something deep and dark inside of you. Don't look at Magnus – he's so hard he might cum in his loincloth." She reaches back to feel his groin. "Yep. Straining at the leash. I know my man."

"Fauna, Pel just married us, so this is our fucking honeymoon!"

"A honeymoon none of us will ever forget. Magnus, you killed your father, not Constantius; sure, he withheld support, but to undermine Julian, not your dad. We'll probably die tonight from your need for petty revenge, so I must satisfy my curiosities

227

now. Oh, Pel, I need you inside me. I want to choke on your fat cock. I'd love anal. Magnus is too big or my ass is too small."

Now nude, Pel looks as shocked as Magnus, beside them and in another world. Fauna roughly pushes Pel onto the sofa and her head bobs up and down on Pel's throbbing prick. The bride loudly grunts and groans with audible desire until he explodes in her mouth. She gulps down his juice and then smacks her lips happily.

"Best man-juice I've ever tasted. Pel, I'm gonna need more of that later. Before Magnus cums in me, I want you to taste me. After so many fantasies, it's past time I got your tongue inside me. I'm already trembling, so it won't take much to push me over the edge."

Pel looks at her like the moon. "Fauna, you're the only woman I've ever loved. Thank you for satisfying me."

"You're welcome. Now shut up and stick out your tongue. Magnus, be a good boy and help me sit on his face."

She sits on his face while he's sitting upright on the sofa, with a stupefied Magnus helping her keep her balance. Fauna rubs herself into him while screaming foreign curses, then roars like a lion and collapses nude on the sofa, her body perpendicular to Pel's, before turning around to get on all fours.

"Magnus, I need more cock. You have me perpetually turned on, so there's never enough cock in the world to quench my cravings. Give it to me, boy. Fill me up. Fuck me like you've never fucked me before!"

Magnus bangs her from behind while Pel watches with a huge smile. Fauna leans in and sticks her tongue in his mouth as if trying to climb in. He reciprocates and they're Frenching until Magnus loses it. He roars, then collapses on the sofa with them.

Pel can't catch his breath. "Fauna, you've ruined me for other women, so I might as well become a monk despite my family's opposition."

"As long as you fuck me first. We have four years to condense into one night. And maybe tomorrow. Once your fat cock stops crying on your leg, I'm gonna ride him like Caesar the Stallion. If we survive the assassination attempt, you both must fuck me until you shut me up or you'll never hear the end of it. Pel, I'll love you forever if you cum up my ass while slapping it hard. Magnus doesn't hit me enough; the hand marks fade before I can show my friends. The harder you smack my ass cheeks, the harder I'll cum."

"Fauna, my eternal love, you own me now. Do with me what you wish."

"Unless Romans execute us, this will be the best honeymoon ever! Magnus, can I hire a whore? A blond whore who looks like me and acts like you? I'm feeling raunchy."

Wearing just mandatory short swords, Pel talks his way into the emperor's palace. Torches soaked in pitch light up the corridor and make shadows dance. Four imperial guards move to block the way.

"Halt, identify yourselves, and state your business."

None of the guards gives young Magnus a second look.

Pel lies his ass off. "Tribune Marcos, sir. Some drunk senator handed me a coin sack if I agreed to escort his favorite whore to the emperor to say he's sorry."

"Which senator?"

"The old, fat, balding one. Whether Constantius enjoys her or not, I've agreed to return her to that expensive brothel on Via Central to earn a freebee. I could never afford those pricy bitches, otherwise."

The head guard senses opportunity. "How much did the lecher pay you?"

"Hell, I didn't count it in front of him." Pel takes out a small sack and pulls out several gold coins. The guards light up with greed. "Which of you is Cornelius? These are for him if the emperor accepts the girl."

"He had an earlier shift, but I'll see to it that he gets it."

Pel chuckles. "It's yours if Constantius likes the girl. If not, back she goes. I get paid the same."

"How are we to know the girl isn't dangerous?"

Pel pulls a string and her bright pink silk tunic falls to her feet, showing her wearing nothing but a smile. Happy and tipsy, Fauna starts dancing as if set free while singing softly in a foreign language. The whore clearly feels comfortable naked. She has nowhere to hide a weapon, but a guard sniffs the pitcher she holds.

"Apple cider. Haven't had that in years. Umm, Marcos, she's leaking. A lot. Damn, how many men did she just have?"

Pel angrily cuffs Fauna and points to a long river of cum slowly making its way to her knee. Surprised, she grabs his cloak and wipes herself clean, putting a hand on the head guard's cuirass breastplate to lean over to gain access to her snatch. She's grunting and groaning loudly in her thoroughness.

Pel had no idea. "Fucking senator! Sir, I didn't know she just satisfied an army."

The four guards talk it over before the head guard goes inside to inform the emperor. Augustus Constantius comes into the hallway looking to get laid. He's a big, handsome, athletic man and Magnus tries concealing his animosity. Pel stands back, rigidly at attention with a submissive face. Fauna ignites at seeing him, speaking approvingly in a foreign language as she checks him out from head to toe. Happy and horny, she turns to Pel and vigorously nods her head yes. That makes the emperor smile.

Chuckling. "Glad you approve. None of my wives were half as beautiful or as eager." He looks at Pel. "She's paid for or are you expecting a cartload of coin?"

"Sire, a drunk senator paid us both and says he's sorry if he offended you. We just have to wait outside to return her by dawn to her masters on Via Central."

"As it happens, I could use help with a headache. I'd have a sexless marriage if it weren't for my affairs." He sniffs the pitcher, smiles in joy, and drinks it all without bothering with a cup. The porcelain shatters when he throws it against the wall. "My mom made me apple cider, but that had cinnamon. Man, I could drink that every day for the rest of my life. Well, come on in, girl. Gaius, please watch in case she's not what she seems. My brother Constantine once sent me a gorgeous dish who turned out to be a bicurious hermaphrodite. I was almost glad when my brother Constans killed 24-year-old Constantine in an ambush. Constans was among the few in my family not killed by my family. Having slaughtered so many of my cousins, next month I need to kill another. What a headache! The problems of government never end."

Except in death.

Not knowing how much time she has before the emperor dies, Fauna laughingly pulls the emperor by the hand to the bed and helps him out of his clothes. She pushes him back roughly and climbs on top to rub his huge penis. Fauna smiles as he gets hard and kneels between his legs to suck him lovingly. Her head goes up and down with loud slurping sounds. Then she climbs aboard and slides down with a satisfying gasp as Gaius watches from the wall. She's fucking enjoying herself, whooping and wailing loudly so Magnus hears. With her long dark wig still in place, she desperately tries making him cum before he goes. He asks for a kiss, but she closes her eyes to avoid his poisonous lips. One of his hands cups her butt cheek and the other massages a nipple until he gets loud and heavy. He comes, sounding surprised, arching his back until he goes limp and loose like a noodle. Fauna lays next to him, without covering her nudity, and massages him until hearing him snore. With that, she sits up and wipes her hands and if saying, that's that. Gaius hands her the silk tunic and she goes out without touching a single thing or uttering a single word.

Fauna exits with Gaius gripping her forearm, but he releases her when a smiling guard clinks the gold coins. Pel and Magnus are at the far end of the corridor. Fauna strolls down as if she just got laid again, but wants to run before the hot emperor becomes a cold corpse. Pel leads them out of the palace complex, but guards stop them at the exit. Fauna shamelessly pulls up her pink tunic to show fresh cum flowing down and the disgusted superior officer waves them through. They head for their clothes, hidden in a dark alley. Changing while walking at night, they navigate several streets and ditch their Roman uniforms, plus her wig and silk robe. Once they feel safe, Fauna begs them for sex in an alley. Imperial troops soon look for them. Gaius spots a man fucking a hottie from behind, on all fours, while she sucks another seated with his back against a brick wall. Even with torches, it's hard to see this late at night.

"Cornelius, that looks like them without clothes. I'd recognize those bouncing breasts anywhere."

"Gaius, you said she was brunette. You think assassins would stop for sex after murdering an emperor? Come on! They're getting away."

Fauna snaps at them in clear Latin. "The fuck are you perverts looking at? We're not doing anything illegal; I paid them both up front."

"No, definitely not them."

The Roman troops run off and the three fuckers finish.

"We should get back to the whorehouse on Central," Magnus whispers.

Whorehouse Master Suite

Roman centurions burst in to startle several nude bodies. Fauna is in a 69 with a gorgeous prostitute; neither pause their fucking sex. The three blond whores look a lot like Fauna. Magnus gets up naked and angry.

"We have this suite and the four girls until noon! How dare you barge in here! I'm gonna tell my father unless he's still drunk."

Pel says nothing, but drinks more wine, burps, then giggles. He certainly doesn't come across like a Roman officer.

One centurion looks at the others. "That's not them. Let's go!"

Watching them leave, Magnus says, "best honeymoon ever!"

Two expensively dressed businessmen and two scantily dressed ladies get into a luxurious carriage. All notice Roman troops posted at every street corner. They reach a seaside restaurant where they enjoy a long, leisurely lunch. Troops roam everywhere, looking for suspicious suspects. Magnus eyes a boat tied to a nearby dock and smiles. As they leave the eatery, Fauna kisses the whore with enough desire to attract an audience. Pel hands her another coin sack and she gets into the luxury carriage feeling infinitely richer. Nearby folks watch the coach go down the street while the three assassins disappear around the restaurant. The three escape down a series of steps to a dock, where a sailboat awaits. Now dressed like a common sailor, Magnus casts off and expertly sails them through Roman galleys, across the bay, while Pel hides under a tarp and Fauna looks like an ordinary passenger in cheap clothes. They reach a small fishing ship and climb aboard. The captain has been waiting for them and the Iberians hug.

Magnus smiles in relief. "Thanks, cousin. I owe you."

The ship captain laughs. "They've been searching every ship, but they can't keep that up. I suggest leaving late tonight after you've dressed like sailors." He smiles at Fauna. "You get to be my daughter for another day."

Magnus looks out the porthole and only sees empty ocean. Sighing again, he turns towards the cot. Grunting when his wife barks his name, he sits on a chair, angrily watching Pel pound his wife to another orgasm. She doesn't just scream, but carries those high notes to the heavens. Her body loses tension and she melts into the mattress, softly singing Girls of Rome. Her feet are over his bare shoulders and Pel goes balls deep before shuddering and shivering like an epileptic. Fauna gently caresses his face while his cock is still inside her.

Pel sounds scared. "Oh, God, that was great. I almost had a heart attack. I haven't been fucked like that since seminary school."

Eyes sparkling, she pulls him down to kiss him lovingly on the lips. "Pel, I'll always love you and I'll always remember how good you made me feel. Too bad we can't repeat it."

She roughly pulls him aside and pushes him off the bed. He lands with a loud thud. She sits up to study Magnus, who eyes her warily, wishing he was armed. Fauna leans back and open her legs to show her husband Pel's cum, but he just sees her naked hostility. Magnus flips her off, but she just laughs. Her hair looks professionally messed up to flaunt her features. Fauna gets up, opens a drawer, wipes herself, and then puts on fresh panties with something sexy that accentuates her nudity, rather than cloaking it. As she bends over to insert her luscious legs, both men moan. The matching red lingerie that she throws on looks eager to fall off. That tiny amount of silk adds a ton of sexiness to her posture and appearance; it almost covers most of her tits, though not her nipples, but displays her flat abs like a challenge.

"I love cotton even more than silk. It soaks up man-juice better. Magnus, I'd appreciate more cotton clothing, especially underwear."

Pel is more confused than usual. "What? That's it? Why can't we do it again?"

The girl's gone. A woman towers over both men. She looks fierce and righteous, with fantastic tits. Turning, she fires verbal bolts at her latest lover that hit him like a catapult.

"Pel, you had years to invite the Heruli to Iberia. Didn't matter if Magnus agreed. A ship could have taken us to any port besides Porto Gordo. If I married you, I would have stayed married to you, whore though I seem today. But you didn't. I had to

231

repay you for long years of yearning and to satisfy my curiosity, but that's done. I'm very satisfied and no longer curious. I doubt Magnus will ever have me fuck another man to get what he wants unless our lives are at stake. I had to punish him for his wicked crime, but now I only want to fuck my husband. Pel, I haven't fantasized about you since the last time you refused to find us a safe home. Four years you could have earned me. Your failure will haunt you. Today I wanted to fuck you silly so you'd appreciate what you lost. For men, sex is often about power or control; for women, it's usually revenge. I enjoyed punishing you both, but now I'm a pregnant wife, soon to become a mother. I had my slutty night and my dangerous adventure; as a teenage mother, I cannot afford more. I must safeguard my baby's future. Magnus, if it's a boy, I will name him Andragathius after my heroic father and no, I'm not fucking asking you. He saved me and Naulo. You can name the next two babies."

Her husband looks horrified and in awe. "My love, I won't argue with you unarmed. I underestimated you and paid the price. I didn't know you were smarter or could see farther ahead. That pricks my pride and rubs me raw more than our last threesome. Most women manipulate men but, no, you just handled us like difficult mules. I'm impressed and terrified. You saw me clearly, but I only see you now. I knew I had blind spots, but not that I had blinders on."

She's not sure how to take that. "I needed to show you who I am and today I fucking did. You never wanted to marry; you only wed me to bind the Heruli to your command. You thought you were getting a sexy girl with a military alliance, not a fucking wife. Yet I doubt you feel married. Decide if you want to spend the rest of your life with me or I'll make that decision for you."

Challenged, the Iberian angrily invades her personal space like an Alamanni raider. She stands her ground on the plank floor.

"I'll never let you go. I'll find you and fuck you so good that you'll never want to leave my side. I'll treat you so good that you'll wonder what I did wrong. I'll drown you in luxuries so you never leave me. I'll never divorce you and I'd rather kill every man on Earth than part with you. You are mine. I just paid for you. Others may mistake you for a cheap whore, but the price I paid for your punishment was painfully expensive. You are my wife and, in time, I hope to make you my queen. You don't command a kingdom yet, but Galicia awaits you. My family gives me enough shit to fertilize a field, but you may bend them to my will better than I can. I admit I misjudged you. I thought I married down – some sexy horse peasant – to get the mounted archers I needed to carve a military career; but, no, I married up. You out-planned me. Me! Fauna, you're terrifying, powerful, and impossibly beautiful, despite Pel's cum dripping on my foot. I'm hopelessly in love with you and can't live without you."

Overwhelmed and horny again, Fauna hugs and kisses him. Dropping to her knees, she fishes out his cock and goes to town. Pel watches, the pain on his face etched like stone. She pushes her husband onto the sofa and climbs aboard. They're both emotional and energetic. Pel rolls the dice like Julius Caesar crossing the Rubican River.

"Magnus, Julian would rather kill you than pay 400,000 gold coins. If you can't think of a safe way to get your gold, I could get it for you for just another night with your hungry wife."

She turns to look up at him, likes what she sees, and nods eagerly with a huge smile without pausing her humping. "Some girls prefer the pursuit; others like getting caught."

Her new husband, however, is more reluctant. "Fuuuuuuuck! Pel, I thought we were dropping you off in Constantinople. Is this a sad ploy to fuck Fauna?"

Pel makes comfortable eye contact with the gorgeous girl who became a wonderful woman before their disbelieving eyes. He's unapologetic. "Nothing sad about it."

With just her back and a boob visible to Pel, the Iberian cums inside her. Magnus shudders uncontrollably, beaten again by his fucking wife.

Port Ostia, 20 miles downriver from Rome

Led by the Sea Horse, the fleet enters the silted harbor like common merchants with 10,000 Heruli and their horses. Eyeing Italy's rich grass, Riders walk their horses off while locals watch them warily. Even after the Heruli greet them in Latin, the Italians seem suspicious.

Pel is nervous. "Magnus, you'll pay me what I'm promised? The second night she gave me after the Christian wedding doesn't count. If I get you the gold, I get another day. I hate working for sex and hope that doesn't make me an anti-prostitute."

Magnus sighs. "I swear it on my mama's soul. It also bothers me that Fauna is looking forward to it so much."

Pel laughs as he goes to find a passenger boat to take him up the Tiber River to Rome. Winston continues chuckling long after Magnus yells at him to shut up.

After Pel leaves, Cousin Theo runs up the gangway looking haggard. Magnus is shocked.

"Theo? The hell are you doing in Rome?"

11-year-old Theo whispers Magnus something that makes him burst into tears, then roar in fury. His rage is real and his Heruli run to find out why.

Theo is furious. "Julian raced here as soon as he heard of Constantius' unexpected death. The entire empire is relieved to avoid an exhausting civil war. The Senate has already recognized Julian as Augustus and those liars even claimed they did so last year. As the new emperor, he's so busy that I doubt Pel can get an audience."

"The sight of mounted archers will get Pel an audience."

The palace looks literally a thousand years old because Romulus himself founded it on one of Rome's seven hills. Aids and officers keep Pel waiting for hours before the city erupts in a startled panic. Everyone had assumed the danger was over, only for an enemy army to encircle the city and sing, Girls of Rome, in an odd accent. He stands up, then nods in understanding. Centurions march on Pel and pin him to the ground to check him for weapons before dragging his sorry ass to an anal probe. Colorfully dressed imperial guards drag the legate like an armed prisoner. Holding a red rose, Augustus Julian glares down at him from a private room after waving away all guards.

"Sire, you risk everything by treating me this way!"

Julian finds offense. "Commander Pelagius, you greet me with a threat? How dare you?"

"Sire, you damn well know how I dare. You hold his rose. You promised

233

something if I brought you a legion of horse archers, but Amsterdam hasn't received anything, so the penalty doubles the price. The Heruli now sing to celebrate your bloodless victory over your rival. If not paid, they will ruin Italy. Commerce will stop and Rome will effectively be under siege. I don't even get a *denarii*. A promotion and pension to complete my 20 would suffice."

The new emperor is outraged that he must pay what he promised four years ago. He just became head of the Roman Empire, the most powerful government the West had ever known. His head still soars in the clouds when, that morning, an assistant gave him a rose and a warning. The new emperor feels old fears.

"After his death, Constantius' third wife gave birth to a daughter, instead of a rival. I long assumed I must murder a baby boy, so the girl, Constantia, was a huge relief. After four years, how did you convince the Heruli to come?"

"I didn't. Max did. He married the Heruli king's granddaughter and married his cousin to the king's last grandson. Max gave them chainmail armor, helmets, and better arrows. If you don't pay, Max will do to Italy what he did to Frankfurt, but he'll enjoy it more."

"Hannibal couldn't get into Rome, so Max can't get into Rome. Fuck Italy."

"Sire, Max doesn't need to get into Rome. His warships can block supplies to Port Ostia while his riders sweep the highways. Rome would starve within weeks and everyone will know it's your fault. Please don't be stubborn. We both saw what that little boy did to Frankfurt. You promised him; I heard you. No one suggested assassinating Constantius until you proposed it. Max did what you wanted, so it's sad that you refuse to honor your word again."

Unsure and unsettled. "Cousin Constantius died of natural causes. The doctors there say so. No one speaks of assassination."

"Julian, I watched Constantius drink poisoned apple cider, just like Gerontius. Gaius was the head guard after Cornelius ended his shift. They suspected murder because they searched for us afterwards. He died nude because a gorgeous girl fucked him to help him sleep it off rather than call for help. Gaius watched her ride him until he exploded inside her. If word got out, both Gaius and Cornelius would be executed for failing their duty. But that's beside the point. Max has 10,000 very good horse archers who will shoot everyone. Sire, just pay what you promised, plus the penalty. I've seen what mounted archers can do and you have nothing to counter them. You're the sole emperor of the Roman Empire; it's not like you must engage in stoop labor to pay him. Keeping your word is smart business. Through Max, you'll have the most dangerous unit that Europe has ever seen. He's invested an enormous fortune in winning them over and transporting them here. Your gold keeps him out of pocket. Don't expect him to do what you asked for free. Sire, I did what you wanted. Constantius would have beaten you badly. We spared you an ugly fate. The Empire has enemies everywhere, so you need more friends. I brought them. Some appreciation is in order. I want a promotion, recognition, and back pay. My father has always wanted a reason to feel proud of me. I'd like you to help him with that. A public ceremony and feasting my family would be nice."

Deflated and pensive. "That little monster has rubbed off on you. I've never heard you speak like that before."

"He's a much bigger monster now. Sire, you now have everything. Don't risk it over a lousy 800,000. Once he starts slaughtering locals, he won't stop until you pay millions in penalties."

Julian grits his teeth. "I must meet him."

"Then go to the south side of the Tiber and he'll find you. But, if you try killing him with a Scorpion, you'll still have 10,000 murderous barbarians and a furious fleet that will ravage Rome."

Julian waits on the tall outer wall where the river flows flush against it so they don't need to yell. Magnus dismounts beyond arrow range and walks with his big bow to the river, where he takes cover behind a thin tree. He sniffs loudly, then sniffles again.

"I smell a familiar piece of shit." He looks up. "Oh, hey there, Julian. Didn't see you lording it over me. Are you here to thank me for saving your life and half the empire? Not having to fight an unnecessary civil war against a superior foe must have left the Treasury with boxes of bullion and crates of coin."

"Your mouth has gotten bigger, somehow. I didn't think that possible. Why is your bow taller than you?"

"To shoot farther. I call it, a longbow. It has the world's longest range. Here, I'll show you."

He has a long arrow notched on his new recursive longbow. To stabilize it, Magnus steps on the end to drive it into the dirt, then pulls it back unnaturally far before releasing an arrow a third longer than normal. It soars over the Tiber and strikes an imperial guard wearing a chest plate. The impact sends him backwards, out of sight and he lands with a loud crash and cry. No way could Magnus shoot this from a horse. Few men have the strength to wield it, but big biceps turn Fauna on, so he trained on the voyage from Constantinople.

Julian is impressed and disturbed. "Show off. I must take Damascus from Shapur II of Persia and reclaim some other cities that Tiberias conquered a few centuries ago. Your horse archers will come in handy."

"They would, but you must first learn to honor your sacred obligations or I'll burn Italy and sink everything afloat. Your grain ships? Gone! With you dead and Rome in rubble, Iberia will rise to govern Europe. Or you could just pay up. Every day you delay doubles the price because I hate lies and liars. I saved your life and you don't even thank me. I spent far more than I ever imagined, getting you out of your terrible predicament. I once hoped for a profit, but now I'll settle on coming out of this whole. I've emptied my coin purse to do what Pelagius could not. If you don't send my payment today, the world will learn what you ordered. I doubt you'd last the month when everyone knows what a wicked weasel you really are."

"That's extortion."

Magnus wants to scream. "Forcing you to pay what you promised is not extortion! Why do you insist on being so difficult?" His posture changes with his mind. "Fuck it. I'll just take what I'm owed. If you kept your word, I could save your ass again in Persia or keep the Germani on their side of our rivers, but you don't like rules applying to you. Goodbye, loser. I'll be in Iberia making an honest living with 10,000 horse archers ruling a new kingdom while dutiful Romans poison you for what you did to Rome's rightful ruler."

"Wait! I'll pay you. I just really dislike you."

"And why should that matter? You govern the greatest empire the West has ever known. How can someone so beautiful be so ugly? Send quality gold bullion instead of the debased crap that Constantius passed off as coin. Pel, I'll trust you to count it. Float it down the river and let's depart not as enemies. One last thing, Augustus Julian. The governor of Iberia imprisoned my Uncle Theo. I need you to dismiss him, imprison him for exceeding his authority, and appoint Theo in his place. Give me those and I'll probably help you conquer your neighbors. I'll remind you that Theo's legion killed thousands of Alamanni. We gave you a decade without having to worry about Germani raiders, time that you can invest in Persia. If you don't include that document, then I'll do what I must to free my uncle and you'll probably never get Iberia back."

The emperor watches Magnus ride off and blow his bugle to signal his riders.

Julian fumes. "I hate that man. Pelagius, what are they wearing?"

"Bear coats over chainmail sandwiched between leather over a leather chainmail vest. His best battalion also wear chest and back plates to offset higher risks. The heavier weight digs into their shoulders, so he plans to design padded undershirts to counter that."

"Do you think he'll help me fight Persia?"

"If you stop fucking with him. You gain nothing and risk everything. Max murdered Europe's most powerful man for you and yet you torment him. Until you reach Persia, I'd advise you to avoid drinking apple cider. It's a killer."

Tarraco Harbor, Northeastern Iberia

The fleet enters the port like a thief in the night. The newlyweds lean against the railing, cool wind blowing through their hair.

Magnus gestures to the shoreline. "Tarraco was Rome's first settlement in the Iberian Peninsula and so became its capital several centuries ago. The Ibera River is not far. Romans called everyone who lived beyond that river Iberians, giving this peninsula its name, though some locals call it Spain, derived from the Latin name, Hispania. That came from ancient Greeks calling it Hesperia, which means Western Land. Both Valencia and Barcelona have better harbors, but Tarraco has sentimental history."

"Arresting the governor at night? Magnus, you live dangerously."

"We live in a dangerous world. I must live day-by-day because my life could end any night. That's why my goal in life is to guarantee everyone food, shelter, and safety."

"And how will you do that?"

"By changing the world. You'll see soon."

"Thank you for sharing me all week with Pel. I've never been so sore. If it weren't for anal, you two would have worn me out. I'm insatiable and I can't take it anymore."

"Pel got me 800,000 extra gold coins and stood up to a tyrant. He's not the boy I met five years ago. I just wish I didn't like him."

As soon as the ships dock, armed men pour out with Young Theo leading the way. He's 11, but does not act like it. Even big men like Magnus and Winston have trouble keeping up. Holding torches, the men are silent as they follow the boy to a mansion on a bluff overlooking the sea. Guards protect the walled compound, but Magnus shows their leader a letter. The guards confer, then reluctantly open the gate. The head guard leads Team Magnus to the luxury home, unlocks the door, and then steps aside.

Wearing helmets, Team Magnus marches in holding lamps and open bedroom doors until they find the governor and his wife, both in their 50s. Wearing chainmail gloves, Magnus punches the man viciously while he's still half-naked, half asleep, and totally terrified. His wife tries interfering, so the Lion backhands her off the bed. She tumbles to the floor and cries pitifully. Winston plants a boot on her center of gravity so she doesn't get up. Magnus puts his hands around the governor's throat and lifts him off his feet, slamming him against the whitewashed wall. He's not choking the man to death, but desperately wants to.

The horrified governor sees Magnus, behind his latest lion helmet, exploding with raw emotion. His sky-blue eyes are a portal to his tormented soul and they are livid. Powerful waves of fear and rage flow across his face; superimposed, a small boy jumps into his happy uncle's arms to receive a kiss on the forehead. In a cruel, capricious life, Theo's kindness made a world of difference to an odd genius finding never-ending obstacles in his way. Speaking softly, Fauna shushes her husband and puts her hand on his. The governor slides slowly to Earth and inhales deeply. Fauna gently pushes Magnus away and steps between them. A very big man in full armor, Magnus towers over him, barely controlling his fury. He keeps clenching his fists and grinding his teeth with a savagery that the governor can't help but inhale. It takes Magnus enormous effort to cool his hot passions. Then Young Theo steps up to kick the governor in the balls. The man crumbles to the ground for the kid to kick him repeatedly while cursing violently.

Magnus hates himself. "My love, you married a monster."

"Monsters don't spend their lives to guarantee food, shelter, and security for everyone on Earth. When given enough power, most men are monsters. The less that men fear consequences, the bigger brutes they become. But you want to make a better world; no monster does that."

Magnus puts a loop of rope over the governor's head, tightens it, and leads him out of the bedroom. Winston lets the lady up. His adult sons shrugs off Iberian guards to attack Magnus, who bobs and weaves while brutally punching both sons until they fall to the floor, groaning pitifully. Stunned servants fear the worst. Young Theo looks at Magnus and nods in satisfaction.

"Thanks, Max. You're too useful for me to hate anymore."

"Thanks, cousin. I think. Fauna, prepare meals and one hot bath. Naulo, please supervise the sons and servants. Theo, we need a set of sandals, a wine sack, and some bread for your father."

As Magnus pulls the governor from the mansion, his Iberians search and stockpile their personal possessions, throwing them into the dirt outside the beautiful archway entrance. The governor's wife, sons, and daughter are also thrown down in the dirt to learn how swiftly lives can change.

Magnus barks an explanation. "Augustus Julian says the governor exceeded his authority by imprisoning Theodosius Maximus and hereby condemns him to 30 days in jail. Another governor is on the way, so you need to find other shelter. Theo will be acting governor until then. If you have personal servants or slaves, as opposed to those employed by Iberia, then call them now to help you carry your shit elsewhere. None of you better be here when I return. Cousin Winston, keep an eye on them."

The prison is not near, but they walk the streets of Iberia's capital so sleepy residents can see their governor publicly shamed. As the sun rises, a few thousand Heruli wait outside the old, filthy prison on the edge of town. The warden has woken and mobilized his men, but the barbarians don't attack. He has no idea what's happening, but then sees the governor being led by a noose, so he steps outside. Magnus hands the warden a document. Shocked and scared, the warden lets them in and leads them to a courtyard surrounded by jail cells.

Magnus is emotional. "Uncle Theo!"

All the prisoners scream excitedly until Magnus quiets them with a primal roar that gives them a taste of his insanity. He sounds like an angry lunatic who misses his mama. A calm voice answers from the shadows.

"I'm here, Little Man."

The warden barks an order and a guard rushes forward to unlock the door. Magnus pulls the governor along and roughly forces him to his knees. Young Theo gets in before his father can step out and they hug, united at last. The dirt floor has straw for a bed, a tattered blanket, and a crappy bucket. Dad kisses his oldest son's head and caresses his hair. They whisper indistinctly. Shirtless, Theo Senior steps out, looking in his 50s instead of his 30s, then eyes the groveling governor on his knees. Though very skinny, Theo does not look like a broken man. Magnus hands him a wine sack and loaf of cold bread. The veteran takes a sip and a nibble while contemplating his words.

"Sir, I told you Max would come for me. I thought he'd kill everyone in his way, but I knew he'd come. Half my family rejoiced at my downfall while the other half did nothing but complain." He smiles at Magnus. "But my sons rescued me, as I knew they would. That is why your beatings could not break me."

The giant Iberian can't believe his eyes, but he stares anyways at his old, starving uncle. Without his lion helmet, Magnus seems emotionally naked, though fully clothed. One strong feeling after another sweeps over him, making him blink, cry, and shake. He seems frozen, both shocked and horrified at seeing his uncle double in years. As his eyes un-glaze, he's still sad, angry, and bewildered. Uncle Theo hugs Magnus before Magnus can hug him. The big teen lifts his uncle off the ground and is shedding tears like a water fountain. Young Theo watches them enviously and angrily.

Theo smiles sadly. "What now, Little Man? Must we run and leave all that we have built behind? I feel bad that you'll lose your life's work. We've invested a fortune in Porto Gordo and Valencia."

"No. You're acting governor of Iberia until your replacement arrives. You only have a month, so work fast. After that, you rule Galicia until I piss off Emperor Julian again. He wants my horse archers to conquer Persia, but I must refuse him."

With a gulp and a bite, the new governor smiles as he reads Julian's order. "As governor of Iberia, I'll confiscate the estates of my enemies to fund better highways and improve freight-handling facilities at our ports. I'm shocked no direct road goes east-to-west from Valencia to Porto Gordo. A wide highway that can handle great weight would be very useful. Little Man, the family built Marc a ship on the Red Sea so he can trade rhino horns, cinnamon, and lions from East Africa for myrrh, nard, cassia, and frankincense in Arabia Felix. The latest cargo had silk from China, tasty exotica from the Spice Islands, and something sweet called sugar from India. A cousin is in charge, but Marc is pushing him to expand to Persia and India to buy those goods directly. His last shipment yielded a hundredfold profit. Marc started a sailing school to expand the fleet in the Indian Ocean. His latest letter spoke of an advanced school for adults called a university. Apparently India has four ancient universities and Persia's is massive. Little Man, can you imagine thousands of our best and brightest teenagers studying useful things instead of theology, rhetoric, geometry, and philosophy? Plato's famous school insisted on students learning geometry before all else, though that's wasted on non-engineers. I'd like to start free universities in Valencia and Porto Gordo since we've bought so much land around those harbors."

Unable to speak, Magnus nods. Old Theo kicks the ex-governor into his jail cell, kicks him some more, then slams the door shut with a satisfying sound. He exhales in contentment at justice done.

The ex-governor resents his humiliation. "Theo, you won't get away with this!"

"Sir, when he first came to Gaul, Julian authorized me to form a legion for Galicia if Galicia funded it. The Iberian government later offered to pay most of their salaries if I deployed them as a rapid-response force across the peninsula. But they were mine. You had no right to replace me and less right to jail me when those troops refused to re-enlist. Galicia paid for their uniforms, arms, and armor, so you had no right to vent your anger at me for having to buy your own. You abused your authority and deserve 30 days in jail. If you come at me again, you must deal with my nephew." Theo turns to study King Naulobatus and other badasses from the savage steppe. "And it seems he finally has friends."

The angry storm rocks the Sea Horse. The dark sky is pissed and the rain feels unnaturally warm. A storm bounces the fleet on swells. Hard rain falls fast and the winds are wicked. Without armor, Magnus climbs masts and adjust rigging as a captain screams commands to his crew. On deck by the main mast, Fauna, Naulo, and their grandfather watch in horror, feeling helpless, hopeless, and homeless against Mother Nature in a pissy mood. Clearly terrified, they clutch each other, soaked to the skin, yet Magnus seems cool and calm as winds whip sails. A rolling deck throws men and one almost goes overboard, but Naulo lassoes him with rope and skill. Grabbing the rope, Fauna circles the mast so the sailor doesn't plunge to his death. Magnus drops down and helps tie the rope in an ingenious knot.

Magnus laughs hysterically. "I haven't been this scared since the world's tallest tower fell on me while burning."

His fucking wife looks at him, horrified.

Porto Gordo (Portugal), Galicia, in northwestern Iberia, 362 AD

The Sea Horse leads the large fleet in. The Heruli pack the foredeck to see their new home. Magnus gestures at concrete catapult towers on either side of the harbor entrance to sink hostile ships. Entering the bay, Fauna is amazed and overwhelmed at several log towers. Having never seen a structure that high, she is not sure what skylines the horizon. Each grouping has a different color. Their patron calls them over. Heruli crowd the foredeck to hear him.

"Paullus Fabius Maximus, a friend of our first emperor, Augustus, conquered Galicia. He founded the city of Lugo in 13 BC, as far up the Mino River that is navigable. The Mino mostly encloses Galicia, making it a convenient border and barrier. Three

239

rivers surround Lugo and my great-grandfather built an outer wall up to 15 meters tall with 71 arrow towers. Paullus was the oldest son of one of Caesar's legates during our painful Civil War. His younger brother, Africanus Fabius Maximus, was named in honor of our illustrious ancestor, Scipio Africanus. Paullus was so liked that residents built him a monument while three distinguished poets – Ovid, Horace, and Juvenal mention him. We moved to the coast to prosper from our merchant and fishing fleets."

Fauna loves Porto Gordo. "Your mountains are perfectly square and of equal distance from each other. Mother Nature is less organized in the steppe."

"The city I sacked had a tall tower shaped as a cube. Their basic measurement is a man's stride, called a meter in their language. They built a structure measuring 30 x 30 x 30 meters, but mine are 100 x 100 x 100; The Alamanni made theirs with logs, but I used Roman cement and iron rebar so they last forever. We spent a few years building modified versions in the interior while prepping a pre-planned port city around this naturally sheltered harbor. Our main water tunnel can fit an elephant. Effective sewage and storm drainage are harder than they sound. Our first few surveys of relative elevations were not precise enough, so rainwater didn't pool where we planned. Today Porto Gordo has more curbs, gutters, and drainage pipes than Rome. The experience was gratifying, humbling, and humiliating. I don't look it, but I'm a century older, wiser, and wearier. Oh, I call them skyscrapers and hope that catches on. Certain Roman concrete lasts forever, withstands salt, but gets tougher over time. Breaking apart old Roman concrete is harder than fresher stuff. Can you imagine a structure that houses several thousand people forever? Each could shelter a thousand generations, rent-free, except for maintenance and repainting. I want to use cheap rent to lure almost everyone worldwide to my pre-planned port mega-cities, each protected by very tall concrete walls. The lower the cost-of-living, the higher the standard of living with families enjoying more money after necessities. Everyone wins and no one loses."

The king is bewildered. "But why? You have all this open land."

"Only massive, impenetrable walls keep residents safe from raiders and invaders. We combined iron rebar with concrete so it stands forever, but length adds to costs. Building skyscrapers means we can put more people in less space. Circles offer the most room per unit of outer wall, but terrain usually dictates where we wall our cities off. Land within a tall wall is valuable, so skyscrapers offer greater value. In violent times, folks will pay more to sleep safely. Plus, building up makes collecting human, animal, and vegetative waste easier, cheaper, and faster. Mixing mulch, compost, or adding soil additives like ash, potash, and bonemeal helps. Planting cover crops like clover and legumes is also good, but nothing can replace crap's magical ingredients.

"I bought all the farmland that I could in Galicia and I got it dirt cheap because yields barely kept farmers alive. Crap from my skyscrapers has suddenly made agricultural profitable. The family is increasingly feeding all of Iberia. We export our grains to other port cities. Big employers, including the government and military, love our skyscrapers. Porto Gordo probably added more new manufacturing than the rest of Iberia combined. We can't build skyscrapers fast enough to meet demand. The more tenants we have, the more fertilizer we get in a virtuous cycle. We're offering absurdly low rent and special amenities to entice the poor and the skeptical. I can't wait to see you lose your shit. Because everything is within easy walking distance, Porto Gordo is the world's only city that doesn't smell like horseshit. Once we fix relative elevations, it also won't have mud or puddles after it rains. Horses are expensive to buy and maintain. Raising oxen, cattle, goats, sheep, and chickens is best left to experts who enjoy economies-of-scale."

The king looks stunned and Fauna stares at her husband like he's brilliant. Even Naulo is quieter than usual. As the ship nears the city, they see wide boulevards and plenty of people walking on high bridges between skyscrapers. Families play in the gentle surf or enjoy shade structures. The only horses pull wagons, coaches, or carriages.

Magnus tries not to brag. "150,000 people live in Porto Gordo now, most of them new. We refer to each neighborhood according to color. So far we have green, yellow, white, and a red that I wish was brighter. Yours is plastered and whitewashed inside and out; you can choose your own color, but we have yet to find a beautiful blue. What looks like separate skyscrapers is actually distinctly colored neighborhoods of eight, aligned in three rows of three with an open, shared center that features a park, plaza, and playground. A short, cemented stone wall controls access to each neighborhood."

He points up at tenants walking between skyscrapers. "Skybridges connect skyscrapers to make it easier and faster to get to work, school, or the market. We help folks work near where they live so that they don't need animals. Those kids are walking home from school. Each neighborhood has shops, grocers, and eateries. Almost everything that people want can be found within their neighborhood. That reduces city-wide traffic so Porto Gordo doesn't feel crowded. Families and companies save money, which they spend on enjoying life. Most families worldwide own animals, except here and Valencia. Everything here we're also doing in Valencia because that has Iberia's best port on the Med, just as Porto Gordo has the best bay on the Atlantic.

"The city's outer wall is concrete held up by rebar, which no one can get through. At 30 meters, it's too tall for besiegers to climb over without the world's tallest siege towers. A deep ditch and big berm protect the outer wall from escalade; the entrance and exit drawbridges go over even greater trenches. We can put catapults on upper balconies and giant trebuchets on roofs. The city's gates are made of iron instead of combustible wood, but set within an iron frame; the entrances are separate from the exits for narrower gates to resist the biggest battering rams. Each entrance and exit goes through a concrete tunnel which can drop several portcullis; defenders can pour burning oil down or shoot invaders through murder holes.

"Each tower has iron doors fitted within an iron doorframe so they can't be kicked in. Each neighborhood has its own walls in case hostiles invade the city. Bowmen on high balconies could shoot belligerents with impunity. Breaching the city's walls is not enough; hostiles must take every skyscraper in every neighborhood; against determined defenders, that'd take forever. Underground granaries, water-chilled fish bunkers, and semi-frozen meat lockers can keep residents fed for years. We put orchards on rooftops and gardens on balconies to maximize food production and minimize food dependence. The Pyrenees Mountain chain blocks off most of the Iberian Peninsula and my family plans to build barriers to wall off the coastal plains. Then not even Romans could invade Iberia, much less Porto Gordo, except by sea. The easier to defend, the less likely a city will be attacked. Sire, how would you raid such a city?"

The Heruli laugh nervously at that.

The king seems unsure. "I wouldn't know where to start. Nomads must conserve their force because dead warriors take 16 years to replace. Raiders depend on surprise and ride away when confronted by superior arms. If we somehow got within the city's outer wall, residents would just flee within these neighborhoods and then shoot us from high balconies. Raiders seek easy prey. Even a big infantry army with siege towers would need many months to take each neighborhood. The outer wall along the bay is lowest, so it'd take a better navy to breach your defenses, but you have many catapults located too high for attackers to hit. I'd say enemies would need to infiltrate thousands of troops and then surprise residents when drunk from celebration."

Their host points to a bigger-than-normal supply wagon. "Each neighborhood has about 50,000 residents, enough to defend their homes. All offer free music and dancing on the weekends because folks should enjoy life while they can."

"What are weekends?"

"Most local jobs are five days a week. Julius Caesar first introduced the 7-day week to help move Rome from their lunar calendar to a solar one. Constantine the Great made it official in 321 AD. He mistakenly started the week on a Sunday, which should be the Lord's day of rest, but the first and last days of the week ended up becoming weekends, for some reason. I want to lure and keep residents because I give a shit, so we maximize free and low cost recreation, amusement, and entertainment. You see the white inland neighborhood on that hill? That's yours to give the Heruli easier access to your ranches in the interior. It's within the tall outer concrete wall, by a gate. Your original skyscraper is as far up the Mino River that boats can sail and almost in the center of our new ranchlands. However, it doesn't take 60,000 Heruli to ranch our herds, so I want your veterans to teach horse archery to trusted Galicians. The rest of the Heruli can live in that neighborhood, doing whatever work they want."

The king confesses. "That last storm terrified me. I don't like the sea. I sure hope you have lots of empty grassland."

"See those concrete docks? They extend into deep water while the rocky causeways around the bay act as breakwaters to protect vessels from ocean swells. Big ships can load and unload there, right next to dockside warehouses. We're planning much bigger ships that can carry more cargo with the same number of sailors. As bulk imports like grain and fuel get cheaper, competition will pass on those savings to consumers. By offering a lower cost-of-living and a higher standard-of-living, organically-grown settlements can't compete with my port mega-cities. Porto Gordo has enough space for a few million folks. Valencia could handle 10 million. Galicia does have vast grasslands between snowcapped mountains that melt into rivers, whereas most of Iberia is rather dry. The foothills are becoming emptier because more and more rural farmers are moving to Porto Gordo for better jobs than stoop labor. Sending a ship-load of cargo to Porto Gordo is much cheaper than sending it into the interior, which means almost everything will be cheaper in our port cities. Rival towns can't compete on either price or quality with my pre-planned port mega-cities. Why would anyone want to live anywhere else?"

Someone roars from a balcony. They all turn to a distant skyscraper. An excited girl slides down an iron cable to the shoreline.

Magnus shouts. "Heeeeeeere's Jaki! Naulo, your pregnant wife finally made her parents happy, so watch your back. Our double-wedding was twice as good. The family looks forward to making sure you're real. Jaki already calls herself a queen because she's a royal pain."

Indeed. The hot teen shows as much skin as she dares and screams in joy as she flies to Earth. Everyone watches, but Naulo's eyes glaze over. He knows all his friends envy him and this makes him feel special.

Naulo is scared to be so happy. "I want a daughter that looks like her and a son that acts like me."

"Magnus, you got more cousins?" Taleg asks.

"Thousands, though most don't have the Maximus name. Over 300 years, our clan mated with many others. We plan to offer free dances every full moon to help the Heruli breed with locals so we can become one big family. Jaki took a zipline because that's faster and funner than walking. There's more within neighborhoods and between them. Ziplines make crossing busy boulevards easier, faster, and safer. We designed the city to improve traveling."

The ships dock and Jaki flies up a gangway to throw herself into Naulo's open arms. He holds the beauty tightly, with her legs wrapped around his waist while they kiss passionately. Magnus walks his boys a mile to the back of the city. Halfway there, thousands of Heruli women and kids run down to greet them, screaming their heads off. The joyous reunion is a tearjerker and Magnus finds it hard not to cry. Together they complete the journey to their neighborhood. Heruli City is several times larger than other neighborhoods because it circles a large grassy hill with a water tower on top. The skyscrapers circle the base of the hill, all equidistant from each other. It must have cost a forest to get so many logs. All other neighborhoods are square-shaped.

Magnus loves their reactions. "Sire, welcome home. You have log towers instead of concrete skyscrapers until we can afford them. The water tower on top irrigates a network of misters to water the grass. Pine gives us the straightest logs, so we varnish them to last longer. Humidity isn't bad here, but salty air eats everything. Protecting the logs behind paint and plaster should help them endure several decades. Yours don't have counter-weight lifts yet – those are tricky and require special equipment. Shops, markets, eateries, and stables monopolize the outside of the ground floor, with the 10-meter-tall interior dedicated to storage. 100 x 100 meters is a massive amount of space until 50,000 folks want food and fuel. That wide tube sticking a meter out of the ground by the outer wall is how wagons fill your granary. A simple padlock secures it so kids don't throw in snakes or mice."

Their patron leads them around a tower, instead of inside. The Heruli whisper in awe.

Magnus pinches his nostrils. "I need to open this door – sorry for the smell, but this is the Shit Room. All human, vegetative, and animal waste ends up in these dirt-covered, cast-iron wagons. Oh, some isolated towers in our northeastern corner have nothing but pigs, poultry, and dairy cows, so we're literally in the lucrative shit business. Teams swap out wagons every night and take the fresh one to a distant field where they mix it to create ideal soil for a particular crop, which grows faster and fuller. You heard me right: we have shit for soil. Independent farmers can't compete with the price or quality of our crops, so they must sell out or work for us as independent contractors. That gives us greater economy-of-scale. Thanks to the Heruli, we have another 60,000 shitters. Walk up the central spiral stairway; I want to show you all some exciting stuff."

The Heruli enter a hallway that leads to an open center that lets in light and fresh air. Residents guide their brothers, husbands, fathers, sons, and cousins to their new

243

homes. Using a wide ramp, Magnus takes his wife and in-laws to the donut-shaped upper floor to show them some serious shit.

"Not including the ground floor, each tower has 30 stories, all 3 meters high. This upper floor is called the penthouse and is reserved for the ruling elite. It has glass windows on the roof to let in more light; moonlight and starlight saves a lot of lamp oil at night. Being on top, the penthouse gets warmer, which is better in the winter than in the summer. The view is spectacular and you have the warmest water for winter showers. I know nomads don't take showers, but you'll learn to love them. Fun fact: you'll have more sex if you stay clean." He takes them to one of the many private homes and they marvel at the marble floors and rich furnishings. "The other floors have plaster, but yours have marble tiles which feel delicious on bare feet. Sadly, oil from skin turns marble yellow or grey, so you'll want to wear socks. Your penthouse has fewer homes, but they are bigger, with larger kitchens, bedrooms, and closets. Each has a few bathrooms with running water. Pumping water to the roof is not cheap, so don't waste it."

He flushes the toilet and then turns a valve to spray water from a shower head. The Heruli moan in shock.

"You don't have to leave your home to pee, poo, or bathe. We've found that folks bathe more often and change clothes more frequently, which reduces illness and contagion. Each bedroom has a heater that vents smoke outside. We use coals now, but I prefer charcoal to repaint the exteriors less often. Coal emits dark smoke while charcoal is light grey. Roman heat their homes via the floors, but Galicia doesn't get cold enough. So: you enjoy indoor water, warm water, and indoor flush toilets. It beats sleeping on dirty ground. Let's visits the roof."

Exiting the ramp, they see big metal containers, fruit trees, and a garden. The Heruli praise the view. To the west they see the bay and the ocean beyond while the east has green countryside with scattered fields with a log Cube in the center. The massive rooftop blows them away. Their faces are full of hope, wonder, and relief as they gaze over the beautiful Galicia interior.

"We assigned several square miles to each farm, with a Cube in the center, so field hands walk less to work. Each mega-farm needs a few hundred workers, including technicians for the heavy equipment. The more we farm, the more valuable our mills become. The sun sterilizes the water in those tanks so they don't breed algae. We drink filtered rainwater and use river water for showers, toilets, and cleaning. The furniture is for folks to enjoy sunrises, sunsets, or just the Mino River. Think how easy it'd be to defend this skyscraper if made of concrete and protected by catapults.

"Imagine hundreds of the world's most sheltered deep-water harbors, enjoying the best climates, optimized for pre-planned port mega-cities, each with several million people. Most of humanity could easily trade with each other to the benefit of all. It's 100x cheaper to distribute products to 100 port cities than to 1 million inland villages and 10x cheaper than to 1000 towns. Moving the most people to the fewest places creates efficiencies from economies-of-scale that enriches residents.

"Kingdoms and countries don't create economies; cities do, and the bigger, the better. Rural countrysides are only good for food production, natural resource extraction, vacation homes, and tourism. The rich can have country villas like what Cicero collected, but they need cities to afford them. Hundreds of port mega-cities trading with each other would negate the need to raid and invade. Armies can't besiege cities supplied by sea and they'd be too expensive to storm, so war would become pointless and unprofitable. Even if Huns took the interior, we'd still be safe. Such a municipal network would create world peace and a global economy, like a tide that lifts all vessels. One city may export certain grains, fruits, or minerals to get different ones. Providing daily seafood would get easier and cheaper with a system of chilled riverside bunkers. An area struck by drought, war, or disease could be supplied cheaply by sister cities having a good year. No longer would regional famine massacre millions. Every skyscraper has a free cafeteria open from dawn to dusk that's included in rent. Families can still cook in their own kitchen, but the cafeterias enjoy economies-of-scale for bulk discounts. Each floor has a dedicated laundry, but we're working on also putting them in our luxury homes. Skyscrapers enable us to not just provide food, shelter, and security, but to do so cheaply. Every geographical region has access to a unique set of natural resources, so the more skyscraper cities we build, the greater value that the whole network provides. Each port city could cheaply distribute natural resources and finished products to wherever they are most needed or to whoever pays the most. In time I hope most of humanity lives in our pre-planned port mega-cities as they out-compete their organically grown rivals."

Magnus expected a louder reaction, but hundreds of Heruli stand there stunned.

Fauna has been crying. "Husband, I cannot reduce to mere words how much I adore you but, when we have privacy, I'll show you."

The king is appalled. "Magnus, you must have spent everything you own to build all this."

Laughing. "Actually, you spent everything you own to build all this, and then some. I'll go over the numbers with you later. The Heruli also collectively own three older skyscrapers centrally located on your ranches. Oh, you own ranches. The Heruli own almost a million horses, cattle, and sheep, plus a lot of land. In return, the Heruli only need to provide me with excellent horse archers. You are not poor, you are not homeless, and you are not alone. In Galicia you have friends, family, and protection. As long as the Heruli and the Maximus clans remain partners, we are both safe, even from the Roman Empire. You can field 10,000 competent horse archers today, but in 30 years, with enough interbreeding, we'll field 250,000 mounted archers by training young Iberians and your own sons."

That moves many to tears.

"I don't understand," the king said, stunned and overwhelmed.

"The Heruli own these nine towers, plus three in the interior. Instead of arriving homeless, you own enough homes to shelter 250,000 people. Did you think you stole all those herds north of the Black Sea for free? A few hundred Heruli died and many suffered wounds. What of all the plunder that Naulo took from Persia? I got my 20%, but we sold several million animals. Ranching is hard work that requires spending all day in the saddle, which is how nomads from the steppe pass the time anyways. At the base of the Pyrenees Mountains, we also ranch sheep that can't be mixed with cattle or horses because they eat grass to the nub. Your older men and kids have been ranching them while we vacationed in the Hun homeland."

His guests are deadly silent, not even whispering, until the king pulls his shit together.

The king's mouth struggles. "Magnus, I don't know how to thank you, but I'm sure Fauna will think of something. I haven't felt such strong emotion since Huns

245

slaughtered my sons. I'll die in peace, knowing my people are safe, thanks to you. I hereby make you an honorary Heruli. Can I please have a hug?"

Magnus wraps the old man in his arms and cries on his shoulder while his people applaud.

Triers, Capital of Roman Gaul, 364

Magnus and Uncle Theo watch Heruli and Iberians compete in horse archery when Governor Sallustius rides up to join them. He's in a good mood.

"Who's winning today?"

Theo angrily spits out an answer. "The bastard's having a lucky day. Magnus bet on a woman getting into the first century and I lost a fortune. I couldn't believe any girl was better than Fauna. Isla alone cost me 100 *solidi*. I was so mad that it cost Max's firstborn, Andry, over 100 huggies before I slept last night."

"Uncle Theo steals my kids as fast as Fauna pops them out. He's trained Baby Gene to crawl after him. Andry calls him grandpa and demands huggies like they're made of gold."

The governor whistles to himself. "I can't remember my last hug. I once wrestled a Saxon to the death; does that count?" He points at the troops. "I like your idea of making them compete annually, then paying more for those who qualify for the 1st Squad, 1st Platoon, 1st Battalion, etc. The 1st Squad of the 1st Battalion makes twice as much as the 10th Squad of the 10th Battalion. You rich boys got money to burn. By putting money on the line, they train harder when no one's looking. Even your cousin Winston can finally hit half the things he aims at."

Theo begs him. "Sir, please don't make his brain explode. I had hoped to humble Magnus today. Yesterday was delicious when Naulo missed a target. He can't concentrate when Jaki goes into labor. He's wishing for a girl this time. Enough Galicians qualified to bring us back up to 10,000 horse archers next year. The competition gets tougher every time. Now we don't accept anyone who can't ride 100 miles a day, every day for a week. The harder we train, the easier we win."

Magnus is pretty proud. "We hurt the Gepids so bad last year that they've given up crossing the border into Gaul, even with the new emperor and our old army in Persia. I had my issues with Emperor Julian, but I wish he didn't die last year getting chased out of Mesopotamia. I've never even met the new emperor, Jovian. The army elevated the head of the imperial guards? Were there no generals in that army to choose from? How did those geniuses decide upon Jovian as our emperor?"

A mounted messenger burns up the trail, riding his horse to death. The beast is in a lather, foam flinging from its lips, and the rider looks just as exhausted. The officers intercept him before he enters the military base.

The governor calls out. "What news, soldier?" The messenger skeptically studies them instead. "Son, I'm Governor Sallustius, Gaul's *praetorian prefect* and I was Julian's consul last year. If you can't tell me, you can't tell anyone."

The messenger anxiously clutches a scroll. "When Julian died, the Eastern Army was still stuck in Persia. As soon as the army left Persian territory, officers poisoned Emperor Jovian because he accepted a humiliating peace treaty that cost Rome its five provinces east of the Tigris. We're without an emperor. Again. And there are no more males in the Constantine dynasty. A summit has been called in Nicaea, just like both Ecumenical councils. All governors and generals are invited."

That disgusts Magnus. "I've had dead fish that lasted longer than our recent emperors. We're going through one a year. Didn't Rome have 25 claimants within 50 years last century? We need a strong general in good health, but I nominate my horse for second-in-command. Upon pain of death, everyone will call him, Caesar Caesar."

The governor sighs. "I'll send word to every commander within easy riding distance. We must choose someone before those idiots in the east give us another loser."

Hundreds of officers argue with each other, often ferociously. Cavalrymen scream themselves hoarse. Commanders are drinking when they should be thinking. Two guys wrestle ineffectively, with comrades laughing at them. The *prefect* bangs his sword against a table to call everyone's attention.

"We must find another emperor with proven military success, who hates barbarians as much as we do. Name, fame, and lineage also count. I'll start by refusing the job and taking my son off the list. We won't kill friends for personal power. I won't offer any names, but I'll veto unacceptable choices. Now, who's the brightest face to lead us in these dark times?"

The governor dismisses names almost as rapidly as they're shouted. Magnus wisely keeps his mouth shut, but higher officers brutally ridicule some applicants: Aequitiuus, the tribune of the Scutarii (imperial regiment), is too boorish; Januarius, a relative of Jovian in charge of logistics in Illyricum, has no combat experience; and Dagalaifus, the magister equitum, is an absolute asshole. Not a partial asshole, which is disgusting, but a complete a-hole. Sallustius is furious. No name earns the support of even a quarter of the commanders.

"There must be someone qualified that we find acceptable! Who's a rising star in the next generation? I'll take young and brave over old and foolish like my friend Julian."

Magnus finds choosing an emperor profoundly enlightening.

Theo whispers to his nephew. "This is how powerful men make history-making decisions: angry, drunk, and scared. No wonder the world is falling apart. For the life of me, I want a man who'll make things right to rebuild civilization. Watch my back and be ready to run."

Theo pushes his way forward and coughs to get their attention. Theo could have nominated himself, as he has the blood, the fame, and the battle smarts. He's well-liked and universally respected, but he had not won any great battles, so he nominates another.

"What about Flavius Valentinian?"

His skin on fire, Theo waits judgment. Unlike everyone else, no one raises an objection. For the first time, Theo sees heads nodding approvingly.

That choice pleases the governor. "Val's a good man, a good general, and a natural governor. He commands our elite infantry, the Scutarii. Best of all, he hates Germani for the death of his father! That man prefers the field to getting fat in luxury. He won't kiss so much Senate ass that he forgets us. If no one has a specific objection, I'd like us to interview him to see what he'd do if given the empire. If he wants to go to Persia, I say we club him to death. Theo, how soon could you get him here, if he's interested in the job?"

"He's in Ancyra, so probably a few days. The Sea Horse is patrolling the Danube from Augsburg. If we support his candidacy, we can sail him to Nicaea."

"Bring him, then. Remember it's only an interview, not an offer. Maybe we'll think of someone better before the summit."

The officers roar their approval, glad that's over with. Some clap Theo on the shoulder or raise cups of wine to toast his nominee. They look more relieved than Theo, who seems suddenly scared. Uncle and nephew wander to the exit in stunned silence. Outside, officers break up into small groups, either relieved or fearful. Theo leads his nephew away for privacy.

"Uncle, Val doesn't like me. Thinks I'm loud, obnoxious, and – I assume – handsome as hell."

"Can you think of anyone better?"

"Yeah. You. Uncle, you'd be perfect."

"I haven't won any battles, I've never been *praetorian prefect*, and I've only governed Galicia, which no one has heard of. Ruling an empire requires a proven general and governor. Do you think they'd choose me over Val?" Magnus makes a sad face. "Then you'll need to make the best of it. Maybe treat him with the respect he deserves and drop the sex jokes. Leave now and come back quick so we can reach Nicaea before they choose someone who hates you."

"Folks hate me?"

General Valentinian does not look up from his paperwork as Magnus enters and executes a crisp salute. His young son Gratian plays with toy soldiers. Commander Jovinus studies Magnus suspiciously at his desk, then stands up as if worried. Both officers seem impressive, fit, and good at their jobs. The office looks tidy, clean, and organized. Clerks handle paperwork in the corners. Val continues speaking with his second-in-command, Jovinus, until Magnus softly coughs.

Val looks up, surprised. "Jovi, it's Maximum Great. No, I checked his name against the registry. Who can confuse ordinary mortals with that?"

"Sir, I have urgent news that requires your immediate attention. It's sensitive, though, so everyone should leave except Commander Jovinus."

Val stands up, wary and wishing he was armed. "Jovi, thank God that Maximum Great says you can stay. Magnus, have you been transferred to my command?"

"No, sir, but I look forward to my horse archers working with your elite infantry again."

Jovinus senses something. "Val, something must be very wrong for Magnus Maximus to show respect to a superior. He hasn't made a single dick joke, yet I doubt he has run out. My favorite is: a man born with five dicks wears his loincloth like a glove." Jovi chuckles. "I still remember the first time I heard Ger tell that gem. Magnus, has Theo died?"

"No, sir. Healthy as a horse and happy as a grandpa."

Val squints hard. "Jovi, he's scared. I've never seen him scared before. He singlehandedly charged those Bulgar spearmen like they couldn't touch him and rode among them until my legion got into position. Magnus was as cool as marble tile on a cold winter night, yet we're making him sweat. He imprisoned Iberia's governor and sacked Frankfurt, but now he's either shitting himself or needs the latrine."

Magnus sounds suspiciously respectful. "General, I apologize for my past and future flippant remarks and insolent attitude. It won't happen again in your presence. I have only the greatest respect for you and Commander Jovinus. If you could only look past my name to see my performance, we could re-start our relationship. As the only commander of horse archers, I'm very useful. As a practical man, you can appreciate my utility."

Val theatrically unsheathes a sword. "Jovi, he's scaring me. Besides an ugly uncle, I didn't think any man could scare me. Magnus, what message have you brought me?"

Sir, I've given you all due respect, but you can't take me seriously because God gave me personality flaws. I've changed my mind. Have a good day."

Alarmed. "Halt or I'll have you arrested! If you were told to give me a message, then you must give it."

"My uncle asked me to ride here in a hurry to tell you something, but you obviously cannot stand the sight of me. I'll be in Galicia with my Heruli if someone appreciative needs my services."

"Guards! Arrest Magnus Maximus for the murder of Emperor Constantius!"

Troops pile in with swords drawn, not sure what to do.

Magnus relaxes with a good laugh. "That old rumor? Please. If you don't hear what I have to say now, hearing it later won't matter. All I ask is gratitude and to keep what I have: legate status, command of the Heruli, and time off to manage my businesses. If you knew my message, I could ask you for anything and you'd give it. I'm your only mounted archery commander. That alone should make you value me. If you cannot, then arrest me and lose 10,000 Heruli."

"Jovi, he's not scared anymore, which scares me. Magnus, I apologize for my rash treatment. Welcome to my office. You are, indeed, a unique commander and you have shown yourself superior on the battlefield. Jovi and I were just having fun, but now we see how serious you are. Something big has happened. I'd be grateful if you'd please tell us."

The big orphan sighs sadly. "Very perceptive of you. That's why Theo thinks so highly of you. I'm gonna regret putting the empire's interests over my own, but after the civil war of 350-353, we cannot afford another." The poor bastard looks like his mama just died. "Furious that he gave away our five easternmost provinces to Persia, officers assassinated Emperor Jovian before he even returned to Constantinople. We need a new emperor. Refusing it for himself and for his son, Governor Sallustius asked his officers for candidates for the ultimate office, but didn't find any acceptable until Theo nominated you."

That chills the room. Even the guards look at their commander in wonder. Young Gratian stands up with big eyes.

Val digests that. "I respect Theo, but he and I aren't friends. Why would he propose me as the next emperor?"

"He didn't say, but I assume because you're the most impressive young general we have. The Empire needs stability to regain prosperity. We've lost three emperors in four years, so I hope you're healthy. The previous three emperors did not have a son, so Gratian helps your candidacy. Young though he is, you even bring him on campaigns instead of him learning to bloviate like spoiled brats in Rome. The two of you could give

249

the Empire decades of stability."

Val sheathes his sword and waves his guards down. "Theo's a good man. What does he want?"

"He didn't mention anything, but I believe he thinks you'll be good for the Empire, though I can't see how our family will benefit."

"You must have ridden all night to get here from Triers. Why do you want me as your emperor?"

"Alamanni killed our fathers, so you despise them as much as I do. Other than that, I think you'd do a better job than anyone else I could think of. My uncle is rarely wrong and Sallustius' judgment carries great weight with me. Avoiding another civil war is also a top priority. You'd start with your elite infantry, my Heruli, Theo's Jovii legion, and the Victores legion that my father commanded, now with Pelagius as legate. I think I can speak for my friend Dutch for the Batavi and for my friend Mallobaudes for the Salian Franks. That should deter ambitious commanders in the West. If the eastern leaders wanted the throne, they would have already chosen one. I doubt they feel good after losing so badly to Shapur in Persia. I can't change horses mid-river, so my uncle and I are now committed if you seek the position. You'll have to win over others, but that'll be easier with so many legates supporting you."

"Magnus, I didn't think you liked me."

"I like you fine. You're a serous commander with heavy responsibilities. But this is hard for me because I know my personality rubs you wrong. I'll try to avoid irritating you and Commander Jovinus, but I fear you will mistreat me because that greatly amuses you, as you two just proved. I have a violent temper that scares me and should scare you."

"Boy, that sounds like a threat," Jovi says.

"You two are too dangerous to threaten; warning you would be suicidal. I'm asking you nicely to not push me too much. You know what I mean and you know what I want. I command Europe's only horse archers, so I'm special, valuable, and irreplaceable. You'll need me and you'll need me often. I'll probably die fighting under your command, so please don't fuck with me."

Jovi sounds deathly serious. "Yeah. Definitely a threat."

Val retreats. "Jovi, he knows something we don't. The sneaky bastard won't tell us unless we rub his coat with a brush like a prized stallion. All right, Magnus. We won't unnecessarily fuck with you if you are obedient, loyal, and competent. Now, what haven't you told us?"

"Governors and generals are meeting in Nicaea to choose the next emperor."

Val laughs and picks up his small boy to kiss him on the forehead. "Gratian, look at Magnus Maximus very closely because he is a clever, ruthless, and violent man who you cannot trust." Val sits down and rests his son on his lap. "Nicaea is in Anatolia, near Cyprus. I'd need a ship to get there. Magnus, you have a ship on the Danube. A big one with a wooden horse."

"Yes. Governor Sallustius and most local leaders are sailing with me to Nicaea. You can come, but not for free. Theo deserves an independent command and public recognition. He'd shine if given the opportunity. Emperor Julian denied him his due to punish me."

"Agreed. Julian disliked you intensely, but never said why before taking a huge

250

army to die in Persia. Magnus, I reward my supporters. I just need a moment to get some things. Jovi, I'd love for you to join me and please bring your sons. I need to convince as many men as possible to become the consensus choice in Nicaea. The more leaders selling me, the better. Thank you, Magnus. I'll try overlooking your louder flaws."

Nicaea, Anatolia

The ship sails into a harbor. Within, Toddler Andry is sleeping in Val's arms again. Excited officers can be heard chatting and chattering on deck. Magnus looks at his precious toddler and the stern general, both sleeping like babies. He gently pushes his boss awake, then picks up Andry and gives him to Uncle Theo.

The toddler greets Theo with a huge smile. "Grandpa, huggie!"

Theo wraps him up and kisses his forehead, madly in love with this child.

Magnus tries not to look down on Val while literally looking down on him. "Sir, we're almost there. Sallustius has more advice that you don't need and acts like he's getting married. You may wish to address the men before we dock."

Val looks sleepy and terrified. He sounds like he's puzzling something out. "I just had the oddest dream. Magnus, I saw your son murder mine near Paris after weeks of skirmishing. Andry ambushed Gratian when both are grown men. Your son is huge and Gratian wasn't much of a general or a warrior. I'm dead and you want my throne."

Shocked. "Sir, your worst fears have infected your dreams. I can assure you that no one wants me as their emperor. I'll faithfully serve Gratian as I've served every emperor. It's just a dumb dream, general. Mine are even dumber. I dreamed you wanted me dead and tried repeatedly to end me, but those are just my fears inflaming my imagination. Go become emperor and I'll show you that I am a loyal officer of the Roman Empire."

Val doesn't look convinced and glares at Andry, who laughs in his face. The general storms off and Magnus reluctantly follows him into Nicaea, looking pessimistic.

Thousands of self-important white men fill the lakeside plaza. Val shakes hands and pats backs, conferring with commanders and whispering in ears. With Lake Ascanius behind him, Val addresses the army and they cheer him. Tension gives way to a festive air as Val consolidates support. He disappears into a sea of men, dominating them like a born emperor. Magnus and his uncle watch Val walk over nervously with armed supporters.

Val acts anxious. "Theo, they're gonna vote soon. If there's anything you want for nominating me, best say it now."

"Secure the empire, raise Gratian to be like you, and don't die in Persia."

The two men, about the same age, appraise each other, then Val nods. "Do I look like an emperor?"

Theo is equally nervous. "By Jupiter, I hope so. As your nominee, if you go down, I go down."

Val laughs nervously, then a distant cheer goes up. Sallustius marches over with imperial guards, a smile on his old, weathered face. Everyone stands as if on eggshells, awaiting the news.

"Sir – sorry, sire – we've agreed on you as emperor and I couldn't be happier.

251

Congratulations, old friend. At the formal ceremony, I'd be honored to be the first to swear fealty. Sorry for the wait, but I wanted to dress the men you chose in imperial guard uniforms so it all looks official. Each has pledged their lives to you. This sounds absurd, but I feel like I've saved the empire by getting you elected emperor, instead of a civil war tearing us apart again. I've fought a hundred battles, but this might be my greatest victory, if anyone feels like congratulating me. Legate Theodosius, I'd like your input in organizing the coronation."

The governor leaves with Theo, happy as a pig in shit. Hundreds of men study their new emperor from a safe distance. The imperial guards stay by their new boss. Magnus looks at them warily, ready to run and wishing he was armed.

Unsure where he stands. "Sire, how does it feel to become the world's most powerful man?"

Val leans into Magnus, his eyes cold and hostile. Whispering intensely. "Good. Very good. You said you'd die serving me. I'd like to see that."

The giant Iberian looks like he's suddenly shitting a kitten. "Sire, it was just a dream. It meant nothing."

Now Val's openly hostile. "Magnus Maximus, I would not have become emperor without you, so I'll repay you with more honesty than you deserve: I can't let you out-live me."

"Wait! What? Sir, I didn't catch that last part."

Val speaks with a menacing expression. "Magnus, if I die before you, then you'll kill Gratian to replace him on the throne, so you must die before me. There. I've repaid my life-debt to you. You should make out your final Last Will. You're welcome."

The new emperor marches off into an army of supporters while four huge guards line up to stop Magnus from following. They all glare at him, looking for an excuse to cut him down. Distant cheering becomes contagious and happy troops start singing, Girls of Rome. Frozen speechless like a statue and looking like Death just shat him out, Magnus watches Val accept delicious ass-kissing from powerful people as if he suddenly rules the world.

Magnus whispers while horrified. "Did the world's most powerful man just say he must kill me?" Throwing his arms up. "Fuuuuuuuuuuck!"

THE END OF BOOK 1.

Now please **give this novel 5 Stars** on Amazon.com and then find out what happens next in Book 2: The Great Conspiracy of 367 AD, which depicts the true events of five neighboring tribes invading Britain!

QUOTABLE QUOTES: "Paying for sex is against my principles, but my wife insists", "I want immortality, but not if it takes forever", "Grandpa was an abusive drunk, so dad abuses me sober", "I feel like a whore selling virginity", "I'm great at lying and I'm probably good at statistics", "I *speak* gibberish, but I can't read or write it", "Luca had great parents, but most babies fuck that up", "Do all women fake orgasm? Or am I doing it wrong?", "I might be crazy, but I don't *suffer* from insanity", "I just had sex for three hours and, man, my hand hurts!", "British food is inedible, but at least there's enough for everyone", "Until I lost my virginity, I didn't know what I was getting into", "If I'm going to Hell, I may as well enjoy the trip", "At work, I grind it out like an ugly whore", "My wife has a body that just won't quit, whereas mine retired years ago", "Tag can't touch this", "Mom, the food you left didn't taste right", "Careful; the ground is slipperier than soft horseshit after a hard rain", "I haven't had a conversation this expensive since I proposed", "I feel like a centipede on its last leg", "I started waking up with raging erections, so my wife stopping letting me sleep in church", "Am I right to go left or wrong to go right?", "I'll procrastinate later", "Ever since mama drank my poison, I've had a pebble in my boot", "Sir, our half-measures are a quarter complete", "Life is precious, but lives are cheap", "I feel like a donkey owner who just kicked his own ass", "Sex is like barley soup: a few hours later, I'm hungry for more!", "Immortality never gets old", "Why do men shake with the hand they masturbate with?", "101% of negative numbers never lie, but 11 out of 9 statistics might mislead", "Are you being facetious or disingenuous?", "The smallest kids give the biggest hugs", "Talking to the dead is normal; the dead talking back is crazy", "I was born with five dicks, so my underwear fits like a glove and my wife loves me grabbing her face", "I feel like a bird, tired of winging it", "I'm busy, so I'll be honest", "I'm often smart", "Numbers don't count", "I'd give you a piece of my mind if I had any left", "To kill time, maybe I'll murder a minute", "Exaggerate? Sir, I wouldn't exaggerate in a million years!", "I haven't been this scared since I proposed", "I've seen the future and, like Archimedes' vacuum toilet, it sucks ass", "I started getting raging erections in my sleep, so my wife no longer lets me sleep in church", "I'm never constipated, but always full of shit", "Sir, you pay compliments as if expecting a receipt", "I haven't felt this dumb since I tried losing my virginity", "Too bad *being* a parent isn't as fun as becoming one", "Every sexy person you see is fucking someone. Else", "Being ordinary doesn't make you normal", "I'm sorry to apologize for the words I regret saying", "I do *not* have a speech impudament", "Happiness is the best cosmetic", "I lost my mind, but it's probably around here somewhere", and "I always finish what I star...".